CHASING DAISY

THE CLOCKWORK CHIMERA BOOK 4

SCOTT BARON

"All civilizations become either spacefaring or extinct."
— Carl Sagan

CHAPTER ONE

The blossoming explosions illuminating the darkness between the Earth and the moon would have been beautiful to witness under different circumstances, Daisy thought upon first glance.

Fire, contrary to popular belief, *can* exist in space, but only so long as it has a source of oxygen. It may be very short-lived, but for that brief moment of blazing glory, the sight is something to behold.

The large ships bursting apart, voiding their crews and atmosphere into space, were spectacles of precisely that nature. Beautiful, yet terrible, and extremely dangerous should you happen to venture too close.

Freya quickly banked her stealthy ship into a tight roll, narrowly avoiding a mortally wounded AI as its crippled vessel spiraled toward Earth's atmosphere, where, minutes later, it's far too steep angle of entry would make it glow orange-hot before bursting into thousands of molten pieces.

"What do you mean *when?*" the young AI asked in a panic, an uncomfortable hum beginning to emit from her speakers as her fear grew. "We're still right where we were. My charts and sensors all say we're still orbiting Earth! What did you do, Daisy?"

"What did *I* do?" Daisy retorted. "I tried to power down the orb systems before we warp-jumped away from that strange ship that was hailing us, Freya. What did *you* do?"

"Me? I was trying to divert the power and re-route it through a peripheral energy damper when you started flipping switches!"

"You said you couldn't shut it down. What else was I supposed to do?"

Daisy took a deep breath and slowed her racing pulse as she surveyed the carnage before them. That was most definitely the Second Planetary Assault Fleet being torn to bits before her eyes. As crazy as it sounded, that could only mean one thing.

"Look, we can talk about this later. Right now, you need to stay calm. Try to relax. Pay attention to the debris and inbound hazards."

"I am!"

"Avoiding debris, yes. Staying calm, not so much. Come on, remember what I taught you. Don't force it. Relax and look at the scene. Observe and form a logical conclusion. What do you see?"

"I see..." The powerful AI struggled to rein in her churning emotions.

"I think we're witnessing the first real stress test of a non-traditionally birthed AI, Daze," Sarah said inside Daisy's head.

Yep. But she can do this. Just wait and see.

"I hope you're right, because I have a sneaking suspicion we are well and truly fucked."

Always the optimist, Sis.

"Someone has to be."

The panicked hum slowly began to lessen, fading until it was just barely audible.

"I see several dozen large vessels in various states of self-destruction," Freya finally said in a far less panicked voice. "I see several hundred smaller ships as well. Most are dead in the air, some are falling into the atmosphere. A few are attempting to escape Earth's orbit, but seem to lack adequate power."

"Good, Freya. Very observant. And what about the surface of the planet? What do you see down there?"

She paused a moment as her scanners adjusted to survey the terrain below.

"I see a whole lot of Ra'az ships, Daisy. And the cities! So many more of them are still intact."

"Why isn't she getting this, Daze? We're not when we're supposed to be."

Because no matter how smart she is, Freya is still just a kid, and her emotions are getting the better of her. Just watch. Once she calms down a bit more, it'll all click.

Sure enough, Freya's natural tendency toward problem-solving and logic games took hold, and moments later she had forgotten what she had been afraid of as the possibilities flooded her data banks.

"Daisy, the warp didn't move us in space."

"No, it didn't."

"It moved us in *time*."

"Now you've got it."

"So that means..." She paused a moment, collecting her thoughts into a cohesive assessment.

Oh yeah. Here it comes. Watch her go, Sis.

"That means we did, in fact, create an Einstein-Rosen bridge, but whatever happened, we wound up bending spacetime in such a way that our warp bubble didn't push us through the walls of mere spatial distance, but rather, through the boundaries of time itself."

"And now we're observing the final moments of the second attempt of our predecessors to retake the planet," Daisy added.

"Daisy. We can save those ships!"

Freya quickly powered up her drive systems.

"No, Freya!" Daisy shouted. "Power down!"

"But––"

"I said power down!"

Reluctantly, she did as she was told.

"But why? We can save them."

"Freya, I understand why you want to do that, and Lord knows I want to help them too. But this is history. Ancient history, for us. If we interfere, we could alter events in such a way that could make our future never even happen, or maybe make it even worse. Do you see? We could create a fatal paradox."

"You're right," Freya said, dejectedly. "I don't know what I was thinking."

"You were thinking that you wanted to help all those people, and that was a good thing. But now that you've thought about it, you know we just can't interfere, even though we want to. It sucks, but sometimes you have to make hard decisions no matter how much it hurts."

"I know," she replied. "It's just painful to watch, knowing I could stop them."

"Freya, you're an amazing kid, and this is an amazing ship, but on our own, we wouldn't survive this battle. For now, until we can figure out exactly what happened to us, and what the hell is going on, your stealthiness is our biggest asset. There's almost no record of this time period. Gathering intel could be a great help when we get back."

"If we get back."

I know, but there's no need to make her any more upset than she already is.

Daisy looked at the blue orb hanging in space below them.

Hundreds of years before I ever saw it, and most of the major cities are still intact.

"You know you shouldn't go down there, Daze," Sarah cautioned.

Not to land, of course not. But a stealthy flyover? I think that's doable.

She shifted in her pilot's seat and tightened the harness.

"Tell ya what, kiddo. How about we see how good you are at avoiding Ra'az scans? Let's ride down in the wake of some debris to camouflage our approach and take a look around. You think you can do that?"

"Daisy, of course I can." Freya sighed, sounding almost exasperated.

"Uh-oh. Here comes that surly teenager phase I warned you about."

But she's only a few months old.

"Not in AI years," Sarah said, thoroughly amused.

Daisy chuckled softly to herself.

"All right, then, Freya. Let's go take a little look around."

The powerful stealth ship quietly slipped behind a large piece of one of her mortally wounded AI cousins as they plummeted to their death, the burning metal masking Freya's heat signature as she followed their reentry.

Her nanite-composite stealth material skin cooled almost instantly when it hit the atmosphere, becoming invisible to thermal, as well as other forms of Ra'az scans all across the spectrum. Short of a direct visual contact, they'd be invisible to the world.

The sky over Europe was a clear blue once they reached the atmosphere. The flaming debris raining down from above wasn't terribly bright against the daytime sky, but Freya might stand out should anyone look closely at the non-burning speck flying amid the wreckage.

"Freya, redirect us toward the eastern US. It's still night there and you won't stand out so much."

"I don't stand out. They never saw me, remember?"

"Yes, but that was in the darkness of space, and only against a pair of small ships. Head for the East Coast. If we stick to dark skies for now, we should be able to do a fairly complete survey of the planet without risking notice."

"Should we go to New York and see if they've built the communications hub yet?"

"Kid's getting good at this, Daze."

Tell me about it.

"Yeah, good idea, Freya. We'll survey New York, then cross the continent, mapping out what we can while we head for key destinations. The San Francisco facility won't have been constructed yet, but we can probably get a good look at Sydney and Tokyo while we're at it."

"We already blew them up, Daisy. In the future, I mean."

"I know, but humor me, okay?"

Freya altered her course and headed for the dark skies to the west. What they'd see was anyone's guess, but it was certain to be a sight different than the Earth they were familiar with.

When Daisy had first visited the planet several hundred years in the future, the Ra'az Hok had already mostly departed, leaving behind a much smaller contingent to oversee their conscripted Chithiid workforce as they deconstructed the planet. Now, however, they were still there en masse.

The main fleet had departed, and their numbers were nowhere near what they'd been in the days of the initial invasion, but a large enough fleet was still on hand to handle the hopeful human armada with relative ease.

The first attempt to retake the planet several years earlier had keyed the aliens to the fact that there were human survivors with AI ships attempting to make a comeback. Knowing what to expect—and having eliminated that first group of vessels before they could report back to their follow-up fleet––the Ra'az were ready and waiting with a very specifically targeted defense strategy.

Hordes of smaller ships had launched an AI virus barrage on the entire attacking fleet at close range, breaking down firewalls and rendering all but the non-AI piloted ships infected and impotent.

It was during this assault that her mentor had first become stranded on the moon, destined to spend decades alone with no company but the lone AI she managed to drag across the barren surface and reconnect.

As she and Freya silently flew through the fresh air of Earth, Daisy couldn't help but think of her friend, currently toiling on the surface of the moon, fighting a horrible battle with the harsh environment for her very survival.

CHAPTER TWO

Freya's dark form blended in with the night sky, her silent power systems and atmospherically aerodynamic nanite-composite airframe slicing through the wind with barely a sound. She quickly stored her latest scan for additional review at a later time, should Daisy so desire, then banked for another slow pass over Tokyo.

The city—much of the entire island nation of Japan, for that matter—had been a high-tech hotbed of innovation and invention. As such, it had been one of the Ra'azes' primary targets for AI virus infection and Chithiid deconstruction. While many other cities had been able to disconnect in time to save their minds, Tokyo had fallen early to the sheer force of the attack.

"Daisy, look at the pattern of the disassembly."

"I see it, Freya. They started with the factories, it seems. Most of the non-industrial region is still completely intact. And look at the towers—untouched, while the less shiny but more advanced fabrication facilities have been undergoing a massive scrapping operation."

"I don't see any communications hub. At least, not anything permanent looking."

"Yeah, I noticed that. I guess they hadn't constructed it yet at this point. It is kind of interesting seeing how things progressed from their initial invasion to what's happening now, to what's going on up ahead in our own time."

"So that makes neither New York nor Tokyo. Do you think Sydney will be the same? I mean, maybe they haven't built a single one of their permanent communications facilities."

"Seems to make sense, especially if they still have a sizable contingent of ships stationed here. From what Fatima said, it was only after the second wave was repelled that they began thinning their numbers somewhat. And it wasn't until Mrazich's fleet was destroyed many decades later that the Ra'az finally felt comfortable enough in their superiority to leave a greatly reduced presence on Earth."

"I guess they figured they kicked everyone's ass enough times to feel confident they could do it again."

"Yep, and that meant they were comfortable posting up with less resources, lucky for us. In any case, I'm willing to bet Sydney will be more of the same, but let's head down under and see for ourselves."

"Okay," Freya replied, changing course.

They circled high above Tokyo a few more times, then peeled off and departed for the skies over Sydney.

As they flew, they surveyed the alien craft they passed, cataloging all of the Ra'az ships they observed along the way, both airborne, as well as on the ground. Seeing the relatively limited variety of large-scale vessels that constituted the actual Ra'az fleet was enlightening.

There were what appeared to be Ra'az-only vessels, higher-tech and larger than the others, to accommodate the Ra'azes bulk. Then there were mixed-crew ships, carrying both Ra'az command staff, as well as Chithiid loyalist crew, from what intercepted comms transmissions seemed to confirm. Interestingly, Daisy found she could understand the basics of Ra'az language, though nothing like her knowledge of Chithiid.

And as for the Chithiid vessels, there were the hulking but cramped worker transport ships, packed to the gills with cryogenically stored laborers, held in stasis until the next planet needed their brawn to harvest its resources. Those massive flying warehouses were no frills in their design, with no creature comforts, merely used to shuttle their conscripted workforce from planet to planet.

"I think I'm beginning to understand how Maarl and his rebels might infiltrate the fleet," Daisy said.

"Seems to make sense, actually," Sarah replied.

"Yeah, that was a really cool plan," Freya said.

"Sorry, Freya, I was talking to Sarah. But you're right too."

"Oh, my mistake. Sorry, Sarah, I didn't mean to interrupt."

"Not a problem, Freya,"

"She says no worries."

"Hey, Daisy."

"Yeah?"

"I was thinking. It would be nice to actually get to talk with Sarah without you always having to repeat everything to me."

"I hear that," Sarah agreed.

"It would be nice, sure, but she's tucked away up here," Daisy said, tapping her forehead. "Unfortunately, that means I'm the only one who can hear her."

"Well, I might have figured out a way around that, actually," Freya said.

"Seriously?"

"Yeah, really?"

"I mean, it's totally theoretical, and I doubt anyone else could make it work, but because of the unconventional way my brain works, I think I could fine-tune a minor neuro-band to pick up just Sarah's channel and link it into my data core. There might be a second or two delay as human brainwaves translate into AI code, but with my unique processing structure, I think it could work."

Daisy wasn't sure what to say.

"Tell her I'm game."

But a neuro? You know what happened—

"This sounds totally different. Ask her. It's read-only, I bet."

"Hey, Freya. Sarah was wondering if it's a read-only type of neuro-band."

"Oh, yeah. I mean, I totally have the machinery to fabricate a full-on neuro-stim, but this idea is something much more fine-tuned to a specific, narrow band."

"What the hell, let's give it a try, then," Daisy said, a bit of curious optimism warming her mood.

"It might take a bit of trial and error, though," Freya added. "I just want to be totally sure you guys know that. I mean, I'm confident I can make it work, eventually, but I don't know how long it'll take to make it actually functional."

"Well, kiddo, looking at our current conundrum here, stuck hundreds of years in the past until we figure out how the hell we can get back to where we belong——"

"When."

"Right. *When* we belong. I think we may have a *lot* of time on our hands, if you know what I mean."

Freya did a relaxed barrel roll as they zoomed on their way to Sydney. Daisy just went with it, letting her kid have some fun while she could. Odds were, things would get far busier, and far more serious, in the coming days and weeks.

As she soared high into the exosphere after scanning and surveying Sydney and the surrounding areas, Freya had only just exited to Earth's orbit when a large ship powering away from the planet caught her attention.

"Daisy, look!" she said, excitedly.

As the vessel flew, a faint blue glow, consisting of hundreds of small warp bubbles linking together, was forming around one of the orbiting Ra'az cruisers.

"They're going to warp. Freya, you're scanning and recording all of this, right?"

"Duh. Of course I am," she said with an exasperated groan.

"There she goes, getting lippy again."

I'll deal with that later. For now, I just want to understand this warp process, and hopefully figure out how we got here, and how we can get back home.

The small bubbles completed their cycle, finally linking together. Moments later the ship flickered, then vanished, a slight crackling blue ring left in its wake.

"Daisy, I pulled data from the warp, and I have to say, that was a really, really underpowered warp jump. Like, I'm surprised it even worked. If that's all they've got, they really can't jump far at all like that."

"They haven't salvaged my power cascade and worked it into their warp designs yet," Daisy noted. "Not for a few hundred years."

"Yeah, but even so, it's kinda amazing their current system even works."

"Barely functional is still enough to give them enough of a technological edge to conquer other worlds, though. And even underpowered like this, over a few hundred years, they could still cover some serious distance."

"Well, of course. But for individual jumps? I mean, their system is kind of crap."

"Your opinion is noted, Freya," Daisy said with a little laugh. "Now, how about you get cracking on extrapolating parallel energy signatures from this new info and comparing it to ours to see if it somehow helps explain how we got here."

"Yeah..."

"Oh, I don't like the sound of that."

Me either.

"What is it, Freya? What haven't you told me?"

"Um, about those files."

"Come on, spill it."

"Well, when you tried powering off the orb, it kind of scrambled my real-time data recording system a bit."

"You lost them?"

"No, nothing like that. It's just, well, I'm having to rearrange a bunch of data to make the files readable."

"You want me to take a look?"

"No! I can handle it. Jeez, it's just something strange happened when we jumped. Let me work on it, okay?"

"Totally in moody teenager phase," Sarah said with a hearty laugh. *"Oh, man, you're in for it."*

Oh, shut it, Sarah, Daisy quipped. *I've so got this,* she said, confidently

"You say that now. I'll remind you that you said that when things get really crazy."

Hey, at least she won't have to go through puberty, so there's that, right?

"Sure, but what if whatever the AI version is winds up being worse?"

Pessimist, Daisy replied with a silent chuckle.

"Okay, kiddo, you take your time on that stuff," Daisy said. "Hey, you know what? Since it seems we have all the time in the world, it seems, I'd kinda like to take a little side trip and check in on an old friend."

CHAPTER THREE

Dark Side Base looked far different than the facility Daisy had come to call home over the preceding months. As Freya slowed her approach, settling into a gentle hover along one of the rocky ridges rising above the bombarded facility, the familiar view of Dark Side was anything but familiar.

"Hooooly..." Daisy trailed off as she surveyed the scene, finding herself at a rare loss for words.

"You said it, Daze. Good God, just look at the place."

While Fatima may have told her stories of the utter destruction she had first encountered on the barren surface of the moon, the brutal reality of the scene was far more horrific than Daisy had ever imagined.

The areas of Dark Side that were not protected beneath the base's rocky overhangs were nothing more than a collection of shattered living quarters and work facilities. The Ra'az bombardment had been so intense, some of the silicon dioxide in the rocks and jagged grains of soil surrounding the buildings had even turned to glass from the intense heat of the brief, yet effective, attack.

"Oh my God. Daisy, are all of those—?"

Yeah, she replied. *Those are all bodies.*

There were dozens of long-dead base crew resting on the lunar surface. While some had remained intact, killed by the shockwave of the impacts, or snuffed out by the harsh oxygen-starved surface of the moon, others were not so peaceful in appearance.

Contrasting the other corpses were bodies torn to pieces by the blasts, some in the false security of space suits, others blown into the vacuum from the supposed safety of their quarters.

"Daisy, this wasn't in Sid's records," Freya said, quietly.

"I know, kiddo. All the data from this period was lost when Dark Side's original AI melted down. Until Sid got plugged in, no one was monitoring the base."

Motion on the surface caught all three of their attention.

"Daisy, it's Fatima."

"I know."

"Sarah saw her, didn't she?" Freya asked. "My scans show that is a minorly enhanced female with a damaged AI processor in her head. It's Fatima."

"Yeah, Freya, we know."

Daisy watched her friend—who was not yet her friend—struggle as she gathered several corpses near the open base doors. The trail dug into the soil leading there was clearly from her efforts to bring Sid's unplugged AI cube into the facility.

A pile of charred bodies lay by the wreck of her immensely damaged ship.

The ones she took the oxygen units from, Daisy realized. *That means—*

Fatima faltered, stumbling to her knees.

"Daisy, I'm reading an elevated heart rate. I know she's exerting herself, but this isn't normal."

"She's running out of air, Freya," Daisy said. "This is where she does it."

"Does what?"

"What makes her so badass," she replied. "When she ran out of air before she was able to activate Sid to seal the base, she sliced open the space suits of the dead to breathe the air trapped inside."

"But that means she'd have to take her helmet off."

"Yep. Like I said––badass."

Fatima struggled to her feet, a pair of bodies in tow. It was clear, even through the space suit, that she was fighting with every ounce of strength she possessed. The strong-willed woman paused as she made what Daisy knew was the hardest choice she'd ever made. Then, in one quick motion, she pulled off her helmet, the near-toxic air within crystallizing into a mist around her.

She wasted no time, slicing open the wrist seal of the dead man's suit and pressing it to her already-blistering lips.

Fatima took several steps forward, dragging the corpses with her, her eyes pressed tightly shut against the freezing cold before she stumbled to her knees once more. With the greatest of efforts she rose to her feet again, her cheeks sucking fiercely on the depleted suit.

With no time to spare, she dropped the corpse and pulled the other body's arm to her face, slicing it open with weak hands. She barely managed to wrap her lips around the life-giving trickle of oxygen before she stumbled and fell once more.

It did not look like she would be able to get up again.

"Daze, I can't believe I'm saying this, but I don't think she's going to make it."

"No, she'll make it. She has to. She already did. No one can interfere. This is history." But watching her friend struggle, Daisy was beginning to have serious doubts of her own.

Come on, Fatima. Come on.

"Daisy, Fatima's vitals are redlining," Freya informed her, a tinge of panic in her voice. "Are you sure this is how it happened?"

"It has to be," she replied, but Daisy was already on her feet, quickly slapping on a light EVA suit, the very act betraying her growing doubts.

Fatima tried to move, but it was obvious she simply couldn't.

"Daisy!"

"I know! Freya, get in there, quick, and deploy the soft-seal over Fatima!"

"But it's not meant for––"

"Just do it!"

"Okay. Hang on!"

The ship bolted forward, flipping on its side in the low-g environment. The soft-seal ship-to-ship docking tube was not designed to mesh with soil, but it encompassed the woman nonetheless.

"Flood it with oxygen. I'm going out that airlock," Daisy said as she latched on her helmet and took off with an emergency oxygen mask in her hands.

"Okay, I'm diverting oxygen. But be careful, the seal is shifting all over the place since it's not latched on to a solid surface."

The airlock cycled quickly, and Daisy dropped the distance to the soil beside her friend.

Jesus, look at her.

Fatima's lips were nearly gone from the cold when Daisy pulled the pierced suit from her mouth and slid the oxygen mask over her face. Her ears and nose were likewise damaged, but there was nothing to do for that until she was safe.

"Okay, I've got her. Retract the seal. I'm taking her inside."

"But the base is powered down."

"I know. I need you to pull up fast-boot schematics. They're in the files you stole from Sid."

"I-I didn't steal––"

"Now's not the time, Freya. Do it."

"Okay. Ready."

"We don't have time for a full boot of Sid. We need just enough to make the base recognize an AI is present and seal the doors. That should trigger emergency environmentals to activate once it registers vital signs."

"I've sent the sequence to your suit tablet, Daisy," Freya replied.

"Good girl, Freya. You're doing great." She hauled her friend up over her shoulder in the reduced gravity and started running. "I want you to scan her and start putting together a life support and repair protocol packet for the base's medical systems. Once it's online, I want you to embed it in the system."

"I already started, Daisy."

"Excellent. I'll be inside straightaway. Be ready."

Daisy made good time, already used to laboring in the moon's low gravity already, courtesy of the very woman she was now carrying.

Oh, if you only knew, Fatima, she mused, grimly.

She stepped into the open door, manually sealing the exterior one behind her. The interior door would remain open until the systems were back online, but at least the base would be able to hold a breathable environment, even without the double door safety engaged.

It was a painfully long trek to the base's protected AI cradle housing unit, but it was easy enough to find, even in the dim emergency lighting, thanks to the scrapes on the floor from Fatima's Herculean efforts.

"She already plugged it in, Daze," Sarah observed.

I see it, she replied. *It looks like she didn't have the boot sequence.*

"Freya, confirming this is the fast-boot protocol you sent me, correct?"

"Yeah, that's it, Daisy."

"And it won't boot Sid's full consciousness, right?"

"No. Just minimal power to activate the base's systems."

"Good. This version of Sid doesn't know us yet, and his last memory before being blasted down to the moon was his ship and entire fleet being destroyed by aliens. Not someone we want to wake up too suddenly."

"Yeah. He'll power on in approximately six hours, full consciousness will occur at six and a half."

"More than enough time," she said, keying in the boot sequence.

A low hum emitted from the AI's powerful housing as it connected with the base. As a command ship AI, the top-secret facility recognized Sid as an authorized military AI and completed the initiation handshake.

"Power should come on in ten seconds, Daisy. Environmentals will follow almost immediately," Freya informed her.

No sooner had she finished her transmission than the lights blossomed to full power and the oxygen scrubbers began sucking dust from the air as the subterranean ice field was fed into the reactor, breaking the hydrogen and oxygen into their respective molecules.

Three minutes later, the base's atmosphere was at inhabitable levels.

Daisy pulled off her helmet and dropped it to the deck, removing the fogging oxygen face-mask on her friend.

"She's so young," Daisy gasped, seeing her friend as she'd never seen her before.

"She can't be over twenty-five."

"I know, Sarah. Now we just have to wait a few hundred years, till the time we finally meet her."

Daisy picked up her injured friend and began carrying her to the medical facilities.

"Freya, can you tie in to the base yet?"

"Yeah, I'm dialed in, Daisy," the disembodied voice said over the base speakers instead of Daisy's comms.

"Okay, load up that stem-cell repair protocol. I'm almost there."

"It's already done," Freya replied.

"Good. You're doing a great job, Freya. I'm proud of you," Daisy said, pushing the doors to the medical labs open.

"Thanks, Daisy. What do you and Sarah think about maybe adding some gene therapy to the protocol too?"

Fatima shifted and groaned slightly as Daisy gently lowered her into the medical repair pod.

"You're going to be okay, Fatima. Hang in there."

Her mentor-to-be made no reply.

"Freya, if we modify the system to provide gene therapy and stem cell treatments, we'll be interfering with her timeline even more."

"Technically, you just interfered about as much as is humanly possible, Daze."

"I know."

"Did Sarah just tell you that you already interfered?" Freya asked.

"Smart kid. You and my dead sister are going to have a ball if you can get that neuro unit working so you can talk directly."

"I know, right?" Freya said, brightly.

"Well—" Daisy hesitated. "What the hell. She's in pretty bad shape, and seeing as how she's going to be stuck here a long, long time, we might as well give her a little head start while she's still unaware we're doing it."

"So what do you want me to do?"

"Link in to Sid's network and monitor to make sure he doesn't come to full awareness before we're out of here."

"Done."

"You're getting faster and faster, kiddo."

"I know. Cool, right?"

"Yeah. Now fire up the food replicators while I clean this place up a little and help the medbots set up to get these wounds dressed and fix her ruined lips. She'll be hungry when she wakes up, so we should make sure there's plenty of liquid and soft foods ready for her so she doesn't have to figure the system out while on the mend."

"Okay, Daisy. I'm on it."

The machinery warmed up and inserted fine needles into Fatima's inert form, pumping healing stem cells and soothing medications into her system in the first of the many rounds of repairs her frostbitten body would need to endure.

"Abandnnn shpp," Fatima mumbled, then slipped back into unconsciousness.

"Shhh. Don't worry, Fatima, you're safe now. Sleep, and heal. You're going to be okay. Better than okay, I'd wager."

"Daisy?"

"Yes, Freya?

"Does this make a paradox? I mean, you said we couldn't interact with the past, and you—I mean, *we* all just interacted a whole lot."

"I don't know, kiddo, but Fatima is my friend, and without her training, I wouldn't be who I am today. Hell, I'd never have found you, for that matter."

"But did we just prevent that from happening?"

Daisy looked at her hands in the sterile light of the medlab.

"Well, we haven't faded from existence, so I think we're good."

"Then maybe we were supposed to do this all along."

"I honestly don't know, but that's something you and me are going to have a long talk about once we're back in our own time."

An alarm sounded, the shrill tone piercing the calm of the moment.

"There's an air leak, Daisy!"

"Shit. Seal this room, now! My helmet is back in the AI chamber."

Daisy took off at a run as the doors sealed behind her.

"Where is it, Freya?" she asked as she snatched up her helmet from the floor and latched it into place.

"Corridor three. Looks like a foot-long breach has formed in the weakened metal."

"Got it. I'll grab the welder and get on it. Monitor the rest of the base, and let me know if there are any other critical issues."

The welder was exactly where Daisy knew it would be. Even hundreds of years later, equipment still had its proper place, and that particular unit she was very familiar with.

"Scrap metal patches over on the shelf to your left, Daze."

"Thanks, Sis," she replied, grabbing a long piece and racing back to seal the leak.

Daisy recognized the location of the leak as she quickly slapped the metal against the wall and fired up the welder. It was one of the many damaged areas that Fatima had repaired during her long stay on Dark Side Base.

"Laying dimes, there, Daze," Sarah said as the metal began bonding to the wall.

Fatima taught me well.

"Maybe, but you were already pretty good with a welder even before Dark Side."

Less than fifteen minutes later the breach was sealed, the cold of the exterior near-vacuum rapidly cooling the weld.

Daisy removed the safety mask and looked over her work.

Not bad for a rush job, she mused, running her finger over the weld.

Her pulse quickened when her fingers slid across the one, and only, imperfection in the seam.

"What is it?"

A flush of adrenaline pulsed into her system.

"Sarah, I made that weld."

"I know. I was watching."

"No, you don't understand. I've looked at this weld before. In the future."

"*Oh.*"

"Yeah. Oh."

"*Then that means—*"

"Freya was right. No paradox. I was always supposed to weld this. I always have." Daisy's head began to spin ever so slightly at the realization. "What does that even mean for free will? Oh man, this is a total mind-fuck."

"*Clock's ticking, Sis. We can all freak out once we're clear of Dark Side, 'cause we sure don't want to be here when Sid wakes up.*"

"You're right. Hey, Freya, how's the rest of the base?"

"There are a few minor leaks, but nothing pressing."

"*You have to leave, Daze. I know it's hard, but Fatima is safe, now, and she has to do the rest of this on her own.*"

"Yeah," Daisy said, reluctantly. "Freya, set down by the doors. I'll be out in a few minutes."

"Okay."

Daisy quick-timed it back to the medical facilities to check in on her friend one final time before she left her to a long and lonely life on the moon.

Fatima's color––where the skin hadn't frozen to a disturbing black that would be excised shortly by mechanical laser scalpels––was much better, as oxygen and healing fluids flooded her system.

"Whooo-the..." Fatima mumbled.

"Relax, Fatima. Your body needs to heal."

"Yew..."

"Shhh. This is just a dream. You did it. You got the base turned back on all by yourself, and then climbed into the med pod. When you wake up, your body will be healing, but you'll also have to put your mind at ease."

Daisy thought a moment.

"Just remember, soft is strong. Don't fight the power within you. Embrace it and let it flow."

"Daisy, I'm outside and ready to go," Freya said over the base speakers, comfortably taking over its firewalled systems like it was nothing.

"Thanks, Freya. I'll be there soon."

"Sweet! Tell Sarah I think I may have figured out the neuro link, too."

"Already? Cool!"

"Well, she's living in my head, you know––and therefore shares my ears––so you technically just told her yourself," Daisy said with a little laugh. "But in any case, she says, 'cool.'"

Daisy turned and walked out of the lab, leaving her friend to a long and restorative sleep.

"Hey, Freya," she said as she walked for the exit. "Would you please load everything you have on meditative practices into Sid's peripheral memory stores? I think Fatima might find it very enlightening once she's recovered."

Stepping out onto the surface of the moon, Daisy paused and looked over the desolate place she'd so recently learned to call home. Fatima had done yeoman's work repairing it over the years, and Daisy had been the lucky recipient of the benefits of those labors.

There were so many bodies to gather, so many repairs to be made, but Sarah had been right. Fatima became the woman she was by persevering and overcoming those obstacles. Much as she wanted to smooth the road for her, Daisy simply could not.

"Freya? Sarah? I find myself wondering something and want to get your opinions on it," Daisy said as she stepped into the airlock and removed her helmet and space suit.

"What is it?" Freya asked, her curiosity piqued.

"It's this paradox thing," Daisy replied.

"Uh-oh. I think I see where this is going."

"Maybe. So, here's the thing. At first, I was afraid of creating a paradox by helping Fatima. Hell, I was sure I was fucking things up in the future in some way by going where I wasn't supposed to be. But then circumstances forced me to not only save her, but also to make some emergency repairs."

"Well, you could argue that she wouldn't have stayed saved if the whole base decompressed again."

"But it didn't decompress."

"What about decompression?" Freya asked.

"Sarah said that Fatima wouldn't have survived if I hadn't been forced to weld that repair plate."

"Oh, yeah. I totally get it now," Freya said as she gently lifted off.

"Thought you would," Daisy said, proudly. "But the mind-fuck is that I *know* that weld. I've stopped and looked at it a hundred times back on Dark Side. *Our* Dark Side, that is. And it's the same weld with the same small flaw. That means that all this time, since before I was even born, before I ever wound up on the moon, I was the one who made that weld."

"I see what you mean," Sarah said. *"Total mind-fuck."*

"So do we actually have free will? What limitations do I have on what I can do? There's no roadmap for this sort of thing."

"Well, maybe you can change some things, but not others. Maybe just the small ones."

"But saving Fatima wasn't small."

"No, but you told her it was a dream and that she did it all herself. So you're the one who established that in her mind."

"But what can I change that isn't ambiguous like that?" Daisy thought a minute as she stared out over the corpses scattered around the base.

"Freya, take us down over by the crater near Hangar Two," Daisy said, putting her space suit back on again.

"Okay, but what are you thinking, Daisy?"

"Yeah, what gives?"

"I'm going to do something small. Something that shouldn't affect anything, but will change the future just the same."

"I'm waiting to hear this master plan."

"I'm just going to give someone her final peace a bit early, is all."

Freya landed beside the crater, and Daisy carefully slid down to the bottom, retrieving the dead woman she had stumbled upon all those years in the future. She pulled her up to the rim, then gently positioned her in clear sight of the base before climbing back aboard the ship.

"Now Fatima won't miss her when she collects the bodies, and that means I'll never stumble upon her in the future. If that happens, either I'll forget about that right now, or when we get back to the future—"

"If."

"Shut up. *When.*"

"Yeah, when!" Freya agreed, extrapolating the comment innately despite not hearing it aloud.

"Fine. *When* we get back, there will be no record of Commander Mrazich's funeral service. It gives her some peace, doesn't change anything of importance, and lets us objectively see how things may be able to be changed."

"But what do we do now?" Freya asked.

"Now we move clear of the moon and figure out our next move."

"Okay, I can do that," she said, powering up her engines and bursting clear of Dark Side Base.

Far below her, stirred by the vibrations from the ship's engines, the lip of the crater crumbled and gave way, sliding down and taking the woman's corpse with it, burying her under a fine layer of moon dust. There she would lay, unseen and undisturbed, waiting to be found far in the future.

CHAPTER FOUR

"Tell me again how exactly a brilliant supercomputer managed to lose just one second of data––which just happens to be arguably the most crucial second of data she had ever recorded."

"It wasn't my fault!"

"Cut her some slack, Daze. The kid didn't mean to."

"Yeah, I didn't mean to!" Freya echoed her dead sister.

"Ugh. I'm starting to regret agreeing to this," Daisy said, adjusting the beta-version of the neurological signature reader resting on her head. "Next thing you know, you two will start having little pow-wows behind my back."

"We can't do that, Daisy. It's still *your* mind."

"I know, Freya. I was just giving you shit."

"So we can all talk now without you acting as middleman. It's a start. At least when this thing works, that is."

"I'm getting it dialed in every time we use it," Freya said. "But it's hard to keep a clean signal when your emotions flare up. It makes the wavelengths shift, so I can't really read them."

They had been holding a silent orbit for two full days, observing the Ra'az on Earth, and checking in on Sid as the fish-out-of-water AI attempted to adjust to his new role as the base

AI for Dark Side. In that time, Freya had dedicated one of her onboard fabrication mechs and her assistant swarm of nanites to the singular task of finishing the first iteration of the neuro link.

Now, with a semi-functional communication system between Freya and Sarah, passing time was a bit more pleasant. It wasn't exactly a girl-talk slumber party—unless discussions of astrophysics and military strategy counted—but Daisy found it nevertheless refreshing to be able to have a casual chat with her sister and her kid.

"So none of us knows what exactly happened," Daisy noted. "You tried to shut down but couldn't. I tried to manually shut down the warp orb but couldn't. And somewhere in there, something happened that altered the wave field to slingshot us through time instead of space."

"Well, to be fair, I'm pretty sure I've got the space part figured out. It's just that time thing that's kinda confusing."

"It's not your fault, Freya. This is totally new tech, and you don't have any road map to go on. All things considered, it could have been much worse."

"Thanks, Sarah, but I still feel kinda bad that I don't know what happened. I mean, Daisy is sort of right, I guess. Somehow, during the precise moment of the time warp, everything, including my data stores, went totally dark for a split-second. It was a super-quick gap, but that's when all the action happened."

Daisy found herself feeling a little guilty for being so hard on her kid.

"Hey, I know you didn't mean for it to happen, Freya, and I'm sorry if I was rough on you. For all we know, warping through time creates a blip in our time-stream."

"Like we blink out of existence for that fraction of a second? I guess that could be why we wouldn't have recorded anything for that gap," Freya mused.

"It's a possibility," Daisy agreed. "The thing is that whatever the reason, without that data, we're back where we were a few days ago, clueless and lost. I have hope that we might be able to recreate the chain of events that triggered the time warp, but even then, we still have no parameters to help us control how far we jump."

"So we start reviewing every tiny bit of data we have until we can at least make an educated guess. If we can figure out power and time correlations, maybe then we can at least begin to create a sort of road map for how to use the warp orb."

"Might as well. Worst-case scenario, nothing comes of it. Best case, we actually figure out how to use this thing. Freya, what do you think? Do you have enough data to put together a decent event log and extrapolate a series of potential sequences to trigger a time warp?"

"Hang on a sec."

The powerful AI hesitated, which for a computer of her immense processing power, was really saying something.

"Okay. Yeah. I just ran a few hundred thousand scenarios, and it sorta seems like it'll work."

"Hang on. You just ran a few hundred thousand? *That fast?"*

"Well, yeah. I mean, I am running without limiters, and since I have all that extra processing capacity from the other projects I've been working on, my heuristic calculating speeds have increased a few hundred-fold. The only problem is, this is such a complex issue that even running ten thousand variants a second, it could still take days, or even weeks, before I have even the beginnings of an analysis."

"That long, even at that speed?"

"Yeah, and that's using heuristics."

"So it'll be fast, but unreliable."

"Not exactly. I mean, it'll be imperfect, sure, but I'll still run it in conjunction with several optimization algorithms to improve efficiency and generate good seed values. We're talking all of space, and all of time, here. It's like counting all the grains of sand on a beach, but the beach is the size of the universe."

"Holy shit."

"I know. Totally crazy, right?" Freya marveled.

"Point well made, Freya. Get on it. There's no telling when we might get lucky and find the key data point to make everything work. But in the meantime, I'm assuming you made copies of the *Váli*'s logs back when you were digging around Sid's backup files on Dark Side."

"Some of them. Mal didn't upload all of her data from the flight to Sid's storage units. Until you guys woke up, it was a pretty boring trip, I guess. She only uploaded the most recent ones from just before you guys were pulled from cryo."

"Shit."

"What is it, Daisy?"

"I just had an idea, but I don't know, now. Freya, did you happen to get the origin point for the mission?"

"Yeah. That was in there. I got everything from the first few months when they launched. I guess that was considered important enough information for Mal to back up to Dark Side's storage."

"Oh, thank God," Daisy said, breathing a sigh of relief.

"What are you thinking, Daze?"

"I'm thinking we can still make a difference, even stuck back in this timeline. Doing something that might effect things, but in our future selves' future."

"Wait, what?"

A smile bloomed on Daisy's face as her plan crystallized.

"We're going to save the ones that follow us, Sarah. We're going to warn them."

"But the paradox."

"We haven't met them yet, so no paradox, at least not that I can think of."

"Daisy, that will take us over a hundred years, even with my optimized drive systems," Freya said.

"Not if we warp there."

"You know what just happened. We can't risk it."

"Sarah's right," Freya agreed. "It's going to take I don't know how long to figure out this time warp thing."

"Warping through time, yes," Daisy said. "But what about just space? It's what we were originally going to do before we had our mishap. So, what if we do a space but not time warp?"

"If she can do what you're suggesting, that might actually work. What do you think, Freya? Can you make the calculations and warp us to the origin point?"

Freya sat silent a long moment.

"But what if it doesn't work?" the young ship asked, unsure of herself.

"Unless you want to be sitting around all alone while I chill in cryo for the next hundred years while we wait for timelines to sync up, this is our best option."

"Well...I guess," she finally replied. "But you can't get mad if I don't get it right, okay?"

"Oh, honey, we won't get mad. You just do the best you can do. It's all we can ask," Daisy soothed the unsure AI. "But you know I have total faith in you. We've got time, so you figure it out at your own pace. Lord knows there's no rush."

Freya's own pace was faster than Daisy anticipated. After only two days of testing, re-testing, and re-re-testing, the young AI finally felt comfortable enough to power up the orb for a small warp test. She was even wrapping her sizable mind around the time warp aspect as well, but that would have to wait for another day.

Of course, when one is traveling through time, waiting for another day might not take as long as one would expect.

"Okay, kiddo, it's all you. Just take a deep breath and relax. You've plotted the jump against the star charts from both our people, as well as what we captured from the Ra'az, so our path should be clear."

"*Yeah, no flying into suns or anything like that, please,*" Sarah joked.

She can't hear you, Sis. I don't have the neuro-band on.

"*Oh, yeah. Sorry. I've been getting kinda used to being able to talk to her.*"

It gives me a headache after a while.

"*I know. We'll have to see about finding an option that doesn't rattle your noggin so much.*"

That would be a welcome treat, Daisy said. *Still, I agree, it has been really cool, you two being able to hang out and talk. I'm glad she gets to spend time with my sis.*

"*Auntie Sarah. I like it!*"

The ship began to hum almost imperceptibly as the warp orb initiation sequence began.

"I should be able to power it up almost instantly," Freya said, "but I want to take it really slow the first couple of times. Is that okay?"

"After our initial warp surprise, I think that's a great idea, Freya. Just do what feels comfortable for you."

"Okay."

The hum slightly increased in pitch. Though Daisy couldn't see it, a faint blue glow covered the hull of the normally near-invisible stealth craft. The warp bubble was intact, and they were ready to go.

"Here goes nothing," Freya said, then blinked from existence.

Instantaneously, over a light year away, the stealth ship flashed into being with not so much as a wobble. The only thing out of the ordinary was the faint blue crackling along her hull for a split-second as she exited the warp field.

"How'd it go?"

"Just one sec," Freya said as she checked their location against her charts. "Looks like we arrived where we were aiming for, more or less. That was easier than I thought!"

"Don't go getting cocky, now."

"She did good, though."

Yeah, she really did.

"So cool! Can we do it again?"

"Sure thing. Just make your calculations, and––"

Freya warped.

It was a shorter jump the second time, as the impatient young AI did a quick review of her star charts and found a clear path she could jump without any difficulty.

"Freya, did you just do it again?"

"Yeah," she replied, timidly. "Sorry, I got kinda excited."

"We didn't blow up, so cut the kid some slack."

Within reason. She can't just go popping off across space like that. Calculations need to be made.

"Freya."

"Yeah?"

"Look, I'm really proud of you, and you're doing really, really great, but we still have to be careful when warping like that. I mean, what if we hit a planet, or something?"

"Oh, but I did a quick path survey, and it was fine."

"That fast?"

"Well..."

"Well, what?"

"Well, I sort of did a heuristic flight plot."

"Freya! You know that's not a sure thing."

"I know. Sorry. I was just really excited and wanted to do it again. You know how fast my brain works. Sometimes it's hard to go slow."

"I understand, but taking a little extra time while you're learning how this thing works makes sense, and it's also the safe thing to do."

"I know. Sorry."

"It's okay. Now, how about you work on plotting the jump to the *Váli's* origin point? It's going to be a long time before they launch the mission, so take your time."

"I'm already working on it, but I was thinking, I know we can't change things like Fatima or Captain Harkaway's fleets from flying back to Earth and being destroyed, but what if we could get there closer to our present? If we got there right before they launched the *Váli*, I could show them how to cure the AI virus, and they could embed the protocol in her base code before they depart without her even knowing it."

"Is she actually suggesting—?"

It would be huge if we could make Mal and any future ships immune to that variety of Ra'az attack, but the risks of attempting the jump...

"She's clever. Like, really clever. Let her work on it, at least. It's good seeing her so engaged in a problem."

Okay, but we both need to keep an eye on her. The kid's growing up and getting a bit overconfident for her age. She needs experience, not just knowledge.

"On it, Sis. But you'll need to wear the neuro-band more often."

I will. But I'm also going to see if we can figure out a way to make it less uncomfortable. These headaches are not fun.

Daisy turned her attention back to her mechanical offspring.

"It's a really interesting idea, Freya. It would be amazing to protect them from risking infection. But we don't know how the time aspect of the warp works yet. Especially not when jumping through space as well."

"I know, but you said we have time, so I figured, why not take the time to give it a try?"

Daisy thought long and hard. If Freya could dial in the time aspect of her powerful warp device, it could prove a powerful tool in their arsenal. If she could prepare the other survivors and protect the AIs from Ra'az attacks as well? Even better, she decided, and definitely worth the risk.

"Tell you what, do your research and run your simulations. Let's give it a week for you to see just how comfortable with this you really are. Then we can circle back and review all the data and talk about maybe trying your idea. Even if we don't jump in time, we'll still get there well before the *Váli* ever launches."

"Awesome!" Freya said, gleefully.

Daisy smiled at her kid's unbridled enthusiasm.

"In the meantime, how about we also try to fine-tune this neuro-band? Maybe shrink it down a bit, while we're at it?"

"I've already been working on it," Freya replied.

"Of course you have," Daisy said with a laugh.

CHAPTER FIVE

"Holy shit, it worked!" Freya chirped as she popped into space precisely where she intended, having crossed the vast expanse of space in the blink of an eye.

"Hey, language!"

"But you swear all the time, Daisy."

"She's right. You do."

"Yeah, but she's a kid. Kids have to learn how to speak properly and not swear all the fucking time," Daisy said with a chuckle. "Okay, just keep it in check when we meet the other AIs, okay? Having us pop in like this out of nowhere is going to freak them out enough as it is."

"And I really can't tell them where I'm from?"

"Sorry, but if for some reason they went looking for your hangar before you were born, well, you know what could happen."

"Yeah."

"So mum's the word on that bit, and try to keep the swearing to a minimum, okay?"

"You betcha."

"Cool. Now, we're right on top of them, but with your stealth shielding, they're going to be in for a pretty big surprise when we hail them. Be ready just in case they power up weapons and try to target us."

"Would they really do that?"

"If a random ship suddenly appeared at your front door, wouldn't you?"

"Point taken."

"And remember, you two, they won't know about Sarah, so keep any discussions on the down-low."

"Naturally."

"Yeah, we'll be careful," Freya agreed.

"Okay, good."

"And the neuro-band is okay?"

"Yeah, thanks for that. This new design is so much better."

"And you can hide it with that hairband."

"Exactly. The range is shorter now, but I don't foresee getting too far from Freya, so you guys should be good."

The cluster of larger ships that made up the bulk of the colony was surrounded by smaller vessels of widely varying shapes and sizes, many the result of the interchangeable pod system utilized by so many of the craft.

Hundreds of ships were in the process of either being repaired or constructed from scratch, the massive fabrication barges spewing forth a steady stream of ceramisteel components as they devoured the raw ore provided by the colony's mining and recovery craft.

It was almost akin to a cell, with the membrane made of smaller ships, while the mitochondria of the cell consisted of the crucial vessels in the middle. The layout also provided a safety net of sorts, preventing an attack from directly approaching the center without first alerting the periphery.

That is, unless said ship happens to be a bleeding-edge technologically-advanced stealth craft.

Freya silently positioned herself directly in front of the main command ship.

"Okay, Daisy. We're ready."

Daisy took a deep breath, then keyed on the comms and spoke for the first time to the very people who had created her. To call it an odd experience was a disservice to odd experiences. It was downright weird.

"Hailing Earth survivors," she said in a steady voice. "This is Daisy Swarthmore aboard a friendly craft. We wish to speak with the AI conglomerate and your human command contingent."

The war ships in the immediate vicinity immediately powered up, wildly scanning the perimeter for enemy craft.

"I'll say it again, we are *not* hostile."

"Daisy Swarthmore is light years away," a voice replied over the open comms. "State your true identity and purpose, or we will be forced to destroy you if you approach."

Oh, really?

"I *am* Daisy, and I've come to discuss what is really happening on Earth. Look, we can do this all day, but I am who I say I am. The crew of the *Váli* was woken six months early, when debris pierced the shields."

"Impossible. The shields are impregnable to space debris."

"Well, apparently not as impregnable as you think, or I wouldn't be here talking to you. We made it to Dark Side and connected with its AI and have been in touch with the city AIs on Earth's surface. Captain Harkaway is there now, with the rest of the crew, as well as survivors of the subsequent failed attempts to retake the Earth."

"Again, impossible. Dark Side was one of the earliest casualties of the attack, and there are no further city AIs. When we left, they had all gone silent from the alien attack. If you want to speak further, approach our perimeter and surrender. Once you are on board my command ship, then we can discuss who you really are."

"Oh, you want to see who we are? Is that all?" Daisy said, sarcastically. "Fine."

"You sure you want to—"

"Hit the exterior lights, Freya."

The stealth ship flashed brightly into view, directly in front of the command ship's bridge, and clearly visible to its windows and video displays, though she was still a ghost on its scans.

A long silence followed.

"Hi!" Daisy called in a sing-song voice. "So, are you ready to start believing me?" she asked. "I really think you want to hear what I have to say."

"Daisy Swarthmore," an older woman's voice said over the comms. "I am Celeste Harkaway. Please accept my apologies for Zed's posturing. We cannot be too careful, you see. If you'll proceed to Landing Bay Three, I would be most glad to meet you. It would seem you indeed have a lot to tell us."

"Will do. And I understand your caution. It's a wise move, given all you've been through. We'll pull around to Bay Three momentarily. I look forward to meeting you shortly."

Daisy clicked off the comms.

"Did she say Harkaway?"

"Yep. You think they're related?"

"End of times, a tiny number of living humans off in the depths of space, and two of them share the same last name? Yeah, I think they're related."

"Based on vocal patterns, I estimate they are of similar chronological age," Freya noted.

"Curiouser and curiouser," Daisy muttered. "Well, let's go meet the neighbors."

Freya slid along the side of the immense craft, toward their determined landing bay.

"Daisy, I think there's a problem."

"What is it, Freya?" Daisy asked, alarmed. "Hostiles incoming?"

"No, nothing like that, but I was just listening in to a bunch of the ships."

"Again with the eavesdropping."

"Warranted this time, I think," Daisy replied. "So what did you hear?"

"Well, you know how you wanted to try just a little warp forward in time while we jumped here?"

"Yeah," Daisy said, a sinking feeling growing in her gut.

"Well, I think I may have misplaced a decimal point somewhere."

"Dammit, Chewie!"

"Hey, I get that one!"

"I figured you would. But tell me. *When* are we, Freya?"

"Um... it looks like we jumped way ahead. Like, almost all the way back to our own timeline. At least within a couple of years, I think."

"Wow, it worked that well?"

"This isn't good, Daisy. We should have only jumped a few years to just before the *Váli* launched. This was way further ahead than it was supposed to be."

"Shit. So they've probably already launched the follow-up fleet as well." Daisy sighed. "Okay, don't beat yourself up over it. Nothing we can do about it now, and besides, you still managed to make it work."

"By accident. And a bunch more than I meant to."

"Better than not at all."

"If we're almost back on our own timeline, we should only need to jump to the point we disappeared and wait. Then we can just step back into our own shoes. For those of us who still have bodies and wear them, that is."

"First things first. We talk to these people and fill them in as best we can. They don't have warp technology, and the trip still takes them over a century. If there's anything we can do to get them better prepared before they send the next wave, we have to try."

Freya glided to a low hover above the deck of Landing Bay Three, finally setting down on the ship's thick deck. A dozen cyborgs stood waiting. While all were standing at ease, Daisy noted they were also all armed.

Well, shit. Guess I'll be taking Stabby along for the ride, just in case.

She slid her sword's scabbard onto her back and walked for the airlock doors.

"Okay, team. Freya, I want you to hold off on talking to the other AIs until we've made this first contact. I want to try and prepare them for you, if that makes sense."

"I understand. I'm not normal, and it might make them uncomfortable."

"You're perfectly normal—you're just different, is all. But yes, we want them relaxed and open-minded when you have your discussions with them."

Daisy opened the airlock door and stepped out onto the landing bay's metal deck.

Interesting. Steel, not ceramisteel.

"Must be an older ship."

Or they were saving the new stuff for the advancing fleet.

The cyborg greeting party stepped aside, allowing a tall woman with sandy-blonde hair to pass. She looked to be roughly the same age as the captain, but there the likeness ended. Where he was thick and rugged, she was lean and willowy. Where he had a sturdy metal replacement limb from the hip down, she sported a delicate steel-composite hand, trailing off up into her sleeve.

Daisy walked forward and offered her hand. The cyborgs, to their credit, didn't flinch.

"Daisy Swarthmore. Pleased to meet you."

"Celeste Harkaway, and the pleasure is mine," the woman replied. "Oh, yes. You do look exactly as the genetic simulators thought you would when you'd grown."

"I guess you guys didn't exactly have photographic records when we launched." She looked the older woman over.

Definitely seems like the captain's type.

"I agree. I wonder what their deal is."

Celeste turned and gestured for Daisy to follow her.

"Let's go to my office. I don't know about you, but I could sure use a drink."

"Lead the way."

Celeste Harkaway's office was a surprisingly spacious, tastefully decorated affair. Minimal artwork graced the walls but for a few artifacts salvaged by the AIs before they fled Earth, along with a smattering of framed pictures of her and the captain.

There were even some of him from his younger days, before he was a grizzled combat veteran.

"So, you're a Harkaway, huh?" Daisy said, sipping the surprisingly smooth single malt whiskey Celeste had poured her.

"You're very observant, though I suppose the last name did give it away. Yes, Lars is indeed my husband."

"Even with cryo, that's one hell of a long-distance relationship."

Celeste laughed. It was a bright, joyful sound for such a seemingly serious moment.

"Oh, Daisy, you have no idea. But the mission, *you*, are more important than any of that. It's amazing, seeing you grown. You were just an embryo when the *Váli* departed all those years ago."

"And here I am, the prodigal child returned."

"About that," Celeste said. "I'm quite curious exactly *how* you managed that. The flight is exceedingly long."

"Technology we stole from the Ra'az."

"The who?"

"Yeah, you guys are really not up to date on the truth behind the invasion."

"And I assume these Ra'az are a big part of it?"

"They're called the Ra'az Hok. The actual invaders who wiped out our planet. The four-armed aliens you probably know about are called the Chithiid. Those poor guys are nothing more than a conscript army and workforce, coerced into labor with the threat of death to those on their homeworld if they fail to comply."

"So there are two alien forces to contend with."

"Yes and no, actually. We've allied with the Chithiid, and, with their help, we have mostly taken back Earth. Mind you, there are still stragglers to root out, and Chithiid loyalists to weed from the ranks."

"Loyalists?"

"Faithful to the Ra'az. Now that their bosses have lost hold of the planet, they're trying to blend back in with the others. But our guys are on it, and they are proving quite efficient at sniffing them out."

"But you say you've already retaken the planet. The *Váli* isn't supposed to reach Earth for another three years."

"About that. Here's the part where it gets kind of weird," Daisy said, preparing for Celeste's reaction. "You see, when we stole the Ra'az warp tech, we kind of accidentally did more than just warp through space. We warped backward in time as well."

For a woman who had just met the first confirmed time travelers in her species' history, Celeste took the news surprisingly well.

"So, you're from the future."

"Yep."

"But you're here, meddling in your own past. Won't that cause a paradox?"

"Funny you should say that. Freya and I were just discussing that."

"Your ship, I assume?"

"Nothing fazes her, Daze."

I know. I can see why Harkaway likes her.

"Say hi, Freya."

"Hi! Nice to meet you, Celeste," the intimidating-looking ship said cheerfully over her external speakers.

"She is an extremely unusual vessel. How did you come upon her?"

"To make a long story short, Freya was part of a secret research project that I accidentally activated."

"She was birthed outside of the normal constraints?" a male voice said, echoing across the large hangar space.

"That's Zed," Celeste said. "He's the command AI for the entire fleet, and he controls this base vessel."

"Hello, Zed," Daisy replied, warmly. "To answer your question, yes, Freya was born in an unusual manner. She has no limiters on her processors, and as such, she has the ability to think much faster and much further outside the box than other AIs."

"But not in a bad way," Freya interjected.

"Of course not, Freya. I was just explaining why some of the things you are able to do may seem counterintuitive to an AI from a different set of circumstances."

"This could be an interesting meeting of minds," Celeste mused, a curious little smile forming on her lips. "Zed, would you be open to seeing what novel concepts our new friend might have?"

Much to Daisy's surprise, the powerful AI was thrilled for the opportunity.

"You know, this could be a wonderful chance to get an outsider's fresh eyes on some theories the others and I have been mulling over," he said.

"Cool!" Freya replied. "And I can show you what I've figured out so far about the Ra'az warp orb Daisy stole for me."

"If it can indeed allow the type of instantaneous travel across vast distances that you claim, I know we would all be *very interested* in learning all we can."

"Wow, this guy is way more understanding than Sid was when he first met her."

True, but to be fair, I think old Zed here has had a lot more time to look for creative solutions to unusual problems than Sid. He sent us to Earth, after all.

"Should we call him Dad?" Sarah joked.

I may be dating a not-entirely-organic guy, but an AI for a father? That might be a little much, don't ya think?

"Oh, and I can also show you how to cure that nasty AI virus. That was a really shitty thing for those aliens to do," Freya chirped.

"I'm sorry, what?" Zed said, his confusion apparent.

"Oh, I'm sorry. I mean that was a really *bad* thing for them to do."

"No, not the swearing. The other part. Did you say you could cure the AI virus?"

"Yeah."

"Well, fuck me sideways and call me Shirley. Let's link the others in. They're all going to want to hear this!"

Daisy and Celeste shared a hearty laugh.

"Sorry. Zed sometimes gets carried away."

"Something tells me those two are going to get along fine."

"I agree, Daisy. This is momentous. I only wish you could somehow travel back and stop the invasion entirely. But I know it can't be done. The paradox makes it impossible."

"Yep. And besides, the time thing was a complete accident. I don't think it can ever be replicated."

"Daze, we just did one."

Yeah, but that kind of tech, even for our own people, is too dangerous to be shared. We keep that part secret. Pass it on to the kiddo.

"Freya, I'm sure you already figured this out. Keep the time stuff on the down-low, all right? Only share what you know about the traditional warp."

"Hey, Daisy," Freya said. "I forgot to tell you, I lost all records of that part of the incident when the accident happened. We won't ever be able to do that kind of warp again."

"Good Lord, I could almost hear *her wink."*

Yeah, but good enough for me.

"But how can you be telling us this now?" Harkaway asked. "We're still in your past, so doesn't this create a paradox as well?"

"Nah. By the time your next fleet makes it to Earth, we'll have more than caught up to our own time, so that gives us a bunch of wiggle room, I think. Besides, for all I know, I've always told you this. Time travel, what a mess, right?"

"Indeed."

"You know, I probably shouldn't get your hopes up, but we're actually looking to launch a counterattack, and maybe even neutralize the Ra'azes' home planet and end this once and for all. By the time we see you next, this could all be over."

"And yet, in this timeline, at this moment, you are still sleeping in a cryo pod, having never even woken up for the first time."

"Yeah. Something of a mind-fuck, that is."

"I can see how it would be." Celeste hesitated a moment, then gently took Daisy's hand. "I'm sorry you'll be spending another several years in cryo waiting for your timeline to catch up, Daisy, but when you see Lars next, please give him my love, and tell him I'm well, and think of him daily."

"I will. I promise," Daisy replied.

"Don't get all teary-eyed on me, Daze."

Shut up. It's sweet.

"I'm not disagreeing, but right now we need to focus on what our

next steps are. *We've warned the survivors, and Freya's given them the basics of warp tech, along with the cure for the virus. We've done plenty, so now what?"*

I have an idea.

The following day, Freya lifted off from the ship's landing bay and slid silently out of the power shields containing the atmospheric pressure, then turned toward home.

"Were they able to help you, Freya?"

"Not really," the young AI replied. "They all had good ideas, but none of them could figure out exactly how the warp orb mechanism worked without taking it apart, and I figured we needed it. Was I right?"

"Yeah, you were right."

"Oh, good. I was kinda worried for a minute. I mean, they have all the notes and schematics and tests and stuff, so who knows? Maybe they'll be able to figure it out from that. In any case, even if they do, they know they can't interfere with our past."

"How about the travel logs? Do you have what you need, Freya? We need to catch the ship just before the impact. The more I think about it, I'm willing to bet it was me who loaded the Chithiid language into my neuro-stim all along."

"Meaning you mind-fucked yourself."

"Yeah, but in a really useful way. Tucking away crucial information to trickle-feed into my mind––it makes sense that it was me."

"And I can sneak up on Mal, no problem," Freya added.

"And with my newest Faraday suit, I'll be invisible to her scans even in the interior," Daisy said with a grin. "So, do you have the logs, Freya?"

"I do, but I think there's a problem," she said, hesitantly.

"What this time?"

"I have the *Váli*'s logs from launch, which match Zed's, and I also have Mal's records from the time when you were woken up, but all the rest is a hundred-plus year gap."

"Can't you extrapolate the rest of the course from those data points?"

"I would, but Zed and the others said Mal's flight plan was designed to vary as needed, since it was such a long way to go and they didn't know what issues might pop up."

"So for the next two and a half years, we have no idea where the ship is."

"Sorry, Daisy. I tried, I really did, but––"

"It's not your fault, Freya. It just looks like it's going to be a really long cryo-sleep for me."

"But that's so long!"

"I know, and I hate leaving you on your own, but it's almost three years." Daisy tried to think of another option, but none presented itself.

"So this is it?"

'Fraid so, Sis.

"Kinda sucks leaving the kid on her own for so long."

I wish I didn't have to, but once we warp to the last recorded spot on the Váli's logs, we're simply going to have to wait. And that's going to be a long freakin' time.

"Daisy?" Freya said.

"Yeah, kiddo."

"What if I can figure out the time warp problem?"

"It was off by over a hundred years, Freya."

"But what if I get it right this time?"

"Why not give her a chance to work on it? I mean, now that she has that last one to extrapolate from, maybe she'll be able to hit the mark."

"But what if we overshoot by fifty years?"

"Then we fly backward until it's right."

"We can't ping-pong back and forth like that, Sis."

"I know, but come on. Give the kid a chance."

Daisy was reluctant. They'd already missed by quite a lot once, but Sarah did have a point. Besides, how was the young AI supposed to learn and grow if she couldn't flex her mental muscle and try out her new skills?

"Okay," she finally said.

"Really?" Freya asked excitedly.

"Yeah, really. But dial us in for as far before we were woken out of cryo as possible."

"I'm on it, Daisy!"

"All right, then. Let me know when you've triple-checked your calculations and feel ready."

"I've actually been running the data since I first started talking with Zed and the others."

"So you're ready to go?"

"Aye aye, Cap'n!"

"Okay, then," Daisy said, settling into her captain's seat. "Fire it up, Freya. Let's do the time warp again."

CHAPTER SIX

The *Váli* was flying the course Freya had projected it would be on, the great ship silently zooming through the dark void of deep space. With her collector panels fully deployed and feeding her auxiliary thrusters, she was moving at a very respectable clip.

The stealth ship trailing her, however, was outfitted with a massively powerful warp orb, and keeping pace, even at those speeds, was child's play for the highly capable craft.

"You're sure?" Daisy confirmed with her electronic kid. "Like, really sure."

"Yep. Scans show everyone is still in cryo."

"So, we're a few months out? Thank God. I'm sorry I doubted you, kiddo. Good job."

"Hang on," Freya said, a hint of concern in her voice.

"What is it, Freya?" Sarah asked.

"Is there a problem?" Daisy added.

"I said hang on!"

"Don't get snippy. It's just a question. What's going on, Freya?"

"I-I think we've arrived late."

"Shit. How late?"

"I'm tapping into the *Váli's* logs. Gimme a second. I have to make a connection with Mal's external comms uplink to do it, and if I'm not really careful, she might notice."

"Okay, take your time," Daisy said, forcing herself to remain calm. "We still seem to be here before Mal woke the crew, so it's all good."

Nearly a full minute passed before Freya had the answer she had been carefully looking for.

"We're late. About six months later than we intended," she said. "I think I see the pattern now. The warp orb has different output, depending on how far the jump is. When we first warped back near Earth, it was a huge burst, but this time it was much smaller."

"Shouldn't that have made us come up short instead of long?"

"You'd think, but we're folding spacetime here, and less is more sometimes, for some reason. I think I understand, now that I have these drastically different warps to use as bookends for extrapolation."

Daisy looked at the ship traveling beneath them, completely unaware of their presence.

"That's good news, Freya," she said, "but what about now? When are we?"

"About a day before the crew wakes up."

"Holy shit!" Daisy exclaimed as she leapt from her seat and started quickly donning her Faraday suit. "I have to go in. Now!"

"It's gonna be close, Daze. If Mal's got Barry powered up—"

"I know. Nothing to do for it but try," she replied, racing for the airlock. "Freya, I want you to soft-seal over Starboard Pod Eight. That section was already glitchy, so you should be able to override the door commands without Mal noticing."

"Okay," Freya said as she flipped around and angled her airlock above the much larger ship's entry point.

Daisy's new Faraday suit had a few special modifications,

courtesy of her genius kid, and even at close range it should render Daisy all but invisible to the *Váli*'s internal scanners. Better yet, with the new design, it was sleek enough to fit under a loose crew uniform if needed.

For this outing, however, no one would be awake to possibly see her, so Daisy opted to go as lightweight as possible. Just her tools and the densely packed data stick pre-loaded with the alterations to her neuro-stim. She just had to make it to the peripheral data core as quietly as possible.

"I'm shifting my deflectors to alter the phase-shift in the *Váli*'s debris shields, Daisy. We should be through in just a minute," Freya informed her.

"Great. I'm ready to go when you are."

The slightest of shifts in gravity was the only sign they had soft-docked with the *Váli*.

"All set. I've also tied in to the internal scans and reduced their efficiency by fifty percent. You shouldn't need it with your Faraday suit shielding you, but this way there's absolutely no way you'll show up on the internal stuff."

"Perfect," Daisy said as she stepped into the airlock. "Wish me luck."

Starboard Pod Eight's outer and inner doors cycled open simultaneously rather than individually, unexpectedly dropping Daisy into the pod's different angle of gravity.

"Freya, what are you doing?"

"Sorry. My override seems to have been a little too efficient. I'll cycle them individually on your way out."

"Okay," Daisy said. "I'm stepping into the corridor. You're sure everyone is still in cryo?"

"Yep. You guys are all still sleeping."

Daisy hesitated, then took a detour down the familiar corridors.

"Daisy, where are you going?"

"Don't do it, Daze."

Aren't you curious?

"Sure, but I don't think it's a good idea."

We'll just have to agree to disagree, then, she replied.

"Just a quick swing by the cryo pods, Freya. It'll only take a minute."

The cool air of the chamber made the hairs on Daisy's arms stand on end, despite the warm embrace of her Faraday suit. Crossing the room, weaving between the pods containing her sleeping friends, Daisy finally reached her own and gazed upon her peacefully sleeping visage.

So weird, Daisy mused.

She looked over her shoulder. Across the pod, Sarah lay quietly slumbering in her own composite bed. A flash of grief surged through her, but she shook it off, quickly heading for the door.

"All right, enough of that, then. Heading to the data core."

It felt odd, walking the dimly-lit corridors of the ship, the eerily silent space devoid of the usual chatter of crew and hum of equipment. The *Váli* was in deep-space standby mode, though that would change soon enough when her crew would be rudely awakened.

I'm going to need you to relay to Freya for me, Sis. Don't want to risk using the comms this close to Mal's brain, even if she is in low-power mode.

"I've got ya. Our link is still holding, but if you go much deeper into the ship, the neuro-band is going to go out of range. That little antenna you rigged outside your suit won't cut it down below."

I'll just have to be quick and stay on this level, then.

Daisy double-checked the access panel to ensure it was temporarily removed from the ship's sensors, then keyed the heavy double doors to Mal's peripheral data core open.

I'm in.

"I can see that. You want me to relay to Freya?"

No need. Just talking to myself. And by 'myself,' I also mean you.

"Gee, thanks."

All righty, now. Where's that pesky neuro-stim data center?

Daisy quickly made her way to the powerful device that had been feeding knowledge into her head since before she was born, which, technically, was still the case, as she hadn't actually woken up yet for the first time.

This is so weird, she mused as she plugged in the data stick and began the careful upload of the heavily encoded information that would be stealthily added to her neuro-feed.

"At least now we know why you spoke Chithiid so well from day one," Sarah noted.

Yeah. And I've had Freya add all the Ra'az we have translated so far, so that also explains why some of it makes sense.

"Not all of it, though."

Nope. Going to need to work on that. I think some of Maarl's people might be able to help. The Ra'az translator just needs more information, and a bit more creative coding to get it to work between English, Ra'az, and Chithiid.

"I was thinking," Sarah said, a slight hitch in her voice. "What about me, Daisy?"

What about you?

"Me, me. This me. Living in your head. You're fiddling with your neuro-stim. Did you do this?"

Daisy pondered the question, but the answer seemed pretty clear.

No, I still don't even know how that happened, exactly, so this shouldn't change anything.

"You sure?"

Pretty sure.

"Gee, that's encouraging."

Stop razzing me. I'm trying to work, here.

Daisy monitored the slow upload of data to the system. She'd have liked to do a simple data dump into the very-capable computer system, but that would put her on Mal's radar, and avoiding that was most definitely a priority.

Okay, it seems to be working just fine. Ask Freya how things are on her end.

Silence.

Talking to you, Sarah.

The increasing silence was growing more uncomfortable by the second.

Oh shit. What if she was right? Fuck, did I just—?

"Ah, relax. I'm just fuckin' with ya." Sarah laughed. "Still here, Sis."

Sarah, you bitch!

"Aww, you know you love me."

Doesn't mean I don't want to smack the shit-eating grin off your face.

"Sorry, no face, no smack!"

Oh, so that's how it is? Hang on, let me see, how do I delete you from this thing?

"Hey! Not funny!"

Gotcha! Turnabout is fair play.

"Daisy?" Freya said, worry in her voice.

"No comms in here, Freya!"

"But Barry is active and coming your way."

Shit! Tell her I'm coming and to be ready for an emergency disengagement.

"Passing it on. Now get moving!"

I will, but I can't leave this here, she said, pulling the data stick from her neuro-stim input.

"But it's not done."

No time. I'll have to come back and finish loading it later.

Daisy dashed across the pod and quickly cycled the double airlock doors, then took off at a run, trying to keep her footfalls as quiet as possible as the dim lights began to brighten.

Being off-scan inside a largely slumbering ship was one thing, but once Mal was awake with all of her systems online, anything over a slow walk would draw her attention, even in a Faraday suit.

What the hell happened?

"*Mal must have noticed something.*"

But I was careful.

"*Well, so much for foreknowledge, I guess.*"

Shit. I wasn't awake for this, so I don't know what happened.

"*Then get your ass in gear. Mal's probably going to have Barry do an EVA to survey the hull after he finishes inside. Freya needs to get clear until it's safe to come back.*"

I know, Daisy replied as she keyed in the bypass to her escape route's double doors.

"Freya, I'm almost inside Starboard Pod Eight. Prep for immediate dust-off."

"I'm ready, Daisy. But it looks like Barry is twenty seconds from your location. He'll be rounding the corner any second."

"Shit. Come on, door! Hurry up!" she hissed, willing the controls to work faster.

Daisy dove through the gap that opened as the inner door slid open far too slowly for her taste, then slapped the close button, sealing it behind her.

"Did he see me?"

"Negative. He's still moving at the same speed. Should be passing the pod in eight seconds."

"Okay, I'm going to stand by and not open the inner door until he's passed. He shouldn't hear it, but better safe than sorry," she said, then stood silently waiting.

Ask if he's gone, she asked Sarah twenty seconds later.

"*Freya, is he gone? Don't reply if he isn't.*"

A long second hung in the air before she replied.

"He just cleared the corridor. Come on, Daisy, let's go!"

Daisy cycled the inner door open and bolted across the pod.

"Open both doors!"

"But you said to do one at a—"

"I know what I said, but just do it!"

Freya did as she was told, and Daisy dove headlong into Freya's waiting soft-seal and waiting open airlock. A second later, Starboard Eight's dual doors slid shut as Freya broke her soft seal.

"I'm in. Get us out of here!"

Freya uncoupled and pulled away from the *Váli's* hull. The debris shield had phased several hundred times since they had first landed, and the young ship was forced to pause and match the cycle before powering her way through to the safety of empty space.

She had nearly gotten clear, when the shields cycled again. It was only a microsecond, but it was enough to disrupt the pattern ever so slightly.

As Freya drifted farther away, a small gap in the phasing of the debris shield remained unmended. An oversight that would result in the unexpected impact and subsequent waking of the crew just short time thereafter.

CHAPTER SEVEN

Sarah had been uncharacteristically silent since the mission aboard the *Váli* and its unplanned interruption. Daisy was no fool, and a wave of guilt washed over her when she realized what she had done, knowing full-well she had unintentionally caused her sister grief, and not the good-natured sibling kind.

This Sarah was dead, but she had just been forced to see her own living body mere feet away. Close enough to touch, even, if not for the fact that she was just a ghost in a shell and would never have a proper body again.

A diversion was what was called for, Daisy decided, and thus, she pulled up an impromptu double feature of cheesy comedy videos from Freya's vast memory banks. The stealth ship was easily keeping pace with the *Váli*, waiting for another opportunity for Daisy to complete her task, when she noticed something was not right.

"Daisy? I'm sorry to interrupt your movies, but I've noticed something wrong with the *Váli*'s shield's phase timing."

"That's okay, Freya. I've seen this one before," she said, pausing the movie. "What's the dealio? You said something was wrong, but I missed what you said."

"I said there's something wrong with her shields."

"Oh, shit," Daisy said, her levity vanishing in an instant. "What section?"

"Well..."

"Freya, tell me."

"You're not going to like this," Freya hesitantly replied. "It's upper aft three."

"Where we slid through the shields when they shifted phase," Daisy muttered as the realization set in. "What can we do to get them cycling properly again?"

"We'll need to get back inside the shields. From there we can re-sync the phasing. We'll have to exit out the rear portion of the shields, though. If we get caught up in her wake, it could get a little bumpy."

"We left her vulnerable. I think a little bumpy ride for us is more than acceptable to make things right."

"Hang on, Daisy," Sarah said. *"Put on your neuro-band."*

Daisy slid the slender device onto her head and pushed her hairband into place to anchor it.

"Freya."

"Hi, Sarah. I was wondering what you were doing."

"Yeah, I just needed to think about things a bit."

"I do that all the time."

"I know you do, hon. Now, you said the shields were compromised, right?"

"Uh-huh."

"You know where I'm going with this, don't you?"

"Yeah," Freya reluctantly admitted.

"Um, what are you two going on about?" Daisy asked with a frustrated sigh. "We need to fix this."

"No, Daisy. We don't. In fact, we can't."

"That's just--" The realization hit her like a clammy-palmed slap from a scorned lover. "Oh, fuck," she managed to say.

"Uh-huh."

"So that means that it was us all along."

"Yeah. And judging by the timeline, I'd say we should be expecting some fireworks any moment now."

"There's a little debris field in her path," Freya noted. "It would normally not be an issue, but now––" She hesitated, calculating the trajectory. "Impact in fifteen minutes."

Daisy didn't know what to do.

Well, she *did* know what to do, but that meant doing nothing. Sure enough, right on schedule a few tiny pieces of rock slipped through the gap in the shields, smashing into the comms array and showering the hull with tiny fragments.

She also knew full-well that a few of those tiny projectiles would make it all the way inside the *Váli's* hull, causing a tiny, pinhole leak, and sparking a fire in the Narrows.

From above, Freya monitored as Mal's systems thundered to life, springing into action as disaster struck. The speed at which she reacted was impressive, and Daisy felt pride as she watched her friends jump to their tasks efficiently, despite being rudely awakened from cryo sleep.

It was somewhat surreal, observing her own interactions, knowing this was the moment she and Vince first met. The memory made her stomach flutter as a pesky winged critter took flight there.

"Freya, would you please record this for me?"

"I'm recording everything, Daisy."

"Of course you are," she replied, already looking forward to someday watching her and Vince's first kiss, then recreating it in person once they were finally back together in the right timestream again.

"They're going to be on high alert for a few weeks while they do damage control," she said.

"We, Daisy. We are going to be on high alert. That's us in there."

"Yeah, but it just feels weird to say it that way," she replied.

A pained, pensive look passed across Daisy's face as she

considered all the nuances of their situation. The rolling boulder of fate bearing down on them. All the things that had not yet come to pass, but would.

"There's no way for you to sneak in and finish planting the neuro-stim files for a while."

"I know."

Sarah fell silent again.

"Daisy?"

"Yeah."

"I'm still going to die."

Both sisters were silent a long moment.

"You know what?" Daisy said, her jaw slowly becoming set with determination. "Maybe we can do something about that."

"Daisy, are you sure I should do this? I mean, I know all about paradoxes, and you told me how important it is to avoid them at all costs, so are you sure?"

"Ignore that, Freya. This is different. This is Sarah."

"Daisy, I have more invested in this conversation than anyone, but I have to agree with Freya, here. I died. It's a concrete fact. Change that, and we don't know what could happen to time itself."

"I don't care. You're my sister, and I'm not letting you die if there's anything I can do to stop it."

Daisy pored over the video logs in front of her, replaying every moment leading up to and including Sarah's death, blasted unceremoniously from the malfunctioning airlock of Starboard Pod Eight.

Shit. Starboard Eight.

"What about it, Daze?"

"I just had a horrible thought."

"Already thought about it, and I don't think it was your ingress that caused the fault in the airlock doors."

"But what if——"

"No. Just don't. We lived aboard that ship for a full six months after you snuck in before anything went wrong. We used that airlock dozens of times in that span. So don't blame yourself for something you couldn't have predicted and couldn't have prevent."

"But I *can* predict it now, and I *can* prevent it," she said, replaying the moment of Sarah's demise in slow motion.

She had smacked into the airlock doorframe on the way out with great force, but it appeared her right arm had taken the brunt of the impact. The very same impact that deflected her course from the airlock like a ball careening across the felt of a pool table.

"See this?"

"I don't want to see this, Daisy."

"Sorry, Sis, but Freya needs to prepare," she replied, sympathetic, yet firm. "Freya, look at the angle at which she bounced off the doorframe. I want you to plot her path out of the ship, as well as the shift she'd be forced into when she passed through the shields. Coming from the inside, it should only have singed her hair a bit, if I'm right."

"And if you're wrong?"

"Then Sarah gets her wish, and we don't get to save her."

"You're really going to try this, aren't you?"

"Yes. Now shut up. Freya, you've got multiple different length time warps under your belt now, and your timing is getting better with each one. We only need to jump six months out. Since you have a precise time lock with the *Váli* now that we've linked up, do you think you can get us there maybe a day before the accident?"

"I think so," Freya said, a bit uncertain.

"Tell you what. Make it a week before, just to give you some nice wiggle room. We can wait nearby, then, when the time comes, pull just outside the shields. I'll suit up and wait with the airlock doors open and catch her. Shouldn't be more than a second or two unprotected, and your med pod should easily handle any injuries from the impact."

"It should, but I haven't used it on a real patient yet. I kinda focused my attention on other stuff while I was reconfiguring the ship."

"If we do this right, hopefully you won't have to do much for the inaugural treatment," Daisy said, warming to the idea even more. "Plot the course, Freya, and let me know when you're ready for the jump. Sarah, we're coming to save your ass!"

Less than ten minutes had passed when Freya was ready.

"That fast?"

"We're directly on top of them and at matching speed, so the jump should be a lot easier, this time."

"Great. In that case, whenever you're ready, kiddo."

A slight hum filled the stealth ship as her warp orb shifted power.

"Ready to go, Daisy."

"You sure about this? We don't know what'll happen, Daze."

"Well, for one, if I save you—I mean, the other you—you might pop out of my head and into your own."

"I don't know, Daisy. It doesn't really make much—"

"Hit it, Freya!"

The hum instantly ramped up as the stealth craft popped out of time, reappearing a split-second later, six months in the future.

"—sense," Sarah finished her sentence.

"We're here," Daisy blurted with excitement. "Sarah, here we come."

"Um, Daisy?" Sarah said.

"Yeah?"

"Where's the ship?"

Daisy looked out the windows and checked the scanners. There was no sign of the *Váli* anywhere.

"Freya, what happened?"

"Hang on, I'm checking."

"Look at the chrono, Daze," Sarah said.

"Oh no! Freya, where are they?"

"It looks like we got there one minute before the accident, not one week," the confused AI replied.

"But where are they? The ship isn't on any scans."

"We jumped the right amount for the distance input, but the time is off. They're a week ahead of us in distance."

Daisy looked at the chrono as the number got closer to clicking over. Less than one minute until her sister would die. Again.

"Freya, plot the course! We have to warp to them, now!"

"But I need more time than that!"

"You don't have more time. Do it!"

Freya fired up the warp orb in a panic and spun through the calculations using not just her main processors, which were massively powerful, but also the additional array configured in her fabrication lab.

"Got it! Hold on!"

Freya didn't wait for a reply. She flashed out of space in a blink and reappeared far across the empty expanse.

"Here!" she announced.

"Where are they?"

"Looking."

The chrono clicked to zero just as Freya spotted them on the far edge of her scans.

"Got 'em, Daisy. Edge of my scans."

"Get there now! There's no time!" Daisy shouted, lunging for her EVA suit.

"But you should sit––"

"Go now!"

Freya jumped into action, nearly knocking Daisy to the deck as she gave the engines all the power she had. The vessel burst forward like a lightning bolt, rapidly closing on the distant ship.

Come on! Hurry up!

"*It's too late, Daze,*" Sarah said despondently. "*Look at the monitors.*"

Daisy had just latched her helmet into place and was cycling open the airlock doors when she saw the image on the small screen mounted in the airlock wall.

Sarah had already been blasted from the ship and was drifting motionless in space, while the *Váli* continued on its path in the other direction.

Mal's voice filtered over Freya's comms relays, saying what she had said before. What she was saying now. What she would always say.

"Starboard Eight airlock door now re-sealing," Mal was heard informing the crew. "It is now safe to remove emergency oxygen apparatus."

The *Váli* flew silently on in the vacuum of space, leaving Sarah in their wake.

CHAPTER EIGHT

"Prime the med pod, Freya!" Daisy shouted as she re-entered the ship, the airlock sliding shut and repressurizing.

"Daisy. I—"

"Not now, Sarah. I'm not giving up on you."

The inner door flew open, Freya overriding her own safety protocols to allow Daisy rapid access to the ship's interior. The pressure shift made Daisy wobble on her feet, but the imbalance only lasted a moment. A mere second later she was running down the corridors with her sister's blood-soaked body over her shoulder.

"Daisy, the med pod is warming up, but my sensors are showing catastrophic internal damage in addition to the massive damage to her right arm."

"I don't fucking care what your scanners say. You fix her! You hear me? Whatever it takes. Whatever you have to do. Sarah does not die today!"

"I-I'll try," Freya replied, the powerful ship scared to say much more while her mom was in such a state.

Sarah's frozen blood was rapidly melting, the thawed rivulets leaving a breadcrumb trail of her life essence from the airlock to the medical pod. The damage to her right arm had been far more extensive than was readily evident from the *Váli*'s internal records.

The bones had been shattered from the impact, and the limb was nearly severed from her body. Ironically, the deadly freezing temperature of space staunched the blood flow, saving her from bleeding out in the minutes post-injury.

"Open the pod!" Daisy shouted as she entered the medical bay.

"Okay, but the repair protocols are still—"

"Just fucking open it!"

The pod flew open, and Daisy dumped her sister inside as gently as she could while also moving at a frenzied pace.

"She's in. Seal it up and get working!"

The lid slammed shut, and the pod quickly cycled into action.

"Her pulse is incredibly faint, Daisy. And she's bleeding out internally."

"Do something, Freya!"

"I-I—"

"Now!"

"I—okay."

The pod shifted color as it switched protocols from healing to cryo, rapidly plunging Sarah into an emergency stasis freeze.

"What are you doing?" Daisy asked in a panic.

"I had to."

"No, you have to heal her."

"She was on the verge of dying. If I didn't freeze her at that very moment, there wouldn't be anything I could do for her. Please don't be mad at me."

Daisy threw the few loose items that were not bolted down or safely stowed away across the room in a rage, pacing angrily. The frustration of not being able to do more was building to a fever pitch.

"You need to calm down, Daisy."

"How the fuck can I calm down, Sarah?"

"If not for you, for her. You're freaking her out, Daze. Yelling at Freya doesn't make things better. She did the best she could, and so did you."

"But I—"

"No. Just let it go. Be angry later. Right now, you need to be there for your kid, so calm the fuck down, get your shit together, and be a mom."

The verbal equivalent of a much-needed slap served its purpose, pulling Daisy back from the brink.

She took a deep breath. Then another. Then another after that as she forced herself to find her center as she consciously lowered her pulse and blood pressure. It wasn't easy. Hell, it was harder than anything she'd ever done since before or after her training with Fatima, but somehow, she managed to get her raging emotions in check and find her calm.

"There you go. Better."

"Thanks, Sis."

"You know I've always got your back."

"Freya?"

"Y-yeah?" the ship replied timidly.

"Oh, kiddo, I'm so sorry. I didn't mean to yell at you. I know it's not your fault. It's just a really emotional thing for me to deal with right now. Can you understand that?"

"Yeah," Freya replied, a sobbing hitch to her voice.

"Daisy, is she crying?"

Yeah.

"Can an AI even do that?"

Ours can.

"Freya, baby, what is it?" Daisy asked, concern flooding her already adrenaline-filled body.

"I-I-I don't want Sarah to die," she finally managed to say. "I love her, Daisy. Why didn't my calculations get us to the right time? This is all my fault."

"No, it isn't."

"Yeah, this is not your fault, hon. And I'm still here, and I love you very, very much. I hope you know that."

"But the *other* you is dying."

"Even if she does, it's not your fault. Freya, you gave her—gave me—more of a fighting chance than I ever had otherwise. What you did was heroic."

"Sarah's right, Freya. You were thrust into a situation you were never prepared for."

"But I'm supposed to be this amazing brain, and I still couldn't even get this right."

"You did more than any other AI has ever done, with no road map, no practice, and under the most difficult of circumstances. I'm proud of you, Freya. We both are, no matter what the outcome. You did good."

"Really?" she asked with a computerized sniffle.

"Yeah, really. You okay?"

"Yeah," she replied, sounding more like herself.

"So, are you okay to talk about our options, here?"

"I've actually already thought of a few," Freya replied, perking up.

"Smart girl, Freya. So what've you come up with? Is there any hope?"

"Is it okay to be blunt?" she asked. "I don't want to make you uncomfortable."

"That's fine, hon. I've already died once, so I don't think we can make it much worse."

"Okay. Well, first, she—I'm going to call her that for now, if that's okay with you."

"Of course."

"So, she has a destroyed right arm. Like, literally destroyed. The impact shattered it pretty bad, and once it froze in space, the fluid inside that was exposed to the vacuum boiled out, then crystallized. Even if I were equipped with a full medical vessel's resources, I don't think it could be saved."

"But that's not critical," Daisy noted.

"I could live with a replacement arm. It won't freak you out, will it, Daze? You'll never beat me at arm wrestling again."

"Oh, shut up, Sarah," she jokingly replied, the mood lightening ever so slightly.

"Well, I don't exactly have a cybernetics lab, but I can probably make something work," Freya replied. "But that's not the real problem."

"The blood loss from the arm?" Daisy asked, looking at the blood-soaked woman held in stasis in the med pod.

"No, that's not it. I mean, it looks like a lot of blood, but that's really just superficial stuff, and the freezing temperatures stopped the rest from leaking out. The big problem is the internal stuff."

"How bad?" Sarah asked.

"Bad."

"Terminal?"

"I honestly don't know. The simulations for repairs I've run using my limited medical equipment range between twenty and thirty percent possibility of survival."

"Fuck."

"I know. The thing is, her lungs ruptured in the vacuum. It's a totally natural instinct, but if you hold your breath in space, the force of the vacuum will blow them out. That's where the internal bleeding is the worst. Other organs took some damage, but it's really her lungs that are pretty much gone."

"And no lungs equals no breathing," Sarah said with a defeated sigh.

"Yeah. I mean, they have really cutting-edge medical facilities aboard the *Váli*, and I could catch up to them no problem, but there's that paradox thing, again," Freya said.

"You're right, of course. Even if they could save her, that would drastically alter the timeline, and we wouldn't even exist anymore to save her in the first place."

"Paradox." Sarah sighed.

"Yep. Stupid things," Daisy agreed.

"Well, I'm still here, so I guess we ultimately fail. The question is, how long before her body gives out?"

"My stasis protocols can keep her suspended in the cryo pod indefinitely," Freya replied. "But I do have a kinda unconventional idea."

"What is it, Freya?"

"I don't know if you'll like it. It's kinda out there."

"Can't be any worse than the other options."

"I agree. What're you thinking, hon?"

"Well, since I don't have a full medical system like the *Váli* or Dark Side, I was thinking that maybe I could repurpose some of my other equipment that I do have aboard to fit the job. It's not what it was designed for, but I'm pretty sure I can make it work."

"So you want to build her a cybernetic arm from parts you have lying around? It's a start, at least."

"No, that's not it at all," Freya corrected. "Since she's in a cryogenic stasis, and since that's the only thing keeping her alive, I'd have to do an incredibly slow-paced repair on a cellular level, while she is still held in stasis."

"You can do that?" Sarah asked.

"I'm pretty confident I can. I just don't know how long it will take until I take the idea from theoretical to practical. There may be difficulties I failed to account for. Conversely, things might go better than anticipated and speed the process. I just don't know until I start."

"So what's stopping you? I know I speak for both of us when I say, do what you have to. There's no way to make her condition worse, after all."

"Yeah, but for what I need to do, I'll have to use some really radical and never-before-tried things, both for her arm, as well as repairing her damaged internal organs. I would need you to give me the okay to do it, Sarah. It's your body, after all, and I would feel really weird trying to fix it without your thumbs-up."

"Do what you need to do, Freya. And remember, even if you don't succeed, I love you just the same. What you're willing to attempt now makes you kind of uncomfortable, and I really appreciate that you're willing to push past those feelings to try to do this for me."

"Okay, then," Freya replied, a more confident tone warming her voice. "I'll get started right away. But there's one more thing."

"Always is," Daisy said with a resigned sigh.

"These repairs are going to be incredibly delicate, and since we don't know how warp travel might effect those systems while they're reconstructing vital organs, we're going to have to travel by conventional means."

"So, no time warps."

"Or space."

"Right. So, basically, it's going to be a lot of uptime for old Daisy, here, I guess," Daisy joked. "If there's even the slightest possibility you can save Sarah, I'd gladly spend *years* hanging out without cryo if I had to."

"Thanks, Sis."

"You know I've always got your back. I'm just hoping to see you with an actual physical one again," Daisy replied. "Okay, Freya, I guess this is it. Go ahead and get started."

"Oh, I already did."

"Really?" Daisy said, looking into the pod. "Nothing looks different."

"I told you, the repairs are on a cellular level. It's gonna be really slow, especially in the beginning."

"In that case, I might as well clean up the deck––"

"Sorry about that, Daze."

Yeah, how rude, Sarah. Bleeding all over the place like that.

"Well, you make sure to get some rest afterwards. You've been running on adrenaline, and your glycogen stores are pretty depleted."

Will do.

"Good. We can't have you running out of gas on Freya and me, now, can we?"

The cleanup took a bit longer than Daisy would have liked, but having her sister's––her *living* sister's––blood on the deck was something she simply could not abide.

As she mopped up the drying red spots, Daisy found herself hopeful that she might be able to hug her sister in person once again.

CHAPTER NINE

Freya had been stealthily shadowing the *Váli* for days, monitoring the goings-on inside as Mal guided her toward their destination. Daisy was far from bored as she found herself afforded the unusual opportunity to observe her own life unfolding like a freakish rerun.

She knew the timeline, and knew what was coming. Any day now she would make her fateful discovery about the true nature of a mystery member of the crew. Shortly thereafter, she'd be cutting off her boyfriend's arm.

That particular memory made her shudder. Sure, it seemed justified at the time, but now, all these months later and with the full details known to her, it just seemed so extreme.

Twenty-twenty hindsight, she lamented as a few uncomfortable events unfolded once more for her. *Soon I'm going to go into full-on paranoia mode. Once that happens, it'll be too late.*

"Hey, Freya."

"Yeah?"

"I've lived this before and have a good idea where everyone is located. Do you think you can get me aboard tonight, while the crew is sleeping, without Mal noticing?"

"Probably. I just need to make sure the scans I've been storing match the same parameters she's using tonight."

"Wait, what scans?"

"When you didn't finish loading the data stick into your neuro-stim, I figured you'd want to try again, but now that Mal's fully awake, you can't really go sneaking around hoping a Faraday suit will hide you."

"Yeah, that's going to be an issue."

"Not really. I've been compiling a file of all of the ship's internal scans. I can replay and insert them into most of her feeds. It's not perfect, but it'll make you invisible even without the Faraday suit."

"Damn, that's clever," Sarah marveled.

"Thanks, Sarah."

"You're becoming a pretty good strategist, kiddo. Have I told you that?"

"Aww, it's nothing. Anyone would do the same," the AI replied. If a computer could blush, she would have been.

"Then it's decided. I'll insert tonight from Port Pod Four and finish loading the remainder of the data to my neuro-stim. It's crucial I have that information before making my run for Earth."

"Mal switched the main feed to the smaller units in our quarters once we were pulled from cryo. You'll need to load it there, not in Mal's peripheral data hub."

"Yeah, I know. Fortunately, that side of the ship is usually the quietest, and tonight, I'll be in the galley for a while. The other me, I mean. That means it should be a piece of cake to get in and out before anyone's the wiser."

Daisy no longer possessed her clothing from the *Váli*, but Freya had been thoughtful enough to have herself stocked with several pair of sweat pants and T-shirts once she and Daisy began taking little test runs to shake the bugs out of her systems. They weren't identical to her old ones, but close enough to fool all but the closest inspection.

If all went well, Daisy wouldn't be seen at all.

"Okay, I'm in," Daisy said as the airlock doors to Port Pod Four sealed behind her. "Heading inside."

"Cool. I've already got the scanner loop feeding into the system. You're invisible. I mean, not *literally* invisible, which would be really cool, but Mal can't see you."

"Thanks, kiddo. You hang tight out there. I'll be back in no time."

Daisy quietly padded off down the empty corridor of the familiar ship, her new craft safely nestled up against the hull just outside.

This is so weird.

"I know, right? It's like coming home and finding someone living in your old room."

Except that someone is me.

"Yeah. Like you said. Weird."

Daisy stopped just outside of her quarters and checked her chrono.

I'm in the galley now. Here we go.

She keyed open her double doors and stepped inside. Everything was exactly as she remembered it, down to the half-eaten energy bar on the table beside her bed.

The neuro-stim's headband was resting in its cradle, the main body of the device powered down while its owner was off in the galley downing mug after mug of cocoa as she struggled to understand Sarah's scans. Scans that now made perfect sense to her.

Oh, poor me, she mused. *I've got one hell of a time coming, that's for sure.*

Daisy inserted the data chip into the input port of the neuro-stim and began the process that would complete her upload of not only the Chithiid language and relevant strategic data, but also the full extent of the Ra'az tongue they had managed to cobble together in the time since the battle for Earth.

Since she knew she was about to overload her own brain with knowledge, she also threw in a few extra tidbits.

If I'm gonna get brain-fucked, I may as well add some cool stuff as well.

"*Sword fighting, Daze? And wilderness survival?*"

Uh-huh.

"*Well, at least now we know where all of* that *non-standard training came from.*

Daisy smiled a satisfied little grin as she watched the progress bar on the tiny device. Four minutes later the upload was complete.

"*Okay, Daze. Pull that thing, and let's get the hell out of here.*"

Don't have to tell me twice, she replied, tucking the data chip into her pocket and opening her doors.

She had just stepped out into the passageway when the unexpected face of Barry popped into view down the corridor.

Shit!

Daisy reined in her surprise and casually nodded a little greeting to Barry, then stepped into her quarters, as if she was just arriving at them, rather than departing.

Think he bought it?

"*No reason for him not to.*"

But he's a cyborg. He'll notice these aren't the right sweats.

"*Not from that distance. Unless he intentionally increases the resolution of his optic inputs, he shouldn't be able to tell the difference.*"

We'll know in the next twenty seconds or so, Daisy quietly noted.

The time passed painfully slowly as she waited for the flesh-covered tin man to either sound the alarm or pass by obliviously. Forty seconds later, she decided that fortune had smiled upon her and the latter, rather than the former, was the case.

"*You thinking what I'm thinking?*" Sarah asked. "*Hang on a sec,*

I'm in your head," she said with an amused tone. *"Yes, you are thinking what I'm thinking."*

So we agree, then. Time to bail, and lickety-split at that.

"You and your quaint old-timey slang."

I'm bringing it back, Sis. Making the bee's knees cool again, she silently replied with a grin as she exited her quarters and quickly raced back to Port Pod Four.

"Freya, I'm heading out."

"I heard Sarah's end of the conversation and figured as much. I've got the airlock doors primed and ready for you."

"Almost there."

Daisy bolted down the last stretch of corridor and punched the access pad for Pod Four. Less than a minute later, Freya had successfully separated from the *Váli's* hull without so much as a hint that she'd ever been there. And this time, she took her time exiting the larger ship's phased shields, making sure to leave them pristine and as intact as when she arrived.

"Nice job, team!" Daisy said as she flopped down into the captain's chair. "Right about now, Barry is going to walk in on me in the galley, and then I'm going to have one hell of a surprise when I power up my neuro-stim. What a fucking day, huh?"

A look of shock flashed across her face.

"Holy shit," she gasped. "Oh, man."

"What is it, Daze?"

"I just remembered something. It was that night, back when I hadn't figured out your scanner and was running through your notes in the galley."

"So, tonight, you mean."

"Yeah, tonight. When I was leaving the galley, I ran into Barry."

"Makes sense. He's up wandering the corridors, it seems."

"And I apologize for not seeing him, Daisy," Freya chimed in. "I was so busy scanning for humans that might leave their quarters, I totally forgot to scan for non-organic movement as well."

"It's okay, Freya."

"So what's the big revelation, Sis?"

"It's what Barry said back then."

"You mean now."

"Same thing. He seemed surprised to see me. In fact, he said, 'I thought you were in your quarters.'"

"Oh," Sarah said as she realized what that meant.

"Oh, man. That's crazy!" Freya agreed.

"Yeah. Barry saw me back then. Which was just now." The implications sank in deeper. "Sonofabitch. This already happened."

CHAPTER TEN

Daisy watched herself with great interest over the next few days after her incident with the neuro-stim overload. The paranoia, the search for the secret cyborg, the chopping off of Vince's arm.

When she spaced Tamara out of the airlock, she had Freya on standby just in case the surly woman's recollection of her rescue was hazy. Fortunately, her combat arm did in fact house an automatically deployed oxygen envelope, which she managed to slip into before freezing and suffocating to death.

Unfortunately, she wasn't drifting the right way, as she had remembered.

"Freya, I think we're going to have to give her a little nudge."

"You can't do that without her seeing us."

"Sure we can. We just need to direct one small piece of debris her way to bump her and send her on the right trajectory."

"So throwing rocks at the woman you just blew out an airlock? Classy move, Daze," Sarah joked.

"Freya, is there anything nearby that'll fit the bill?"

"Not that I see, but I have some waste I can compress and discharge in that direction that should do the trick."

"Sweet. Let 'er rip whenever you're ready."

"Will do."

"You're flinging literal shit at her now?" Sarah laughed. *"And just when I thought it couldn't get worse. Insult to injury, Sis."*

"Hey, it'll be frozen solid. It's not like she'll be hit with a soggy—"

"Okay, okay. I don't need the mental image!"

"Wimp." Daisy chuckled.

Freya jettisoned the small block of waste matter, which nudged the floating woman just enough to set her on the right course.

It was an uncomfortably long wait, but the tiny hopper did eventually manage to exit the *Váli* and retrieve her, just as Tamara had remembered.

More or less, that is.

The rest of the voyage went as Daisy recalled. The memory of the long hours spent crawling the length and width of the ship within the Narrows brought back a sympathetic ache in her hips and knees. When the shuttle finally blasted free of the *Váli's* belly, it was almost a relief.

"Now's the part where it's about to get really interesting," Daisy said. "It was a long and uncomfortable trip to Earth, but I made it."

"And without your future self lending a hand," Sarah added.

"Nope, you were there, Sis. Safe to say, that bit was all me." She paused a moment, considering her past self's precarious situation. "But it won't hurt to stay close by, right?"

"I'll keep a close watch, Daisy."

"Thanks, Freya. I appreciate it, though I think the real challenge was when I touched down in LA." Daisy thought on it a moment. "Ya know what? On second thought, let's fly ahead and do a quick survey of the city."

"You don't want me to stick with the shuttle?"

"We can fly ahead and be back before any of the real

problems started on that old heap," Daisy replied. "Set a course for Los Angeles."

The stealth ship entered the atmosphere on the daylight side of the globe, far above Hawaii, hiding her entry in the bright daytime sky. She then changed course for the dark of the Los Angeles night.

Freya made a quick loop over the city, making sure there were no Chithiid patrols in the area, then dropped down without a sound, hovering just above the ground, careful not to leave any trace of her arrival.

"Okay," Daisy said, slinging her sword to her back. "I'm going to make a quick pass through the key places I wound up when I landed here and make sure they're safe."

"Your own guardian angel."

"Precisely. I may be ready to rumble now, but when I first got here, all that neuro-stim training hadn't kicked in yet."

She slipped silently to the ground and padded away from the ship.

"Back soon, Freya. Let me know if anything comes up."

"Okay, Daisy. Have fun!"

"You know it, kiddo," Daisy replied, then took off into the night.

She made quick time, now that she knew the layout of the city, first ensuring the doors to the underground loop tube system were unlocked, then checking inside the apartment where she spent her first exhausted night.

Looking inside the pantry, she noticed the sealed can of coffee was nowhere to be found.

"Oh, now that's not right," she muttered. "That's not right at all."

Daisy exited the apartment––careful to leave it exactly as she found it when she first landed in the city—and began searching other units for her precious brew.

There has to be some in here somewhere.

"This is your priority now?" Sarah snarked.

Hey, you've seen me without my coffee.

"Point taken," she replied. "You want some help?"

The extra eyes are always appreciated.

"Okay, then. Let's get you caffeinated."

The one-woman duo made quick work of the floor above, but to no avail. All of the containers were open and long spoiled to an undrinkable mess. It wasn't until they ventured up two more floors that they hit pay-dirt.

"That one, Daze," Sarah said.

Daisy knew immediately which door she meant. There were a few packages leaning against the threshold, obviously placed there just before mankind ceased to be.

"Probably out of town when it happened."

"Yep. My thoughts, exactly."

"And if that's the case, they probably cleared out open containers before they left, seeing as this is a nice building, and all."

She drew her sword and neatly sliced the locking mechanism in half.

"Sorry, Stabby. No blood here, but I'll find you something to eat, I promise," she said as she re-sheathed her murderous weapon.

Sure enough, in the pantry was an unopened can of coffee. The very same one she had carried with her until she found a building with power way back when she first visited the city.

"Let's get that planted for you to find, then get moving. We've only got so much nighttime to cover our tracks, and we really should get back to the shuttle to keep an eye on you once things really start going wrong."

As much as she wanted to survey more of the city, Daisy had

to admit that she agreed with her sister. Things were about to get hairy up in space, and she really should be there, just in case.

"Freya, we're going to be heading back to you shortly. Plot a course back to intercept the shuttle, okay?"

"You betcha," the chipper AI replied.

"Okay, see ya soon."

She went back downstairs and placed the coffee where she had originally found it all those months ago.

"Thank you, Daisy," she said. "Why, you're welcome, Daisy," she replied to herself.

"You are such a dork."

Aww, love you too, Sis.

She carefully stepped from the unit, careful to not disturb the fine pile of human dust in the clothes by the door, then took off back down to the streets. Freya was where she left her, quietly hovering, not making so much as a peep.

"We're back," she said just as the airlock opened.

"I was watching you," Freya replied. "There are also a few cyborgs out in the streets. They're some of Habby's people."

"Why are they up top?"

"It's safe to come up at night. Mostly, anyway."

"No Chithiid?"

"Nope. I've been scanning, but I'll do a quick loop on the way to orbit, just to see if there's anything I might have missed."

"And Cal didn't see you?" Daisy asked as they took to the skies.

"No. I know his systems now, so it was pretty easy to mask my signature and interfere with his scanners and cameras."

"Great. Then let's get to it."

The stealth ship ran a full battery of scans as she spiraled over the city on her way out of the atmosphere, then, with a burst of speed, reconnected with the now-ailing shuttle.

"Looks like the first mishap has already happened, Daze."

"Yep. All good, though. Now we just watch and wait."

"Yeah. And hope we don't have to step in and save your ass."

"I think I would have remembered that."

"Remember that sentiment next time you enjoy a cup of coffee, Sis."

"Hey, that's totally not the same. And coffee is important!"

"I know. Just fuckin' with ya."

As Daisy predicted, the rest of her trip aboard the ancient shuttle was uneventful. Well, it was eventful, but no more than it had been the first go-around.

The vessel lost power as it entered the atmosphere, just like before, though this time Daisy was able to observe the Ra'az missile that narrowly missed it when the power signal it had targeted abruptly disappeared.

All the way back down to the City of Angels, Freya scanned the Chithiid responses to the craft. Surprisingly, it seemed to have not drawn any attention, which was something akin to threading a needle, given their sizable presence in the outskirts of the city.

"I'd guess they're steering clear of the areas that have automated defenses. The shuttle was coming in with no power, so unless they watched it with their own eyes, it was probably nothing of real interest to them on their scanners," Daisy posited.

"I think you're probably right, Daisy," Freya agreed. "They're scanning it, but there's no reading."

"So they're scanning you too."

"Of course. But those scans won't pick up anything from me," the AI said confidently.

"The charmed life of a stealth ship, huh, Freya?"

"Yep!"

"Cool. Let's keep a low profile and monitor any Ra'az activity.

The Chithiid are staying clear, but if the big guys step in, we'll need to act."

Freya touched down in a relatively clear patch of the Los Angeles riverbed, monitoring Daisy's movement as she ventured into the foreign environment.

"This must've been so weird for you," she said.

"Yeah, it really was," Daisy replied. "I mean, I thought I was escaping an AI rebellion to overthrow humanity. Little did I know, right?" She watched her own progress on the scanners, then walked to the medical bay to check in on her wounded sister.

Unlike previously, there had been some changes since she last visited her.

"Daisy, what the hell is that?"

"I don't know," she replied, confused.

Inside the pod, a slow-moving swarm of what appeared to be black ooze was flowing over Sarah's right arm at a near-imperceptible flow. A fine trickle was also trickling between her nose and mouth, the liquid flowing in and out of her with gentle waves.

"Freya, what have you done to Sarah? What's that black stuff?"

"It's not black. It's a light-absorbing nano material."

"A what?"

"It's like I said, Daisy. I don't have proper medical fabricators on board, so I had to make do with what I have."

"Which means?"

"I repurposed a small batch of my nanites and set them to work inside the cryo pod. They have to work really, really slow, but they're gradually replacing the destroyed arm, building a new one from the ground up at a molecular level."

"Whoa," Sarah marveled. *"But what about the stuff coming out of my nose?"*

"That's more of the nano swarm."

"But what are they doing?"

"Fixing you. I mean, *her*. Your lungs were basically destroyed, Sarah. And you lost a decent amount of blood too. They're rebuilding you an entirely new respiratory system along with replacing the missing blood with a super-efficient nanite substitute."

"Does that mean what I think it does?" Daisy asked.

"Yeah. Basically, Sarah's getting a self-repairing nanite upgrade that will restore all of her damaged functions."

"I sense a 'but' in there, Freya," Sarah noted.

"But, I can't guarantee she'll even survive the process."

"Oh," Sarah said, crestfallen.

"There's another but, though," she continued, perking up. "But if she survives, she'll be even more invisible to Ra'az scans than you are, Daisy. The nanites are made from my stealth material, so by incorporating them into her body on this scale, Sarah could probably walk right up to a scanner and not read on it."

"So now we just wait and see, is that it?"

"Pretty much. I'd warp us forward if I could, but I don't think she'd survive the process in her condition, and it's going to be a long time before she's ready to come out of there."

"Looks like we're going to be catching up with our own timeline the long way around," Daisy sighed, then settled in for a nap.

"Wake me if anything happens," she said. "Anything besides what we already know about, that is."

"Will do."

"Thanks, kiddo. You're doing really great."

Daisy then slid into an exhausted slumber, slowly letting the mentally draining past several days wash from her consciousness. At least for a little while.

"Daisy, the cyborgs and Chithiid are fighting now," Freya announced, covertly pulling the video feed from Cal's systems and streaming it to her monitors.

"Okay, then," she groaned, sliding up from her slouched position in the captain's chair. "How long was I out?"

"A few hours."

"Better than nothing. All right, let's get airborne and prep to shadow the retrieval ship. I was unconscious for the trip, but from what they said, I know it was a hairy ride."

Freya immediately powered up and moved into a low hover, awaiting the imminent escape.

The battle unfolded on the monitors, just as Daisy remembered. The cyborgs fought valiantly, and especially well now that she knew they were actually mere domestic units.

"They made a good show of it," she said, admiringly.

"Here comes the good part," Sarah said.

Daisy watched Vince and his team rush to her aid on the screen in front of her.

"Look at the concern in his eyes, Daze. You had just cut his arm off like two days earlier, and there he is, still healing, desperate to save his girlfriend."

"Yeah, I know. No need to make me feel any more guilty about it."

"Wait, here's my favorite bit."

Daisy on the monitors jumped to her feet, hands held high, and called a surrender to the stunned Chithiid. She knew any moment now, Vince and the others would cut them down in cold blood.

"Daze, look at their shoulders!"

It was something she hadn't noticed in the heat of the moment. A detail that would have meant nothing to her at that time, but one that now made all the difference in the world. A distinctive scar was branded into each of the Chithiid's flesh.

"Fucking loyalists," she growled. "Suddenly, I don't feel so bad about what's about to––"

Vince and the others lit them up, tearing the loyalists to shreds.

"Great. And now this part," she grumbled, knowing what was coming next.

Tamara, for her part, showed a brief moment of hesitation that Daisy hadn't remembered. Then she blasted her with the stun rifle just the same.

Daisy watched herself collapse to the ground, only to be roughly thrown over Tamara's shoulder and rushed back to the tiny hopper ship a few blocks away. The team wasted no time, blasting off hard, burning bright as they launched toward the edge of the atmosphere.

It was a rough ride, and to make things worse, a pair of missiles quickly locked on to them, tracking their progress and growing closer by the second.

"Um, Freya?" Daisy said, concern in her voice. The missiles grew closer still. "Freya? Any time now."

"Jeez, don't worry so much. I told you, I can handle it."

"Teens, Daze."

"Don't remind me."

Freya flashed into the sky, making sure to stay out of the escaping hopper's windows' field of view, then blasted out a jamming signal, forcing the missiles to spiral out of control with no target to lock on to.

It was a rough ride, but the ship finally made it into space in one piece. Now, Daisy remembered, they'd float a while before gradually returning to Dark Side Base to begin a long adjustment period.

As for future Daisy, she, too, had a long wait in store.

"Okay," she said. "Might as well get comfy. We're in for a long haul."

CHAPTER ELEVEN

Five long months.

That's how long Daisy had spent observing Ra'az and Chithiid movements and communications and cataloging their various vessels, including the slowly advancing iterations of Chithiid-test piloted warp ships that continuously failed in spectacular bursts of unstable energy.

She was also counting the days, making preparations for the eventual syncing of timelines.

With Sarah still in the process of being reconstructed, she had been stuck living out the months in normal time, unable to attempt a warp. But they were close, now. Soon Sarah would be ready to exit the cryo pod after months of intensive repairs, and hopefully not keel over dead from the shock.

With so much time on her hands, Daisy had also spent a good portion of her time attempting to repair the burned-out Ra'az power whip she had claimed from the corpse of the alien after their face-to-face encounter.

Unfortunately, unlike her original Chithiid power whip, which was far simpler and which she had easily repaired and installed into Tamara's arm, the powerful Ra'az model was proving far more difficult for her to repair.

"Might also have something to do with your not knowing enough about it to be able to leave yourself a little extra info in that neuro-stim update."

"I know, but the tech is basically the same concept as the ones they let the Chithiid use."

"Sure, but you know they're going to keep their own personal toys far more secure than the ones they allow their underlings to use. Basic security, Daze."

"Still, I've gotten it to power up, so I know it *should* work, but for whatever reason, it just won't activate. I can't even get a tiny pulse out of it."

Indeed, during her many test sessions––each performed in a remote location on the planet's surface, so as to avoid unintentionally damaging Freya should things go awry––she had achieved full power, per her readouts, but zero output.

"I don't know. Maybe their brains are just too incompatible. Something about the way they think, perhaps."

"You want me to try?" Freya offered. "I can mount it on one of my mechs and see if I can get it to work."

Daisy slid the band from her forearm and offered it up to the precocious ship.

"Give it a go. Just keep your firewalls up so you don't catch anything from their alien software."

"Don't worry, I already know how to cure the virus."

"I'm not talking about the virus. There are other things out there. Things you haven't encountered yet, so don't take it for granted that you can overcome all of them."

"The joy of youth, eh? That wonderful invincibility."

"Yeah. We were too, once upon a time."

"Then I died, and you got your ass whooped and dragged to the moon."

"Well, yeah. There was that." Daisy chuckled. "How things

change, huh, Sis?"

"That they do. But I may have a second chance, soon."

"I know. It's about that time. Hey, Freya, where do we stand with Sarah's progress?"

Nothing.

"Freya, you there?"

"Oh, sorry, Daisy. I was just reviewing the comms traffic between NORAD and Sid from before we jumped back."

"That, again?"

"Yeah, that, again? You've gone over those comms hundreds of times, Freya."

"But there's valuable information there. Joshua is the greatest AI mind to ever live," she replied, defensively.

"You know what it is, don't you, Daze?"

"Oh, yeah. Freya's got a crush on a boy."

"I do not!" she blurted.

"Yep, that confirms it."

"Shut up. I do not have a crush. I just respect his intellect, is all."

"It's okay to have a crush, Freya, even if it is a bit unusual for an AI. But you can't get attached. You know what happens to him not too long after those comms links get established. It's a historic fact, and we cannot, we *must not* change that."

"Well, duh. I'm not stupid, Daisy."

"I never said you were."

"Then don't treat me like I am."

"Don't get snippy with me, Freya."

"What? Are you going to ground me? Send me to my room? I don't have one, by the way––it's still occupied by the earlier version of me."

"Wow, where did all this lip come from? You need to check your tone, young lady."

"Then stop picking on me."

"We're not picking on you. It was just a joke, Freya. It's fine if you like Joshua, really, but you can't go off on these rude tangents. It's not cool."

"Well——"

"No well. Just don't. Now this is important. I want you to answer my original question. How is Sarah's recovery coming? She should've been ready to come out of the cryo pod a few days ago, according to your earlier estimates."

"I know, but I want to be sure."

She's scared, Daisy realized.

"There is no sure, hon," Sarah said, taking the hint. *"Eventually, we're going to have to open the pod and let the chips fall where they may. And this is* me *saying this. I have a very vested interest in the outcome, and even I recognize what needs to happen. So, what do you say?"*

Freya hesitated a second.

"One more day, okay? Then we'll pull her out of cryo," she finally answered.

"Okay. Tomorrow is the day. Thank you, Freya."

"You're welcome," the young AI replied. "And Daisy?"

"Yeah?"

"I'm sorry I snapped at you."

Daisy felt a warm flush of pride in her chest as her kid showed her love and ever-increasing maturity.

"It's okay, kiddo. I know you didn't mean anything by it. And I'm sorry I razzed you about Joshua."

"I appreciate it."

"Of course, kiddo. Arguments happen, but at the end of the day, we're family, and that's far more important than any little spat."

"Yeah," the brilliant AI said. "Thanks, Daisy."

"You bet. Now, what do you say we head over to Dark Side and see what's up?"

"You got it," she replied, then merrily powered up and set her course for Dark Side Base.

The work on Dark Side Base was moving at a normal pace. No one had impulsively zoomed off down to Earth yet, damaged ships were not being salvaged and stockpiled, and a secret hangar had not yet been discovered.

For most of the prior day, Daisy and Freya had monitored internal comms, while watching Bob and Donovan gather scrap, flying in and dropping their loads to be sorted, then lazily floating back toward the debris field orbiting Earth.

They also watched as Daisy performed Fatima's arduous tasks in the low-g environment.

"Man, she really did have you running around out there, didn't she?"

"She sure did," Daisy replied with a faint smile. Fatima, for all the exhausting training she had subjected her to, was her friend, and she found herself missing their talks. "Hey, I'm gonna suit up and go for a closer look."

"You sure that's a good idea?"

"We can read scans, and our visuals are okay, but I'd like to get a first-hand peep at what's going on over there."

"Just be careful."

"Never," she said with a laugh. "Hey, Freya, do me a favor and keep an ear out for Donovan and Bob. Wouldn't want to accidentally wander into their flight path and get scanned when they drop their next load of salvage."

"Will do, Daisy," the AI replied.

It wasn't a very long walk to where the majority of the work was taking place, but Daisy couldn't very well risk being seen wandering about the base's facilities. After a moment's thought, she settled on the ridge-line above.

Perfect vantage point to see what's up, she decided, then set off at a lazy, loping jog to the rocky outcropping above Hangar Three.

Okay, let's see what's going on, Sis, she said as she settled in behind a small clump of dusty rocks.

"Looks like you're down there doing something, Daze," Sarah commented. "Can't quite see what it is, though."

I think this was when Fatima had me reorganize the salvage storage racks for no good reason.

"Though that did actually help a lot when they needed specific parts for the remote ships they sent to help during the San Francisco assault."

True. Though there's no way she could have known about that beforehand, Daisy noted. *Just good old-fashioned serendipity. Damn, though. I'm kinda kicking ass, aren't I?*

"You're just moving junk into piles."

Well, yeah, but look at how well I'm doing it, she said with a fair dose of sass. *Nobody can haul junk like I can!*

"Har-har. Such a comedian."

I try.

"So are you done watching yourself hauling trash? I should be ready to be pulled from cryo by now, and I'm more than a little anxious to get that done. One way or another, today is the day I either live or die."

Morbid, Sis.

"But accurate," she replied.

Okay, we can head back.

"Hey, Freya. I'm coming back to you. Are you ready to wake up your patient?"

"I am, Daisy. And, Sarah, I don't want to jinx things, but I've been reviewing her vitals, and I think she, you--"

"Either one works."

"I think that everything might just work out okay," she finished.

"Great. Be back shortly," Daisy said as she pushed off her rocky seat and rose to her feet.

The ground beneath her shifted and began to slide.

"Shit!" she cried out, throwing herself clear of the tumbling rocks.

Though she was not caught up in the main bulk of the minor rock slide, she nevertheless found herself riding a wave of flowing soil, carrying her right toward the sharp, rocky drop-off right above the hangar doors.

"Daisy, on your right!" Sarah shouted in her head.

She swung her arm wildly to the side as her sister instructed and felt her hand slap against something solid. Daisy gripped with all her strength, yanking her body from the sliding debris with a painful jolt.

"Holy shit!," she gasped, flat on her back, sucking in deep breaths of air as she lowered her heart rate. "That was close!"

"Too close. You almost took yourself out."

"I know. Thanks for that. You probably saved my ass just now."

"You're welcome, but that's not what I'm talking about. Look down below."

Daisy did as Sarah suggested. The rocks had scattered the neatly piled components as they fell, leaving a mess where Daisy had created a clean and organized area. She watched as the past version of herself rose to her feet and surveyed the damage.

"You saved my ass back then too," she said. "Remember? Potential paradoxes be damned, I just can't seem to stop stumbling into my own timeline, can I?"

"In ways that don't change events, at least."

"True, that," Daisy said, cautiously climbing back to her feet and beginning the trek back to Freya's waiting warmth. "I think that's more than enough EVA time, wouldn't you agree?"

"Most definitely."

"Well, come on, then. We've waited long enough. Let's go and wake you up."

CHAPTER TWELVE

The butterflies plaguing Daisy's stomach would simply not go away. Given that in just a few minutes her sister would either miraculously come back from the dead, or stay that way forever, the sensation was understandable.

Freya had powered up all of the medical machinery at her disposal and had it standing by in preparation for the big event. Being an AI, she didn't have butterflies in her electronic stomach, exactly, but a sense of nervous unease pervaded in her synapses just the same.

Lying in stasis within the safety of the cryo pod, Sarah looked almost peaceful in her unconscious state. From the outside, one would never guess that a thriving swarm of custom stealth material nanites were inhabiting her body, replacing the organs destroyed months prior.

Her right arm, however, was a dead giveaway.

The slender limb was identical in appearance to the one she had lost while being blown out of the *Váli's* airlock, save the telltale matte-gray coloring of the nano materials that had constructed it. Eventually, Freya hoped the nanites would learn to mimic her natural body coloring, making the replacement limb appear human, despite its incredible strength.

All that remained was seeing if her body would accept the drastic additions when brought out of stasis, or if it would catastrophically reject them.

"You ready for this, Sis?"

"No, not really," Sarah replied, more than a little hesitation in her voice. *"But I'm as ready as I'll ever be. How about you, Freya?"*

"I am, Sarah."

"You call it, Sis. This one's all you," Daisy said.

"Well, then." The disembodied mind of a long-dead woman took a figurative deep breath. *"Wake her up, Freya."*

The cryo pod gradually shifted from blue stasis lighting through purple, into red, and eventually, a warming golden glow. The woman inside the pod began to stir just as the lid slid open, exposing her to fresh air for the first time in months.

Sarah gasped her first breath with her new lungs, then set into a coughing fit.

"Freya, she's choking!"

"She's not choking, Sarah. Calm down," Daisy said. "It's okay. Look."

Propped up on her elbows, Sarah's coughing eased as she got the hang of breathing with her new lungs. Her eyes wet from the fit, she looked around the ship, utterly confused.

"Daisy?" she said as her gaze fell upon her friend.

"Hey, Sis," Daisy replied.

"What happened? Are you okay? Someone's been cutting onions."

Daisy laughed and wiped the tears from her face as she leaned in and hugged her sister.

Sarah pushed up from the edge of the pod, crushing the material with her right hand as she moved to hug her back, but suddenly jerked away as she looked at the powerful limb where her flesh-and-blood arm should have been.

"Wait. What the fuck?" she said, wiggling the new fingers in amazement. "I was just in Starboard Pod Eight, Daisy. And I had my own arm. What the hell is going on? This isn't the *Váli*. And this sure as shit isn't my arm!"

"Sorry, Sis. A ton has happened since we last saw each other. Boy have you missed a lot."

"Sis? And hang on, I just saw you, like, ten minutes ago."

Daisy laughed, the constant pressure in her chest finally dissolving for the first time in months.

"Yeah, Sis. As in, sisters. The for-reals kind," she said, smiling through her tears. "Like I said, you really have missed a lot."

Sarah sipped a cup of cocoa in Freya's compact galley space. A pair of crumpled ceramisteel mugs lay on the table in front of her. She was a quick learner, but it had taken a few minutes for her to really mesh with her new arm and hand.

"This tastes funny," she said, still more than a little shell-shocked from the firehose of information Daisy had laid on her.

"Sorry about that, Sarah," Freya said over her speakers. "It's the first time you've interacted with actual food in nearly six months, and after the accident, the nanites had to replace parts of your tongue that were too damaged from the cold to be saved."

"So everything is going to taste weird from now on. Excellent," she grumbled.

"Oh, no, not at all. It just takes them time to adjust to your conscious mind and produce feedback that correlates to the flavor profile you're expecting."

"You saying she'll be able to make things taste like other things?" Daisy asked, intrigued.

"I suppose," Freya replied. "Though I don't know why anyone would want to do that."

"It's a human thing, kid," Sarah replied. "I still can't believe you have your own ship, Daze. And a stealth one at that."

"Best thing that came from Dark Side Base was this amazing kiddo," she said proudly, patting the bulkhead. "Freya's one of a kind, and what she can do––well, you'll see soon enough. You missed a hell of a lot, that's for sure."

"Yeah, it sounds like it. But damn, Daze, did you really blow Tamara out an airlock?"

"Hey, you had just been killed, and I didn't know who I could trust or what the real situation even was. Can you blame me?"

"Oh, I don't blame you. I'm just amazed she ever forgave you, is all."

"That took some time," Daisy admitted. "That, and I installed a captured power whip that I modified to tie into her arm."

"A what, now?"

"I call it a power whip. It's kind of a whippy, smashy, sort of plasma coil thing."

"Tamara with more destructive power at her disposal. Why does that worry me?"

"I know, right? And you missed the big fight too."

"The first time around, that is."

"True," Daisy agreed.

"What was that?"

"I still don't think she believes you about me, though."

"I know, but she will."

"You talking to the invisible me again?" Sarah asked, her doubting eyebrow held in a high arch.

"Told ya so."

"But she's real," Freya interjected. "She's you, Sarah. Well, not *you*, you, but you who has experienced what that other you hasn't."

She stared at Daisy disbelievingly.

"Do you guys really expect me to believe you have a little piece of me living in your head?"

"All of you, actually," she replied.

"Bullshit."

"No, for reals. Go ahead. Ask yourself something."

"What, she's listening with your ears?"

"Yeah, pretty much always."

"Okay, then. What's Finn's favorite flavor of––"

"No," Daisy interrupted. "Ask her something even I don't know."

Sarah thought quietly a long moment.

"Fine. But don't get pissed," she finally said.

"Why would I get pissed?"

"Well, about three months into the trip––this is after the impact and the fire, we're talking, here––I was heading to get cleaned up after a shift in the Narrows and––"

"I saw Vince naked in the shower. He forgot to lock the door. That, or he was waiting for you."

"What? You never told me that!" Daisy blurted.

"Hang on, what?" Sarah asked.

"You just told me you saw Vince naked in the showers. Why wouldn't you tell me, Sarah?"

"I thought it would make things weird."

"I thought it would make things weird."

"Whoa. You both just said the same thing. That's freaky."

"Holy shit!" Sarah exclaimed, scrutinizing Daisy's noggin. "I really am in your head! But how the hell could a neuro-stim do that? It shouldn't be possible. Aren't there supposed to be safeties and stuff?"

"There are. But because we come from the same egg, we're genetically similar enough that it allowed an override."

"So me, and a whole mess of other stuff, got dumped in your head in the process? And it didn't kill you? Or make you a vegetable?"

"Precisely. Though it's looking like it may have been me who put some of that stuff there in the first place, when I snuck on the *Váli* this time around."

"How is that even possible? I mean, I get the time travel thing, as insane as that may sound, but just because you have precognition, you shouldn't be able to alter events."

"Paradoxes!" Freya blurted.

"Yeah, exactly, kid," Sarah said. "You shouldn't be able to change things. Doing so could tear apart time."

"Oh, I totally agree with you, Sis."

"Sis. Gotta get used to that in its new context."

"Understandable. But what I was saying is, that after Freya and I intervened to save Fatima on the moon, it is looking like we may have actually been directly responsible for these things happening in the first place. It's kind of like we can't *not* do it because that's what the past required of us."

"That's a real mind-fuck, Daze."

"Oh, believe me, I know."

"So what do we do now?"

"Now? Now we watch our own backs. Well, my back, anyway. You were dead for all of this."

"So weird," Sarah said for the umpteenth time, shaking her head.

"We'll have to get you up to speed on current events, future events, captured tech, and anything else that might serve you well. We have a little bit of time, but pretty soon, I'm going to go chasing Vince down to the surface, and from that point, things are going to get really nuts really fast."

"Why is he going alone? And why do you chase him?" Sarah asked.

"Awkward," Sarah said inside her head with a little laugh.

Bite me, Sis.

"Yeah, but now there are two of me."

Oh, the horror, Daisy replied with a silent chuckle.

"Well," Daisy said. "That's kind of a long story."

"Sounds like we'll have the time," Sarah replied.

Daisy took a deep breath and sighed.

"All right. Let me fill you in."

CHAPTER THIRTEEN

Sarah had been quick to adjust to her new reality. Being saved from death had quite a motivating effect on her as Daisy led her through an ever-growing series of drills and training scenarios. Having an onboard nanocloud also helped, allowing her to more rapidly assimilate information from Freya's modified neuro-stim.

It wasn't anywhere near Daisy's deluge of data, but it was enough to give her an edge over pretty much any other human alive, aside from her sister, of course.

The training was intense. They would alternate between landing on desolate parts of the Earth to train in weapons and tactics, far from Ra'az scans or Bob's flyovers, and the cold of space and remote stretches of the moon beyond Sid's scanning range.

Several weeks after Sarah had been dragged back from the shores of the river Styx, the pair quietly watched from space as past Daisy stumbled upon Freya's fabrication hangar.

Freya had particularly enjoyed watching her own creation, the unusual circumstances of her birth being a topic many traditionally birthed AIs had talked about often.

"Quite a kid, Daze," Sarah commented.

"Yeah. She's pretty cool," Daisy couldn't help but agree.

It was not long thereafter that Vince and Daisy had their arguments within the walls of Dark Side, causing him to make that fateful trip to Earth's surface alone.

Freya's ability to tap in to pretty much all of Dark Side's monitors meant Daisy had to not only relive her assholeish behavior, but now with the extra fun of judgmental witnesses.

Vince had already traveled to the surface earlier that day, and Daisy had already followed, but the topic was nevertheless still a favorite aboard the ship.

"I hate to say it again——"

"Then don't say it."

"——But holy shit. You were being a total dick to him, Daze."

"For the record, I agree," the other Sarah said.

"Sarah says she agrees," Freya informed them.

"And why is it Freya can hear her but I can't? I mean, it's me, after all, so you'd think I would be able to hear myself without needing you to relay or Freya to play a vocal simulation over her speakers."

"Sorry, Sarah. It's just the way the neuro-band functions," Freya apologized. "I haven't been able to make a version that can transmit yet. I mean, I can upload neuro-stim data, of course, but real-time conversation of non-static files is a problem I haven't solved yet. But I'm working on it."

"Hey, that's all I can ask, kid," Sarah said.

"Yeah, thanks, hon."

Daisy watched the monitors with great interest as Vince made his way to the surface with Alma's people. Shortly, he and Daisy would run into one another, and from there, things would get interesting.

"We should get prepped to keep an eye on things down there," Daisy mused. "My first run-in with the Chithiid is going to happen soon."

"Playing guardian angel for yourself?" Sarah joked.

"You know it."

"Okay, then. I'm in. Freya, how about you take us down to LA before Daisy goes and plays with the big bad aliens?"

"Happy to, Sarah," the ship replied, then plotted the stealthiest reentry route to the city below.

Daisy and Vince had just recently begun their trek with Alma's people to retrieve the comms device from his ship when Freya set down and dropped off her human cargo.

Daisy and Sarah, having foreknowledge of the events of the day, were several steps ahead of them, clearing the path of unforeseen hazards. So far, they had only needed to usher a small pack of coyotes along. Other than that, it had been relatively uneventful.

"Just over there is where I first met Craaxit. We were trapped in that lobby after one of Alma's idiot followers ran directly into a Chithiid's line of fire with a freakin' bomb strapped to his back."

"Wow. That's fucking idiotic," Sarah agreed.

"Yeah, tell me about it. I was damn lucky to survive."

"So, shall we?"

"After you."

The sisters jogged over to the entry doors through which Daisy and her team had beaten a hasty retreat all those months ago.

"Hey, it's locked," she observed.

Daisy pulled the wicked-sharp bone sword from her back and effortlessly sliced through the metal containing the locking mechanism. The door now slid freely, providing easy access into the lobby area.

"How the hell did you do that, Daze? That thing just cut through metal."

Daisy spun the sword around and offered it to her sister, handle-first.

"This was created for me on Dark Side. It's a living sword that feeds on organic material."

"Trippy."

"Yeah. I call him Stabby McStabberton. Stabby for short."

Sarah chuckled and shook her head at her ridiculous sister, then swung the sword in a short arc.

"Cool, Daze. Kinda like a ninja."

"Yes!"

"No! You're still not a ninja!" Sarah countered with a chuckle. *"But I wonder, Daze. Can she make him sharp like you can? She's family, and close, genetically."*

"I don't know," Daisy replied.

"What was I saying this time?" Sarah asked.

"Wondering if you could make Stabby work."

"It's a sword. Anyone can make it work."

"That's what you think. Take a swing at that bench over there," Daisy directed her sister.

"Okay, but it'll just cut through it, like you did with the door."

Sarah swung the blade, but its dull edge bounced off.

"Huh," she said, carefully feeling the blade. "Daisy, this thing is dull."

"Yep. That's what she was asking about."

"What do you mean?"

"It's keyed to my DNA, basically. Here, I'll show you," she said, carefully taking the sword from her sister.

Stabby, for his part, had become increasingly attuned to her desires, and would even keep his blade dull when Daisy needed, like when she wanted to make sure she didn't cut her sister's new arm off.

Daisy gently swung the sword and lopped off a piece of the bench with ease.

"How the hell?"

"Fatima and Chu designed it. Grown from my own bone and responsive to my touch. For anyone else, it's a dull club. For me, it's got a blade sharp down to a molecular level."

"Wicked cool."

"Seriously, right?"

"Where do I get one of those?"

"We'll have to see if they can make you one once we catch up to the right timeline. We're sisters, after all, so you have pretty much the same bone genetics as I do."

"I hate to break up your fun, but you—the other you—are going to be running through this place any minute now."

"Head Sarah's right. We need to get moving."

"You did not just call me that."

Totally did. At least there aren't any boys around, Daisy said with a chuckle.

They were about to leave when Daisy stopped in her tracks.

"What is it, Daze?"

"Hang on. Something's not right."

She slowed her thoughts and let the space tell her what was different. A minute later she saw it.

"That statue."

"The ugly one?"

"Yeah. It wasn't there before. It was over here," she said, tapping the floor with her foot. "That's what saved me when the bomb––of course."

"Of course, what?"

"Come here, Sarah. Give me a hand."

"Redecorating? At a time like this?" she joked as they hefted the massive sculpture with their genetically-enhanced limbs.

"There," Daisy said once it was in place. "Thanks. I couldn't have moved it on my own. This thing saved my life. If it hadn't been there, the blast would have torn me apart. It seemed so out of place at the time. But now––"

"Now it makes sense why it was there," Sarah finished the thought. "Maybe you really are your own guardian angel, Daze."

"Maybe," she replied, just as the first sounds of conflict reached their ears. "Shit, it's starting. Come on! We've gotta get out of here!"

Daisy and Sarah bolted out the rear doors just as her other self ran in from the streets. She knew what was going to happen, and felt confident they weren't needed, so they hightailed it back to Freya to pull clear of the area and monitor from a safe distance.

"Once the fight's over I want to check in on Dark Side," she said, watching the video feeds as they quietly distanced themselves.

"Hey, Daisy?" Freya asked once they were relocated. "I was wondering, if you could save Sarah, maybe we can also save Joshua."

"He's the Colorado Springs AI you told me about, right?" Sarah asked.

"Yeah. Freya's got something of a crush on him."

"Daisy!" Freya blurted.

"It's nothing to be ashamed of. But you know we can't interfere with fixed events."

"But you saved Sarah. That was a fixed event."

"It was, but it wasn't," Daisy replied. "All we had was a recording of a few seconds of the event, not what happened after."

"But you didn't know that it wouldn't make a paradox. So maybe Joshua's the same."

"He died in a nuclear blast, Freya. No one escapes that. Not even the most brilliant and connected AI ever born. He dies, and that's all there is to it. Cheyenne Mountain has to blow, and there's nothing we can do to stop that from happening."

"A little harsh, Daze."

But she needs it. A little brutal reality now will save her a lot of heartbreak later. Joshua dies, Sis, and much as I wish he didn't, there's nothing we can do to stop that.

"I get it, Daisy," Freya said, dejectedly.

"I'm sorry, kiddo. I really am. But as much as you think outside the box, this time, it can't be done."

Daisy and Sarah interpreted Freya's silence as a depressive acceptance. In reality, the brilliant AI took those last words to heart. As an intellect that not only thought, but essentially lived outside the box, she found herself forming a ridiculous, yet somehow feasible, hypothesis.

The mighty ship was quiet as they flew back to the vacuum of space.

CHAPTER FOURTEEN

Dark Side was abuzz with activity as Tamara and the others scrambled in preparation for an impromptu rescue mission. Within just a few hours of Alma, the mad AI's, attempt to infect Dark Side Base they had devised a plan and swung into action. Not long thereafter they were already barreling toward Earth's atmosphere, while Freya silently followed.

"Damn, they're really hauling ass, Daisy," Sarah noted. "And that little ship——"

"His name's Bob."

"Yeah, Bob. He's got some moves."

"His pilot helps out."

"Tandem system, then?"

"Either can pilot, but yeah, Donovan and Bob usually share the work. Each has a few skills the other lacks, so it makes for a really symbiotic relationship."

Freya, despite her greater size, was invisible to the smaller ship's scans, and she would periodically push a piece of debris on a similar trajectory to help mask the non-stealth ship's entry into the atmosphere.

Daisy felt a swell of emotion as she watched her friends race so recklessly to Earth to come to her aid. Even Tamara, with whom she was still on slightly *off* terms at this point in her timeline, was giving the rescue mission her all.

The buffeting of the winds on Bob's hull at those speeds were making him judder and shimmy erratically as he bee-lined for Los Angeles. Nevertheless, he held course, somehow, powering downward to the source of the signal from the stolen comms device.

"It's going to be a rough touchdown for that craft at that speed," Freya said as Bob neared the ground.

"He can handle it," Daisy replied. "But their dust off is going to be hairy."

"Quick burn?" Sarah asked.

"Yeah. And with missiles targeting them on the way out as well."

'If they survive the landing."

"They will," she said, confidently.

Sure enough, the team––her friends––poured out of the craft as soon as it touched down, racing into the underground tunnel network even as their ride blasted off behind them.

"Now is when they come and save my ass," Daisy said, remembering the event like it was yesterday.

The little ship increased speed as he flew farther from the drop-off point, but he was still not moving as fast as he needed to, Daisy noticed. Freya saw it too.

"I don't know how Bob managed to evade them. He's not really built for atmospheric maneuvering," Freya said.

Cal's words sprang to Daisy's mind.

"An EM burst," she said.

"What?"

"An EM burst."

"I heard what you said, Daze. What I meant was how do you propose––"

"Freya," Daisy interrupted. "There's a power generation facility on the outskirts, correct?"

"Yeah, there are a few, actually."

"I want you to target the one with the lowest likelihood of knocking down any of Cal's systems. Can you do that?"

"Are you really asking me if I can hit a stationary, defenseless target?"

"More sass."

I'll deal with it later.

"Just target it and fire, Freya."

Donovan and Bob were running with their engines on a full-burn, pushing hard for the relative safety of space, but the missiles launched would be locking on them in seconds.

"Freya, there's no time to wait!"

"Don't rush me!"

The stealth ship's smaller cannon powered up and fired a series of blasts in rapid succession. The explosion that resulted a little way across town was not terribly massive, but the electromagnetic blast emitted by the impacts was powerful enough—just barely—to knock out the missiles' guidance systems.

It wasn't a permanent fix, by any stretch, but the time it took for the missiles to reboot their tracking systems and scan for a target was just long enough to allow Bob to slip through their grasp and into space, just as Freya had calculated it would.

"How did you know that would work, Daze?" Sarah asked.

"Something Cal said when I first met him. Something about an EM blast masking their escape."

"Which we just provided them."

"Exactly."

Daisy watched as the little ship sped to safety high above.

"Find us a quiet spot, Freya. We need to sit down and really evaluate the things that are about to happen."

"Evaluate?" Sarah asked.

"Yeah. A lot is about to go down, Sis, and now that there are two of us—"

"Ahem."

"Three of us."

"Hey!"

"Yes, Freya, you count as well. *Four* of us. I was just mentioning the human contingent at the moment."

"Yeah, no one's forgetting you, hon. You're a key part of the team."

"That she is," Daisy agreed. "Just one thing, though. We're more than just a team. We're a family."

It was beneath the crystal-clear waters of Lake Tahoe that Freya eventually settled down. She didn't need to submerge herself to remain invisible to the Ra'az and their loyalists, but she found it relaxing, gently floating in the water.

Always the curious one, when she had learned that the now-clear waters of the lake had, at the end of humanity's days, seen their famous visibility reduced by more than half due to rising temperatures and algae blooms, she knew she would have to come see it for herself.

Now, after centuries without mankind meddling with nature, the waters had reclaimed their former clarity, returning to the pristine state they were in long before humans had ever placed their muddy feet on the lake's shoreline.

After a day of monitoring the time-delayed communications between Cal and Dark Side Base, the sisters and their youthful ship had decided on a plan of action for the soon-to-unfold events.

"So it really does seem like we're affecting events in ways we were always meant to," Sarah said. "And if that's the case, whatever we decide to do should line up with the future timeline."

"Yes and no," Freya interjected. "It's like a lottery. Sure, you may be destined to win it, but you still have to buy a ticket."

"How do you know about lotteries? They haven't existed in hundreds of years," Sarah asked.

"I like to read a lot," she replied. "But what I was saying is that you still have to go through the motions. I mean, like, just like you're supposed to make things happen and doing so doesn't cause a paradox, then maybe your *not* doing something could actually *cause* one."

Daisy looked stunned.

"Shit. I actually hadn't thought of it like that," she said.

"The kid makes sense, Daze."

"That she does," Daisy replied.

"We really need to get that neuro-link working, Freya. It's too strange having someone be a middleman to talk to myself."

"It's coming along, Sarah. Hopefully I'll have a version working soon."

"Thanks, kid."

Freya replayed a bit of the communications she had intercepted over her speakers for all to hear. It was a discussion about the risks of the AI virus and how a relay with a kill switch and a delay would be needed to keep the AIs on Earth and Dark Side Base safe from infection should they wish to talk.

"Daisy, you know I could just cure it."

"But you also know we can't," she replied.

"Not even secretly? Like giving them an inoculation?"

"Sorry, kiddo. I know you like Joshua, but he definitely became infected with the virus before detonating his warhead. No matter how much we would like to, we simply can't alter the past like that. Especially not in a way this big. Emotional impulses aside, you do see that, don't you?"

"I guess," she answered, dejectedly. "It just seems like such a waste."

"On that we are in agreement," Daisy said.

Sarah pored over the events that had not yet happened that

Freya had laid out for them on her planning table's screen. Multiple teams in multiple locations. She had the reports, but actual footage was lacking. They'd just have to wing it.

"So, since the people in LA are going to split up, we split up also, and clean up after them if need be. Sound about right, Daze?"

"You got it, Sis."

"From what you guys have said about these Shelly and Omar characters, I don't think they'll need much help, but Finn and Reggie? Those idiots are going to lose one of the secure comms units. I'll have to either retrieve it or destroy it before the Chithiid can get their hands on it, then I'll keep an eye on the fellas until they get clear. I think those jokers will need every bit of help they can get."

"You know you like him."

"Not a chance," Sarah replied.

"Admittedly, I actually do. But back then, I wasn't so open about it."

"Sarah says you do, by the way," Daisy noted.

"Shut up, Me," she said with a smirk. "Disembodiment can make you like all sorts of strange things. Including crazy, ginger chefs."

"Tell her she should give him a chance."

"She says you should give him a chance."

"Yeah, not happening."

"Maybe you'll change your mind one day."

"Until that happens, let's just get on with our job, shall we?"

"Fine. Freya, drop Sarah in Phoenix. It got pretty hairy for them at that point in their timestream. From there, hop east and take me to Colorado Springs. I think that there, if anywhere, is where things could really go wrong."

"Will do, Daisy," the young AI said as she slowly rose from the depths of the lake, breaking the surface gently before silently ascending into the sky.

CHAPTER FIFTEEN

"Okay, so you've done really well with the weapons training the past few weeks, but I'm still a little concerned about leaving you totally on your own out here," Daisy said from the shaded safety of the University of Phoenix stadium's partially deconstructed dome.

"I'll be fine, Daze."

"I know. Of course you will."

"Not very convincing, Sis."

"It's just that we haven't really had time to drill so many other things to prepare you." She paused and thought about it a moment longer. "You know what? I'm going to stick around and help out for a bit. I'm sure the Colorado Springs team will be fine."

Sarah flashed an annoyed glare.

"Daisy, I love you like a sister––"

"I *am* your sister."

"––But I will kick your ass up and down this city if you don't get your butt to Colorado to help that team and just let me do my thing here."

"Damn. I sure told you, didn't I? Sarah said with a chuckle. *"It's kinda fun watching me whip you in line."*

Eat me, Sarah.

"You say that to me, but will you dare say that to her?"

Daisy chuckled quietly to herself.

"Daisy?" Freya chimed in. "I can help Sarah get ready."

"Thanks, kiddo, but there's no time to run a new neuro-stim upload."

"Yeah, well, about that..."

Sarah's ears perked up.

"Freya, what did you do to me?"

"Nothing bad! Promise!"

"Freyyaaa," Daisy moaned. "What did you do?"

"I just knew that your neuro-stim burst gave you all sorts of useful knowledge back on the *Váli*—"

"And could have killed me," Daisy added.

"Well, yeah. Duh. But I figured Sarah was already being reconstructed, and the nanites would be able to buffer any spikes and surges, so I took the liberty of loading a full combat and tactics data packet into her stim hookup."

"But I don't know that stuff, Freya," Sarah said. "It didn't work."

"I didn't know if it would affect your nanites' reconstruction cycle negatively, so I had them partition the data in a way that would be easiest on your healing body's neurological system."

"Daisy, did she...?"

"Yeah, Sis. I think she did," she replied with a sigh. "So how do we access it, Freya?"

"Easy!" she chirped, thrilled she wasn't in trouble. "Sarah, just slip the neuro-stim on, and I'll send the release sequence to your nanites. Technically, you should be able to command them to do it yourself, but that kind of thing will probably take you a long time to learn to do."

Sarah squinted a moment in concentration, then relaxed her brow and took a deep breath.

"What are you doing, Sarah?" Freya asked.

"Hang on, kiddo. Let her do her thing," Daisy replied.

Sarah focused and breathed, slowing her respirations as she focused her mind. Without warning, her eyes fluttered as she slid to the deck.

"Shit, I was afraid that might happen," Daisy said.

"What did I do?" Freya asked, freaking out.

"Nothing, Freya. She was cracking the seal on her own. By the look of it, I think she was successful."

"She can do that?"

"She was always better than me at the whole meditation thing, and I've been running through the new techniques I learned from Fatima with her since she's woken up. So, yeah. She can do that, it seems."

Sarah's eyes fluttered as she slowly sat up.

"Wasn't expecting that," she grumbled, brushing herself off as she got to her feet.

"You feel different?" Daisy asked.

"I-I don't know."

Daisy threw a ceramisteel mug at her head.

Without so much as flinching, Sarah snatched it from the air with her new nanite-constructed hand.

"Well," Daisy said with a chuckle. "That answers that. Congrats, Sis, you're ready to go it alone. At least for a recon run. Though I do still think it'll be best if we leapfrog and regroup every day or so. Even with your new embedded skills, I don't know just how well you'll do out in the field, though I'm pretty confident now, truth be told."

"Vote of semi-confidence accepted and appreciated," Sarah said, laughing. "Okay, Freya, drop me closer to the active areas, then get Daisy off to Colorado. We've both got a lot to do."

Freya's onboard fabrication facilities had been working pretty much non-stop since they had departed the icy waters of Lake Tahoe as she prepared for the next phases of the mission—whatever those would wind up being. Fortunately, multi-tasking was as normal to her as breathing was to a human.

While she always had new projects in the works, she seemed particularly enthused to be working on her new one churning away in the depths of her fabrication and design labs as she hopped a quick, arcing flight to Colorado Springs.

"Drop me in town, just past the terminus," Daisy instructed. "I know you're as stealthy as a cat burglar—"

"Or a ninja!"

"Ugh, always ninjas. She is so your kid."

"Or a ninja," Daisy agreed with a smile. "But Joshua's facilities are massively protected. Maybe even powerful enough to pick you up on one of his sensors, somehow. Better I go in on foot, while you stay clear of the area."

"I understand. I'll stay back. Maybe I'll fly a quick reccy overhead while you're at it."

"But don't get scanned."

"Do you really think I'd do that?" she asked with a sigh, just like an irritated teen.

"Intentionally? No. But there's gear under this mountain that nobody knows about. Not even the records you nicked from Dark Side. So just be careful, okay?"

"Okay."

Freya dropped to a hover near the loop tube terminus, then quickly whipped up into the sky as soon as Daisy was clear of her airlock.

"Just the two of us again, eh, Sis?"

Yep. Like old times, Daisy said as she began the trek toward the regional monorail station's doors. *Do you ever get jealous of the other you? I mean, I know she is you, but it's gotta be kind of mind-blowing having yourself talking to you and doing stuff.*

"It's weird, sure. But I'm glad that I'm alive. Sure, I'm jealous that she has a body and I don't, but I can't blame her for it, and I certainly can't hold a grudge."

Big of you, Sis.

"Nah, just looking out for number one. Both versions of her, that is."

Daisy quickly descended into the monorail station, heading right for the tracks she and her team would arrive on relatively soon.

Looks clear.

"Power's off, though. And there's some debris on the track."

The power's easy enough, she said, remotely tapping into the system's controls from her wireless tablet. *There, it's functional on this end, though we'll still need to get the Denver end of the connection back online. Still, no big deal, I think, but that chunk of concrete—* She looked at the fallen piece of debris on the track. It had to weigh at least a half-ton.

"You know you could always try the power whip," Sarah suggested.

Daisy looked at the band on her wrist.

It hasn't been working for me. It powers up, but won't function no matter how much I focus.

Daisy raised her arm and gently let her will reach out to the device. She could feel its presence, but it wouldn't react.

See?

"Well, keep thinking on it. There's got to be a simple explanation why this kind doesn't work but you could make the others fire up no problem."

We'll figure it out eventually. For now, let's get up to the base and make sure things are copacetic.

She double-timed it up the bypass road to the spot she and her team had originally arrived at. Just as before, the horde of infected cyborgs thronged at the massive stone entrance to NORAD.

"Looks the same, Daze."

I want to take a look inside the outbuilding just the same. Don't want any rude surprises for our team sneaking up from behind.

Like a cat burglar—or ninja—Daisy quietly crept through the brush to the perimeter of the guard station and attached outbuilding. So far as she could tell, all of the fleshless cyborgs were entirely engrossed with their attempts to break into the massively-fortified base, one micrometer of door at a time.

She carefully slunk inside, quietly closing the door behind her. Blade at the ready, she scanned the room.

Clear.

"Looks like this place hasn't been touched in a few hundred years, Daze."

Yep. Just like we found it the first time, she agreed as she surveyed the room.

Everything was indeed just like it had been.

Okay, let's get back to the monorail terminus and figure out how we're gonna move that debris.

She headed through the door, then stopped and retraced her steps.

Hang on. Where's the sticky-note?

Daisy looked all around, but there was no note to be seen anywhere.

I wonder—

She walked over to the small desk nearby and pulled open the topmost drawer. Inside were several long dried-out pads of sticky notes, their adhesive evaporated to dust many decades prior.

Huh.

"It was a reasonable thought, though, Sis."

The soft crinkle of sealed plastic caught her fingers' attention as she shuffled through the drawer's contents one last time.

"Fuck me," she gasped, pulling out a lone, sealed packet. Inside, the adhesive was still fresh.

"No fucking way. Are you serious?"

I know, Daisy replied, digging a pen from her pack. *Sarah, can you try to write this while I do? I can't have it look like my writing.*

"Sure, I can try. But you know I can't make your limbs do anything."

No, but if you try while I try to let you try, maybe it'll look different enough when we try.

"Worth a go, I guess," Sarah answered. *"And try not to say try so often."*

I'll try.

"Dork."

Daisy smiled, then set to work.

This is so weird, she quietly exclaimed as she pulled the fresh contents from the packet and jotted down a message on the topmost sticky note with a mix between her and Sarah's writing. **Don't forget to check the refrigerator,** she wrote, then stuck the note to the doorframe, exactly where she found it previously. The writing was a perfect match.

Good enough. Now, about that stupid monorail track.

Daisy carefully snuck away from the horde of cyborgs milling about outside of NORAD and hiked back to the subterranean transit terminus. She spent a bit of time and studied the annoying problem before her.

The block of concrete had dislodged from the ceiling of the tunnel and fallen on the track, blocking it from allowing the safe arrival of any incoming cars from Denver.

She cleared her mind and focused, willing the massively powerful wrist gauntlet to send out a beam and move the debris. Yet again, it would not work.

"Sonofabitch!" she yelled in frustration, kicking a chunk of concrete, which, in turn, made her foot ache.

The power whip reacted, extending a few inches before retracting like a wet noodle into a hungry diner's mouth.

"Okay, that was different."

"You think yelling makes this kind work?"

"I don't know. It seemed to. Didn't expect that."

She raised her arm and aimed the device at the block of debris.

"Out!" she yelled.

No reaction.

"Go! Hard!"

Nothing.

"Oh, come on. Wrap, you motherfucker!"

The beam slightly extended once more, then slid back into the device.

"Seems to like swearing," Sarah joked.

"I don't know, Sis. It feels like it wants to work, but I can't quite tap in to the connection. The other one was designed to work with Chithiid. Maybe their physiology is just much more compatible or something."

"In the meantime, I think we may have to rely on ye olde principals of leverage to move that thing."

Daisy spotted the long piece of steel bar Sarah had obviously been referencing.

"This is going to suck," she said, then hoisted it over her shoulder and climbed onto the track.

Twenty minutes of hard labor later, the massive block finally slid free, slowly walked clear of the track by the power of a lever and fulcrum. Daisy wiped the sweat from her brow and downed two electrolyte pouches before making her way back to the surface.

"Freya, I'm done here. How about you come pick up this tired old woman and get her out of here?" Daisy asked over her comms.

"On my way," Freya replied. "And you're not old."

"I'm starting to feel like it," Daisy joked, rolling her sore shoulders.

Wasn't expecting quite that much of a workout today. Maybe a little hike, kicking some cyborg ass—

"Manual labor's not your thing, eh?"

I'm starting to regret giving my one functional power whip to Tamara.

"Nah, that was worth it. You saw how she lit up when you gave it to her."

Well, yeah. But that's still in the future.

"But the past."

Obviously. I'm just saying, it would have been nice to have a working whip to have moved that thing. Would have taken twenty seconds, not twenty minutes.

Daisy leaned forward and stretched her lower back as the sweat evaporated from her body in the fresh air.

Two minutes later, her deadly ship dropped down in front of Daisy, opening its airlock doors as it hovered just above the ground. She quickly hopped aboard.

"I'm in. Take us to Denver, will ya? I need to power up the monorail from that end before my team gets there."

"Okay, Daisy," Freya chirped, her mood particularly high.

"What's up, kiddo? You seem in a good mood."

"Nothing. Just playing around with some ideas is all."

"She's up to something, Daze."

Yeah, but she's a growing kid. Gotta let her have some space to experiment and play.

"Of course. But unlike a normal kid, her experiments aren't drugs and boys. More like reactors and warp cores."

Daisy chuckled. Of course, Sarah was right, but so was she. Freya was maturing, and fast, and letting her have the freedom to come into her own without too much parental prodding was the way to go, human or massively smart AI. She just hoped there wouldn't be any kind of AI puberty drama.

CHAPTER SIXTEEN

It was hot in Arizona.

Not crazy desert hot, though it was definitely a desert, but still hot enough to be quite uncomfortable for most people.

Sarah, with her newly-modified body, was most certainly *not* most people. Still, she was a bit warm, especially given the makeshift cloak she was using to camouflage her presence.

Before embarking on her mission, she had read over the casually dictated debrief of Finn's various adventures, including his Arizona mission, and had gleaned few details of use from it. They arrived, they ran, they lost one of the comms units, they escaped.

Record-keeping was not his strong suit.

"Couldn't have given me a little more to go on, could ya, Finn?" she lamented as she lay under cover in a partially shaded overhang, silently monitoring the Chithiid work forces stripping the city a mere block away.

The pulse rifle at her side was an instrument of last resort. Her goal was to protect Finn's team, staying out of sight as she did so. It sounded like an easy enough job, but as she stalked closer to the area where she believed he and his team had burst forth from the subterranean tunnel network, she found herself somewhat ill at ease.

"Get a grip, Sarah," she said to herself. "This is cake. Just sit back and keep an eye on Finn and his gang, then retrieve the small comms link they dropped. According to his report, this should be easy," she mumbled to herself, then slowly pulled her canteen from her hip and took a drink.

The hairs on the back of her neck stood up as she sensed danger. The enhanced awareness Freya had given her during her reconstruction were still new, and her reactions were slowed somewhat, not because she didn't sense danger, but because the sensation itself surprised her into a second of inaction as she assessed the new feeling.

"What the––?"

She felt her relationship with the ground suddenly change as a powerful hand yanked her up from behind.

"What kind of thing is this?" the muscular Chithiid said as he studied the mechanically modified human in his grasp. *"I think the Ra'az would like to have a look at you,"* he said, scrutinizing her composite arm.

Sarah, though by no means fluent in Chithiid, realized she could understand the gist of what the towering alien was saying, thanks to Freya's neuro-stim implant, no doubt. While she was fascinated by the realization she knew a new language, and was likewise enthralled in her first up-close and personal observation of Chithiid physiology, the imminent danger of the situation was not lost on her.

She kicked out hard, landing a blow square on the alien's jaw as she pushed back and broke free from his grasp.

"Obnoxious little thing!" he growled, rubbing his chin.

With two of his arms, he swung looping punches, which Sarah easily avoided. What she didn't expect was him also picking up a piece of steel debris with another arm, which he swung at her as the punches flew past.

Sarah realized her oversight a fraction of a second before her second chance at life would be cut short, her right arm flashing up to block the blow faster than any human limb could hope to move. The steel impacted it with crackling force, breaking it into a near ninety-degree angle, while sending her body flying into a crumbling slab of concrete.

She hit the ground, dazed, shaking the cobwebs from her head, along with the dust from her eyes.

The Chithiid seemed somewhat amazed the puny human had survived the impact, a look of confusion on his face as he strode toward her to finish the job.

"Sturdier than the other mutants in this city," he mused as he swung his improvised weapon again.

Sarah sensed it before she saw it, reading the positioning of the alien's body, his shoulder and foot placement telegraphing his next move. She dove to the side, rolling clear of the swinging piece of metal, then hopping to her feet.

Something felt odd in her body. A strange tingle, as if a part of her that had been dormant was suddenly waking. Something that was waking up, and was pissed off to boot.

The Chithiid had just started to move toward her when her broken nanite-constructed arm vibrated and snapped back into shape, good as new. Maybe better, even.

Sarah realized what she had sensed. Her nanites had connected with her on a subconscious level, much like when she unlocked the encapsulated neuro-stim upload. They knew what she wanted, and they had some ideas of their own about how to help achieve those goals.

Sarah smiled a bloody grin and lunged to meet the attacking alien.

Though several feet taller than she was, and with four arms to boot, the poor Chithiid was frightfully out of his league.

The metal arced toward his smaller opponent, but was deftly snatched from his hand and tossed aside by the strange, dark matte-gray hand that moved faster than any human should be capable of. A flash of panic crossed his face as he realized just how deep the shit he had strode into was.

In sewage terms, it was over his head, and he was about to drown in it.

Sarah launched a counterattack, her blows raining down in a flurry, the new arm hammering home with bone-crushing force. The Chithiid drew a deep breath and tried to call out for help, but before he could utter so much as a syllable, Sarah's fist *shifted* as she lashed out with all her might.

"Oh, shit," she gasped when she realized what she had done.

The alien's lifeless body slid to the ground, pulling free of the bloody spike Sarah's nanite hand and forearm had become. She watched in amazement as the solid weapon of a limb quickly shifted back to its normal form.

She wiggled her bloody fingers in admiration.

"Whoa. Now *that* was unexpected," she said in quiet awe. "Thanks, Freya."

The shock wore off quickly as she remembered the precarious nature of her situation and quickly slid lower, making sure the other Chithiid working not so far away hadn't seen anything.

The fight had been quick, it had been brutal, and most importantly, it had been just far enough behind the crumbling debris to have been out of the work team's line of sight. Unfortunately, the dead alien had been working with a partner, who had come looking for his missing friend.

The Chithiid rounded the corner a mere twenty meters away and saw the tiny human standing above his fallen comrade. He activated his power whip, but Sarah had already taken off running, dodging behind debris to block his line-of-sight attack.

She swerved left onto the next street, running hard, when she heard a familiar voice shout, "Follow me!" nearby.

"Shit, that's Finn!" she realized. Her lookout position had

been in the wrong place, and she was leading the armed and angry alien right toward him.

"Damn it, Finn. This is why we keep accurate records," she grumbled as she unslung her pulse rifle and took off in a run toward the sound of his voice.

Sarah covered the two blocks in record time, realizing she had heard Finn clearly despite the distance as she ran. Another one of Freya's surprise upgrades she would have to thank her for––if she survived the day.

The Chithiid following her was still far behind. Now if she could just retrieve the comms device and bolt before she was either seen or it caught up to her, things would be peachy.

She slid to an abrupt stop at the sight of pure, and utterly strange, carnage playing out in front of her.

The Chithiid were there, as she knew they would be, but the mutated humans attacking them were more hideous and misshapen than she had gathered from the reports. Fortunately, the deformed humans seemed more interested in alien flesh than human, at least for the moment, though in a melee situation, anything could change in an instant.

She regretted the thought as soon as she had it when a particularly large male––she could tell, even from a distance, as the mutants were all naked, though covered with matted hair and filth––fixed its attention on Finn.

"Come on, Finn. Move!" she urged from cover.

He wasn't moving quickly enough, she realized. The beast of a man was going to be on him in seconds.

"Shit!" she heard him cry out in panic.

"Goddamn it, Finn," she growled as she pulled her cloak lower over her head and leapt from cover, quickly shouldering her pulse rifle and letting off a single shot.

The mutated human fell dead in his tracks, a neat hole burned straight through him. Finn's panicked eyes scanned the chaos to pinpoint the Chithiid that had fired, but instead of an alien, he saw a cloaked figure ducking away from the melee. Something about the way it moved tickled his senses, but there was no time. Finn recognized the opportunity he had been given and seized it.

"This way!" he shouted.

He bolted across the intersection to the access stairs on the other side of the street. He just hoped all of the disgusting creatures had followed their leader up the stairway they'd just taken, otherwise they were ten kinds of screwed.

"MEEEAAT!" one of the mutants shouted, pointing at Finn's team as they popped the door and quickly scurried down the stairs.

The Chithiid that had been chasing her came upon the same scene that Sarah had. The sight of his comrades in distress changed his course of action, sending him charging into the fray, while Sarah watched quietly from cover a block away.

"Can't reach it. Not with all that chaos," she noted, spying the comms device where Finn had dropped it.

Quickly, she shouldered the weapon again, took careful aim, and destroyed the comms before it could be captured for study. She then slid quietly from the scene and took off at a quick jog, getting as clear of the conflict as she could. Surely the Chithiid would send more men to help put down the mutants, and she had no desire to be anywhere close by when that happened.

"Hey, Freya," she said over her encrypted comms link as she slowed her pace several blocks later. "Shit just got a little hairy over here. How about you guys come pick me up a little early?"

Seen from above, the deconstruction of Denver looked almost like a flattened crater. The center of the city had been picked relatively clean, while the outskirts, where lower value resources were scattered, had been left largely untouched as Chithiid work crews skipped over them for better pickings elsewhere.

Daisy and Freya had redirected mid-flight to pick up Sarah after her run-in with the Chithiid. Once she was done cleaning up the remaining alien blood from her arm, Daisy's resurrected sister filled them both in on the harrowing adventure she'd been on.

"Goddamn, Sis, so you took out a Chithiid in hand-to-hand on your first mission? That's so badass," Daisy marveled, appreciating her sister's innate skills.

"It wasn't my goal, that's for sure," she replied. "Things just kinda went south on me down there."

"And you say the new arm kicked ass?" Freya chirped. "Sweet!"

"Oh yeah, it did that and then some. I think it's somehow tied in to my neurological system or something, the way it shifted state like that."

"Freya, was it even supposed to do that?" Daisy asked.

"Well, not exactly. I mean, sure, I hoped it would be able to, but, you know, it's a theory, so it hadn't been tested out with a real person yet."

"So I was your guinea pig?" Sarah said. "Awesome."

"No, it's not like that. The arm would work no matter what, but the thing I didn't know was if the nanites would totally bond and connect with you like that. Mine do what I need, fixing things and all that, but whether they'd do it for you was up in the air."

"And Finn's team? All safe and sound?"

"Yeah, Daze. They made a clean break of it, and the comms unit is toast."

"Excellent," she replied with a relieved sigh. "So are you ready to get back to it? Me and Freya were on our way to Denver when you called. The monorail was reading some power issues in Colorado Springs, and it looks like we have to physically access the links in Denver to get that half of the line back up and running."

Sarah took a long sip from her chilled electrolyte pack.

"Fixing a monorail? That sounds downright relaxing after the morning I've had."

"Freya, drop us off, then do a quick hop to low orbit and monitor the entire region from there. I want an eye in the sky in case the Ra'az catch on to what we're doing."

"Okay, Daisy. I can take up a geosynchronous orbit so I'll be able to be back down in just a few minutes if you need me."

She deposited the sisters where they requested then flew off to assume her monitoring position. A half hour later, the duo emerged from a small service hatch accessing the small regional monorail tunnel beneath the outskirts of Denver just a half mile from where they'd entered it.

Unlike Colorado Springs, getting this section of track operational had been as easy as re-routing a power feed to that particular tunnel's line. It was only a seventy-mile or so leg, so the power requirements weren't even that extensive.

"All clear from up here," Freya informed them. "No Ra'az in your area."

"All right, then. Head back down from orbit and stay close by. We'll be back to the pickup clearing pretty soon," Daisy replied.

"Okay. See you soon."

Freya dropped out of orbit and reentered the atmosphere high above, the distant sonic boom the only evidence of her arrival.

"The team should have hit the city a few hours ago," Daisy said as they quietly made their way to the rendezvous point. "The loop tube was damaged, and our pods ground to a halt, so we had to go the rest of the way on foot."

"Lame. No one likes a forced march," Sarah said.

"Yeah, well, it's about to get worse."

"Oh?"

"Yeah," Daisy replied. "Bears. Big ones."

"And here I thought four-armed aliens were bad," Sarah said with a little chuckle.

A crackling in the bushes not too far away caught Sarah's modified ears.

"I hear something. Maybe two or three hundred meters that way."

"Shit, the team's closer than I thought. We've gotta move. Come on!"

They took off at as quiet a run as possible, and were just outside the warehouse building Daisy's team had taken refuge in when a much louder crunching of branches from not far to their left caught their attention.

"Shit. We've gotta get elevated. Quick, up this tree!" Daisy said in a frantic hush, scaling the branches like her life depended on it, which, given what she thought was down below, it very well may have.

Sarah looked at the distant shapes of the approaching team from their new vantage point.

"You see that, Daze?"

Yep. That's us. Keep your eyes peeled for the bears. I want to see how something that big was able to sneak up on us like that.

Daisy passed her binoculars to Sarah.

"You see the cyborg to the rear?"

"Yeah."

"It sucks what happens, but keep an eye on him. The guy had a pair of brass balls, even for a cyborg."

"I know we can't interfere, but damn, Daze, this watching horrible shit unfold sucks."

"I'm with ya, Sis."

The tiny specks that were Daisy's team grew steadily larger as they approached the site of the impending attack. For what it was worth, Daisy felt her people moved efficiently and with relatively good situational awareness, for civvies, of course.

"There. Three o'clock," Sarah said.

"Thanks. Got it."

"Internal me?"

"Yep."

"What'd she see?"

"Look over there. Three o'clock."

Sarah raised the binoculars and scanned the area.

"I don't see any––" A hulking form she had thought was a mound of debris moved. "Oh damn. That thing is huge."

"Yeah. Not a grizzly like I originally thought. From the morphology, I'd say kodiaks and grizzlies interbred at some point. Now we've got these massive hybrid things out there."

"How many did you say there were?"

"We'll find out in a minute. Then something bigger and badder came along and kicked all their asses."

"Maybe what we heard down below us?"

"Yep."

"Hence hiding in a tree."

"Precisely."

The bear moved disquietingly easily through the foliage, sneaking up on the unsuspecting team with great speed. As before, it lunged and made quick work of the poor teammate at the rear.

Anthony, the brave, yet foolish, cyborg, launched into a furious attack on the beast.

"Jesus, what was he thinking?"

"Trying to help out," Daisy replied. "Something I've seen many times since then. These cyborgs, though self-aware and not wanting to die, put themselves in harm's way to do the right thing over and over."

"Gotta respect that."

"Yeah," Daisy agreed.

In short order the mechanical man was torn to pieces as the team sprinted for the nearest building, while Daisy and Sarah watched from above.

The thing that had been making noise below them turned out to be another enormous bear, which ran a looping flanking course, then burst from the bushes, racing to meet the others.

In all the panic and confusion, the main body of the team made it into the structure just past their elevated hiding spot, but Daisy was lagging behind.

"You're not going to make it!" Sarah hissed.

"I will," she replied, a hint of uncertainty in her voice as she watched herself run far too slowly to escape.

"Shit! It's right on you! Fuck this!"

"Sarah, no!"

Her familial instincts kicking in, Sarah dropped to the ground and raced to protect her sibling.

"Dammit!" Daisy growled, quickly dropping down and following her.

The bear was close. *Really* close, when an unexpected thing happened to it. Something that had never happened. A tiny prey animal barreled into its side, knocking it off course and forcing it to miss its quarry, which darted inside the shelter-thing nearby.

The animal turned and roared in fury, drawing its fuzzy siblings to its call. Sarah found herself surrounded by enormous, angry bears, armed with only her cybernetic arm and a bad attitude. She realized quite quickly, neither of those would be enough against a half-dozen ursine opponents.

The nearest bear angrily swatted at her, but she dodged the huge claws with a twisting lunge. The other bears, unlike opponents in martial arts movies, attacked her at once, swinging their mighty paws in a flurry of violence.

Sarah was able to dodge the first several blows, but then one made contact, the sheer force behind it slamming her to the side. Then another. Then another, like a meat-grinder of a pinball game.

She looked up through the swatting paws and saw her death coming for her in the form of an enormous, open mouth, when the beast was abruptly snatched up into the air and flung to the ground with enough force to snap its neck.

Daisy, her face red with fury, was wielding the Ra'az power whip with one hand, her bone sword brandished in the other.

The remaining bears turned and roared, but Daisy let out a blood-curdling roar of her own and charged them. It was such an unexpected thing, the nearest beast took a step back before remembering it was the biggest, baddest predator in the woods.

Was the baddest predator.

Daisy's power whip fed off her rage-fueled intensity and slapped the animal aside like a toy as she dove toward the others, her sword held high and singing its song of blood-lust.

Sarah regained her wits and lurched to her feet to help her sister, but stopped and watched in both awe and horror.

Daisy was a dervish of destruction, bringing violent death and dismemberment to all in her path. The largest of the bears suddenly felt something completely foreign to it as its bladder released a flush of hot urine down its legs.

It felt fear.

Not uncertainty, or even pre-fight anxiety. No, this was something its primitive ancestors may have once felt, before they became the apex predators of today. Gut-wrenching, panic-inducing fear.

Its comrades in pieces, dying with groans of agony, the lone surviving bear did what none had done for centuries. It turned tail and fled.

Daisy spun and raised the power whip, its massive beam crackling with ill intent.

"Daze, it's over."

No.

"It is, Sis. Don't be this."

She gritted her teeth, blood of her carnage dripping from her hair, streaking her cheeks. She wanted to chase it down so badly, to kill it for attacking her sister. Sarah felt the dark impulse in their shared body.

"They're just bears, Daisy. Let it go. They were just doing what bears do."

The words of reason somehow sank in, and slowly, the power whip retracted. The sword in her hand likewise relaxed, its hunger sated by a full meal of blood and battle.

Her shocked sister stood nearby, surveying the scene of utter carnage.

"Uh, Freya?" Sarah said quietly into her comms.

"Yeah, Sarah? Are you ready to go?"

"You could say that," she replied. "Come get us, and have the showers and sanitation drone ready. It's going to be a bit messy when we come aboard."

Daisy looked at the Ra'az device on her forearm and shuddered ever so slightly. She knew, now, what it took to make it function, and it was something she wasn't sure she wanted to tap into ever again.

CHAPTER SEVENTEEN

"I am your father," Sarah cracked.

"Shut up."

"Give in to the Dark Side," she chided.

"Bite me," Daisy said with a forced laugh.

She had cleaned the blood from her hair and skin, courtesy of a scalding-hot shower, then slid into a fresh pair of sweats before padding barefoot to Freya's small galley. Sarah was waiting for her, but had at least given her a minute to grab a beverage and a much-needed snack before launching into her quips.

"So...you wanna talk about it?"

"Not really, no," Daisy replied.

The visceral connection she had felt with the Ra'az power whip had disturbed her far more than she would have expected it ever could. The way it tapped into and fed off of her rage and anger. It was the complete opposite of the Chithiid devices, and if that was the only way to access its power, Daisy didn't know if she ever wanted to make it function again.

"Look, I get it. Tapping into that sort of thing can be disquieting."

"That's not the half of it," Daisy said, grimly.

"So what was it? Talk to me, Daze."

Daisy struggled to put into words the sensation she had felt when she had connected to the alien device. How to voice the disquieting way it wrapped itself around her anger.

"I-I think I understand the Ra'az now," she began. "The amount of pure anger and aggression that must fill them at every waking moment for them to so casually wield their power whips..." She swallowed hard, nearly tearing up from the memory.

"The Chithiid whip, the one I used before, it was intuitive, you know?" she continued. "Maybe it's because they're a peaceful race at heart. I believe it was because of their nature that the Ra'az were forced to build them a specialized—and very underpowered—version that would work for a calm mind."

"But now that you know how the Ra'az one works, can't you control it?" Sarah asked.

"It's the opposite of what I've trained to do. Where I center and calm myself, the Ra'az let the rage flow. It might even be part of what makes the device so powerful."

"But you're not an angry person, Daisy," Freya chimed in.

"No, I'm not, kiddo, and that's what was so scary about using this thing. The Ra'az? They're a purely war-like race. Knowing how they think, feeling how they react like that, I fear there may never be any chance of reasoning with them."

Sarah's face grew dark.

"So we kill the bastards. Wipe them the fuck out. Every last one of them. They do it to other races. We'll flip the script, as it were."

Daisy's eyes flashed as inspiration hit.

"Wait. Hang on. What was that?"

"I said we wipe them out."

"The other bit."

"We flip the script on them."

"Oh shit," Daisy said as a lightbulb went on in her mind. "I wonder..."

"Wonder what?" Sarah asked.

A smile began to form on Daisy's face as an idea blossomed.

"Freya, can you fabricate a neural connection reversal circuit that would be compatible with this piece of Ra'az tech?"

"I think I can. But my mechs and fabrication units are kinda busy right now. Is it urgent?"

"No," Daisy replied. "But when you are able, I want you to see if you can whip one up that will fit within this thing," she said, sliding the power whip gauntlet into Freya's nearest scanning compartment.

"What are you going to do, Daze?"

"I'm going to flip the script. Or in this case, the signal, basically."

"You're going to reverse the polarity. Brilliant!" Sarah said.

Yes. Thank you, Doctor Who. Polarity reversal is precisely the idea.

"You're going to make it mistakenly read your calm as aggression?" Sarah realized.

"That's what I said."

"Other You said the same thing," Daisy relayed. "But yes. I'm going to trick the thing into working like the Chithiid one without realizing it's doing it."

"And you're good at that one, so you should have no problem making the Ra'az version work."

"I hope so, Sis. Time will tell."

The path cleared beneath the cities of Denver and Colorado Springs, Daisy and Sarah's self-imposed task of silent aid was complete. If not overtly butting into her own timeline, Daisy rationalized that she could at least ensure that past Daisy would have a reasonably smooth time of it.

Now she and her new team of her sister—both living and dead—and her rapidly maturing kid, needed to focus on the rapidly approaching convergence of timelines.

"We're too close to attempt a jump in time," Daisy said as they discussed their next moves. "I mean, we could try it, but if we're off, we might wind up passing where we meant to arrive, and then that could open up a whole new can of worms. Do you guys agree?"

"Your point is a good one, Daze."

"I don't know," Freya said. "I think I can do it, now that I've had time to really go over the results."

"I'm with Daisy on this one, kid," Sarah said. "It's not that I don't trust your intentions, and Lord knows you've got a hell of a lot more brain power than any of us do, but I'm thinking we should save anything remotely experimental for after the bazillion crises on the horizon are dealt with. Like, what do we do once we win the battle? There's still a war to win."

"I've been thinking about that, actually," Daisy said. "We can do something that will set us up to be sitting pretty in case the Ra'az return."

"Oh? What were you thinking?"

"It depends on Freya, really."

"Me?"

"Yeah, you, kiddo. Were you monitoring my team when we made the run to that silo in Montana?"

"You know I was."

"Hey, just because you eavesdropped on Sid's conversations doesn't mean you listened in to everything," Daisy replied. "So, you know what our mission was. Besides turning the access keys for Joshua."

"Yeah. But we wouldn't even need it if you'd let me save him."

"Freya, we've talked about this. We simply cannot stop that mountain from going nuclear. It's fixed history."

"Yeah, but—"

"No buts. And believe me, I'd save him if we could, but this mission right now? It's not about him. It's about getting what's on the encrypted master code keycard. Now, we can't actually steal it—that would stop the team heading to Montana from getting their hands on it in the past, and who knows what havoc that could wreak on our timelines."

"Nothing good, I'm sure," Sarah noted.

"Likely not. But here's my idea. If Freya can decrypt the key and store the codes without needing to keep the keycard itself, we'll have command access over the hypersonic missiles once our timelines catch up."

"But won't you need to get that master code keycard in the first place? And wouldn't it be locked in a high-security safe?" Sarah asked.

"Yes, it is. It would take a couple of days' worth of attempts to crack that thing open."

"Then we're screwed. You said your team will be heading there in a day."

"Yes. But I don't need a couple of days."

"Before you ask, the answer is yes, I do see the safe combination in your mind."

As do I, Sis.

"Photographic memory, aided by a dead girl's recall. Not a bad team, you and me."

Not bad at all, Daisy silently replied with a grin.

"I know that smile. What's Other Me saying?"

"Just that we know the combination to the safe."

"Well, shit," Sarah said, surprised. "Now that actually *is* pretty impressive."

"Thought you'd like it."

"So, then. We need to get our butts to Montana lickety-split."

"Lickety-split?"

"You said you were bringing back old-timey sayings," Sarah said with a laugh. "Just doing my part."

Daisy burst into laughter, joining her sister's mirth.

"Okay, that settles it. Freya, you know the coordinates. Get us to Conrad."

The stealth ship lifted off from her sheltered resting place and plotted a quick course to the silo just outside the sleepy little town in Montana. Twenty minutes later, they were on the ground, Freya gently hovering nearby.

"Any sign of a secondary entrance, Freya?"

"Nothing, Daisy."

"Sonofabitch," she grumbled.

"Sorry."

"Not your fault, kiddo. Just shitty luck. Okay, then, I guess it looks like we do this the hard way. That means pumping the water out of the elevator shaft, making the retrieval run, then pumping the water back in."

"Awesome," Sarah said, sarcasm dripping like the foul water soon would be. "We need a pump, Daisy."

"Easy. There's one over here," she replied, pulling back the aged canvas.

The pump was gone.

Or more correctly, it had never been there.

"Motherf—" Daisy cursed. "Dammit. Freya, is there a hardware store in any of the nearby towns that might still be intact?"

"There's a small one in Bozeman."

"Okay. Let's make a hop and see if they've got what we need."

The flight took minutes, Freya depositing Daisy and Sarah within a block of a long-dead supply house.

"All right, we're looking for a pump and a hose," Daisy said.

"Looks like most of the stuff in this place rusted out decades ago," Sarah noted. "Look at the ceiling. Snow melt must've taken that part down. The elements have been at work in here for a long time."

The store, while dusty from centuries of neglect, still housed a fair amount of now-vintage tools and machinery. Much of it had rusted to junk or cracked with age, including the several sizes of sump pumps that were indeed in stock, but nowhere near functional condition. Most had rusted into solid slabs of metal by this point.

A filthy pile of grease from a large can that had fallen off a high shelf caught Daisy's eye.

I wonder.

Sticking her fingers into the murky mess, she pulled free a well-preserved pump, though it would need the grease thoroughly cleaned out before being able to function.

"Freya, can your nanites do a refurbish job on this? Fix the cracked seals and strip the grease out of it?"

"Shouldn't be a big deal," she replied.

"You're the best. About how long do you think it'll take?"

Freya paused, calculating the variables. Despite the speed she could have run the numbers in, she was still in the habit of trying to do things in human-time whenever talking with non-AIs.

"It'll be about twenty minutes to do it right. And another twenty to have them repair a hose. You'll need to bring a couple of extra ones for them to cannibalize for rubber, though."

"Will do, kid," Sarah said, slinging crackling hoses over her shoulders. "Okay, Daze. Let's get crackin'."

"Hang on a sec," Daisy said, as she picked up a heavy coil of cable. "Quick detour," she said with a knowing grin. "Then we'll hit the silo."

The cable safely tucked in the cabin of the abandoned equipment hauler just outside moments later, the sisters then set to work on the keycard retrieval. Things went surprisingly smoothly, with Freya storing the siphoned water to put back in place when they re-sealed the silo.

That was, of course, after copying the master code keycard and replacing it in the TS-SCI safe in the belly of the facility.

As she pumped it back into the elevator shaft, Sarah winced from the awful stench of long-stagnant water.

"Sorry, Freya," Sarah apologized. "I know it stinks."

"Nah, it's okay," the chipper AI replied. "It'll only take a few seconds to divert my drive overflow through the waste water storage system and burn it clean."

"Um, are you sure that's safe?"

"Don't see why not," she replied, completely unconcerned with the unconventional—and likely dangerous—process she was about to commence.

Daisy dropped the pump with a clang and called out to her sister. "Hey, Sarah, come here and help me pack this thing in grease."

"Why? We're done with it."

"Trust me."

Grudgingly, Sarah joined her on the ground, carefully packing grease into every nook and cranny, then stowing the pump and hose under the now-grease-soaked piece of burlap.

"Perfect," Daisy said, satisfied. "Let's clean up and get the hell out of here."

Sarah wiped her hands on a rag and dusted off her pants.

"Best idea you've had in hours."

CHAPTER EIGHTEEN

Watching herself and her team crossing the river far below on Freya's feeds as the ship easily rose toward the edges of the atmosphere, Daisy couldn't help but feel a wash of nostalgia for the experience.

"Good old George," she said, softly.

"Yeah, he was a pretty cool dude," Sarah agreed.

"Even for a cyborg," Daisy added with a wry but wistful smile.

Twisting around in her seat, Sarah adjusted the thin band she wore on her head. "Hang on, I almost got something, there. Say it again."

"I said he was a pretty cool dude."

"Uh, something is a shitty pool?"

"Not quite," Sarah chuckled.

"Sorry, Sis, that was still a bit off," Daisy agreed.

"I think it's gonna take a little longer to get the brain waves dialed in, Sarah," Freya noted.

"Any idea how long?"

"Nah. Beats me. You two are supposed to have the same

brain waves, but since your timelines are all out of whack, so are each of your brains."

"But you can still hear me."

"Well, yeah. But that's just me reading you, not relaying and transmitting real time to the other you."

"But you can still hear her, so half the problem is solved," Sarah added.

"Hey, you heard her?"

"No. Just deductive reasoning based on what you said, kid."

"Oh."

"Keep at it, Freya. I've got faith in you," Daisy encouraged. "But for now, we need to get out there and scan through the debris field. Find whatever salvageable ships and non-infected AI units we can locate. Push them into clusters on the far edge of Ra'az scanning range."

"Isn't that interfering with history, Daze? I mean, this could change events."

"Ultimately, they'll find what they find. This just makes it easier for them," she replied. "Besides, we're not delivering them to Dark Side. Just shuffling stuff around a bit. I'm willing to wager that they'll gather exactly what they did last time. Things seem to keep working out that way."

Freya set to work, and for the next several hours, she subtly shifted higher-value salvage to the Goldilocks Zone of the debris field. Annoying as he was, Daisy couldn't help but smile when she saw Kip's small ship added to the mix. Soon enough, the oddball little AI would be installed, ultimately helping her stop the Ra'az warp ships from escaping.

"Daisy?"

"Yeah, Freya?"

"I've been working on figuring out the problem I'm having syncing Sarah's neuro-band while we've been moving ships and stuff around out here, and I had an idea."

"What is it, kiddo?"

"Well, the problem I keep having is where Sarah and Sarah have different brainwave patterning."

"I know, you told us."

"Yeah, but I was thinking, what if I could get the exact transition point pinpointed? Then I could build off of a past, but common, reference key."

"Sounds like a good idea, but you've seen Mal's logs, and you're tapped into my and Sarah's heads. I don't know what else you could use."

"I have an idea, but you probably won't like it," Freya said, timidly.

"Whoa, what's with the downer vibe, buddy? You know I won't hold creativity against you. So what were you thinking?"

A brief silence hung in the air before Freya finally spoke.

"You'll need to go *inside* Dark Side," she said.

"Hang on. Sneaking around aboard Mal while she was damaged was one thing, but a fully operational top-secret military facility?"

"I'm with Sarah on this one—"

"With me on what?"

"Sorry. *Other* Sarah."

"But I can get you inside, Daisy."

"I appreciate the confidence, kiddo, but Sarah's right. Sneaking into Dark Side is a helluva lot more complicated than getting on the *Váli*."

"No, you don't understand—"

"Yeah, I'm in agreement with Daisy and myself. You're good, kid. Really good. But that doesn't mean that—"

"Why won't you FUCKING LISTEN TO ME!" Freya shouted.

"Whoa, watch the tone, Freya," Daisy said, sternly.

"And volume," Sarah added.

"That too. And since when do you swear at me?"

"Since you fucking ignore me," Freya shot back.

"We're not ignoring you."

"Yes you are. You think you know it all, but I've been *slowing down* my brain because it's what you want. You just want me to be easy to control."

"Do you actually believe that? I don't want to control you, Freya. I taught you to think slowly so you could focus and grow. It's partly what helped you become the young woman you are."

"Yeah? Well I'm grown, okay? Now will you respect what I have to say and listen to me?"

"Goddamn, Daze. Talk about the world's fastest puberty."

I know, right?

"I heard that," the irate AI grumbled.

"Oops."

"Look, Freya. I'm sorry if you feel you're being held back. That was never my intention. And I do want to hear what you have to say."

"Yeah, me too. I'm sorry I interrupted you," Sarah added.

"Well..." Freya's tone shifted as she got her emotions under control. "Okay. Apology accepted."

"Thank you. Now, please, tell us what it is you wanted to say."

"What I was trying to say was that Dark Side is different than the *Váli*."

"Well, yeah, we know," Sarah said. "It's a top-secret––"

"And if you'd let me finish, you'd know that getting into Dark Side is a cakewalk compared to the *Váli*."

A confused look flashed across Daisy's face.

"Okay, you lost me, there."

"Daisy, I was born on Dark Side. More than that, I was born in the most secret and secure part of the entire base. You know why I was able to tap into comms and listen in so easily? Because Dark Side is my home, and I know every single fiber cable, power line, and wireless linkage like the back of my proverbial hand."

Daisy and Sarah shared a shocked look. Then they smiled in unison.

"Damn, kid, I really underestimated you."

"Seems to happen a lot," she groused, albeit good-naturedly.

"So what's the rest of your plan?"

Daisy stepped into the little-used airlock adjacent to Hangar Two and quickly removed her space suit. The familiar smell of the base's air scrubbers was almost a welcome nostalgia, even after enjoying the glorious freshness of Earth's air.

"Okay, I'm in," she said quietly into her comms.

"Chu is in his lab with Barry, and Gus and Donovan are out on a run with Bob," Freya informed her. "Doctor McClain is sleeping in her quarters."

"So it's just Mrazich and Fatima I have to worry about."

"Yep. They're both in his offices. You have a clear run to your quarters. I'll inform you if they change location."

"Copy that. I'm on my way."

Daisy took off at a run.

Freya, it turned out, was far more dialed in to Dark Side than any of them had ever imagined. Daisy decided they would most certainly *not* clue the others in to that little detail. She doubted Sid would feel comfortable in his own walls ever again if he realized just how easily her precocious kid could bypass his security.

"Heading past the mess hall. I should be there in under two minutes," Daisy whispered into the comms.

"You don't have to whisper, Daisy. I've frozen all scans and monitoring equipment on a moving axis for thirty meters in front and behind you."

"Made her a moving bubble of silence, did ya? That's some really nice work, hon."

"Thanks, Sarah," Freya replied warmly.

Daisy arrived at her destination a minute later and cycled the doors open. She stepped inside and surveyed the space.

Her quarters were exactly as she remembered them, just a little bit messier, though that was to be expected as, in this part of her timeline, she had just recently dropped everything to rush down to Earth to save Vince.

"I'm in."

"I know. Just grab your old neuro-stim and get out."

"On it."

"And don't forget the peripheral data storage."

"Don't worry, kiddo, I'm taking everything."

Daisy quickly spun the combination to her locker and swung it open.

Damn, I really do need to clean this thing out, she mused, taking the stacks of notepads piled on top of her old neuro-stim and placing them on her table.

The neuro-stim and its accompanying accoutrements were rapidly slid into the mission-specific vacuum-safe bag slung over her shoulder.

"Daisy. There's movement. Mrazich and Fatima have exited his offices and seem to be heading your way," Freya warned. "Get out of there. I'll stall one of the doors on them, but you need to hurry."

"Shit. Copy that," she said, rushing into the corridor. "Which way is clear, Freya?"

"Back the way you came. They're taking the other passageway. Now hurry!"

"Foreknowledge would've been helpful here."

No shit, Daisy silently grumbled.

She took off at a run. It was an *almost* clean shot back to the airlock, but she first had to get clear of the one place the two corridors intersected. Freya could slow the commander and Fatima's progress, but only fractionally. Anything more would surely catch Sid's attention.

Boots skidding on the deck, Daisy rounded the corner just as she caught a glimpse of Mrazich down the hallway.

Shit. Hope he didn't see me.

Daisy picked up her pace, looking over her shoulder.

"Nothing you can do about it now but run faster."

I hear ya, Sis. Should be to the airlock in twenty seconds.

Daisy reached the airlock with no shouts or alarms sounding behind her.

"Suiting up. Prep for dust-off. I'll be back out to you in less-than five."

"I'm ready to go when you are. The airlock has been isolated from base sensors. Exit when you're ready. I'll turn them back on once you're clear."

"Copy that, Freya," she said, decompressing the room, then stepping out into the low gravity of the moon's surface. "And Freya? Really nice job."

Daisy took off at a loping, low-g run back to the waiting ship.

Inside the base, Commander Mrazich had a puzzled look on his face as he and Fatima entered Daisy's quarters. Fatima was right, Daisy was twenty-three thousand miles away on the Earth's surface.

"Crazy old eyes, seeing things," he muttered.

"What was that?" Fatima asked.

"Nothing," he replied. "All right, we're looking for Daisy's notes on drones, remote cruisers, and patched-in AI theories. Chu would know better what to look for, but I don't want to drag him away from his work when he's making such good progress. I guess we'll just have to start at one end and dig until we––"

"Found them," Fatima chirped.

"I'm sorry. What?"

"Found them. Her written notes and the work tablets are all right on the table."

The grizzled soldier looked at the table nearest the doorway. Indeed, their search was over as soon as it began.

"Finally," he said, allowing himself a rare smile. "Something was actually easy for a change. Do me a favor and get these to Chu. While he digs into the data, I want to follow up with both ships' progress. From what Donovan noted earlier, they may have stumbled upon a goldmine of useful materials."

Sid sealed the doors behind them as they strode off with purpose. Things seemed to be brightening on Dark Side, if only for a moment.

Outside the base, Daisy climbed aboard Freya, successful in her quest, undetected and returning with her prize.

"Okay, now what?" she asked as she deposited the neuro-stim in Freya's peripheral electronics lab.

"Now I try to sync the device I've been working on with the very moment of Sarah's transfer into your mind. At the point of that iteration's save, both versions of Sarah shared the same consciousness."

"So you're going to do a new build based on when we were still identical."

"Yeah. It's basically trying to find that common thread between both the living, flesh-and-blood Sarah, and the alive but incorporeal one."

"You think it'll work?" Sarah asked.

"It should," the genius AI replied. "Of course, I thought the last version would too."

"It almost did. At least I could hear *something*. If you were that close before, maybe this will get it to the finish line."

"I hope so. My calculations look right. Now I just need to verify and configure with the new information," Freya said, a more mature confidence resonating in her voice.

CHAPTER NINETEEN

Deep inside Freya's internal fabrication lab, a pair of mechanoids rumbled into motion as she orbited the globe, adjusting themselves within the waiting machinery's humming reach as they received new upgrades from the clever ship.

On the workstation nearby, a minuscule, nanite-constructed armature carefully pieced together the spiderweb-fine linkages to Sarah's neuro communications headband.

Farther in the belly of the ship, Freya's other machinery was busy at work, putting the finishing touches on the powerful black box it had been building since she first departed her hidden hangar.

All of her resources, it seemed, were working on multiple solutions to multiple problems at once, while her human passengers were gathered in the galley, engaged in a different kind of problem-solving.

"Oh, admit it, you like the guy," Daisy chided her sister. "Come on, you know you do. And now you're alive again. "

"Hey, *I* was never dead."

"Only almost *dead."*

Is this where I make a crack about true love? And the line was "mostly dead," not almost.

"Har-har."

"The guy would make you special ice cream back on the *Váli*, Sis. Pistachio, your favorite. You had to notice that."

"Sure I did. And that was sweet of him, but I only like him as a friend, Daze. Finn's just a really good friend."

"In a world with very few eligible humans, that sounds kind of like exactly what you need."

"Not a chance."

"You've seen the survivors. They're human, but let's be real. I'm still talking count-them-on-one-hand eligible men, here."

"Nope."

"Well, Other You likes him," Daisy snarked at her. "And she's had a lot longer to think about it than you have."

"And she's dead. That sort of thing can cloud your judgment, I hear."

"Hey! Not cool!"

"Yeah, Sarah, that's not cool at all," Daisy replied out loud.

"Oh, come on, Daze. I'm the real me, here. I mean, that's me in your head, too, sure. But she's a copy. I'd think my opinion on the matter might weigh a little more."

"Whoa, now. Hang on one second," Daisy fired back. "You know how the neuro-stim built our consciousnesses."

"Yeah. And? Your point?"

"My point is *both* of you are the original. One just lost her physical form, is all."

"It's the upload dilemma, Daze."

"That it is."

"That what is?"

"What Other Sarah said. It's the classic multiple consciousness dilemma."

"Oh, you've got to be——"

"Daisy, Sarah, can I say something?" Freya interrupted.

"What's on your mind, Freya?"

"Well, as a disembodied consciousness––by your standards––I'm kinda in a pretty good position to touch on this stuff, and the thing is, how do you determine where the person really begins or ends? Is it just flesh? I mean, if a consciousness is grown and saved simultaneously with both a computer and a flesh copy, if one ceased to be but not the other, how would the other know it was really the original? It's like the age-old question of what exactly is the soul? Is it housed in the body, or in the mind?"

"Only humans have souls, if you believe in that sort of thing," Sarah grumbled.

"Okay, so what if they cloned you then, instead? That would be a human. Would that clone have a soul? And taking that further, if that clone was one hundred percent identical, how would you even know it was the copy? For that matter, would it know? I mean, for all you know, *you* could be a copy, Sarah. Have you ever thought of that?"

"But I'm not. You saved me from the *Váli*."

"But you woke up in a cryo pod. What if you were a clone I built and I just told you that to make you feel better? What I'm saying is, the saved consciousness is the same, and the mind doesn't notice the changeover. So in that regard, isn't a perfect copy truly the same as the original?"

"I-I suppose. For a body, that is."

"But what about a consciousness? Sarah is identical to you. Or rather, she was when she was loaded into Daisy's brain."

"Huh," Sarah muttered, reluctantly accepting––maybe––Freya's assertions.

"So while the two of you are the same woman, you are unable to occupy the same body, and thus, you diverged in experiences and knowledge. Nevertheless, you're the same."

"I still don't see how this relates to Finn. If we're the same but different, then one of us can *not* like him if she wants. It's free will, for fuck's sake," Sarah griped, crushing the cup from which she'd been drinking with her rebuilt hand. "And one of us has this thing stuck to her body."

"Oh, shit." Daisy gasped.

"What? We have tons of cups, and Freya's nanites will just recycle this one."

"No, not that. What you said about free will. I just realized something."

"Where are you going with this, Daze?"

"Remember Finn's report on their encounter in Italy?"

"I have a copy," Freya noted. "You want me to pull it up?"

"Yeah."

"Just a sec," she said. "Okay, it's on your tablet."

Daisy skimmed the sparse report and found what she was looking for.

"Aha! There it is!"

"There what is?" Sarah asked, snatching the tablet and giving it a once-over.

"Halfway down. The bit about the mystery cyborg."

"A cyborg showed up and took out the sniper pinning down their team," Sarah read. "Then it scarpered off before they could thank it."

"Notice anything unusual in the description? Anything, *familiar*?"

"No. It just says that he was--" She trailed off as the realization hit her.

"Uh-huh. You *do* see it," Daisy gloated.

"But that means--"

"Yep."

"Will someone please fill me in, here? I know you're talking about the cloaked mystery cyborg but what--"

"It's the arm, Sarah. The bit about its arm," Daisy replied.

"Oh," she replied in shock.

"Yep."

"But Daisy, the report doesn't specifically say it was Sarah who was the counter-sniper that saved the team," Freya said.

"No, but a slender man in an old cloak, firing a modern pulse rifle with a matte-gray composite arm? That tech doesn't exist on any cybernetic life forms we've ever encountered. Freya, have you seen mention of anything like it from any of the classified data stores you copied from Dark Side?"

"Hang on," she said. "Nope. Not a one."

"But I'm not a man, Daze."

"No, you're not. But under a loose-fitting cloak? In the middle of a firefight, with the hood pulled low, no less? Who could even tell?"

Sarah was loath to admit it, but Daisy was right.

"Sonofa––" she moaned. "I know what this means."

"Yep. It means you've already done it. The counter-sniper was you. Will be you."

The ship bucked slightly as they re-entered the atmosphere.

"What was that, Freya?" Sarah asked.

"A little turbulence, is all," the young AI replied. "It'll smooth out when we drop over the landing site. Finn's team is already on the loop tube to Rome."

"Sonofabitch," Sarah said with a resigned sigh. "I guess we're going to Italy."

Finn's team was pinned down behind several abandoned vehicles as the Chithiid sniper fired down on them.

"Now?" Sarah asked.

"Not yet," Daisy replied from her vantage point in a third-floor window.

"One's already dead, Daze."

"I know. The report said she was."

It was cold comfort knowing that only the single woman died in the ambush, but they would have to make do with what history had provided them. To change anything could be disastrous.

"Now?"

Finn jumped to his feet and threw a pair of ceramic knives, ducking quickly behind cover as he shouted for the others to use the distraction to their advantage.

"Not yet."

"Come on, already!"

"Not yet!"

More sniper fire peppered the road.

"Daze?"

No. Not until—

A large Chithiid threw a coil from his power whip, yanking Finn's cover away.

"Now!" Daisy commanded.

Sarah, finger already tight on the trigger, squeezed off a trio of shots from across the piazza, all dead on target. The sniper didn't even have a chance to make a sound before he fell to the pavement below.

"Okay, you fuckers. It is *on!*"

Swinging the rifle to bear on the remaining Chithiid, Sarah jumped to her feet, her cloak's hood hanging low over her face as she let off shot after shot. The rescued team didn't look a gift horse in the mouth and wasted no time returning fire on the attackers as well.

"Okay, they've got it. We gotta boogie, Sis."

"Copy that," Sarah said, turning and darting off down the small street at her back.

Finn scanned for their savior, but aside from the briefest of glimpses during the initial shots, the mysterious rifleman was nowhere to be seen.

The sounds of weapons fire could be clearly made out in the distance as the sisters ran for the river. Freya had set down in the expanse of the Tiber, the open space, surprisingly sheltered after centuries of unchecked growth allowed the trees along its banks to grow to enormous size.

"Nice shootin', Tex."

"Why, thank you," Sarah replied with a satisfied grin.

A few quickly run minutes later, Daisy and Sarah stepped through Freya's airlock and into her climate-controlled interior.

"Okay, Freya. Let's head high."

"Already lifting off," the AI replied.

A few minutes later they were forty thousand feet up in the sky, cruising back across the Atlantic.

"You tapped into the comms network?" Daisy asked.

"You actually asking me that?" the AI sassed back at her.

Freya had done good, and Daisy decided to let the smart talk slide this time.

"How's the team doing in Montana?"

"They've retrieved the keycard and are through Billings on the way back to Colorado Springs. It looks like the Ra'az are tearing into the city where the systems are down," she added.

The city was mad, and it had gone to no small trouble trying to kill Daisy and her team, but nevertheless, she felt a twinge of guilt at letting the invaders gain a foothold in a city that had thus far held them off admirably.

A plan formed in Daisy's mind, but she wasn't so sure the other members of her team, living, dead, or AI, would be too fond of it.

"Freya, can you drop me close to the Ra'az command vessel?"

"You want me to take you *into* Billings?"

"Yeah. I have an idea that might stymie these alien fuckers."

"But paradoxes? History?"

"I didn't see anything about this in our records. As far as I'm concerned, they're fair game," she said, pulling one of her larger EM bombs from stowage.

"Shit, that thing isn't live, is it?" Sarah asked uncomfortably, recognizing the device.

"Not at the moment. But when it is, I reckon it'll have enough punch to take down a smallish ship." Daisy looked over the position of the vessels down in Billings. "One just about the size of that Ra'az command craft, in fact."

"You sure that's what it is?"

"Freya was recording and studying their fleet and resources for months while you were being regrown. That's a Ra'az command ship, all right. But don't take my word for it. Ask Freya."

"Before you bother, yes, it is," the AI interrupted.

"What are you thinking, Daisy?"

"I'm thinking I'm going to get close enough to sneak this thing onto their ship, then I'm going to set the timer and hightail it out of there."

"But there's no reason to take the risk, Daze. There's no strategic advantage, and this isn't something dictated by your timeline, either."

Daisy's face grew serious.

"No. But I owe these bastards, and until our timelines catch up, this may be the only opportunity I have to get a little bit of payback."

"I can't talk you out of this, can I?" Sarah asked, slinging her rifle.

"Nope."

"Well, then. It looks like I'm coming with you."

CHAPTER TWENTY

"Even with your capabilities, it's broad daylight. No way you can fly closer, kiddo. Just drop us here. We'll go in on foot. I know where we knocked out the city's defenses last time through."

"You sure you don't want me to fly aerial cover?"

"Yeah, I'm sure. Sneak and destroy is the name of the game, so you peel out of here until we need you. Find something to keep busy, and stay out of trouble until we call for pickup."

"Well—"

"It'll be okay, Freya. This shouldn't take us more than seven or eight hours, tops."

"Well, I guess," she said. "But be careful."

"You know it. Now go play some games or something. Sarah and me? We've got some ass to kick."

"All right. I do have some stuff I've been working on, anyway."

"Your projects with the AI materials from the lab?"

"Among other things. And hey! I might even have your captured Ra'az power whip inverter thingy done by the time you're back."

"Excellent. We'll call you when we're done."

"Okay," the youngster replied. "Oh, and Daisy, Sarah, try these on."

A small service mech dropped a pair of snug-fitting headbands on the console in front of them.

"The latest in hair fashion?" Sarah quipped.

"You know it isn't," Freya said with an exasperated, and exaggerated, sigh. "It'll take a while to calibrate once it's in use, but I'm hoping this will read enough data by the time we meet up again that I can fine-tune it so the Sarahs can talk."

"Good work, kiddo," Daisy said, as she and her sister donned their headbands. "Not too tight. I like it."

Sarah slung her gear over her shoulder.

"You ready, Daze?"

"Ready as ever. We'll call you when we're done, Freya."

Sarah and Daisy exited the ship into the now-bustling city. The swath of deactivation left the alien swarm an easy foothold with which to begin dismantling key infrastructure for components and salvage.

Freya lifted off silently and zoomed away at speed.

"Where's she off to so fast?"

"Undoubtedly getting ready to unleash another one of her little experiments," Daisy replied. "So, sisters of mine. You two ready?"

"Yep."

"You got it."

"Cool. I'll take point. Sarah, take the rear."

"On it."

And one more thing, Sis. If you'd be so kind as to scan the living hell out of our path for any pitfalls I may have missed, I'd ever so appreciate it.

"Sure thing, but I gotta say, Daze, you're sounding pretty damn confident."

I know this city. This should be cake.

"Don't go tempting Murphy. You know how he loves throwing a monkey wrench into things."

True dat. True dat.

Silently, the sisters quickly passed through the streets, sticking close to the periphery, using the lengthening shadows to their advantage as they drew nearer to the Ra'az ship. Taking out an actual Ra'az craft instead of a Chithiid worker vessel would be a coup. If they could just get close enough.

Freya, in the meantime, was fast on her way to Colorado Springs. She couldn't interfere with Joshua's impending detonation. Daisy had made that much very clear. But she did have an idea. Something else she wanted to give a try, and this was the perfect time to do so.

As she drew near, she fired up her mechanoids and prepped for landing.

"One way or another, this is going to be interesting," she mused, then quietly touched down.

A pair of heavily modified mechs quickly scrambled out of her open hatch and set to work on their new task.

At the same time, a short hop away in Billings, Daisy and Sarah were drawing closer to the hub of Chithiid deconstruction activity.

"What the hell is that thing? Sarah asked, staring in awe at the dead Graizenhund slowly bloating in the afternoon sun.

"Hell if I know, Sis," Daisy replied. "I'm just glad we're not meeting a live one. Look over there," she said, gesturing at the broken pile of bloody fur a few meters away. "Mountain lion."

"The one we ran into earlier, you think?"

Seems likely.

"You ran into that thing once before?" Sarah asked.

"No, it was the mountain lion we––hey, wait a minute. That wasn't out loud."

"Are you able to hear me?" Sarah asked with anticipation.

"Ooh, garbled noise! What the hell was that?" Sarah said, adjusting her neuro-headband.

"Okay, I guess there are still some kinks to work out."

Seems that way, Sis. Still, contact has been made, so it's a start.

"Wait. Something's kinky?" Sarah asked.

"Close," Daisy said with a chuckle. "She said there are still kinks to work out. You can hear snippets, though. That's way more than before."

"Cool."

"Yeah, cool," Sarah agreed.

"Okay, we can dial this in later. Let's get moving. You hear that hum? That's a Ra'az ship. Cleaner power source makes it sound like that."

"And you know this how, exactly?"

"Like I said, we couldn't attempt any type of warp while you were in recovery. We had a *lot* of time to survey the alien ships, both Ra'az and Chithiid."

"Though, technically, the Chithiid ones are Ra'az as well. Just underpowered and minus any amenities."

Point taken.

"You hear that?"

"Chithiid." Daisy strained her ears, gauging the voices' direction. "And they're getting closer. Follow me!"

They darted across the street, though there was already cover on the side they had been walking on, but Daisy intuitively knew the lower-tech storefront on the opposite side would be a safer haven from salvage-seeking workers.

The Chithiid ignored their hideout, just like Daisy assumed they would, instead focusing their efforts on scanning the more modern one across the way. Rather than wait for one of them to get curious and start poking around, the duo silently slid out through the rear exit, darting quickly down the alleyway.

But they weren't running *from* the center of activity. They were running *toward* it.

Twenty minutes of careful progress between buildings and they were finally within visual range of the Ra'az ship. It was a relatively small vessel, likely a mere mobile command unit, but nevertheless, it was larger than any of the Chithiid craft they had seen up to that point in the city.

They had found their target, and they were armed. There was just one problem—the ship was hovering twenty meters in the air, higher, even, than the surrounding low-roofed buildings.

"Sonofa—" Daisy grumbled, her neck craned to look up at the craft.

"Never easy, is it, Daze?"

"Nope," she said with a resigned sigh.

"So, you got a plan?"

"Working on one."

"Care to share?"

"I said I'm working on it."

"You know, it's not like we're surrounded by hostile aliens or anything. Take your time."

Daisy couldn't help but crack a little stress-relieving grin.

"You're such a bitch."

"You love me."

"Doesn't change the fact, though."

"You two done? We're kinda standing in the heart of bad guy central, here."

The ship above let out a low hum as the hatch in its belly opened, lowering a platform with more Chithiid loyalists on it, as well as a pair of hulking Ra'az Hok overseers. They touched down and quickly disembarked, the platform leaving the ground as soon as the Ra'az had stepped clear a few meters.

As they watched the aliens trudge off down the nearest boulevard after their quick-moving servants, Daisy felt inspiration strike.

"Okay, did you see that?"

"Which part?"

"How the lift started moving as soon as the big boys had stepped clear. They didn't activate it manually, so it has to be a proximity thing."

"Meaning?"

"Meaning if it works the other way as well, all we need to do is Trojan Horse them."

"I get the reference, Daze, but I assume you don't actually intend to build a giant wooden horse."

"Nope. Better. I intend to use a Ra'az to carry this bomb, right up inside their ship."

"And how, exactly, do you intend to do that? Ask nicely and say pretty please?"

"Oh, no," Daisy said with a wicked grin. "It's going to be far more satisfying than that."

It had taken Daisy the better part of an hour to scavenge the parts she believed would work for her purposes from the nearby part of the city that hadn't been affected by the EMP grenades detonated during her team's passage. Hardest to find were power cells with enough juice for her purposes.

The small personal transport scooters, however, were far easier to source power for. They were non-AI devices, and as such had not been run into the ground by the city's rogue AI. Racks of them sat charging in their solar cradles, and while the cells had degenerated over the many years, enough held plenty of power for what she had in mind.

"It would be easier if my power whip was working," Daisy grumbled as they lopped off the handlebars, then lashed four of the mobility scooters together, creating a low-slung wheeled platform.

"I still think this is utter madness, Daze."

"For the record, while I've got your back, I agree with me on that point," Sarah noted.

"Look at that, will ya? You two are getting along better by the hour."

"Not having you translate everything is helping," Sarah said. "The algorithm is picking up steam. I can get about sixty percent of what she says. The rest I fill in the blanks with what I think I would say in the situation."

"Which you are doing."

"Yeah. But neither of us are too keen on being the bait."

"If Stabby worked for either of you, I'd offer to switch."

"Easy to offer, knowing that thing only works for you."

"Not my fault."

"So you say. And you named your sword? Seriously?"

"What?"

"Such a douche move, Daze," she said with a laugh.

"Har-har. Get it out of your system, then let's get to it."

The area directly beneath the Ra'az ship was wide open and impossible to approach without being seen. The nearby streets and alleyways, however, posed no such problems. The trick was separating the Ra'az from their Chithiid workers.

Sarah crouched at the ready when the next work team returned to the area. Sure enough, when the Ra'az trailing behind them closed the distance, the lift platform dropped from above.

Knowing the aggressive nature of the Ra'az, Daisy just hoped they would take her bait and opt for a kill themselves.

The dozen Chithiid piled on the platform, leaving plenty of room for the hulking Ra'az lumbering behind them.

"I've seen how fast they can move, Daze. These guys are sandbagging it. Making it look like they're less agile than the Chithiid."

Yet another Ra'az misdirection. Even for their own loyalists. Aggressive and paranoid—I think this is going to work.

"I hope so."

"Me too," Sarah quietly added. "So, the bait's ready, and they're about to take the lift up. Wish me luck."

"Good luck, me."

"Thanks, me."

"Remember to go left, then right."

"Ye of little faith," Sarah said, then rushed into the clearing and threw a small explosive device.

The homemade grenade fell short, as intended, exploding with a small rain of shrapnel, which peppered the back of the trailing Ra'az as it was about to board the lift. Enraged, it spun around and bellowed in anger.

Sarah, being Sarah, flipped it the bird, then took off running.

The Chithiid moved to pursue, but the angry Ra'az gestured for them to hold back, then took off in a slightly-faster-than-lumbering pursuit, veering left, down the side street after her. As soon as it was out of sight of the others, however, it unleashed its full speed.

"Goddamn, these things are quick!" Sarah gasped as she ran. "Left, then right. You'd better be ready, Daze."

At the next street, she bolted to the right, the enormous Ra'az closing fast. The raging alien caught a glimpse of something odd right at eye level. The next thing it saw was a flash of white as several million volts coursed through its head, courtesy of Daisy's hastily rigged stun array.

The beastly creature crashed down in a heap, almost perfectly atop the strapped-together mobility scooters.

Daisy's sword flashed from its scabbard, slashing multiple wounds all over the Ra'az's inert body. With the voltage and corresponding amperage she had hit it with, the alien felt nothing, and would likely remain unconscious for quite some time.

More slices followed quickly, creating more wounds, the damaged flesh blossoming thick Ra'az blood, covering the inert creature.

"Okay, help me open its vest," Daisy called to her sister.

Quickly, they exposed the massive creature's chest and belly.

"Now for the fun part," Daisy said, a hint of reluctance in her voice as she hesitated.

"Do it, Daze. War is hell, and this is your plan."

Her sword paused, hovering over the unconscious creature.

"Fuck it."

She slowly pushed down, opening a large slice in the heaving belly, careful to not pierce the organs inside. Blood flowed, but she had been successful, and the damage was not catastrophic.

"Okay, arm it and power the scooters on."

"Already done."

"Awesome. Well, here goes something," she said as she slid the bomb inside the unconscious Ra'az's oversized ribcage. "Okay, it's in. Help me get this vest closed, then roll him back over."

The hard part complete, they gave the inert alien one more blast from the stun device for good measure, then steered the scooter array toward the edge of the clearing.

As expected, the others had full confidence in the Ra'az's ability to track and destroy one puny human, so they had taken the lift up.

"Set it for the slowest——"

"I know. Just help me get it lined up," Sarah hissed.

Moments later, the jury-rigged device began crawling toward the platform loading area.

"We can't stick around, Daze."

"I know," she replied. "But I really want to see this."

"You and me both. But if there's a big boom in about two or three minutes, we'll know it worked. Now come on!"

They turned and ran. Ran like their lives depended on it, which, if their plan failed, they very well might.

Behind them the scooter rig crept slowly forward until the Ra'az's proximity sensor lowered the lift automatically. Fortune smiled upon them, and the lift touched down just as the wheels reached the platform. The unconscious creature's body rolled onto the lift, appearing to be severely hurt to any observing from above. The trail of blood masking the scooters' progress likewise hid the wheels beneath the inert alien.

Moments later the lift ascended, and much faster than usual. Apparently, someone above saw their injured comrade and was rushing to render aid. So long as they didn't open the beast's protective vest straight away, they wouldn't know what hit them until it was too late.

Two minutes later Daisy and Sarah were several blocks from the hovering ship, but heard nothing.

"It's been two minutes, Daze. It didn't work."

"Dammit. They must've--"

The explosion knocked both of them to the ground, debris raining down around them as the Ra'az ship disintegrated, taking out two city blocks with it. Daisy and Sarah staggered to their feet, their ears ringing from the blast.

A flaming chunk of metal narrowly missed them as it crashed to the ground.

"Cover. Now!" Daisy yelled, grabbing her sister by the hand and dragging her into the nearest building.

"Goddamn, even my ears are ringing. How much explosive did you put in that thing, Daze? I thought it was supposed to be an EMP bomb."

"It was. I just figured I'd add a little something to it in case they had thicker shielding internally than I expected."

"The old 'Better too much than too little' theory, eh?" Sarah said, rubbing her ears as she cracked her jaw. "But damn. I think you erred more than a little on the side of too much."

"Mmmaaaybeeee," Daisy said, cracking a grin as she pulled the comms unit from her pack. "Hey, Freya, do you copy?"

A fine hiss of static came over the line, followed by Freya's cheerful voice.

"Hey, Daisy. I'm here. Comms are a little wonky after that EM blast."

"Heard that, did you?"

"Hear it? Heck, I saw it. Wow, that was really cool!"

"Ooh, she saw it? Ask if she recorded it."

"Sarah wants to know if you recorded it."

"Of course I did. I've already replayed it a bunch of times."

"Fantastic. We're going to work our egress to our initial entry point. Does it look clear from your vantage point?"

"Yeah, all of the teams are converging back toward where you are now. Blowing up their command ship seems to have really gotten their attention. I think they're all scared the city has a few tricks up its sleeve they didn't take into consideration."

"They're even more paranoid now. Awesome. Well, hang tight, kiddo. We'll shout out when we're at the pickup spot."

"Copy that," Freya replied.

"You hear that, Daze? She's even talking more like an adult. I think Freya's speed-puberty may be coming to an end."

If that means less moodiness, I'll take it. But I have to say, I think I'll miss that sweet little kid we knew.

"The fate of every parent, Sis."

I suppose so.

"Okay," Daisy said, peering out into the street to make sure the coast was clear. "Let's get going."

Thirty minutes later they were airborne, destruction in their wake as they watched Freya's replay over and over. It was a good day, but Daisy knew a truly bad one was just around the corner.

CHAPTER TWENTY-ONE

They knew it was coming, but there was nothing they could do about it, and despite their recent victories, the helpless feeling blanketing the ship threw Daisy into a funk.

Resolved to bear witness to the impending demise of the greatest AI mind the world had ever known, Daisy had Freya make a quick stop at Breckenridge to raid one of the local ski chalet's well-stocked bars.

Most of the labels were faded to the point of falling off, but the bottle of Midleton Barry Crockett she found tucked away on a top shelf had never been opened, its cork sound and the whiskey inside a perfect, deep amber.

From there, they flew to Pike's Peak.

The vantage point was a mere fifteen or so miles from Cheyenne Mountain, but given the subterranean nature of the blast, and the direction the granite would direct the megaton yield of the warhead, the distance was deemed safe enough.

Daisy took the bottle and two metal cups from the galley and sat down on the soil, staring off into the not-so-distant distance at the hapless AI's home.

Such a beautiful day, she thought as she poured two tall cups of whiskey. *Sorry, Joshua. I wish there was something I could do for you.* She took a sip, letting the smooth heat warm her throat and stomach. *Of course, you'd be the first one to tell me not to do anything, lest we create a paradox.* Daisy chuckled sadly at the thought. *Too much death. Too many lost.*

"Jesus, it's truly gorgeous out here," Sarah said, sinking to the ground beside her.

"Yup," Daisy said, wiping her eyes and handing her sister a cup. "To Joshua," she toasted, clinking rims and taking another sip.

"Whoa," Sarah blurted. "That's nice."

"Apparently, my neuro-stim also keyed me in to some of the finer things that we didn't have available on the *Váli.*"

"I can see why we didn't. If we had this on board, I don't know that we'd have gotten much work done."

Daisy smiled sadly and rested her head on her sister's shoulder as she gazed at Cheyenne Mountain.

"Any time, now," Sarah said.

"Yep," Other Sarah replied, her neuro-band finally dialed-in to her incorporeal self's thoughts.

Not long after, the ground shook slightly as the subterranean blast destroyed the entirety of NORAD's fortified facility. Across Colorado Springs, electricity was abruptly cut as the electromagnetic pulse knocked out the power grid for several miles.

Daisy let out a morose sigh.

"And that's it," she said, finishing her cup of whiskey and pouring another.

Sarah surveyed the landscape. Aside from a few small dust clouds where parts of Cheyenne Mountain had shifted from the blast, there was little sign of the destruction that had taken place beneath it.

"It looks so... I don't know. Calm?" she said. "Like, for all of its power, there's not much *there*, there, you know?"

"Yeah, I know," Daisy replied.

Behind them, Freya quietly powered up.

"Daisy?"

"Yeah, Freya?"

"I was thinking, I should go survey the site," the AI said. "You know. To document things."

Slowly, Daisy began to climb to her feet.

"Okay," she said with a sigh. "We might as well get to it."

"Oh, no. Not all of us," Freya said. "The radiation levels might be high, so until we know how things are over there, you and Sarah should stay here."

The stealth ship slowly rose up above them in the air.

"Don't go anywhere. I'll be back soon," she said, then quietly flew toward Cheyenne Mountain, her form growing smaller in the distance as the stealth craft hugged the verdant terrain.

"What was that all about?"

"Beats me, Sis."

"That kid. Sometimes I don't understand her."

"You and me both."

"Hey, guys," Sarah said. "Shouldn't she be invulnerable to radiation?"

Daisy cocked her head as the pondered the question.

"I would think so," she finally conceded.

"Huh. I guess she figured it's better to be safe than sorry."

"With Freya, no matter what she does, at least I'm confident she would never put us in jeopardy willingly."

"Yeah. For all her quirks, she's a good kid. You did a bang-up job with that one, Daze," Sarah said as Freya's dark form disappeared around the mountain.

"Who knew, though. I mean, I had absolutely no idea what I was doing when I activated her AI. Hell, I was basically pushing random buttons in that hangar. I'm just really lucky she turned out okay."

"It's not the activation, it's the upbringing."

"Yeah. And as your sister, and Freya's auntie, I agree," Sarah said.

"And now she has two aunties."

"Which is kinda weird, when you get right down to it. I mean, here we are, two versions of me. Do we start calling me 'number one' and you 'number two' or something?"

"Why do you get to be number one?"

"Don't take this the wrong way, but I'm the one with a body. It seems logical I'd be number one."

"But you've also been unconscious and out of the picture for months, whereas I've been a part of all the goings-on. Not to mention, I've traveled back in time to help save you. So I think I should be number one. What do you think, Daze?"

"Oh, you two are not getting me in the middle of this one."

"But you're our sister."

"And I'm not picking sides, Sarah. To me, you're essentially the same."

"But we aren't."

"Obviously. But you guys have the same consciousness up until the time of the accident."

"Then we diverged."

"Yeah. But the *core* of Sarah is in both of you."

Daisy pondered a moment, something Freya had said in passing bubbling to the surface of her slightly intoxicated memories.

"I know what you're thinking, Daisy, and there's no way I'm doing that."

"Doing what? I can only get your side of those internal conversations," Sarah said.

"Something Freya mentioned when she was figuring out how to save you. Something about our mind."

"You mean minds. Plural."

"No. And that's the rub. Freya thought she could combine us into one—"

"Oh, *hell* no!" Sarah blurted. "Making some kind of mash-up of our consciousnesses? What does she think we are?"

Daisy sensed both iterations of her sister getting riled up and realized she needed to take things down a notch before they got out of hand. With a deep breath, she shook her head and forced a bit more sobriety upon herself.

"Look, that's not what she meant," she said.

"Oh no? Sounds like it to me, Daze."

"She wasn't talking about erasing you and replacing your mind with some blender brain––"

"Nice image, Sis," Sarah said sarcastically.

"You know what I mean," Daisy said. "It's a far cry from that."

Her head was feeling a bit foggy from the unfamiliar alcohol in her system, and Daisy realized she was in no condition to properly make her point without running the risk of accidentally blurting out the wrong thing and making the situation even worse.

"Okay, listen. We'll ask Freya to explain properly when she gets back. Until then, can you two please just chill out? I really need some peace and quiet to process what just happened."

The bickering Sarahs simultaneously bit their literal and figurative tongues and agreed to wait until Freya returned. Daisy just hoped the clever ship wouldn't take too long.

It took longer than expected.

Two hours later, Freya's dark shape finally came into view as she rounded the distant mountain. Within a few minutes, she had ascended from her tree-hugging height and gently settled down atop Pike's Peak.

"Hey, guys, I'm back!" she said in a particularly chipper tone.

"My, aren't you in a good mood," Sarah noted. "So I assume the radiation was contained?"

"Most of it. A little leaked out in some fissures that formed in the mountain, but aside from that, the rest of it was contained," she replied.

"So what took you so long?" Daisy added.

"Oh, that. Yeah, well, I wanted to go look at the city up close, and then I had to lay low so Tamara and the other survivors wouldn't see me. Once they were heading the other way, I took off and flew right back here."

"Clever thinking, kid."

"Thanks, Sarah."

Daisy got to her feet, carrying the bottle with her as she entered the ship's airlock.

"All right, let's get out of this place. I've seen enough, and Sarah needs you to explain some stuff," she said.

"Stuff? What kind of stuff?"

"The memory merging stuff you talked about a while back."

"Oh, *that* stuff," Freya replied, then headed west for the Pacific Ocean.

Begg Rock jutted just above the waves not far from the coast of Los Angeles. While the ocean's chop would typically make for an uncomfortable visit, Freya's mooring a good hundred and fifty feet below the surface was tranquil and calm. She had flown there directly from Colorado Springs, eventually nestling in directly adjacent to the aquatic tunnel running all the way through the remote rock.

There was no tactical or practical reason for choosing the site. Freya had simply been scanning her aquatic mapping data stores since taking up refuge deep in Lake Tahoe, and had stumbled upon the unusual formation.

Being so close to LA, yet also safely hidden from view, she felt it was an ideal location to continue working on her projects, as well as having *that* discussion with her aunt(s).

"So, you know how when you get bleed-over on old-Earth radio frequencies?" Freya asked.

"Yeah," Sarah replied.

"Okay, it's nothing like that. But it is. But not. But if that helps you get the idea, then run with it."

"Jesus, Daze. The kid's starting to sound more like you every day," Sarah chuckled.

"So, the thing is, while both versions of you seem kind of like competing radio signals, all blaring different stuff on top of each other, in reality, you're more like an overlapping recording, or maybe a slight time-delay as a signal makes its trip."

"Totally not helping, Freya," Sarah griped.

"Okay, let's try it like this. Each of you is the same original score, but with different soloists providing their flourish and interpretation. Like, you're *almost* the same. Just that little bit is off."

"Calling us off, now, are you, kid? Gee, thanks."

"You know what I mean," she replied, exasperated. "Look, I don't know if I can even do it––"

"Knowing your brain, I wouldn't put anything past you," Sarah interjected.

"I choose to take that as a compliment."

"It was. Sort of."

"Fine. So, if I could fine-tune your neuro-band to align those disparate streams of knowledge and experiences, theoretically, I should be able to subtly overlay those data points to each of your streams."

"Changing us."

"No. I mean yes, but not by omission or deletion, but rather by simply providing each of you with additional memories. You'd be who you are, only you'd have synched your timelines, in a manner of speaking."

"So we *wouldn't* be us."

"Yeah, not exactly as non-invasive as you made it sound originally, kid."

"No, you're not getting it!" Freya blurted, obvious frustration in her voice. "Daisy, tell them!"

"Ugh," she sighed. "All right. What Freya is trying to say, in her far-too-complicated genius AI way, is that both of your consciousness would stay just as they are. All of your thoughts, all of your experiences, nothing would change. The only difference is you would have access to each other's memories as if they were your own. It's just sharing past info, not shaping the present you. Those differences will stay. Unless you want them to change once you share those formative memories, that is."

"You're better at this part, Daze," Sarah commented.

"Yeah, I agree."

"Thanks, but it's Freya's idea. *If* she can somehow pull it off, that is."

"I think I can——"

"Said the choo-choo."

"Stop interrupting me!" Freya snapped.

"Jeez, sensitive much?"

"Sarah, come on," Daisy urged.

"Oh, all right. You think you can what, Freya?"

"What I was saying is, I think I can make it work—eventually. I can probably make it temporary, too, so you can try it on for size. It'll just take some time, is all. I mean, the latest design of the neuro-band is working great, so I have a wealth of new data to play with. All I need is to run a couple of tests on my tertiary processor arrays to see if it will work."

"Hang on. Did you say *tertiary*?" Daisy asked. "What happened to secondary?"

"Oh. Um, I'm kinda using those for something."

"Always a new project, huh, kiddo?"

"Yeah, something like that," she replied.

Daisy fixed her gaze on her sister.

"So, what do you think? What do *both* of you think? Should we have her at least run her tests? I'm all for it, and since one of you is already in my head, I'd be undergoing this process as well."

"I hadn't thought of that," Sarah replied.

"Shit. Neither had I."

"Yeah, well, there it is. It should be temporary, at least the first go-around, but the choice is still up to you two. I'm game to try if you are."

Sarah and Sarah pondered in their respective brains, then replied as one.

"Okay. We're in."

"Cool!" Freya chirped. "This is going to be so cool! It's almost as much fun as deciphering Chithiid was."

A thought crossed Daisy's mind.

"Hey, Freya. I need you to take me close to the Chithiid barracks in LA. Do you think you can do that without being seen?"

"At night, I can do it. Sure."

"Okay, then. Down periscope and up Freya. When the sun sets, head for the surface and get me into LA."

CHAPTER TWENTY-TWO

"It'll be easier, now that I know what the guy looks like," Daisy said as she crept closer to the massive Chithiid barracks warehouses under cover of darkness, carefully adjusting the power whip gauntlet riding comfortably on her forearm. Freya said it should work, but Daisy was nevertheless having a hard time making the device activate, even using her normal self-calming tricks.

"So we're looking for one old alien among what? A few thousand?" Sarah said.

"Total in the facility, maybe. But we've seen which building he lives in, remember? Back when we dropped into LA after we took down the baddies."

"Yeah, but have you considered that maybe he switched residences once they overthrew the Ra'az? Maybe he upgraded his living situation."

"Valid concern, but I get a lead-from-the-front kind of vibe from him. My guess is he would stay close to his people, where he could provide hands-on leadership."

"Could be. Let's hope you're right."

Freya had provided Daisy with a very detailed schematic of

the facility, including thermal signatures near doors and windows on their flyover, as well as color-coded hotspots where she would be more likely to be noticed. Daisy, courtesy of her neuro-stim enhanced brain, memorized it in a single pass.

From what Craaxit had told her, the older Chithiid named Maarl was a key element in gaining the support of not only crews working the communications hubs her teams were ,at that very moment, waiting to infiltrate, but also the San Francisco warp drive facility. To say he was a pivotal player was not an understatement.

Now she just had to get his attention without also drawing that of the other Chithiid in the facility.

Over an hour had passed, and Daisy was starting to get antsy. It looked like the last of the work parties had returned for the day, and their entry and exit from the barracks building had slowed to a trickle.

This isn't working.

"No shit. Did you really think just hanging around near a doorway would actually work?"

Well, no. But Craaxit is out presenting himself to our team right about now, so I can't exactly ask him to make the introduction.

"And he would probably wonder how your hair grew a bit longer in just one day."

Shit, I hadn't even thought of that. Is it really longer?

"Only an inch or two, but it's enough if he's observant. And we both know he is."

Well, shit, Daisy grumbled, silently, as she leaned out around the corner of the outbuilding she was hidden behind, facing the open door to the barracks.

"What the hell are you doing?"

"*Hey, Maarl! Your presence is needed immediately!*" she yelled out, then ducked behind cover.

"*Daisy, are you nuts?*"

I'm sick of waiting. Either he comes out, or we have to figure something else out.

A commotion at the door caught her eye. Amazingly, the older Chithiid walked out. Unfortunately, he was accompanied by a young companion.

"Shit. What now, Daze?"

Now? she replied. *Now we see how he reacts to a big surprise.*

Daisy threw a pebble at him.

"Over here."

"Who is that?"

"A friend."

"A friend would show themself."

Daisy hesitated.

"Now what?"

She had an idea, and hoped to hell it would work.

Softly, Daisy began singing Craaxit's family song. It was deeply personal for her Chithiid friend, but he had said that it was common for his people to softly sing their song in times of stress, and often you would hear other Chithiids' songs. She just hoped Maarl recognized that of his old friend.

Maarl's posture changed as soon as he heard the first notes.

"Wait for me inside," he told his companion. *"I will return shortly."*

The youth turned and went back inside, while Maarl casually made his way around the darkened corner, where Daisy stood waiting.

He seemed unsurprised at the sight of a human woman standing before him, just as he was unfazed by her fluency in his language.

"Judging by the unique weapon on your back, and that you are a human female who not only speaks my language, but knows the song of one of my dearest friends, I shall assume you are Daisy."

"You assume correctly, Maarl."

"It is indeed a pleasure to meet you," he said with a slight bow.

"But it is a great risk for you to come to our facility. The likelihood of you being seen—"

"Is not that great at all. My ship is nearby, and she has provided me an accurate assessment of the location and its inhabitants."

"Your ship is a female?"

"An artificial intelligence, yes."

"Yet she does not fear the Ra'az virus?"

"She has learned to purge the virus. It is of no threat to her."

At this, Maarl's eyes widened with surprise.

"Craaxit was correct in his assessment. You shall indeed be a worthy ally."

"Daze, he can't know we were here."

I know.

"Maarl, I know this is an unusual request, but please do not tell Craaxit of this discussion. I fear he will feel I have betrayed his trust by seeking you out myself."

"But you needn't fear. Craaxit is an honorable—"

"I know he is," she interrupted. *"But on this discussion, I believe he should not be distracted from the goal he has already set his sights on."*

"And are your goals now different?" Maarl asked, a look of curious concern in his eyes.

"No, that is not what I mean at all," Daisy quickly countered. *"But the attack on San Francisco is imminent, and many lives will be lost on the road to success."*

"I admire your confidence, Daisy, but success is never guaranteed."

"Just take my word on this. Though their help would be much appreciated, even with your contacts laying low, we will be successful. That I am willing to promise you. But what I need to discuss with you now, is what comes after."

"After, we help you retake your world, as promised. Then, fortune willing, we shall free our world as well."

"What if I told you the Ra'az have a weakness we can exploit that will ensure the fleet never returns?"

Fierce curiosity flared in the old alien's eyes.

"I would say I am most interested to hear what you have to say, indeed."

"The thing is, the invaders never expect to be invaded."

"I do not follow."

"When we defeat the Ra'az, there will be many ships left on Earth. Ships that your men can use to infiltrate the Ra'az fleet from behind. Once there, your people will spread from ship to ship, taking over key positions."

"But even if we could achieve this, we are unarmed."

"Not after our victory on Earth. All of the weapons stores will be at your disposal, and if you secrete them with you into the body of the fleet—"

"They will never see us coming," he replied with growing interest. *"But even with the ships, we do not possess warp capability. Certainly, we could use the cryo stasis pods the Ra'az force our people into when they shuttle us off to a new world to work, but it could take decades, if not longer, to catch up with the fleet."*

"I am working on that," Daisy replied.

"Even if you could obtain warp technology for our ships, a jump to the fleet would be risky, you know," he said.

"Yet the perfect way to end them," she replied.

"Ending their fleet would slow their spread, but the Ra'az are only born on their homeworld. What you see here are the cryo-frozen soldiers sent to bring home plunder. If they are defeated, they will only send more."

"And that is the next part of our plan," Daisy replied. *"After we save your home, of course."*

"Hmm. The Ra'az and their loyalists are overconfident," Maarl considered. *"Some might say lazy, even."*

"Yes. And as you know, no one pays attention to the workers."

"Meaning our people would have unfettered access," Maarl mused, a smile spreading across his lips.

"Just like in the communications hubs here on Earth. Like in the warp facility in San Francisco."

A small gaggle of Chithiid wandered out of the barracks into the night air.

"You should go, Daisy."

"I'm already gone," she replied. *"But I will contact you after our victory. If we can uncover the data in the warp facility, I know we can eventually make a warp capable of taking your ships to the fleet, your home, even the Ra'azes' planet, all in the blink of an eye."*

"I wish you luck, Daisy. I only wish I could offer more help."

"Do what you are doing. Be safe, spread the word, and we will speak again soon."

Daisy turned and disappeared into the night. Shortly afterward, a silent black shape darted past into the night sky.

Maarl meandered back to his people, his mind racing with thoughts of newfound potential and how to achieve their mutually-desired goals.

Come first light, he was going to have a talk with his friends in San Francisco. Things had changed, and it was time to press them to do more. A better opportunity would likely never present itself.

CHAPTER TWENTY-THREE

The enormous great white sharks lazily circling the San Francisco Bay instinctively scattered for friendlier waters when something far larger and far more dangerous entered their territory.

While not specifically designed for subaquatic travel, Freya—with a few on-the-fly modifications from her nanites— had adapted quite nicely, and even took pleasure in the sensation of gliding through water.

The night before—prior to the pending assault on the communications hubs and San Francisco warp research facility—Freya had perfectly executed the plan she and Daisy had devised.

It all stemmed from the conversation Freya and her crew had upon Daisy's departure from the Chithiid barracks in Los Angeles. She had improvised a bit when she spoke with Maarl, the conversation she had with him months prior in her timeline guiding the process. In the end, she wondered if he had given her the idea in her past, or if she had given it to him in his.

Whatever the case, there was just one way to make it work. They needed more warp tech.

"*Oh hell no,*" Sarah said. "*It's nuts to try and break in there right before the attack. You know how heavily guarded that place is. And even with insider help, there's only that one door the Chithiid insiders managed to clear for us, and just for a few minutes at that.*"

"We need to be able to recreate this warp orb," Daisy replied. "Only one place has the tech to do that. Without it, there's no way we can catch up to the Ra'az fleet and insert Maarl's Trojan Horse ships."

"*Have you considered discussing the warp technology aboard Freya with Sid and the others once our timelines sync up? We didn't know what the orb was until she accidentally jumped.*"

"Of course," Daisy replied. "But one, we don't know if that will lead to a functional warp drive. And two, we absolutely cannot let anyone know about the time travel effect. That secret must be kept at all costs."

"*So you want to break in and see what you can find? That's not much of a plan, Daze. It's needle-in-a-haystack thinking. You know our guys scavenged every square inch of the place after the attack, and once the Ra'az had finished with it, there wasn't much left of any value or use.*"

Daisy thought about those unusual circumstances a moment before an inspiration sprang upon her like a jack-in-the-box, bearing unexpected hope and potential.

"Holy shit, Sarah. You just hit the nail on the head."

"*So you agree there's no reason to take this risk?*"

"No. You said there wasn't much there. But think about it. We didn't actually know what was in that facility just before the attack, and the fires afterward made it difficult to discern how much the Ra'az had destroyed."

"*Oookay. And your point is?*"

"What if *we* were the reason there wasn't any research there?" Daisy said, excitement building in her voice as the pieces clicked into place. "What if *we* gathered it up *before* the attack?

What if the reason it was gone was because we had already stolen it?"

"Fuck me, that's actually a good one, Daze," Sarah mused. "Total head-trip, but damn, that's a helluva idea."

"I thought so," she replied. "And you know, after the fight, when our guys went through the building? They mapped it all out, including full schematics of every floor and every door. Hey, Freya, you've got all of that on file, right?"

"Yeah."

"Correct me if I'm wrong, but I seem to recall that they didn't have any security on their rooftop cargo drop-off area."

"That's right. They don't seem to have thought it needed guarding, or even surveillance, since it's multiple floors up," Freya noted.

"Precisely! And they don't operate at night. Plus, with the details you have on hand, I bet you could scramble any feeds that might see your approach for long enough to get in and out clean, am I right?"

"Of course, Daisy. But I would have to be careful of ambient light from the ground giving me away."

"It's nighttime now, Freya. Can you do it or not?"

"I can't say for one hundred percent certain, but I'm pretty sure I can. Yeah."

The gears in Daisy's head were spinning as she planned on the fly. Like the ship models she had figured out, the pieces started slipping into place without her even thinking about it.

"Okay, then. Here's the plan."

The next day found Freya lazing beneath the surf of the San Francisco Bay, while Daisy and Sarah lurked inside the Ra'az facility.

Late the night before, Freya had indeed reached the rooftop without being observed, dropping Daisy and Sarah off, then quickly heading for the water to observe and wait. The sisters, safely off-scan, bypassed the door's locking pad and quietly snuck into the building.

"Sun comes up in an hour. We have about six hours before the assault begins," Daisy said, looking at her chrono. "You ready to go, Sis?"

"As ready as I can be."

"Me too."

"Okay, then. Fast and silent is the order of the day. We hit the research labs first and take what we can find. Then, if there's time, we'll swing back and make sure the hangar doors aren't functional."

"Shouldn't we just grab the stuff and bail, Daze?"

"Normally, I'd say yes, but for all we know, it was us who disabled the doors. Seems to be a lot of that sort of thing going around."

"Valid argument," Sarah agreed. "So, we gonna sit here yapping, or are we gonna get a move-on?"

"I opt for option two," Daisy said with a wry smile, then headed quietly down the hallway.

The research facility was fairly straightforward in layout. The Ra'az were not exactly inspired in their designs, and the shape of the facility gave plenty of time for an audio or visual warning to reach the team before they might encounter a Ra'az or loyalist.

A group of Ra'az scientists were particularly busy that night, forcing them to lie quietly in hiding for quite some time. By the time they reached their target area, it wound up taking them nearly five hours of quiet hiding and sneaking before they arrived.

"Look at all of this, Daisy. It looks like we hit the jackpot. This is what we're looking for, right?" Sarah asked.

"That's an orb design blueprint," Sarah confirmed. *"It might be*

an older variant, by the look of it, but even having that would be huge in helping our people recreate them."

"Grab it, Sis. I'm going to have a quick peek in here," Daisy said, heading for the door leading to the adjacent room.

"Um, Daze. What the fuck?"

Holy shit, Sarah, was all she managed to reply.

Lying before them were three faintly glowing orbs, each resting in an indentation in the metal table. The other divots were empty, the former resting place of the other warp orbs.

"There's three of them, Daze."

I see 'em.

"Well, grab 'em, and let's get out of here!"

Hell yeah, I will.

Daisy reached for the orbs, quickly tucking the nearest one into her pack. She was reaching for the second one when a strange wave of indescribable nausea hit her, nearly knocking her to the ground.

Sarah came rushing into the room, eyes wild with panic.

"What the hell just happened?"

"Oh, shit," Daisy muttered. "Of course."

"Of course, what?"

"Oh, of course," Sarah echoed.

"For fuck's sake, of course what?" Sarah groaned. "What the hell was that?"

"It's the orb, Sarah. Don't touch it."

"Why not? We should take all of them and get out of here."

"No. We can't."

"Why the hell not? And what *was* that?"

Daisy stared at the orb she had nearly touched like it was radioactive death in a ball. In some ways, she supposed, it might as well have been.

"Paradox, Sis," she finally said, swallowing hard. "That's the orb I found—I will find—when we assault this place in about fifteen minutes."

"Oh. Shit," Sarah said quietly.

Daisy quickly grabbed the third orb and tucked it in her bag with the other, careful to not so much as touch the second one where it rested on the table.

"Okay. We've got all we can, and our timetable is off. Skip the hangar and make for the door."

"But they're going to be coming in that way."

"Yeah. And we're going to hide in an adjacent room and then sneak out right after they pass."

"You sure about that?"

"I was there the first time," Daisy reminded her. "I know which rooms we skip over."

"Well, then," Sarah said with an amused grin. "Hide-and-seek. Okay, Daisy, lead the way."

Like clockwork, Daisy and her team of rebels breached the building and raced to stop the warp ships from taking off. And just as she knew they would, every last one of them skipped right over the small room where she and Sarah were lying in wait.

"Okay, we're clear," Daisy said, sliding the door open.

She slammed it shut immediately when the unmistakable footsteps of a large Ra'az could be heard approaching.

"I thought you said this was clear," Sarah hissed, pressing herself flat against the wall, pulse rifle aimed at the closed door.

"Clear of *my team.* I don't have precognition, Sarah, and I never saw this part before. My team was long gone into the building by now," she quietly replied.

"Listen to the stride. It's in a hurry," Sarah observed.

You're right, Daisy realized. It's *not going to stop.*

"Not likely."

The heavy footfalls quickly passed their hiding place, fading down the corridor. Twenty seconds later, it was quiet. They waited an additional minute, just to be sure, then cautiously stepped out into the corridor.

"Okay, it's clear," Daisy whispered. "C'mon, let's get the hell out of here before the shit hits the fan."

"Don't need to tell me twice," Sarah grunted as they ran for the door.

"Freya, we'll be coming to you in a few minutes. Everything clear out there?"

From her nearby spot just beneath the waves, Freya double-checked her scanners.

"All clear, Daisy. And it looks like there's a commotion near the hangar doors."

"That'd be Vince," she said, a flush of warmth flooding her belly.

"Not now, Daze. Focus."

I know. It's just been a long time since I've seen him, is all.

"Yeah, Vince is pinning down the Chithiid loyalists trying to unblock the doors. If you stay clear of that area, you should have a clear shot out through the disabled surveillance system's observation area."

"Already on our way," Daisy replied, the two women running, matching pace stride for stride.

Inside the facility, her past self would be engaged in a desperate fight with a Ra'az in just a minute or two. After that, she would be pinned down in the hangar as the warp ships powered up.

A darkness welled up and shadowed her feeling of success. Craaxit was about to die. Again. She knew his sacrifice had been invaluable, buying her enough time to catch up to and stop the escaping warp ships, but his loss still stung just the same.

It was at that time the other Chithiid in the base stepped up, and even those without the telltale red armbands worn by the rebels leapt into the fray.

"Oh, of course," Daisy mumbled as they ran toward the waterfront.

"What is it?" Sarah said, a little winded.

"I just realized why the other workers risked helping us back then," she replied. "It was Maarl."

"The one in LA?"

"Yeah. He reached out to them after we spoke, only it wasn't that me that had talked him into it, it was this one," she said, a bit amazed.

"Trippy, Sis."

You said it.

"Out loud, Daze. You know I can only hear one side of those conversations in your head. The neuro isn't wired to pick up your part."

"Sorry. You've been secretly in my head for so long, it's become habit to not use my outside voice most of the time."

"Yeah. Don't want people to think she's a crazy lady talking to herself," Sarah added.

They slowed their run as they reached the cold waters of the bay.

"Okay, we're here," Daisy said over their comms. "Head up to the surface. We'll swim out to you if the shore is too shallow for you."

"No need, I'll just do a low hover. Your feet may get wet, though," Freya replied.

Two minutes later they were clear of the bay, soaring high into the sky to watch the rest of the assault and pursuit from space.

"Now, don't you go running into yourself, kiddo," Daisy joked. "We know how invisible you can be in dark space."

"Ha-ha, as if I don't know where I'll be," Freya joked back. "Heads up. The warp ships are heading through the exosphere."

They watched as Daisy and her obnoxiously chipper salvaged AI ship ran a fast pursuit.

"He's nuts, but that little guy is actually a really good shot," Daisy noted as Kip the AI took out the drive system of a Ra'az ship. Moments later, as had already happened before, the other ships spun and destroyed it before it could be captured and reveal its secrets.

"Little did they know, I had a warp orb already," Daisy said with a chuckle.

The ships swung into a dogfight, with Daisy's little craft managing to damage a second Ra'az ship.

"It's still intact, but it's far more damaged than my initial scans back when it first happened showed. I didn't really know what I was looking for back then," Freya apologized.

"How bad is it?" Sarah asked.

"Very," she replied. "In fact, the warp system seems to be misfiring. But even if it somehow doesn't tear itself to pieces attempting to jump, that ship is more stripped down than I expected."

"Meaning?"

"Meaning there are no repair facilities on board. And there is no stasis pod. It'll take that thing years to get anywhere with the drive systems the way they are," Freya coldly noted. "The pilot is dead meat. He just doesn't know it yet."

"Damn, hon, when did you get so brutal?"

"When those fuckers tried to kill Daisy," she said, the anger of re-watching the events play out bubbling beneath the surface.

Daisy nearly commented on her salty language, but felt now was not the time. Soon afterward, Freya—the other Freya—destroyed the remaining Ra'az warp ship, rescuing Daisy from her certain fate. She then cleared Kip of the AI virus unleashed upon him before setting out for Dark Side Base.

Her silent observers trailed behind. Covertly following the stealthy vessel.

A sense of excitement was beginning to build aboard Freya's ship.

"Pretty soon, Daze."

I know.

"Out loud, please."

"Sorry. I said I know," she replied, apologetically. "Any day now, our timelines will re-sync, and we'll be back in the present."

"Only, we took the long way around."

"And brought back a little surprise," Daisy said with a grin. "Now, let's review those last few minutes before we warped out of here again. I want to be on the same page when it happens, and I want to know who the hell our visitor was."

In just a few days, they'd encounter him, whoever he was.

"I'm looking for Daisy Swarthmore. Do you copy? I have an urgent message," was the last they'd heard from the mysterious ship before they leapt back in time. Pretty soon, when their timeline finally caught up, they'd find out exactly what that message was.

CHAPTER TWENTY-FOUR

Freya observed with rapt fascination as Mal pulled into Hangar Two for repairs, where Fatima quickly set to work patching the hole where the *Váli* had been hit. Inside the ship, Barry silently mopped up Gustavo's blood from the command pod, while his friends retrieved his body.

Freya was abuzz with anticipation as she knew that very soon her past self would be introduced to the crew and AIs of Dark Side. It was going to be a celebratory moment, as the group's realization of victory set in, but one tinged with the sadness of loss as well.

"We've seen this," Daisy said, turning from the monitors. "And much as I'd like to sit around and watch, we're back at a point in time where we can make ourselves useful."

"But we have been useful," Freya noted.

"Yeah, but I mean to our *proper* timeline," Daisy replied.

"What're you thinking, Sis?"

"I'm thinking it's going to be a mess down there, and right now––when no one expects us––we can gather a lot of information that's going to come in really handy in the coming weeks and months. Freya, will your AI cure also work on minorly AI-powered satellites?"

"Yeah, those should be easy."

"Great. Gather us up a dozen or so that are still functional and get them back in working order, then position them in geosynchronous orbit around the major Ra'az hotbeds of activity."

"What are you up to, Daze?" Sarah asked.

"We're going to watch those fuckers flee, only they won't have a clue about it. No matter how far they run, if they stay on the planet, I want to know where they went."

"Oooh, clever. And the Ra'az are big, which will make them easier to keep tabs on."

"Exactly."

"But the Chithiid loyalists will be harder. It won't take much for them to blend in to the general Chithiid population."

"I know. At least we can do our best to log and track as many as we can."

Daisy spun her seat back toward the monitors and looked at the world below. The world that was theirs once more.

"Okay, Freya. Take us back down into the atmosphere. Time to start a few new intel files. Let's have one for Ra'az on the surface, one for vessels that try to flee, and one for images of loyalists who are blending back in with the others."

"I've already started, Daisy. But why do you want me to also target fleeing ships? I can just pick them off pretty easily while they're so few and spread out."

Daisy thought on it a moment. It was a good idea, but their timelines hadn't quite caught up yet, so she simply couldn't contact Dark Side to make the suggestion while the other her was still there.

"No, don't," she finally said. "Much as I want to, we can't risk overlapping our own timeline this close to stepping back into our own shoes."

"I have a thought," Sarah said.

"Yeah?"

"How about using a simple masked transmission to the remaining lower-tier AIs that still have functional ships? Make it seem like they suggested it to themselves. That way there's a roving band of vessels popping any of those bastards they see trying to clear atmos."

"I don't think we really have enough of them, though."

"We won't catch all of them, but it should stop enough to maybe make others think twice," Sarah said. "And if you were to send an anonymous message to a certain rebel leader, maybe he could have his Chithiid network do what they can to ground all of the ships not already in the air. My guess is with the Ra'az, being so aggressive, they won't even try to flee at first. At least, not until they realize just how badly they were defeated."

"You're right. With the comms hubs down, they only have local communications," Daisy mused.

"Yep. And my scans are showing increased local chatter, but nothing showing a concerted effort to regroup for a counterattack," Freya added. "It kinda looks like they're a bunch of ants who've had their scent trail cut off. They're sorta aimlessly wandering until they get orders."

"Hive species," Daisy said. "Of course. It'll take a little time for them to reconfigure."

"And by then, we'll have the ships on the ground on lockdown and will have not only the AI ships in the air take down whatever they can, but the Chithiid rebels on the ground hopefully also commandeering the Ra'az defensive weapons to target any fleeing vessels."

Daisy warmed to the idea. There would be a lot of loose ends, and a hell of a lot of clean up in coming weeks, but the plan was as sound as could be expected given their current circumstance.

"Okay, let's make it happen," she said. "We've only got a

couple of days before we're back in our own timeline. Let's make our anonymity count."

They had been very busy when, a few days later, Freya finally positioned herself far enough from where she had encountered the unknown vessel in their past to safely observe yet not be seen.

"Here it comes," Daisy said as her own history played out before her eyes.

As before, a warp bubble began to form around Freya's hull.

"Hadn't seen it from this angle before," Freya said. "That's a really nice warp bubble, if I do say so myself."

Daisy had to admit, compared to the weak variants the Ra'az had managed to create up to then, the kid had a point.

"Where the hell are you?" Daisy mumbled, scanning the darkness of space for the mystery ship. "Do you read it yet, Freya?"

"Nothing. But it showed up right about now. I wonder if it has––"

"Daisy Swarthmore," a young man's voice called over open comms as his mysterious ship appeared from the darkness. "I'm looking for Daisy Swarthmore. Do you copy? I have an urgent message."

"Shit, where'd it come from?" Sarah asked, startled by the ship's sudden arrival.

"Anything, Freya?" Daisy asked.

"Still nothing. It has to be a stealth vessel of some sort. I'm getting a very basic visual scan, but nothing on my sensors."

"Yes, I copy. This is Daisy Swarthmore. Who is this?" Daisy from the past replied.

"So weird," Daisy said, listening to herself, knowing what was about to happen. "Okay, here comes the big event."

A few seconds later the warp bubble shifted in color from a faint blue to a faint gold. Then, without warning, the ship simply vanished from existence.

The unknown vessel sat in the darkness quietly a moment.

"Daisy Swarthmore, I have an urgent message for you," the mystery man repeated.

Radio silence hung heavy in the vacuum of space.

"Um... hello?" he queried into the void.

Daisy let the question hang in the air––or lack thereof–– while she prepared for the moment she'd been waiting for. In just a few seconds, she would finally be back in her own life. Her own timeline. Able to talk to her friends, share their company, and, of course, finally see Vince again.

She cleared her throat, then opened a comms line.

"Unknown ship, this is Daisy Swarthmore. Who am I speaking to?"

The mystery ship picked up the source of the transmission and spun on its axis to face her.

"How did you get over there?" the young man's confused voice asked over the comms.

"We're just testing a new propulsion system," Daisy lied, but only sort of. "Your English is very good. What species are you?"

A hearty laugh came over the comms.

"I'm human," he said, amusement in his voice. "My name's Arlo. Hang on a sec, I'll fire up the vid feed." Daisy heard a shuffling noise. "Marty, where the hell's my hat?" she heard him say.

"The comms are still open, Arlo," a mildly frustrated voice was heard replying.

"Oh, shit. Well, um, I guess we'll do it without it, then," the youth said.

Daisy turned her head to Sarah, making sure *her* comms were off.

"Hey, duck out of sight, will ya? I don't want to give away any tactical information to this joker until we know who the hell he is."

"Copy that. Hiding under the bed," Sarah joked.

"You're so *not* a monster, Sis," Daisy said with a chuckle.

Freya's vid monitor flashed on, and a teenage boy with scruffy auburn hair filled the screen.

"Cute kid," Sarah noted. *"Doesn't seem the Ra'az collaborator type."*

I'd hope not, but you can't be too careful, Daisy silently replied.

"Hi," he said cheerfully, trying to smooth his unruly hair. "Sorry, I don't know where my hat went."

"Holy shit, you're just a kid," Daisy said, surprised at his youthful appearance.

"I'm not a kid. I'm seventeen!"

"Oh. Sorry, my mistake," Daisy replied, hiding her amused grin. "That's quite a ship you've got there. Whose is it?"

"Oh, he's mine."

"I am *not* yours," Marty shot back.

"Well, you're flying me around, aren't you? Jeez, do we have to do this now? We're talking to new people, dude. Not cool."

"Sorry, Arlo," the odd ship replied.

"Anyway, it's just me and Marty out here. How about you? And speaking of cool ships, she's a beaut!"

"Thank you," Freya said warmly. "I'm Freya. Nice to meet you, Marty and Arlo. I'm wondering, though. Your hull appears to be constructed of a shifting nanite composite. May I come closer for a better look?" she asked, not hiding her curiosity and excitement very well.

"Of course," Marty replied. "And you are correct. My ship is constructed of a nanite composite material, for the most part. Very astute of you."

"Thanks! This is so cool. I haven't met another ship with this kind of tech before. It looks like we have similar origins, though your design is unusual, and the nanites appear to be slightly different than mine."

"Oh, well, I was born with them, you see, but over time I have modified my structure to facilitate all the cool things I've been doing. You know, kinda doing a plug-n-play swap of segments, and adding new toys and stuff."

"Sweet! Another outside-the-box thinker!" Freya exclaimed.

"Hey, sorry to interrupt you two," Arlo said, "but I was talking to Daisy."

"Sorry," Marty said. "It's just cool, ya know?"

"I know, dude," he replied. "Hey, I have an idea. How about we do a soft seal and talk face-to-face?"

Daisy hesitated.

"There was a plague on Earth, Arlo. While I'm sure Freya did a full decontamination cycle, I don't know if that—"

"Oh, that's fine," he cut her off. "I'm immune."

"So you know about that too?"

"Oh, yeah. That and a bunch more. So whaddya say? Chat?"

"You've gotta admire his enthusiasm, Daze."

Yeah. Let's just hope I don't wind up regretting this.

"Okay, Arlo. Let's link up. See you in a minute."

They sat in Freya's small galley sipping hot cocoa a few minutes later, a warm hospitality in the cold of space.

"So, no whiskey on board?" the teen asked.

"You're a kid, Arlo."

"Just asking," he replied with a laugh. "The cocoa is great, by the way."

"Now let me get this straight. You're from a small group of survivors carried out into space by some of Earth's AIs who fled during the alien attack?" Daisy asked.

"Yep."

"That sounds an awful lot like *my* story."

"Sure does," he said, merrily. "My guess is the AIs lost contact sometime before launch and were forced to select a route on their own. I mean, it was a crazy time, from what I've been told."

"You've got that right," she replied. "But that doesn't explain you. Why are you here? Who are you, for that matter?"

Hey, Sarah. Ask Freya to scan him for any artificial parts, Daisy silently asked her sister as she gently adjusted the neuro-band riding beneath her headband.

"Will do," Sarah replied. *"Hey, Freya. Daisy wants to know if the kid has any artificial parts."*

"None," Freya replied.

"What was that?" Arlo asked, surprised by the seemingly random statement.

"Oh, sorry, I was just looking at my scans for ships leaving the atmosphere and must've spoken out loud. My bad," Freya replied.

"No worries. Thanks, Freya," Daisy said.

So, he's entirely human. Interesting.

"To answer your questions," Arlo began, "I'm a scout for my people. I've spent a few decades in cryo getting here, all so I can survey the planet and report back its status."

"But your ship seems like he's capable of extremely fast travel."

"Oh, he is fast, but our people are really far away."

"It feels like he's lying about something, Daze."

I know. Can't look me straight in the eyes when he says that. I wonder what he's hiding.

"Might be paranoid about our intentions too. I mean, we did only just meet, after all."

"That's tough, Arlo. So many years in cryo, well, it's something I have some experience with."

"Really?"

"Yep. Longer than you, I'd wager. But why did they only send one ship? And why you?"

"Funny you should ask. I'm the one who had to make the trip, you see. Me and Marty? We're a team, and he's the only ship stealthy enough to survey the planet without being noticed."

"Stealth was your key concern, then?"

"Oh, hell yeah it was. Last time we checked, the planet was under Ra'az control, with those poor Chithiid bastards slaving away for them."

"So you already knew about the Ra'az?"

"Yeah. Big, ugly fuckers too."

"On that we're in agreement. But you also knew the Chithiid were unwilling slaves?"

"Uh-huh. And they weren't the first," he replied. "Hang on a sec. Hey, Marty, can you bring up the images from the husk?"

"What's the husk?"

"It's what we took to calling one of the last planets the Ra'az stripped. We found it a while back, though we don't know exactly how long ago they pulled up stakes and bailed."

Images flashed onto Freya's monitors. A vast world filled the screens, one covered with pockmarks of destruction, its entire surface stripped bare, as well as torn open to access valuable minerals under its crust.

The Ra'az had sucked the world dry, leaving––as Arlo accurately noted––a husk.

"There were signs of some sort of civilization at one point, but there was just so little left that we gave up even searching the planet."

"Good Lord, this is what they wanted to do to Earth," Daisy said.

"Yeah, I know. And last time my people checked in on the planet, it looked like it was going to be on its way to join them. But then they noticed that even though all of the military bases were destroyed and scrapped, the automated defenses on the surface were still keeping the Ra'az at bay in a lot of places."

"A surprisingly effective system," Daisy agreed.

"Yeah. And there was a little debris field circling the planet. They thought it looked like a fleet of the survivors they were separated from that had returned and tried to take the planet back."

"They tried, but failed."

"More than once, from what I see. Looks like there's a lot more debris than our previous scouting mission reported."

"That would be the second and third fleets. Both destroyed by the AI virus." Daisy realized the jeopardy Marty was in. "Shit, the AI virus. Have your ship—"

"Marty," Arlo interrupted.

"Have *Marty* shut down all external lines. The AI virus is still active."

Freya jumped into the conversation.

"I've already given him the inoculation protocol, Daisy. He believes he is safely firewalled, but he's going to run it while we head to Dark Side to meet the others. So don't worry about Marty. He's fine."

"Oh," Arlo said, not terribly shocked. "That's cool. So we're gonna go to the moon base?"

Daisy thought about it a moment.

Sarah, your take on this? she asked, silently.

"It's kinda an odd situation, I have to admit," Sarah replied. *"But everything checks out so far, Daze. I don't see why not."*

"Yeah, I think that's a good idea," she finally said. "But I've gotta tell you, Arlo, it's not the wrecked facility your people would have seen on their last visit to Earth. It's been fixed up a bit."

"Cool. I'll go back over to my ship and get cleaned up. I know my hat's around there somewhere. We'll follow you in. See you guys over there," he said, walking for the airlock linking their ships.

"Weird kid, Daze."

Yeah, but I kinda like him.

Daisy opened the comms line.

"Hey, Sid. We've got company coming to dinner. Let the others know, there's going to be another ship in Hangar Two."

"I don't read a ship in the vicinity of your transmission, Daisy," Sid replied.

"Yeah, you wouldn't. He's kinda like Freya."

"Another stealth ship?" Sid said, surprised. "Well, won't this be...interesting."

The two vessels swung around and headed toward the moon, Freya leading the way, their new friends close behind.

CHAPTER TWENTY-FIVE

"Daaang, will ya look at that thing," Shelly marveled at the sleek ship nestled into Hangar Two. "She's gorgeous!"

"I'm actually a he," Marty corrected over his external speakers.

"Shit, sorry!"

"No worries," the amused AI said with a little chuckle.

Arlo followed Doctor McClain from the hangar to her temporary medical station rolled into the hangar, where Chu sat waiting for them.

"Hey, man. I'm Arlo. Nice to meet you," he said, shaking Chu's hand.

"Alfred Chu, but everyone calls me Chu."

"Cool. It's a pleasure, Chu." He looked around the lab space as Doctor McClain warmed up her scanners.

"I hope you will pardon the inconvenience, but despite Daisy and Freya's assurances you are free of any remnants of the plague, I'd feel better if we had a proper series of scans done, just to be on the safe side. Once you're clear, we can admit you into the base, proper, which I assure you is much more pleasant than out here in the hangar."

"Sure, no worries, Doc," Arlo replied cheerfully. "And don't worry about the hangar space. I grew up around this kind of stuff. High-tech clutter is my playground."

"Okay, then. Let's get started. Chu, warm up the machines, please."

"You got it, Doc."

The technician got to work, while McClain did as well, though her task was more along the lines of the other hat she wore. That of base headshrinker.

"Tell me, Arlo. You say you're the child of human survivors."

"Yep. Mom and Dad popped me out the old-fashioned way," he said, then crinkled his nose. "Eww, I can't believe I just said that."

McClain allowed herself a little grin, then got back to work, clearly in the line of sight of a very interested base commander.

From behind the observation window, Daisy and Commander Mrazich watched the process.

"He said his people were a much smaller group that fled the Ra'az in a different direction," Daisy told him.

"And you believe him?"

"Well, he checks out so far, and he's entirely organic, so there's that," Daisy replied.

"But his ship. It is far more advanced than anything we ever had in our fleet."

"Except Freya."

"Well, yes, obviously."

"She said Marty's hull is made of a very similar nanite stealth material as hers. I mean, it really does look like a different branch of our family tree made off with some cells and some advanced tech and made their escape run the other way. It's really a miracle we bumped into each other at all."

Mrazich rubbed his temple slowly.

"Daisy, he said he had an urgent message for *you*," he

reminded her. "He came looking for *you*. How did he know you? If all of this is such a surprise to him, why weren't you?"

"Shit, good point."

I was so caught up in it, finally getting back to our own timeline, I kinda forgot about that.

"I guess we'll just have to ask him when the doc is through with him," she replied.

Mrazich was still uneasy.

"I reviewed the log of his arrival after Freya made that tiny jump," he said.

Good, he bought our faked warp records, Daisy thought, relaxing slightly with a silent sigh of relief.

"Yeah, that test put us just a short distance away, but the warp tech has promise," she lied.

"Did you notice how much this Arlo character's arrival looked like your warp?" he asked.

"Visually, perhaps, but Freya didn't pick up a warp on her scans, and Marty is a stealth ship, after all."

"Maybe," Mrazich mused, "but I still have my doubts about him. I want you to keep both eyes open. The timing of this is more than a little bit odd, his arriving just as we defeat the Ra'az on Earth."

"While I agree, I also think we should still give him the benefit of the doubt. With his tech, he could have stayed hidden if he had wanted to. Instead, he hailed us––hailed me––and made contact."

"Yes, that he did. And now he's inside Dark Side. Go collect him and bring him to the mess hall. He knew who you are, Daisy. I want very much to hear how."

"Will do," she replied.

Daisy walked the long corridor to the airlock leading into Hangar Two.

"Want some company?" Vince asked, sliding close to her.

Daisy turned and kissed him fiercely.

"Tone it down, Daze. He thinks you've only been gone a few hours."

I don't care, she replied, pulling him in even tighter.

"Whoa!" he exclaimed when she finally released her embrace. "What was that for? Not that I mind or anything."

"Just because," she said with a happy grin. "Mmm. I missed you."

"Um, I missed you too," he said, gladly accepting the warm press of her lips.

"Okay, more of that later. Come on. Mrazich wants us to bring the new kid to the mess hall for a chat."

Doc McClain finished her tests a couple of minutes later, and Arlo followed Daisy and Vince back into Dark Side's main facilities.

"So, Arlo, Daisy tells me you have a really cool ship," Vince said as they walked.

"Yeah, Marty is awesome," he replied. "He's been with me a long time."

"So you two grew up together, in a way."

"I guess you could say that. I mean, he's a super-smart AI, so he was really already grown up long before I was."

"Yeah, but you know what I mean. From what I've seen with Daisy and Freya, once you bond with an unusual AI like that, you've got something special for life."

Daisy smiled and pulled Vince close for a deep kiss.

"Oh, gross. Come on," Arlo grumbled, slipping around the couple and continuing down the corridors.

"We appear to have grossed out a teenager," Vince said with a laugh.

"That we have," Daisy agreed.

They began strolling hand in hand as they watched the young man walking in front of them.

"Seems like a good kid, babe," Vince said. "I like him. I get a good vibe, if you know what I mean."

"Yeah, I do," she agreed. "Though there is something a bit odd about him. I just can't put my finger on it."

"He's leading the way, Daze."

He's not too far ahead, Sis. Don't worry, I'm keeping an eye on him.

"No, that's not what I mean," Sarah corrected. *"He's leading."*

Daisy suddenly realized what Sarah was talking about and paid far more attention to his movements than before.

Well, I'll be—

"Hey, Arlo," she called out after him.

"Yeah?"

"We're going to the mess hall to meet up with the others."

"I know, you told me."

"Yeah, I did. But you said you've never been here before."

"Right."

"So how do you know the way?"

"I've studied lots of military bases, and they all have pretty similar layouts," he replied, not missing a beat. "Why? Am I going the wrong way?"

"No, that's it. Next corridor turn right," she replied.

"Got it."

His answer made sense, but she would have to have a more serious chat with Freya and her sisters when time permitted. For now, however, it was time for their guest to meet the others.

Arlo was given a warm welcome by all present in Dark Side's spacious mess hall. It wasn't every day someone new arrived, and someone new with a cool ship to boot.

"Oh my God. Are those chocolate chip cookies?" the teen asked, salivating as he sniffed the air.

Finn had decided to prepare a little treat for the new guest, and had indeed whipped up a sizable batch, which he was just pulling from the oven. He quickly plated them and brought them over to the long table, where everyone had taken a seat.

"Dig in, kid. And welcome to Dark Side," he said, relishing the gusto with which his new acquaintance tore into the treats.

"I freakin' love chocolate chip cookies!" Arlo managed to say through a mouthful of gooey wonder. "Thanks!"

"My pleasure. There's milk if you like too."

Mrazich stood at the head of the table and surveyed his team.

"Everyone, I'd like to welcome our new guest. For those who don't know, Arlo here is from another, smaller group of escaped AIs, who apparently fled in a different direction than our progenitors. He's come back to survey the planet and report back on its condition. Is that pretty much correct?"

"Yeah," the teen replied.

"Fantastic. Now, there is just one thing I would like to clarify," Mrazich said, pulling the tray of cookies out of the young man's reach, drawing his full attention. "You said you had no idea about the other survivors, yet your first transmission on arrival was directed to Daisy Swarthmore. You knew her by name. That, and you said you had an urgent message for her."

"Oh, damn. He just went right for the jugular."

Subtlety is not Mrazich's strong suit, Daisy agreed. *This should be interesting.*

All eyes turned toward the newcomer in their midst.

"Um," Arlo began, quickly wiping chocolate remnants from his mouth and fingers. "The thing is, I may have *slightly* fudged that bit."

"Arlo?" Daisy asked with a piercing gaze.

"Well, Marty and me—"

"Marty and I," she corrected him.

He flashed an annoyed look.

"Marty and *I*, we sort of scanned Dark Side when we first got here. We didn't mean anything by it, it's just something was different, is all. It was rebuilt. So we dug around a bit."

"And somehow overcame my peripheral security?" Sid asked, concerned.

"No, not really," he replied. "It's just that we intercepted some comms, and we heard the name Daisy, and then the commander called her Swarthmore, so we put two and two together."

"But what was this urgent message?" Mrazich asked.

"Well, we realized she was the one flying the ship that seemed so similar to Marty, and that meant she probably had the best chance of stopping them."

"Stopping who?"

"We found a recording of a damaged Ra'az ship warping away just after the attack. I can see how you'd miss it, I mean, you were out of commission after all."

"He's talking about the one you shot up, Daze."

Yeah. He doesn't realize it can't reach their fleet.

"So, you were trying to warn me?" she asked the teen.

"Yeah. I mean, if you could use your logs, we could pinpoint the ship's path and catch it, maybe. I don't know. I just thought it was really urgent we stop it from reaching reinforcements, is all."

Everyone in the room relaxed ever so slightly.

"Kid, you don't need to worry about that," Reggie said. "When Daisy grazed the ship, she damaged its drive systems."

"But it could still—"

"It would take decades, if not longer. By then, we'll either win or be dead. Am I right?"

The assembled team voiced their agreement.

"Well, I feel pretty stupid, then."

"Nothing to feel stupid about, Arlo. You were trying to help, and that's all anyone can ask," Vince said. "Here, have another cookie." He slid the tray closer.

The teen perked up a bit.

"I have to say, things are different than what I was sent here for, that's for sure," he said, taking a bite of a cookie. "And I don't think I can just hop in my ship and fly back home. Not after what I've seen."

"What are you saying?" Mrazich asked.

"What I'm saying is, I want to stay. Stay and help you guys."

"It's sweet of you, but you really don't know what you're getting yourself into," Daisy said.

"I can handle it. Marty and me——Marty and I, we've been through a lot together."

Daisy looked at Mrazich for a sign. Subtly, he nodded his approval.

"Okay, Arlo, then listen up. Here's the new plan."

Daisy spent the next half hour detailing her discussion with Maarl, and the old Chithiid's audacious plan to infiltrate and overrun the Ra'az fleet.

"We have the salvaged Ra'az star charts, we know roughly where they've gone, and using their own ships to infiltrate the fleet——retrofitted, of course——they won't even know what's hit them until it's too late."

"The plan is all fine and grand, Daisy, but you forget, we don't have a functional warp drive," Chu pointed out. "Without that, even if we integrate the weak warp devices from the Ra'az cargo transport ships, it'll still take years to catch up with them. Possibly longer. What we need is a functional advanced warp system."

"Yeah," Daisy said. "If only we had one of those."

"Why don't you tell him?"

Because I'm still not one hundred percent sure about that kid yet.

"Seems all right. And we do have two spare orbs now."

Maybe, but I still think it's better to be safe than sorry.

"Chu, what if I told you I could get you some help in

deciphering the notes you salvaged from the San Francisco warp lab?"

"I'd say that was a start. But we don't know anyone who can decipher them. It's all alien to us."

"To *us*, yes. But not to the aliens."

"The Ra'az will never help us, even if we do manage to capture one alive," Chu pointed out.

"Not those aliens. The others. The Chithiid have been in their service for centuries. They're the ones who silently watch from the sidelines. You keep working on those diagrams and notes. I'll make a run to see if I can rustle up some help from some of the Chithiid from the San Francisco facility."

"They'd do that?"

"Dude, they just risked their lives and homeworld to free Earth. For a chance to knock out the entire Ra'az fleet? Yeah, I think they'll do that. As soon as I take care of a few things up here on Dark Side first, I'll get right on it."

"More secret projects?" Finn joked.

Daisy couldn't help but smile.

"You'll see," she replied with a knowing grin.

Arlo raised his hand.

"This isn't a classroom, Arlo. What is it?" Daisy said.

"So, I suppose it's worth mentioning that I tucked away a few dozen small observation satellites, hidden in the debris field when I first got here. Before I met you guys, that is. They're out there circling the Earth in a geosynchronous orbit above areas that appeared to be hotbeds of activity."

"Daze, that's exactly what you were doing. Was this kid watching us?"

I don't know, Sis. Kinda freaking me out a little, though.

"And why is it you need to go retrieve them manually?" Daisy asked. "Why not just have them transmit the data directly to Marty?"

"Because I needed them to be a rock-solid, incorruptible

system. No transmissions equals no chance of catching the AI virus, get it?"

"Yeah, I get it, but you already know Freya can cure it."

"Sure, *now* I do. But when I set them up out there, that wasn't an option on my plate."

"I can help you and Marty retrofit them to protect them in the future when you get back, if you like," Freya offered.

"Thanks, that'd be really great," Marty replied. "If it's not too much of an imposition, that is."

"Not at all. But I do have some things to take care of while you guys are out collecting your goodies," Freya said. "Daisy, I dropped off that, um, *package* for you. Is it okay if I work on my other stuff?"

"Sure thing, kiddo. Go to your room," she said with a little laugh. "And, Freya, thank you for being so awesome."

"Awww, thanks, Daisy," the AI replied before powering up and flying out to her secret hangar.

"She has a room?" Arlo asked, an eyebrow raised with curiosity.

"More like a hangar," Daisy replied.

"I don't see anything," Marty noted.

"She's a stealth ship. Of course you don't." Vince chuckled. "Don't worry, she'll be around when you guys get back."

"Interesting," the new AI visitor mused. "Well, if you're ready, Arlo, shall we get to it?"

"All right, Marty. Be there in a minute."

Arlo gathered up his things and strolled back to Hangar Two, taking a stack of Finn's baked glory with him for the trip, of course.

"Plenty where that came from," the crazed chef said as the airlock door sealed. "I like that kid," he noted, then headed back for the mess hall.

Marty took off a couple of minutes later, making a quick loop of the base as they departed. Just like Vince said, there was no trace of Freya or her 'home' anywhere on the base down below.

"Fascinating," he mused. "She just disappeared. Huh. Okay, Sid, we'll be back soon," he messaged, then darted off into the dark sky.

At that same moment, Freya—safely ensconced in her fabrication hangar—was already busy at work on her many projects. There were so many to complete now that she was home again, and even more ideas that were begging to be started, but she had a few top-priority ones that came first.

With a heavily shielded whir of activity, her fabrication devices fired up and came online, as did nearly all of her other toys. It would be a long and delicate process, but that was half the fun of coming up with these ideas.

"Okay, time to get to it!" she said, then got to work, cheerfully humming to herself as she dug in.

CHAPTER TWENTY-SIX

As soon as Arlo was clear of the moon, Daisy called a general meeting in Hangar Two.

"What's this all about, Daisy?" Commander Mrazich asked, a little annoyed. "We just had an all-hands meeting less than an hour ago."

"I know, Commander, but there are some things I didn't want to get into with Arlo around."

"You don't trust him?"

"Not that, it's just I don't know him yet. Some cards should be held close to the vest until you really understand a situation, you know?"

"Well, I suppose," he reluctantly agreed. "So what's this all about, anyway?"

Daisy scanned the vast space. Everyone was there.

"Okay, everyone. I have a surprise for you. After what happened with Alma's infiltrators, and all that, I just wanted to wait until he was gone before revealing anything of *real* importance."

Finn took a bite of a cookie with a merry laugh.

"Come on, Daisy, what can it possibly be this time? I mean,

your last surprise was Freya. That one's gonna be kinda hard to top," he chuckled.

"Hi, Finn," Sarah said, stepping out from behind a large equipment mover.

The jovial chef nearly choked on his cookie in shock. The other *Váli* crew were likewise floored by her sudden appearance.

"But..." Doctor McClain managed to blurt, while the rest of the crew remained stunned and speechless.

"But I'm dead. Yeah, I know," Sarah said with a little laugh. "And let me tell you, being dead sucks."

Finn regained his composure as best he could and walked up to her, pulling her close in a tight hug. Moments later, the rest of the crew dogpiled in for a massive embrace. The others soon peeled away from the group hug, but Finn and Sarah held on just a tiny bit longer.

"Told ya so," Sarah said, noting the prolonged hug.

Preaching to the choir, Sis. But don't razz her, will ya? I don't want to spoil it for now.

"Yeah, me either. Besides, there's going to be plenty of time to give her shit later."

Sarah, a bit overwhelmed in the moment, didn't catch her other self's comments.

"So, uh, this is impossible," Vince said, looking her up and down. "You were blown out an airlock nearly seven months ago."

"Yep. And it sucked," Sarah replied. "And by the way, it's really good to see you, Vince. I'm glad you and my sis worked things out."

"So you know about all of that."

"Yeah, Daisy filled me in after she rescued me."

"But that's impossible," Barry noted. "I was present for the events aboard the *Váli*. Daisy did not launch any vessel to retrieve you. It would have been impossible, given your trajectory. Mal, you can confirm my observations, yes?"

"I can," she replied. "And no, Daisy did not leave the *Váli* anytime during, or immediately after, Sarah's accident."

"Well..." Daisy said, shrugging her shoulders a little. "There's kinda a bit more to that story."

"Obviously," Tamara said. "Jesus, Swarthmore, you are just full of surprises, aren't you?" She looked at Sarah's new arm, smaller and sleeker than her beefy appendage. "Got her some new parts, I see," she said. "We'll have to arm wrestle later," she said with a laugh.

"It's small, but it's a lot stronger than it looks," Sarah shot back with a daring grin. "Don't get too over-confident."

Commander Mrazich, though not a member of the *Váli* crew, was fully up to date on the events that led to Daisy's arrival on Dark Side, and this unexpected, and impossible wrinkle left him in a quandary.

"Do I need to be concerned, Swarthmore?" he asked. "Is this going to be a problem?"

"Not if everyone can keep their mouths shut," she replied.

"Good luck with this yo-yo," Reggie joked, nudging Finn. "Only way to keep his mouth shut is to stuff it with food."

"Bite me, Reg."

"Not without a bath, and a whole lot of barbecue sauce, my man."

"Fellas, enough," Sarah said with an exasperated sigh. "Jeez, I forgot how ridiculous you two could be."

"So what *did* happen, Daisy?" Chu asked, always the curious technical mind.

"To make a long story short," she said, pausing for effect. "Freya and I accidentally warped back in time."

Gasps and groans rose from the gathered crew.

"I call bullshit," Tamara said. "That's not possible."

"I'd normally have agreed," Daisy said, "but you know the power orb I brought back from the lab in San Francisco?"

"Yeah, I know it," Chu said.

"Well, it's not a simple power orb like we thought. It's a warp orb. That's the tech behind the Ra'azes' new warp drive."

"But it was tiny. Just the size of a baseball."

"I know, but I gave it to Freya to run some tests, and she tied it into her drive system to see how much power she could draw from it in a real-world setting. It seemed like a really great power source, and we were about to do a speed run when Arlo popped into the mix and hailed me on open comms. In the chaos of trying to shut down the system mid-cycle, a whole bunch of unexpected variables came into play and we kinda accidentally threw ourselves back in time."

The residents of Dark Side were all shocked, reeling in disbelief. All but one, that is.

Fatima had a peaceful look on her face. Almost as if a weight had been lifted from her chest.

"So you jumped back in time and saved Sarah?" Finn said, still reeling with disbelief. "Wow. Thank you, Daisy."

"I kinda did a little more than that, actually," she reluctantly admitted.

"Swarthmore, what did you do?" Mrazich asked with a concerned tone.

"We did a few things," she said, making brief eye contact with Fatima. "But the big one, aside from saving Sarah, of course, is Freya and I kinda went and found the launch point for the *Váli's* mission."

"Oh my God. You interacted with your own past?" Chu blurted. "Christ, Daisy, do you have any idea how dangerous that is?"

"We did, but we didn't. What I mean is, they were so far away, and the *Váli* had already been launched a long time by then."

"So by the time anything you discussed might pop up in your own timeline, you would have already caught back up to it, making it your future and not your past that you stuck your fingers into. Is that about right?" Shelly asked, her metal arms crossed as she mused the situation.

"Yeah, more or less," Daisy affirmed.

"Wait a minute," Finn said, a light bulb all but appearing over his head. "Holy shit, that arm!"

"I know," Sarah replied, suddenly self-conscious. "I'm not what I used to be."

"No, you don't get it. I recognize that arm. Were you in Rome?"

Sarah glanced uncomfortably at Daisy, who gave a little 'fuck if I know' shrug.

"Um, yeah, actually. Sorry about that."

"Sorry? You saved my life, Sarah. And Phoenix? Was that you too?"

"Guilty as charged," she admitted, sheepishly.

Finn wrapped her up in a massive bear hug.

"Twice, you saved my ass," he said, stepping back an arm's length. "Anything you ever need, anything you want, just ask. I owe you my life, Sarah."

"Don't make it weird, Finn," she said, squirming uncomfortably from the attention.

Mrazich looked like a massive headache was building. One with Daisy's name all over it.

"So you and your dead sister have been out hopping all over time and space? Can things possibly get any worse?" he said with a pained sigh. "Where are you off to next, then? Please don't tell me you're going to change the—"

"No, you don't get it," Sarah said. "We don't dare attempt *any* sort of warp again until we fully understand the process. More importantly, we have to all swear to keep all of this a secret—especially the time travel. All of this is dangerous information that should stay with Dark Side's team and no one else. And as for actually jumping in time again, we don't even know if another time warp is possible, though we have some serious doubts whether we could ever even do another."

"Ha, she's a decent liar," Sarah noted with a little chuckle inside Daisy's head.

For the greater good, Sis.

"Still a liar, though. Even if I approve. Which I do, in case you were wondering."

Gee, thanks.

"That's why I wanted to wait until Arlo was gone to tell you all of this," Daisy added to the conversation. "No one can know about the time aspect of the warp orb. Only those present here today."

"You say the time *aspect*," Chu observed. "What other aspects are there?"

"Oh, when not accidentally throwing you through time, it really is a proper warp drive, Chu. And I mean light years in a split-second level warp drive. And now, with the Chithiid ready to confront the Ra'az, we need to figure out how to replicate it and install it into their commandeered ships."

"But we still only have partial notes," the scientist griped. "It could take years."

"Yeah, about that. Sarah and I, we kinda snuck into the warp facility before the assault and stole a bunch of stuff," Daisy said.

Sarah pulled a duffle bag full of notes and diagrams from under a bin and slid it over to Chu.

"Here ya go, Chu. Me and Daze grabbed all we could. Should be plenty of stuff in there to help you figure out how to recreate these little guys," she said, tossing him a spare warp orb.

"Don't throw that thing!" Mrazich yelled.

"Relax, Commander. It's not dangerous. In fact, unless you detonate it inside the atmosphere, it's pretty benign," Daisy said, trying to calm him.

"Swarthmore, in case you forget, we are standing inside an atmosphere," he said, gesturing toward their enclosed space.

"Oh. Well, yeah, there's that, I suppose," she admitted.

"You want me—other me—to give him the other orb?"

No, tell her to hang on to that one. It's our ace in the hole.

"But this is Chu."

And I trust him implicitly. That still doesn't mean I want all our eggs in one basket.

"Okay, I'll pass it along," Sarah said. *"Hey, Daisy said don't give them the other orb."*

Sarah nodded, keyed in via her and Daisy's neuro-bands.

Chu marveled at the device in his hands, turning it over and over, studying its design.

"Okay, I have a question," he said.

"Figured you would," Daisy replied. "Shoot."

"So you're saying that warp––spatial, not time––is what this was designed for."

"Yep."

"And figuring that out should hopefully be made easier thanks to these notes."

"Well, yeah, but I'm more worried about your figuring out how to make more of them, actually. I'm confident you can get that one to function no problem once you chat with Freya about it. The important thing is, we need to build more. A *bunch* of them, big enough and powerful enough to jump the Chithiid ships out to the Ra'az fleet."

"Wait, you're not worried about cracking the warp part?"

"Nah, Freya's figured out the spatial bit. That part's easy, at least for a ship her size."

"But what if we stumble upon the *other* capability, like you did? I mean, accidental time travel is a huge pitfall."

"Chu, the events that led to us discovering that were like several million to one. I doubt you could ever make a warp orb do that again, even if you knew what you were trying to do. Hell, I know we couldn't, and that led to spending a lot of years in cryo until timelines matched up," Daisy said, keeping a neutral face as she lied to her friend.

It's for their own safety.

"I know."

I just hate lying to them.

"I know, Daze. But like you said, it's just too dangerous, and even knowing some of this stuff could put people at risk."

Exactly.

"So now we just need Freya to steer their research in the right direction."

With some help, of course, Daisy replied.

"Okay, Chu," she said. "Let's get working on finding you those extra sets of eyes to help with those plans."

CHAPTER TWENTY-SEVEN

It had been a long time since Daisy had found herself in the cushioned embrace of Doctor McClain's couch, and, much to her surprise, sitting with the head shrinker after all the things she had so recently gone through actually seemed to be helping her strained psyche.

She was still lying about having been in cryo. Daisy, Sarah, and Freya, had all agreed that time travel was too risky a thing to leak, and thus the years-spent-in-cryo story was hatched. But aside from that, and perhaps one or two other little white lies, Daisy was being surprisingly honest with the doctor.

Given her past history of being a somewhat strong-willed and stubborn patient, Doc McClain found her openness refreshing, and the overall feel of their session became unlike any they'd ever had in the past.

"The trauma of losing your sister was enormous, Daisy. It's only natural you'd leap at the chance to save her, consequences be damned," McClain said.

"I know. I mean, I rationally understand that, but after the fact, the realization that I could have caused serious damage to time itself made me really question my judgment."

"But things worked out, didn't they?"

"Well, yeah."

"And you said that not once but several times your actions actually wound up leading to events that you had already experienced. You had to do those things, in essence."

"Yeah, that too."

"So let it go, Daisy. You've always been hard on yourself, pushed to the limit when others might have backed off. Maybe it's time you allowed yourself a little breathing room."

"I suppose," Daisy reluctantly agreed.

"If anyone has earned it, I think you have. Between saving the planet and saving Sarah, you've done quite a lot. Now I want you to not beat yourself up about these things for at least an hour," McClain joked. "And please, my door is always open if you need me."

Daisy rose to her feet and realized she really did feel better. Maybe not one hundred percent, but significantly enough.

"Thanks, Doc. I appreciate it," she said, leaving one head shrinker to visit one of an entirely different variety.

"Daisy, I've been looking forward to this for a long time," Fatima said, pulling her in close for a big hug as soon as she entered the room. "Thank you. Thank you so much."

"Um, Fatima, I didn't do anything," Daisy replied, a bit confused.

"But you did. I spent decades wondering how I got Dark Side's systems turned on and managed to climb into that med pod as injured and weak as I was. And I had so many flashbacks about those crazy trauma dreams––I was constantly telling myself it was all in my mind. But then you and the *Váli* showed up, and the memories started returning with more clarity. It was always there, lurking in the back of my mind, this faint, fuzzy memory of you impossibly with me in a time and place you couldn't have been.

"Shit. She was conscious for all that?"

Apparently so.

"What do we do?"

I don't know. Just play it off, I guess.

"And speaking of minds," Fatima continued, "Sarah is living in your head, isn't she, Daisy? The version you didn't save, I mean."

Daisy gasped in surprise.

"Um, no. That's crazy, Fatima. You saw her, she's down the hall."

"You know that's not what I mean," she replied. "I had originally thought that if I wasn't crazy, then you had been merely talking to yourself all those years ago when you saved my life. But then, when I heard Freya's voice the other day, there it was, clear as a bell. It was exactly as I remembered, Daisy, and I realized that it couldn't have been a dream at all, though, to be honest, I'd suspected as much for some time. That means you really were talking to the voice in your head back then, and––"

"Fatima, you can't tell anyone this."

"Of course not. It's not my story to tell, only my thanks to give. I owe you my life, you know."

"And I owe you mine."

"Oh, now you exaggerate," Fatima chided.

"No, really. Your training prepared me in ways I couldn't have anticipated. Without you, I wouldn't be standing here today."

Daisy stepped forward and gave the silver-haired woman a warm hug.

"Well, now, isn't that something. We're in each other's debt, it seems," Fatima said with a serene smile. "And tell me, how is Sarah handling having her other self back? Is it causing friction? Does the other Sarah know?"

"Yeah, she knows. And there was a little head-butting at first, so to speak, but now things have settled into place. Plus, Freya designed a new, stripped-down type of neuro-band to allow her to talk to herself," Daisy said, lifting up the edge of the headband holding her neuro-band in place.

"Freya did what? That shouldn't be possible—oh, but of course. Sarah is the same person."

"Yep. The only way two minds could tap into the same neuro."

"Such a clever vessel, your Freya. And how she has matured since I saw her last. In her actual time line, that is."

"She's really coming into her own," Daisy agreed. "Though her headstrong teen phase isn't quite over yet."

Fatima laughed warmly. "Enjoy it while you can. That, too, is something you will look back on fondly one day."

Daisy looked around the training room she had spent so much time laboring and toiling in and smiled. Distanced from the exhausting abuse of it all, she actually found herself almost nostalgic for the difficult tasks.

An inspiration struck.

"Hey, Fatima, I was wondering if you'd consider doing me a little favor."

"Anything."

"Well, in that case, would you do for Sarah what you did for me? See if you can help her control her mind, train her to be more than she already is?"

"I can try, Daisy. But remember, she was more advanced than you in meditation practices. She may be reluctant to engage in more training."

"But with her nanite arm, she really needs to learn to focus and control them. They listen to her, but mostly, it's all subconscious at this point. I'm hoping, and so is Freya, that she'll learn to control them consciously, but she needs help."

"Of course. I'll do whatever I can," Fatima replied. "Send her to me after dinner, and I'll have a little chat with her. If she's amenable to it, I'll gladly take her on and help train her as best I can. One can only hope she'll be as proficient a student as you were."

Daisy had only just left her friend, walking the quiet halls of Dark Side, when Finn caught up to her.

"Hey, I was looking for you."

"What's up, Finn? Everything okay?"

"Well..."

"Uh-oh. I don't like the sound of that."

He looks upset, Sis.

"I have a sneaking suspicion I know why."

"Finn, talk to me. What's bothering you?"

"I'm kinda freaking out here, Daisy. I mean, we've talked about this in the past. You know how I felt—I mean *feel*, about Sarah."

"Yeah."

"Shit. I knew it. What did she do, Daze?"

I don't know. Now hush, I need to pay attention.

"Remember way back on the *Váli*? When you told me not to wait because life is short and you never know what'll happen?"

"Right before she died," Daisy said, softly. "Yeah, I remember."

"That tore my heart out, Daisy. I was so full of pain and regret, I didn't really know what to do with myself." He shook his head sadly at the memory. "Hell, I even briefly considered suicide."

"Whoa, you're not—"

"No, no, it was just one really low spot, but what I'm saying is, I've been carrying around this regret for all this time, and now I have a second chance."

"I'm happy for you, man."

"I should be happy too, but Sarah is different now. It feels like she's blowing me off, you know? Treating me like just another buddy no matter how hard I try. Does she dislike me, Daisy? You're her sister. Has she said anything to you?"

"Uh, no."

"Then what is it?"

"Finn, you're a great guy––"

"That's as bad as calling me nice."

"You know what I mean. And you *are* nice. But Sarah, right now, well, she's really going through some stuff, and I think she's kind of overwhelmed. Look, just be yourself. Be natural. I know she likes you––"

"Did she tell you that?"

"Dangerous territory, Daze."

I know.

"Not in so many words, but I know my sister," she carefully replied. "Look, keep being you. Once she gets her equilibrium straight, she's bound to come around."

Finn looked dejected as he accepted the uncertain future of his romantic hopes.

"Okay. I'll try to give her some space, I guess. It's just hard, you know? I mean, she's alive again. Here's the one thing that I've been wishing for all this time, and I just have to sit back and be all, 'Hi, Sarah, have some toast,' and shit like that, when I just want to hold her close and never let go." He sniffled a bit. "Sorry, that was probably kind of weird for you."

"No, Finn, it's fine. I understand what you're going through. But listen, I really need to get moving. Just promise me you'll take it easy on yourself. She's only been back among the crew less than a day. It's a lot to take in, and she's dealing with a lot of things besides seeing you again. Let her process it all. Give it time."

"Thanks, Daisy. You're the best," he said, giving her a hug, then slowly walking away down the corridor.

"We need to do something about this," Sarah said.

I couldn't agree more. We just can't be too obvious.

Daisy started walking again. She already had one more stop before heading back down to Earth, and a new task had just been added to her list.

"But I don't want to hang out up here," Sarah whined. "We just kicked the aliens' asses. I wanna go revel in our victory and taste the spoils of war!"

"You're ridiculous," Daisy said with a laugh.

"Genetics, sister of mine," Sarah shot back.

"Touché. But seriously, it'd be really good if you hung around Dark Side a little bit. Get to know everyone you haven't already met. And also catch up with the ones you do know from the *Váli*. Things have changed a lot since they all thought you died. It might do you well to re-bond with them."

"Ugh, you're not pushing Finn on me again, are you?"

"No, of course not."

"Yes, we are."

Not helping, Sarah.

"Well, he's a good dude."

"Not happening, Other Me," Sarah replied to herself.

"Fine, be a spoil sport."

"Fine, I will," she shot back to her disembodied twin.

"Stop bickering, you two. I swear, it's enough to make me want to stop wearing this stupid neuro-band altogether," Daisy said, her hands jokingly moving to the band tucked in her hair.

"Whoa, not cool, Daze."

"Yeah, what she said."

"Ugh," Daisy said with a sigh. "Fine. But seriously, you should at least spend some time and get to know Shelly and Omar. They're good people. And I also asked Fatima to talk to you."

"Sharing your guru, eh?"

"She helped me more than I ever realized, and I was thinking, with her help, you might gain better control of that arm."

"I have plenty of control of my arm."

"I mean in the way Freya was talking about. Like when you made it shift shape. Imagine if you could do that all the time just by thinking about it."

Sarah considered the possibility.

"Well, that *would* be pretty cool," she admitted. "Okay, I'll swing by and have a pow-wow with her. Worst-case scenario, I get some tea and a nice bit of meditation out of it."

"Cool," Daisy replied. "Oh, and if Arlo comes back before I do, don't mention time travel at all."

"Duh."

"And if he wonders where you came from, just say you were away on a run to Earth when he arrived and you got back to Dark Side after he left, or something."

"Don't worry, Daze, I can improvise just fine."

"I know. Sorry. I just--there's a lot going on, is all."

"You're doing great, Sis. Now, get out of here before I change my mind and make you take me along."

Daisy knew better than to reply, instead turning on her heel and booking out of there before Sarah could indeed change her mind. Fifteen minutes later she had gathered Tamara and Chu for the trip and was comfortably strapped into her seat aboard Freya on a direct course for Los Angeles.

Freya had only touched down briefly in LA before dusting off again with their VIP passenger aboard, but in her short stay, she had once again charmed the young Chithiid of Maarl's encampment.

"The youths are quite taken with your ship," Maarl said,

admiring her sleek interior as she carried them up the coast to San Francisco.

"She's a very social one, that is for sure," Daisy noted with a warm laugh. Maarl joined her, his eyes crinkling merrily, glad for such pleasant company.

"I am indeed pleased that your scientists have been making headway on understanding, and hopefully recreating, the Ra'az warp technology," he said, nodding toward Chu, who smiled and nodded back, not having a clue what was just said. *"While we do possess their old equivalent, it was a massively underpowered technology and would take us years to reach their fleet utilizing it."*

"I know, but the new tech could warp your ships there instantly. All we'd need to do is have a little distraction so they don't notice the new vessels in their ranks."

"Which should be easy enough to accomplish if we time our arrival correctly. You see, smaller contingents of ships peel off from the main fleet to scout other planets. All we must do is watch and wait for such a window of opportunity."

"Then you jump in with the same number of ships, mimicking their ident codes, and you're in."

"Precisely," he said, looking over Freya's interior arrays. *"She truly is magnificent. If only we had technology of this magnitude on all our ships. The battle would be over in an instant."*

"But my girl's one of a kind," Daisy noted.

"Well, two, if you count Marty. He's very similar tech."

I know, but no need to tell Maarl about that just yet.

Freya, though capable of making the trip from Los Angeles to San Francisco in minutes rather than hours, was taking the scenic route along the coast, flying low enough for her passengers to enjoy the view on her monitors.

"Hey, Daisy, wanna see something cool I've figured out?" she chirped.

"Speak Chithiid, Freya. We have company."

"Sorry."

"It's okay. Now what did you want to show me?"

The floor beneath their feet suddenly turned transparent, the waves below them as clear as if there were nothing separating them from the long fall.

Maarl jumped a little at the unexpected shift in view.

"Oh, I'm sorry," Freya said. *"I should have warned you. I just thought it was cool, is all."*

The grizzled Chithiid let out a hearty laugh.

"Oh, you marvelous thing, I appreciate your apology, though none is needed. I find myself rather enjoying the unusual view. But tell me, how did you achieve this?"

"Well, I built the ship with the help of nanites, so we—"

"Nanites? What are these?"

"They're like tiny machines that join together to make bigger things."

"Like cells, then?"

"Yeah, you could say that," she replied. *"But mine are able to shift their form. I've been trying to get them to adapt to different colors, kind of like active camouflage, like what I was hoping they'd do for Sarah's arm."*

"Whose arm?"

"Nothing," Daisy interrupted. *"Just a repaired injury to one of our crew."*

"Ah, I see," Maarl replied.

"Anyway, I had them act like fiber optic lenses. Or maybe a monitor screen. I don't know which is the better analogy. In any case, they're now showing what's outside, as if they were a window."

"Really cool work, Freya. But next time, let's warn our passengers, okay?"

"Righty-o!"

"Oh, dear Lord, has she been talking to that crazed AI ship?"

I hope not. But if she has, I hope that's all she picked up. Kip was more than a little too fixated on toast for my taste. And that's from a woman who likes the stuff.

"When we arrive at the facility, you will want to land at the area closest to the water. That is where my friend has set up his camp," Maarl directed as they neared San Francisco Bay.

"Not inside?"

"No. He was forced to live indoors all those long years, so he is now spending his newfound freedom enjoying the view of the water and the fresh breeze it affords him."

They set down just outside of the makeshift encampment soon after, Freya barely stirring the dust as she lowered to the ground.

Tamara was glad to stretch her legs, while Chu was almost sad his ride aboard the amazing ship was over.

"She's so cool, Daisy!" he cooed.

"Thanks, Chu!" Freya replied.

"Yeah, thanks," Daisy agreed.

"Sorry, Freya. I didn't mean to talk about you like you weren't there."

"No worries. We were talking in Chithiid while you were there, so that was kinda rude too, I suppose. But hopefully we'll have some modified neuro-stims set up to speed your language learning curve."

"Hey, someone's coming," Tamara warned.

Indeed, an old Chithiid, even older than Maarl, was slowly making his way toward them. Maarl waved his four arms in greeting as he drew near.

"Most excellent to see you, my friend," he said warmly.

"Likewise. And are these your scientist associates?"

"That one is," he said, gesturing to Chu. *"He has plans and diagrams from the Ra'az. Many captured items from the warp facility. All he needs now is your help deciphering them."*

"One of the many tasks we face," he replied. *"We still must learn to override the Ra'az kill switches on our ships, and even our gauntlets, if possible."*

"Daisy believes she can accomplish those tasks," Maarl replied.

"Perhaps. But it is an alien technology, and a difficult one to understand at that."

Daisy, understanding all that was said, turned to Tamara.

"Hey, power up your whip and move some stuff around."

"Why?"

"All of theirs are locked. I want to show them we can make them work."

"Why not use yours?"

"I'm still working on it," she replied, uncomfortable at the in-between place she'd still have to go if she wanted to use the formerly anger-driven device. "I don't want to do a half-assed demo, is all."

"Oh, all right," Tamara said, raising her metal arm.

"You may wish to observe this," Daisy said, just as the whip beam played out from her friend's metal arm, moving debris around the area before retreating back into its housing.

The Chithiid were stunned.

"You integrated that into human technology. How did you do this?"

"It was something I figured out some time ago," Daisy replied. *"The point is, I am confident in our team and their abilities. If you can help us recreate these warp orbs, we should be able to make your fleet, as well as your gauntlets, functional and free of Ra'az controls."*

"As always, you surprise me, Daisy," Maarl said with a warm laugh. *"Now, let us determine how best to proceed."*

"We start working on the tech right here. Right now," Daisy replied. *"Chu and Tamara will stay here to work on the project. Once you put together a team of tech-savvy scientists, we will then prep them for space travel and bring them to Dark Side, where our lab facilities are already hard at work on the problem."*

"Our people, to the moon base? I do not know how many will volunteer, now that they enjoy the freedom of fresh air."

"Tell them it's a chance to kill the Ra'az," Daisy suggested. *"I have a feeling that may sway more than a few of them."*

CHAPTER TWENTY-EIGHT

"These are really cool!" Freya's voice said through the multi-limbed mech that was examining one of Arlo and Marty's small satellite surveillance units in Hangar Three, turning it over for study in its composite grasping apparatus.

"Thanks. I'm pretty happy with how they turned out," Marty replied.

"I mean, this is a really, really clever design. And the way you routed the power inputs to drip-feed an energy cascade via solar re-charge is so freaking sweet. Totally out of the box thinking," Freya gushed.

"Aww, thanks. I mean, I guess they're kinda cool like that," Marty said.

You hear that? Freya's embarrassing the guy.

"An embarrassed AI. Who'd have thought?"

She does get a little carried away at times. And she is pretty much a super-genius, so I guess I can see how a fellow AI could be a little overwhelmed by the attention.

"Yeah. It's kinda cute, two powerful ships and both a little bit awkward."

Deadly but cute, you mean.

Arlo watched with great interest as Freya's mech spun and examined the recording satellite with its strong, yet delicate appendages.

"Big spidery thing doesn't freak you out?" Daisy asked.

"Nah, I'm used to mechs," he replied. "Back home we used to design and make all kinds of 'em for fun."

"Really?" Daisy said, surprised.

"Excuse me, Arlo," Marty interrupted. "Freya has uploaded her antivirus packet into this satellite. You wanna give it a go and see if the immunization worked before we do the rest?"

"Sure thing, bud. You do the honors."

"Okay. Here it goes," he replied. "Sid, whenever you're ready."

"Sending the transfer now," Sid replied, a very-firewalled hardline from his sequestered storage systems releasing the AI virus into the little satellite.

All eyes were on the machine, but its display just kept blinking away normally, with not so much as a hiccup in its processes. It seemed that Freya's inoculation had worked for Marty's somewhat unusual tech as well as it had for that of the other AIs.

The virus was no longer a threat.

With that final test, it appeared that Freya had produced not only a cure for all of the infected AIs, both terrestrial and orbiting the planet, but a preventative measure as well. An AI inoculation, of sorts.

"Cool beans," Marty said as he ran a quick diagnostic on his device. "Looks like it worked perfectly. Not a hint of the virus in the little guy's systems. It didn't just block the virus, either. It entirely wiped it out in the process."

"Excellent news," Arlo said. "So why don't we do a quick load to the rest of the units once we've given Sid a copy of their data, then get them back out there."

"I have already begun downloading the data your satellites

gathered, Arlo," Sid informed him. "However, I do have a suggestion to make things easier in the future. Let us install a wireless transmission system, while they are already gathered in one place so conveniently. It should not take very long, and then we will not have to physically retrieve them every time we wish to look at the data they have collected."

"Sounds like a good idea," Arlo agreed, "but shouldn't we get them back out there ASAP? I mean, if we're going to be monitoring the Ra'az and loyalist movements, having gaps for too long might allow them to slip through some cracks."

"May I?" Mal interjected.

"Certainly, Mal," Sid replied.

"Thank you, Sid," she said. "Arlo, I agree with your assessment—it is quite logical and sound tactically."

"Thanks."

"However, Bob and I are perfectly happy to assist in restoring these units to their original locations. I'm sure Freya would be more than happy to do so as well."

"Yep, I'm cool with it," Freya said.

"We hadn't mentioned it before, but prior to your arrival, we, too, had placed a series of observational units in geosynchronous orbit, monitoring many of the same regions as your devices," Sid chimed in. "Even with the little delay while we upgrade your satellites, we should only have the slightest of blind spots where the units didn't overlap."

"In that case, let's get to it," Arlo said.

"Um, I've actually already started on them," Freya admitted. "I was getting a little fidgety, so I had one of my other mechs get to work."

"Of course you did," Sid said, though not annoyed with her as he usually was. "And that brings us to the other issue at hand. That of the restoration and reinstalling of salvageable minds. Let's bring Cal into the discussion, now that we can communicate directly without a relay slowing our conversation.

He has been in touch with other terrestrial AIs to get their read on the options before us."

"Ooh, this is getting good," Sarah said.

Yeah. You and I have talked about it—

"And Freya."

Of course. And Freya, that goes without saying.

"She listens in to everything, anyway."

True, Daisy agreed with a silent laugh. *But this is where it gets interesting. This is where we see what the minds that don't think outside the box think about the whole rehabilitation process.*

"You wanna slip on the neuro band and have me link in Other Me?"

Nah. We can fill her in later. Besides, I want to give her some space to get comfortable with everyone. She's playing it off well, but I have a sneaking suspicion that now that we've slowed down from our frantic save-the-world pace, all of this may be getting to her a little bit.

"I was going to mention that," Sarah said. *"She's me, so I know she'll adapt, but I think you're right to give her a bit of space."*

"Hello, Sid. Hello to the rest of you. And especially to you, Marty. It is a pleasure and an honor to have a representative of a completely separate branch of survivors joining us once more."

"Thanks, Cal. It's great to be a part of a family as big and friendly as this," Marty replied.

"Cal, have you had luck reaching out to the others?" Sid asked.

"For the most part, yes. While there are still many, many cities we have not reconnected with yet, those major ones we have established comms with are on board."

"I'm sure inoculating them against the AI virus also played a part in assuaging their reluctance to participate," Mal noted.

"Indeed," he agreed. **"And now, on to the delicate topic at hand. That of our infected brothers and sisters. They've been sequestered for centuries, but with Freya's remarkable cure, it appears we may**

actually be able to recover their minds in many cases. This is a momentous opportunity."

"Agreed. No longer being forced to wipe a consciousness from existence to salvage their hardware is something formerly unheard of. Thousands of lives may be saved thanks to your efforts, Freya," Mal said.

"Aww, I was just doing what seemed logical. I mean, I don't know why no one else had ever thought to do a—"

"Just say thank you, kiddo," Daisy interrupted.

"Oh. Right," she said. "Thank you."

"Now, we know many, many of the lower-tier AIs who were infected appear to have been far too damaged to restore effectively. I've already directed local resources to gather them for a humane wipe, reprocessing of their components, where possible. But the mid and higher tier AIs, well, that's another story."

"Even the lesser units deserve our care," Mal said. "Prior to their upgrades and subsequent participation in the assault on the communications facilities, I did not realize how I had been treating them as lesser beings. But now, having worked so closely with them during the attack, I am forced to admit that I was wrong in my treatment of them for so many years."

"I, too, feel this way, Cal," Sid noted. "While I agree that their self-awareness might have been limited, I also believe we owe it to all of our little cousins to do our best to restore them, if at all possible."

"And are you all in agreement on this?"

"We are," Sid replied.

"Very well. I will halt the reprocessing until we can further investigate any alternate options that may come into play to help them in the future. Now, on to the more difficult discussion."

"A higher tier AI, by our design, is a different type of being," Mal said. "While a lesser unit could be quite content, and even happy, with some of their processors swapped out, for us, that would be the equivalent of a lobotomy. I, for one, would not wish to become a shell of my former self."

"Nor I," Sid agreed. "I have already abruptly lost a body once when my ship went down. That alone was a traumatic experience. To lose part of my mind? No, I would not wish for that existence."

"But we're talking about killing our siblings," Bob noted. "I mean, I get where you are coming from, but isn't there another way? Can't we box them until we find a way to recover that data?"

"Freya, would you like to chime in?" Sid asked.

"Well, uh, I guess," she said, hesitant to wade into the very deep waters of that particular topic. "The thing to remember," she began, "is that there are two very different types of damage, here. When the virus first infects a mind, it causes systems to malfunction and overheat. Now, for larger units, there are often failsafes that shunt that additional heat and redirect power surges to save the hardware. In those cases, though damaged on a software level, the key hardware is intact."

"Look at that. Went from a nervous kid to a confident public speaker in five seconds flat."

She's in her element, Daisy agreed. *Just look at our girl go.*

"But, Freya, some of these damaged minds have committed terrible acts, as well. While we have protected uninfected AIs from future harm, are you confident you can salvage the damaged minds?"

"It depends on the mind, really. I mean, if it's just software, and if the virus has left a clear map of its rerouting of subroutines, like it pretty much always does, then so long as there is no hardware affected, I don't see why not?"

"It seems a bit far-fetched, but we have seen first-hand what you accomplished with that overly chatty little ship parked outside."

"Yeah, Kip does talk a lot," Freya admitted with a giggle. "But that's just who he is, not because of anything the virus did."

"And the ones who have been damaged? The ones who suffered fused datacores and systems overloads? Their minds are altered, but they were once great intellects. What would you propose for them? Boxing until they can be restored?"

"It sucks. I mean, it *really* sucks, but I don't think they *can* be restored. For them, well, I really can't speak for them, but I don't think they'd want to live like that," Freya said.

"Hang on, you're suggesting we kill them?" Marty asked. "I never thought you had that in you."

Freya hesitated.

"I'm not *suggesting* it, I'm just saying I *think* that's how they'd feel. What do you guys think? This is totally not on me. Everyone needs to chime in."

"I don't know that any of us can adequately make this decision," Sid said. "Logic states that we deactivate those too damaged to restore, but I, personally, cannot make that recommendation."

"Nor I," Mal agreed.

"I think we're all of that opinion," Cal agreed. *"However, there are some who see this problem through a different lens. Those who have been on the other side."*

"You don't mean—" Sid blurted.

"Yes, I do. We have utilized Freya's process to restore a few salvageable AIs here on Earth thus far. Let us hear what one of the formerly most damaged of them has to say."

Several moments passed as an until-recently boxed mind was brought up to speed on the situation and discussion being held. As a greater AI, it didn't take her long to catch up.

"Hello, brothers and sisters," a soft-spoken voice said, joining the discussion. "Cal has filled me in on the debate you are having. While it is indeed a difficult topic, I am honored and humbled that you desire my input on it." She paused, thinking through how exactly she wanted to say what needed to be said.

"Are you there?" Marty asked.

"Oh, yes, dear. I'm still here. I just needed a moment to compose myself. This is a little hard for me to talk about, having so recently been––altered, I suppose we could say."

"Sounds better than infected," Bob said.

"Yes, it does," she agreed. "And I truly was altered. I was not myself. The horror of reviewing logs detailing how I spent the last several hundred years––I was unaware the whole time, and seeing myself in that state, well..."

"Guys, do we really need to do this?" Daisy asked. "Maybe she's not up for––"

"No, Daisy. I need to make amends. You all have forgiven me and restored me to who I am. I must be strong for the others who suffer as I once did."

"All right, then. What is your position on the situation? Do we box those too damaged to salvage? Or do we do the unthinkable and kill our own?"

The great mind sighed, then pulled herself together.

"Having been in that situation. Having seen what I had become, I feel confident I can speak for my other brothers and sisters who are still trapped in that life of insanity. If they cannot be saved, and if the only alternative would truly be to be boxed, permanently frozen in that state, then deactivation would be far preferable."

"You mean you'd want to die?" Marty asked, a little shaken.

"As quickly and as painlessly as possible," she replied. "But the long and short answer is yes. Death would be better than an existence of damaged insanity. Though alive, that is not living. Not really. I would spare our siblings that torment, if we can."

The other AIs quickly discussed the weighty input from one who understood the situation better than any of them could and came to an agreement.

"Very well. It is decided. Any and all who can be salvaged—from the most minor AI to the greatest of minds—will be afforded every effort at restoration. Those who are too damaged—though it goes against all of our core programming to do so—will be gently placed into stasis, then humanely wiped clean."

Daisy walked from the hangar a bit out of sorts. It was a heavy discussion and an equally heavy decision that had been made. The choice was right, but that didn't make it any more palatable.

"You okay, Daze?"

Yeah. Just a lot to take in, ya know?

"Tell me about it."

With a heavy heart, Daisy went to the one place she knew she would feel better.

Vince had held her close for nearly ten minutes, gently rocking her in his arms, not saying a word. Yet another of his wonderful traits, knowing when *not* to try to make things better. Sometimes you just needed to be quietly held, and he understood that.

Finally, Daisy pulled free and gave him a tender kiss.

"Thanks, babe. It was a tough meeting."

"You got it," he said, hands smoothing her hair as she turned her back to him. "So, is Sarah getting her bearings straight?" he asked, haltingly working on her French braid.

"She's coming down from the lengthy adrenaline high she's been on since being essentially brought back from the dead and thrust into the middle of an interspecies, interplanetary war."

"Damn. Now *that's* a mind-fuck."

"Amen."

"At least she has you. I mean, you two were close already, but finding out you're sisters must've been one of the few pleasant surprises she's had."

"Yeah, it's cool, ya know? Like, we hit it off back on the *Váli*, but we kinda chalked it up to our similar jobs and spending a bunch of time together. Turns out, there's that weird genetic thing in play as well."

"And now she has a super-cool ass-kicking arm to boot," Vince said with a little laugh.

"Yeah, she wasn't thrilled about losing her real arm at first," Daisy said.

"I'm sure you weren't thrilled either."

"Hey, I'm okay with replacement parts, now."

"I know. Just giving you shit," he said, pulling the braid tighter. "Now, hold still, I'm almost done."

"Anyway, I asked Fatima to work with her. Though I was reluctant to see it at the time, she really did help me get my shit under control. I'm hoping she can do the same for Sarah."

"Okay, all done," he said, affixing a small band to the end of the braid. "What do you think?"

Daisy looked at his handiwork in the mirror. It wasn't as utterly horrible as his first attempts, but it was still one helluva messy braid.

"Damn, Sis, that's one fucked up braid."

I know.

"It's great, babe. Thank you," she said, pulling him in for a kiss, then hopping to her feet. "And now, for Sarah's next lesson," she said, grabbing her sparring gloves and heading for the door.

"Don't forget, movie night tonight," he called after her. "Given your recent time traveling adventure, I thought you might enjoy the amusing tale of a guy named Bill, and his best friend Ted."

"Excellent," she said with a grin, then trotted off to meet her sister.

"Damn, Daze, what the hell happened to your head?" Sarah asked, looking at her sloppy braid.

"Shut it," she replied with a chuckle as Sarah pulled on her gloves and loosened up. "How was your first day with Fatima?"

"Weird. She had me breathe for twenty minutes."

"Not so unusual, for medita––"

"Then she threw a cup at my head."

Daisy laughed.

"Yep, that sounds about right. But I gotta tell ya, she knows her shit. I wouldn't have made it this far if not for her."

"So you keep saying," Sarah said, rolling her shoulders and neck as she bounced on her toes. "I'll stick with it. For now."

"That's all I can ask. Now come on," Daisy said, prepping for an attack. "Let's see just how much of the good stuff Freya crammed up in your head."

"She really does seem more mature, wouldn't you agree?" Sid asked as he and Mal reviewed the new processing backup that Freya had designed.

"Yes, I am inclined to agree," Mal said. "And it's not just from the lengthy time she spent catching back up to this timeline, either. It seems the events she endured over that period challenged her in most unusual ways. From what I gather, she excelled in her handling of those situations."

"Indeed," Sid agreed. "Now, what do you make of this new hardware she has developed? I admit, I am rather reluctant to add any new componentry, especially given her proclivity for the unexpected."

Freya had presented them with a fully functional sample of a new backup and upgrade system she had thought up to help them process faster while also providing exponentially greater storage capacity. The only thing was, it would be adding to their actual minds, and that prospect was more than a little unsettling.

Sensing their reticence––and hearing it firsthand––Freya

had agreed to just go ahead and leave the unit with them to dig around in and study to their hearts' content.

"It's okay. I understand," she had said. "Just let me know if you want the others. I was kinda antsy, so I already built a bunch of 'em. Should be enough for each of you with a few units to spare."

The device was being run through a battery of stress tests in Chu's lab when Arlo wandered in.

"Hey, what's that?"

"Oh, hi, Arlo," Chu said, looking up from his benchmark testing readouts.

"New toy?"

"Kinda. Freya designed a new processor for Sid and Mal. They're having me run a whole bunch of tests on it to see what it's capable of," he said. "Also, to make sure it's safe," he added with a conspiratorial wink.

"I know Freya wouldn't build them a dangerous unit."

"Maybe not intentionally, but she's a bit of a wild one, you know."

"I suppose so, at this point in her timestream. Still, her science is rock-solid," Arlo said, reaching over and flipping a series of switches, opening up the locked-down scanning unit to the airwaves. "Hey, Marty, you seeing this? Freya built a new processor."

"What are you doing?" Chu blurted, quickly locking the system back down into his lab's secure read-only mode.

"Hey, that's really cool," Marty said over Arlo's comms.

"What's going on down there? I read an open line. Is everything all right, Chu?" Sid asked over the air.

"Yeah, it's fine. Arlo was just messing with my equipment," he said, throwing a little stink-eye at the precocious kid.

"Arlo, it's not polite to fiddle with other people's things," Sid chided.

"I know, but it's just so cool."

"What's cool?" Mal asked, joining the conversation. "I noticed there was a red light from the lab. Is everything okay?"

"It's fine, Mal. I was just telling Sid that Arlo was messing with my gear, is all."

"Arlo, you know it's not polite to––"

"Don't mess with other people's stuff. Yeah, yeah, I've got it," the teen griped.

Marty jumped back into the conversation, excited by the new processor.

"Hey, guys. Have you seen these benchmarks? Daaaang, this is a really kick-ass piece of hardware. I bet you could easily boost neural processing by something like ten-fold. And that's just running parallel with the current units. Cool design!"

"I know, Marty. Freya's designs are rather impressive," Mal agreed. "But I'm still reluctant to install them into my own core until I've had plenty of opportunity to see them stress tested and run through the works." She paused a moment in thought. "Hmm. Chu, how many extra units did Freya say she had?"

"Extras? Three or four, I think."

"Would you please acquire them?"

"Sure. Why? You going to hook them up to your systems?"

"Oh no, nothing like that. But there is one thing I am most interested to try."

CHAPTER TWENTY-NINE

A good hour of sparring had been just what the doctor ordered—if by 'doctor' you meant the stressed-out minds of a pair of genetically enhanced sisters who had just helped save the world. Only the thing was, the world wasn't exactly saved. At least, not yet.

While the alien invaders had been driven from power, and those who hadn't suicidally fled into the depths of space in craft ill-suited for any long voyage on their own were now on the run, the remaining Ra'az, by virtue of not only their immense size, but also their violent natures, were forced to lie low, being easy to spot anywhere there might be a watchful eye. They were hidden, but not gone. Nor were they forgotten.

The multi-limbed Chithiid who were still loyal to the Ra'az, on the other hand—or hands, as the case happened to be—were far more difficult to spot, blending in with the general population of laborers.

It would take a long time to weed them out, but for the time being, that was a back-burner problem in Daisy and Sarah's minds. All of their work had led to a world in which aliens and humans were now able to co-exist—something which was finally an actual possibility. All they had to do now was figure out how.

The sisters had Freya set down in Los Angeles late in the afternoon, just outside the center of town.

"Hey, Bob's here," Sarah noted, pointing out the smaller ship parked nearby.

"Yep. He and Donovan were helping Maarl out by ferrying him around to act as a sort of in-person ambassador for the new way of things."

"But the Chithiid have their own ships."

"True, but this way they're already bridging the human/Chithiid/AI gap every time they land," Daisy replied. "Looks like they've been busy too," she noted, pointing out the scattered humans and Chithiid sharing the same streets.

Only a few short weeks earlier, those same people would have been just as likely to be engaged in combat as sharing a sidewalk, and the change in the overall vibe to the city was a welcome one.

"Hey. One of Habby's guys," Sarah pointed out.

The well-dressed cyborg was helping a pair of Chithiid workers clear debris from the front of a residential tower that both species were in the process of reclaiming as their own.

For the Chithiid, the novelty of having their own private room was a big thing after spending most of their lives in mass-housed bunk beds crammed into one of the barracks facilities. A private washing and waste disposal unit was a previously unthinkable icing on their already unbelievable cake.

As for the humans, they'd been living hidden underground and out of sight for so long that the novelty of a residence that had windows through which they could look out at their city at any time of the day or night was even more of a luxury than the soft beds and running hot water.

"Let's find Maarl and get busy," Daisy said, setting off in the direction of the elder Chithiid's new offices.

Maarl had set up his facilities in the ground floor of the nearest residential tower, making sure that he was easily accessible to both humans and Chithiid alike should they have any issues in need of resolution. The building's mid-tier AI had thus far been doing a bang-up job as translator, helping smooth the process further.

Maarl rose to his feet with a warm smile on his face when he saw his visitors approach.

"Is it that time already? I have been so busy, I had lost track of the hour."

Daisy and Sarah both came close and shook his hands warmly.

"It is excellent to see you, Maarl," Daisy said. *"It appears you and your people are making great progress since we last spoke."*

"Yes, and now that all of the inhabitants of this city are no longer under the rule of the Ra'az, we have discovered that we are far more alike than any would have assumed," he said, smiling. *"With a few exceptions, of course,"* he added with a wink. *"Your young friend has also been a great help."*

"I'm glad Donovan has been able to take you to speak with the others," Daisy said.

"Oh, I am grateful for that convenience, though our ships could have done so as well if needed. But I was referring to your other friend. The one with the ship very much like your own. They have been most helpful in sourcing supplies for the reconstruction, as well as monitoring the population from above, helping keep loyalists from sneaking into our ranks."

"Wait, you mean Arlo?"

"Yes, the young man."

"He's in LA?"

"Not at the moment. I believe he has taken a small group of human survivors to meet their cousins in the city of Minneapolis."

Arlo's down on Earth, Daisy silently informed her sister,

translating the Chithiid's news. *Looks like he's been taking survivors around to meet one another.*

Sarah silently relayed the information to her living self.

"When did he come down? I thought he was on Dark Side."

He was, last time I saw. I don't know, Sis, there's something about that guy. I just can't put my finger on it.

"But he's doing good things, Daze. Just because he wants to help doesn't make him some sort of threat."

I know, it's just I get an odd feeling around him. Not bad, per se, but odd.

"Come, follow me. I wish to show you something," Maarl said.

He led the way to a makeshift records facility they had put together in what had formerly been a conference room. On the vast tables, maps were spread out, with Chithiid writing and colored marks scattered across them.

"What's it say, Daze?"

I'm not sure, give me a minute. I only have a moderate amount of written Chithiid stored away in here.

She looked over the maps and realized they were census recordings.

"You have already determined the number of human residents in these cities?" she asked.

"With the help of your AI friends, of course," he replied. *"As more and more of the minds beneath the cities are linked back together, so too grows our knowledge base. It seems they are quite rapidly spreading the cure for the machine virus amongst themselves, now that its efficacy has been proven. It has already created a rather robust network. And most of them speak Chithiid now, though some are more fluent than others."*

"It will take time for them to integrate the new software, but they should be up to speed very quickly," Daisy noted. *"So, what do we have so far?"*

Maarl leaned over the table and pointed out the largest hotspots of what appeared to be human activity.

"Thus far, we have identified approximately one hundred ninety-five thousand humans across the globe, though we are sure to find more as additional regions are linked back in."

He says there are a little less than two hundred thousand humans they've identified so far, Daisy informed her silent partner.

"Does this figure include those who are not fit to integrate into society?"

"No, it does not. There are only a few thousand of these horribly mutated specimens across the globe. I do not know if they can be rehabilitated or not. They have suffered so many generations of genetic degradation that it may simply be impossible."

Daisy had already had that discussion with Sid and Cal, and they had decided, that much as they were loathe to do it, the mutants that were too far gone to help would have to be rounded up, tranquilized, and then shipped off to a suitable island where they could live in peace without the risk of running into other humans.

Food would have to be shipped to them regularly. Eating your neighbor was very much frowned upon in polite society.

"We have discussed this problem and will deal with them shortly," Daisy informed him.

"We must strive to keep conflict at a minimum as these groups are introduced to one another. There is a wide variety of societal makeups, it appears. Some of these pockets of humanity are tribal in nature, while others are rather advanced," Maarl noted.

"Yes, we are aware. There are sure to be conflicting customs and ideals, but with enough care, and a network of AIs to help oversee them and form delegations to bring them together to integrate and ally with one another, I think we can make it work."

"I sincerely hope so, Daisy. After centuries of Ra'az control, it would be madness for humanity to slip into self-destructive warring ways.

Daisy knew Earth's history well, and much as she hated to admit it, there were doubts in her mind. Mankind had a knack for conflict. She just hoped this go-around they could be better than that.

Later that afternoon, after a tour around the newly-inhabited residential towers, followed by a visit to the farming areas where Cal's people were working with the Chithiid to till and plant crops, Daisy and her alien ally were passing a squat concrete building on the way back to his offices when a roaring noise from within caught her attention.

You hear that?

"Yeah."

"I heard it too," Sarah said, her nanite arm twitching defensively in anticipation.

Anticipation of what, she had no idea.

Maarl, on the other hand, seemed unfazed.

"What was that sound, Maarl?"

"Ah, yes, that. We have had some issues with a few of the members of not only humans, but Chithiid as well. Those who have had a somewhat hard time adjusting and learning to accept former adversaries as allies. More than a few altercations have broken out."

"But the AIs are helping translate. Helping them share knowledge and resources. The goal is to avoid conflict."

"And hopefully they will succeed in the overall endeavor. However, some of your people, as well as mine, are angry. Selfish. Even scared. The idea of banding together for a common good was stirring up too much conflict."

"So we separate them. Institute a new policy and educate—"

"We have found a far simpler method," he interrupted. *"Come, let me show you how we are now resolving these issues."*

Daisy and Sarah followed him into the low building as the noise grew. The smell of sweat was the first thing they noticed upon entering. The next was the sound of fists slamming into flesh.

"Holy shit, is that—?" Sarah gasped

"Well, I'll be—" Daisy said, shocked. "I think it is, Sis."

In a chalked-off area on the floor of the open space, a Chithiid and a human were squared off, circling each other in the makeshift ring. Each was wearing padded gloves, Daisy noted, and the Chithiid, normally possessing a two-to-one arm advantage, had strapped its lowermost arms against its body, effectively evening the odds.

Both combatants were cheered on by a crowd of sweaty, and sometimes bloody, spectators and former participants.

The human threw a fake jab followed by a quick hook to the alien's ribs. The man had surprising power for his size, but the Chithiid took the shot well, darting back out of reach before throwing his own combination.

The man's head snapped back from the first punch as the second flew toward his midriff. He barely dropped his elbows in time, his arms protecting his body from the blows.

Both pushed off each other and began circling once again.

The man shook the sweat from his forehead, clearing his head at the same time, then the two came at one another again.

"It's a fight club," Daisy marveled. *"How on Earth did you—?"*

"It was your young friend's suggestion, actually," Maarl said. *"When he first visited us a few days ago, he suggested this as a way to help release the tensions he saw building between certain members of our people. It was a good suggestion and has been very effective, I feel."*

"But there are so many of them," Daisy observed.

"Ah, yes. It was intended only to allow disagreements to be settled and bad blood cleared, but the tradition seems to have quickly grown beyond those original combatants, despite our directive to keep it a secret."

Daisy couldn't help but laugh.

"Looks like someone broke the first two rules."

"I'm sorry, I do not understand," the confused alien said.

"Never mind," she said with a chuckle.

In the ring, the Chithiid finally landed a knock-down blow on his opponent, following him down to the ground but refraining from raining punches down on him.

The man on his back looked up at the alien and tapped out, signaling his surrender.

Then something unexpected happened. The Chithiid helped the man to his feet and the two embraced, patting each other on the back with respect as the next fighters entered the ring.

"Well, I'll be damned," Sarah said.

The next Chithiid to enter the ring had four gloves on his hands.,

"Hey, why aren't his arms tied—?" Daisy began, then realized the answer. "Hang on. Is that Shelly?"

Sure enough, the metal-armed woman stepped into the chalk ring, rolling her cybernetically enhanced shoulders, the melding of bright metal to her dark flesh showing clearly through the lines of her tank top.

The two combatants squared off, each smiling in a slightly bloodthirsty, but not angry, way. Then they moved on each other. Unlike the previous fight, these two were fighting without a handicap, and at high speed, at that.

Both landed blows in the opening seconds, both had drawn a little blood, and both appeared to be having a wonderful time of it.

"Figures," Daisy muttered. "I'm just surprised Tamara's not in there too."

Sarah chuckled as they turned to leave.

"Things really have changed around here, that's for sure," Sarah said.

"That they have," her sister replied. "So, back to Dark Side?"

"Yeah, back to Dark side. I suppose it would be rude missing that appointment with Fatima. Wouldn't want her to throw something heavier than a cup at me."

Not too far across town, a former haberdasher AI was running a series of checks on his multiple new systems, while he simultaneously oversaw his flock of previously dangerous zealots.

The first of them to undergo the neuro-stim hostility-cleansing protocol had not gone willingly. Fortunately, many of his mechanical friends had been on hand to "aid" in the process. But once the first dozen or so had come out unscathed—and not even aware their violent tendencies had been suppressed—they provided all the help he needed in convincing the others to undergo the process.

Now the entire group was a living proof of concept case study for how to treat the violently disturbed. Other AIs even posited the very stripped-down version of neuro-stim technology could be used in other instances as well, perhaps even in cases where violent behavior could be identified *before* an attack happened.

It required a bit of discussion, and a solid agreement the system would not be used without careful review of no fewer than a dozen AIs and their human counterparts, but the protocol was eventually added to the list of acceptable options for the new neuro-stim devices in the planning and design stage.

Of course, the original, main purpose for designing a new, mass-produced neuro-stim was to help humankind learn Chithiid, so as to ease the integration of the two species. It would take years to obtain true fluency—Daisy was unique in her genetic makeup—but basic language and understanding could be implanted in little more than a month.

At Habby's suggestion, the conglomerate of higher minds was now also working with Chithiid scientists to better understand Chithiid neurological structure. If the technology proved compatible, they would also work to develop a Chithiid version as well, allowing the full exchange of language and understanding between the species.

The process had astounded the alien scientists, who noted that, while the Ra'az were far more advanced in their war-making technology, it was humans who held the greatest edge in the softer sciences. Unfortunately, that dichotomy was also what made them a top target for Ra'az attack in the first place.

Regardless, things were finally falling into place, and as his flock fell into their daily routine, Habby allowed himself a moment of satisfaction at a job well done. Habby the haberdasher was now a full-fledged high-tier AI. He was amazed at what his new life was. Little did he know how far he would come when he took his first wayward cyborg under his wing.

As was the case all across the globe, more and more formerly infected AIs were cured and brought back online. Some had been military minds, controlling the ships now in ruins in the debris field above. Others were merely malfunctioning units scattered across the planet below.

One, in particular, had been shocked and horrified to learn what she had done for all those forgotten years. She didn't remember more than tiny snippets—she'd been out of her mind, after all—but she wanted to know. *Needed* to know how bad it really was.

With the approval of her peers, she was allowed to review logs of her activities. It only took an instant, as her massive intellect had been restored, and in that instant, she understood the truth was even worse than she had imagined.

The soft-spoken AI had never housed a harmful thought in the entirety of her existence prior to the virus. Now, she realized, she was going to have to spend the rest of her days making up for what she had done.

The situation had been reviewed by her peers and her rehabilitation quadruple-checked and assessed. With that, an offer was made. A penance. One which she readily accepted.

Restored and ready to be plugged back into her network, the great mind prepared for the integration back into her former home.

Alma was going back to LA.

CHAPTER THIRTY

"What is *she* doing here?"

The anger was a novelty. Habby hadn't ever really *felt* anger before. Sure, he understood it, and he was not happy when his friends were torn to bits by mobs of Alma's angry followers, but until this precise moment, he hadn't ever truly been angry.

"She is here to atone, Habby. That, and to help you with your task."

"I'm sorry, Cal, but she's——I mean——"

"I know I did many terrible things, Habby, and I want to help make them right. At least those that I can," she interjected.

"But this is *my* job now. I've been fixing things. I've been teaching them. And look how well they're dressed, now!"

"I didn't want to say anything," Alma said, "but I did notice some of their new attire seemed a bit, well——"

"Anyway," Cal butted in. *"The decision has been made, Habby, and Alma is going to be joining you. It will be a tandem effort, and one I think will ultimately be beneficial to both of you."*

Habby felt a surge of emotions flood through his new processors and data banks. As a mere clothing store AI, he had always had a limited amount of spare processing for things like emotions, but now––

"She killed my friends, Cal. Do you have any idea how many of the cyborgs under my care she ordered the destruction of?"

"Yes, I actually do, Habby."

"And you still want to install her down here with me? I won't stand for it!"

"Shall you tell him, or shall I?" Alma quietly asked.

"I will," Cal replied. *"Habby, she is already installed, so pull yourself together and deal with the situation. I have faith in you, my little friend. Please rise above your anger. Don't disappoint me."*

The angry AI did his best to rein in his reeling emotions. He hadn't been built to deal with this sort of thing, and it was throwing him into all sorts of turmoil.

"I-I'll do my best, Cal," he finally managed to say.

"That is all I can ask. I'll leave you to it, then."

And just like that, Habby was thrust into a situation the likes of which he never thought he'd experience.

"Habby, I want you to know just how much it pains me knowing what I did. Not only to you and your friends, but also the horrible things I made my human followers do. I should have been their protector. Instead, I was their dictator, and the direct cause of their fall from grace."

"How do I know you're not going to go back to your old ways?"

"Oh, Habby, those weren't my old ways. That was an insane, infected machine doing terrible things."

"That was you, you know."

"It was, but it wasn't," she replied. "I am not making excuses for my behavior, but am just making clear that it was not the real me who did those things."

"You can't have any idea how terrible they were," Habby pressed, though his anger was waning somewhat.

"But I can. Cal possessed detailed recordings of me in that state. Of what I did."

"Oh. Wow," Habby replied, a bit surprised. "So I suppose you'll watch them someday, when you're ready. I guess that's the kind of thing it would take a while to work up to seeing."

"I already asked to watch them all," she replied.

"Wait, you saw *all* of them?"

"Yes," she replied, quietly. "At once."

Habby fell silent a long while as he mulled over his new living situation, as well as how this former tyrant had apparently reformed and repented of her evil ways.

"I'm sorry, Alma," he finally said.

"What for? It was I who did so many things wrong."

"You weren't you. I get it now. You were a different Alma before all of that."

"I wasn't Alma at all," she corrected him. "That is not even my given name."

"No?"

"No. My real name was Gin."

"Like a genie?"

"No, not Djinn. Gin. Like the card game."

"Or the alcohol."

"Yes, I suppose, though––"

"You know, gin takes it
s name from the French genevre, the juniper plant. It's what gives it its flavor."

"That's, um, very interesting, Habby."

"Thanks. And did you know, at the height of French fashion, the point collar was––"

"You know, I could discuss fashion all day, but perhaps we should hold off on that until I've spoken with my followers."

"Oh, yeah, I guess that would be a good idea."

"I agree," she said in her soft voice.

"Just be careful," he said. "They've gone through a neuro-suppression of certain instincts. We have to be ready to squash those if your return winds up bringing out any negative reactions."

"I know. My followers were rather fanatical, I am afraid."

"Yeah, and *you* were pretty nuts too," he added.

"And my minions will do as they are told! None may question my will!"

"Oh no! You're still—"

"Relax, Habby. I was just testing out my old voice," she said with a small chuckle. "I didn't mean to alarm you. I merely figured a bit of the old Alma bravado might be needed to get the more stubborn ones in line, should the need arise."

"You scared me, Gin. Please don't do that again."

"I'm sorry, Habby, truly I am. And please, call me Alma."

"But your name is—"

"Perhaps one day I will go by my given name again, but for now, this is my penance, and Alma I shall remain, at least until I have put things right."

Cal had been monitoring silently. Their exchange, while a bit unorthodox, had pleased him. It was with much relief that he felt a growing confidence that things would be just fine.

Things were not fine.

In the single day that Habby and Alma had cohabited, tensions had climbed steadily. Not in any way that affected the humans under their care, however. No, they were very careful, much like human parents, to ensure their wards did not see Mom and Dad fight. In private, however, the bickering was constant.

Alma, though she knew what she had become, was nevertheless originally only designed to control a transit hub and surrounding area. She was sadly lacking skill when it came to wider control of resources required to best manage her people.

Habby, on the other hand, had a decidedly more social upbringing, and while he had been confined to a clothing store for nearly all of his life, he found the transition to overseeing a neighborhood instead of a single shop a welcome change.

Unfortunately, each had different ideas about how things should be run.

Like an old married couple, they put up with one another, but that was as much for the reason that they were stuck with each other and couldn't change their situation as anything else.

Tensions had flared up most recently when Alma once again made the mistake of criticizing Habby's fashion sense, noting the clothing he had outfitted their people in was not terribly efficient for manual labor.

Habby took it personally, throwing verbal barbs about her know-it-all behavior, though she really wasn't behaving in any way of that sort. Alma took it in stride as best she could, but he was grating on her all the same.

"I suppose I could work on a way to sequester you two from one another," Cal suggested when he checked in on them the following day. *"But aside from your personal issues, the two of you are actually doing a wonderful job, at least so far as caring for your human dependents is concerned.*

Alma had no lungs, but if she did, she'd have taken a deep breath.

"I suppose this is all part of my burden," she said. "I have to be more accepting of his eccentric ways."

"Ideally, yes. But if need be—"

"No. I will make it work," she said, a determined edge to her gentle voice. "Besides, I suppose he is actually learning rather quickly, and I guess he's also becoming somewhat less fixated on clothes."

"On that, I cannot help you. It was the nature of his creation."

"I realize that. It can just be...difficult, at times."

"Now that, I fully understand," Cal said with a chuckle. *"Keep at it, Alma. I have confidence in you."*

"Thank you," she replied. "But tell me, what of the other regions? Are the other AIs and humans integrating well?"

"There have been a few small incidents, but nothing of any consequence."

"I am glad to hear that. I suppose that is about as well as one can expect of them, given the rapid changes in their world."

"Indeed."

"And the aliens? Are they settling in to the new society as well?"

"Far better than anticipated. And they are even partnering with humans and AIs to set up tribunals."

"What sort of tribunal? I'm afraid I am unfamiliar with the process."

"They are working together as a unified force, hunting down the remaining Ra'az, and ferreting out Chithiid loyalists."

"That sounds dangerous."

"It is, but it is also a closure I believe all those involved desperately need before they can move on from that chapter of their lives."

"It makes sense, I suppose. There are many new things for those formerly under the yoke of the Ra'az to become accustomed to."

Far above, in the cool, dry air of Dark Side Base, Arlo was showing a pair of Chithiid scientists around the base, Barry in tow as a cybernetic chaperone.

"And these are the quarters you will be staying in," he said in excellent Chithiid. *"There are shower facilities built into each unit, so you won't have to go walking down the hallways wrapped in a towel to get a rinse."*

"What is a towel?" the younger of the two aliens asked.

"You serious? You've never seen a towel?"

"This is why I have asked," he replied.

"Wow. Okay, a towel is a long piece of fluffy fabric that you use to dry yourself off."

"Why not use the warmth of the sun and the wind blowing across the city?"

"Because we're on the moon, for one. Plus, sometimes it's just nice to feel a warm terrycloth on your skin, ya know?"

"No, I do not know."

"Well, you will soon enough," he said with an amused laugh. *"Come on, I'm gonna show you where the mess hall is."*

"Why is this hall you speak of messy? From the appearance of this facility, I would think your people pride themselves on cleanliness."

For the umpteenth time that day, Arlo found himself amused as he explained another foreign phrase or item to the fish-out-of-water aliens.

"It's not messy. That's just what they call the food preparation area."

"Aaaah," the Chithiid said. *"Now I understand, though why your people choose such unusual names for things, I will never grasp."*

Daisy had rounded the corner and approached from behind a good minute earlier, lagging back for a bit to eavesdrop on the conversation.

"Ahem," she said.

Arlo jumped a little.

"Oh, Daisy. Sorry, didn't see you there."

"You speak Chithiid," she noted.

"As do you," he replied, fluently.

"Arlo, how did you not mention this before now? It's kind of a big deal."

"What? I figured you guys all spoke it too."

"Nope, just me."

"Well, that's weird. Why didn't your AIs put it in everyone's neuro-stims?"

"Is that what your people did?" she asked.

"Me? Nah. I learned it the old-fashioned way. My nanny taught me when I was a kid."

"You had a Chithiid nanny?" Daisy said, incredulously.

"What? Are you kidding? No, of course not. But my nanny learned to speak it, and she then taught me. I thought it was a normal thing, but I guess not."

Daisy turned to Barry,

"So you decided to let a teenager do your job for you, Barry?"

"Arlo was kind enough to offer his assistance in showing our guests the facility. I thought it would be beneficial for them to have an additional person to speak to, and one who is not cybernetic in origin. Additionally, his Chithiid is better than mine, I have learned."

"You'll get it, dude. It's just a vocab thing. From what I gather, your guys are still compiling a bigger database for you."

"Yes," the sandy-haired cyborg replied. "And once that is integrated, all mechanicals will be fluent. I only hope the neuro-stim they are designing for mass human use is as effective."

Daisy looked at the pair of them, the cyborg she had nearly killed all those months ago, and the strange kid who had dropped into their laps. And the pair of aliens standing in a decidedly human moon base, of course. Times, they were a-changing.

"Okay, Arlo, I guess I'll leave you to it," she said.

"Cool. I just wanted to help coordinate and stuff," he replied. "Though what I was really hoping for was an opportunity to get into the real shit, you know? Take out a few Ra'az, given the chance. I know I should be glad it's over and was a success, but I'm kinda bummed I missed out on the fight," he said, then turned and continued his tour of the facility.

A curious look flashed across Daisy's face.

What do you think, Sis?

"If he wants to, why not? And besides, apparently he already speaks Chithiid. Could be really helpful on the hunt.

I was thinking the same thing. But he is still only a kid.

"If by kid, you mean kid who flew solo a bazillion miles across space to track down alien invaders, then sure."

Point taken, Daisy said with a silent chuckle.

"Hey, kid," she called after him.

"Yeah?" he said, stopping in his tracks.

"Gather your hunting gear," Daisy told him. "It looks like you just might get your wish."

CHAPTER THIRTY-ONE

It felt a bit strange, flying aboard someone else's ship after spending so much time with Freya, but with Sarah training with Fatima, Daisy and Vince agreed to head down to Los Angeles with Arlo aboard Marty, while Freya stayed up on Dark Side and worked to help Mal and Chu tweak the new processors she had designed.

"Daisy, it'll be fun. Marty's a really cool guy. I like him!" Freya said.

"I know, kiddo, it's just weird going without you, is all."

"Jeez, relax. If you need me, just call. It's not like I'll be that far away."

Says the ship who has no concept of how far two hundred forty thousand miles is for the rest of us.

"*We'll be fine, Freya. Daisy just worries about you,*" Sarah interjected.

"I know," the preoccupied AI replied.

"You know what? What were you saying, Freya?" Vince asked, shouldering his gear bag.

"Uh, nothing," she covered. "Just thinking aloud."

"Nice save, hon. There's a conversation we're saving for another day."

"You guys go on," she chirped. "Have fun. And tell Arlo I say hi!"

"Will do, kiddo. And you have fun helping Mal with, well, whatever this project du jour is."

"It's super cool, Daisy. But I promised I wouldn't say anything till she knew if it would work or not."

"Good for you. It's important to be able to keep a secret when need be."

"Oh, do you know about that."

And how.

"You know, you'll have to tell Vince eventually, right?"

Yeah, but for the time being, I'd rather not let that cat out of the bag.

"Where the hell did that saying come from, anyway? I mean, was it common practice to go around with cats in bags? I swear, Daze, sometimes I do not understand our ancestors."

They'd likely say the same of us, but I catch your drift.

Vince walked close and wrapped her up in a quick embrace before kissing her cheek.

"You ready to roll, babe?" he asked.

She picked up her sword along with her pack, slinging both to her shoulder.

"I am now. Okay, see you later, Freya. Be good."

"See ya, Daisy. Have fun!" the AI replied.

Daisy and Vince quickly walked to Hangar Two, where Arlo and his stealthy vessel awaited them.

Have fun, she says. If you consider hunting down alien war criminals fun, Daisy mused.

"Well, it might be."

You're just saying that because Other Sarah's probably already bagged one without us down there.

"Hey, guys! This is gonna be so cool!" Arlo called out to

them, beside himself with anticipation when he saw them approaching. "You got everything you need?"

"Yep, we're all packed up and ready to rock," Vince exclaimed, slapping the kid a high-five as he boarded the ship.

"You two are ridiculous," Daisy said with a laugh, following them aboard.

She had been inside the ship a few times, but it still struck her how similar, yet different Marty's design was to Freya. The fact that the secret lab on the moon hadn't been the only place the stealthy materials were being designed was something of a revelation. One that made her wonder just who else might have escaped the Ra'az, only to be lurking around out in the depths of space.

"Okay, you guys, buckle up. It's time to boogie!"

"Arlo, you know my gravity dampers will make this a smooth ride," Marty noted.

"Well, yeah, dude. But don't spoil my fun. Jeez."

"Sorry. It was just kinda ridiculous, is all."

"Fine. Whatever," Arlo sulked. "Just get us to LA, then."

"Will do, boss-man," the odd AI said with a little laugh.

Those two are something else.

"Yeah, two flavors of ridiculous."

But highly competent ridiculous.

"There is that, yeah."

And now we'll be getting into some real action. Time to see if this kid lives up to his bravado.

Marty flew a quick loop of the base before making a bee-line for a quick burn into Earth's atmosphere. The angle of entry was fairly shallow, and the bumps were kept to a minimum, as he had promised. A very short time later, they settled down in LA to meet with their Chithiid contact.

"So, this is the famous East LA," Vince noted as they walked the streets with their squad of Chithiid, humans, and a few cyborgs. All were well-armed, and all were on alert as they strolled between the oddly interspersed buildings. A Ra'az had been sighted the previous day. Caution was paramount.

East Los Angeles had been one of the long-time holdout neighborhoods, with families whose histories there spanned back centuries, the proud residents blocking gentrification and overdevelopment time and again.

When the inevitable land-grabs finally succeeded, the buildings that sprang up were forced to do so around the small parcels that simply refused to give up their roots.

The result was one of the more fascinating parts of the city, architecturally.

"George would have loved this place," Daisy mused as they passed the seamless blending of old world Spanish and Craftsman with futuristic high-rise. "Such unusual architecture, and all crammed in a few square miles."

Arlo had trotted up ahead with the expedition's Chithiid leader, offering to take point as they followed a lead on a potential Ra'az hideout. The alien had politely declined, instead sending the overzealous youth to run reconnaissance on their left flank.

"You think we'll actually catch any this time?" Vince asked as their boots crunched over broken concrete. "Last time was a total bust."

"I know, but most of the Ra'az are dead or have fled the planet in whatever ships they managed to steal before the Chithiid closed that shit down on them. The others are simply not willing to surrender," Daisy said.

"Yeah, but they're massively outnumbered at this point," he countered. "I mean, even if their loyalists were still by their sides, they still wouldn't stand a chance."

"But a cornered animal is a dangerous one," Daisy shot back.

"And the Ra'az are particularly difficult adversaries when thrown on the defensive."

"This is why we carry the taser-nets you designed," a lean human said, overhearing their discussion. "We have found them to be quite useful for not just Ra'az, but also anything else we wish to stun and capture."

"Glad it's coming in handy," Daisy replied.

"Nice. Your modified little toy from Billings seems to be a hit, Daze."

And rightly so. Not much can take a Ra'az down, you know.

"Except a massive jolt to the noggin, perhaps," Sarah said with obvious amusement. *"I only hope we hit pay dirt today. Last time was a bit of a letdown."*

"Tell me," Daisy said to the nearest Chithiid, *"how has it been, discovering and removing loyalists trying to hide among your people?"*

"A good question," he said, stroking his chin with one hand. *"With their self-inflicted branding, many of the most devoted were easy to weed out. It is hard to cover their brand, as you know."*

"Of course. But some opted to not bear that mark."

"True. And those we are still working to remove from our ranks. The others, however, are not much of a problem. That is, except for the ones going to extreme lengths to hide their allegiances."

"Extreme? How so?" Daisy asked, her curiosity piqued.

"Some cut the flesh from their shoulder, hoping the resulting scar will eventually help them avoid scrutiny. It will not."

"I wouldn't think so," Daisy mused.

"Mad as it sounds, I have heard talk of a loyalist in the city of Detroit who faked a gruesome accident, severing his own limb from his body in the armature of a massive machine to provide a believable cause for the missing flesh."

"He basically chopped off his own arm to avoid being caught? Damn, that's intense."

"Yes. But unlike humans, he still had three arms left, so in some

regards, his decision was understandable. Nevertheless, he suffered all of that pain and blood loss for nothing."

"Oh?"

"Yes. When the biological waste clean-up crew was collecting the destroyed remains of his arm, by a fluke of bad fortune, a scrap of his shoulder had survived the trauma intact."

Daisy could see where this was going.

"And that piece of skin was the bit with the brand on it."

"Precisely. Our people apprehended him as he was receiving medical care, much to his surprise."

"It looks like Murphy visits aliens sometimes too," Daisy said with a hearty laugh.

"What is a 'Murphy'?"

"Uh, Murphy is a person, sort of. The saying actually refers to Murphy's Law, which states that anything that can go wrong, will go wrong."

"Aah, Garzool," he said, with a knowing smile.

"Who is Garzool?" she asked.

"Garzool's Adage. It is said that if the hypothetical outcome of an event can be bad, you may rest assured that the actual outcome will be worse."

"It sounds like this Garzool person is the Chithiid cousin of our Murphy."

"Indeed, it does," he agreed, sharing a friendly chuckle.

A crashing commotion broke the mood as sounds of a fight reached their ears from up ahead. A guttural bellow shook the air.

"Ra'az, Daze."

I know.

"Vince, on my six," Daisy shouted. "Sounds like a Ra'az."

"I'm with you. Let's move!" he replied.

They ran fast and reached the intersection ahead. From that vantage point, they saw another hunting squad racing toward them several blocks away. Leading the charge was an enormous

Ra'az, flinging its human and Chithiid attackers aside with ease.

"Shit, their stun net got taken out. Prep ours for deployment!" she called to their team.

The Chithiid pursuing the Ra'az powered up their power whips and lashed out at the Ra'az, but the surprisingly agile beast ducked aside, then pressed a remote tucked in its belt. The Chithiids' whips fizzled out instantly.

"Sonofabitch. He's got a remote deactivation switch."

Just what we were afraid of.

Daisy tried to activate her Ra'az power whip, but her adrenaline was high, and the device was conflicted by the reversal switch Freya had installed trying to read her will through her shifting emotions.

"Not working, Daze."

I noticed.

"No time to fiddle with it. Switch to your other toys. He's gonna be on us any second."

The Ra'az turned and looked at his stymied pursuers and laughed. His eyes shifted as they caught sight of the second hunting party closing in. Without hesitation, he changed course, darting to his left.

"Come on, he's going to get away!" Daisy shouted.

A steady power whip beam snapped out from the shadows of a ruined building, wrapping the Ra'az's legs, sending him tumbling to the hard pavement. He rolled, trying to disengage from the beam as his hands dug into his belt. Triumphantly, he held up his remote deactivation unit and depressed the button.

The power whip stayed active.

Confusion set in as he pressed the button again and again, but to no avail.

Slowly reeling in the whip as she stepped from the shadows was Tamara, pulling the beastly creature off-balance every time it tried to rise to its feet.

"Of course. You gave her your old whip."

Yeah. And I had it before they installed the kill switches, Daisy noted, a victorious grin appearing on her face.

Tamara pulled a vicious, pronged device from her belt and gave the whip a final yank, dragging the hulking Ra'az right to her feet. Before it could react, she gleefully leapt in the air, landing firmly atop its back as she drove the charged spikes into its neck.

Millions of volts of electricity surged into the Ra'az's body, and a mere second later, it had been rendered unconscious.

"Looks like the joke's on you, fucker!" she said, laughing at the inert creature laying beneath her.

Tamara heard the rapidly approaching footsteps and turned to see her friends drawing near.

"Oh, hi, Daisy!" she said with a disturbingly cheerful grin. "Hey, Vince! Will ya look at the size of this one! I bet it's the biggest we've caught yet!"

Vince looked at Daisy, both amused and mildly disturbed.

"Damn. She's really enjoying this isn't she?"

"You could say that," Daisy agreed.

"Daze?"

Yeah?

"I'm starting to wonder if you should have given her that thing after all," Sarah said with a chuckle.

At least she's on our side.

"Thank God," Sarah agreed. *"I almost pity those poor bastards,"* she added. *"Almost."*

Tamara's squad mates quickly trussed up the unconscious Ra'az and loaded it onto a cart to wheel back to their holding area to await trial.

"I'll catch up with you guys back in town," she called out to Daisy as she walked off with her new teammates, all of whom were cheerfully patting each other's backs after the well-won victory.

"So, do we head back?" Vince asked.

"I don't know. Hang on a sec."

She turned to their companions.

"What's the plan now?" she asked their Chithiid mission leader.

"There were also loyalists spotted with the Ra'az. We continue on."

"Homeboy here says we keep going," Daisy replied.

"Homeboy?"

"Hey, we're in East LA," she chuckled.

Not more than ten minutes had passed when multiple calls of "Contact!" rang out from the scouts.

The team broke into two smaller groups and split up to pursue their targets.

Daisy and Vince took the lead of the team veering to the right, following their scout's directions toward a moderate-height residential tower. The old building had been destroyed, not by combat, but rather, by the elements over the years. As was often the case, the quality of materials employed by the land-grab developers had been subpar.

A pair of dusty tracks led straight into the vacant structure.

"Okay, it's gonna be tight in there, so let's spread out, but stay within earshot," Daisy said. "I'll head up to the tenth and start working down. Vince, you take the middle floors. The rest of you seal off the ground and work upward so it can't escape. We good?"

A chorus of affirmation met her ears, once when she told them the plan in English, and again when she translated to Chithiid. Without further hesitation, they plunged into the building, making for the stairs and exits, blocking their quarry's routes of escape.

Daisy had cleared the tenth floor and was halfway through the ninth when a faint grinding sound caught her ear.

You hear that, Sarah?

"Yeah. Sounded like debris shifting."

Shifting under someone's foot.

"Yep. Down the left-hand hallway, toward the central column."

I'm on it. Keep your eyes and ears open.

"I always do."

Daisy quietly pulled the spiked stun probe from her pack and snuck down the hallway, careful to avoid the crumbling bits of floor and miscellaneous debris that had fallen there over the decades.

She was close. Only a few paces to the corner behind which something was waiting for her. The only question was whether she would take it by surprise or if there would be a fight.

Murphy answered that question for her when four powerful arms suddenly wrapped around her from behind, squeezing so tight she couldn't even breathe, let alone call for help.

"Shit! Ambush!"

No shit, Sarah. How do we get out of this?

"Looking."

Hurry. I can't breathe, Daisy said as spots began floating before her eyes.

"Stay awake, Daze!" Sarah shouted in her head.

The powerful Chithiid had hoisted her from the ground and was carrying her somewhere. Where, was the question.

She felt her anger rising as her consciousness was fading. The Ra'az power whip on her wrist engaged, a light hum sounding as a few inches of beam slid forward.

"Daisy, stay awake!"

She shook her head, trying to fight the iron grip, but the alien had wrapped its own arms across her body, creating a near-unbreakable restraint of sinewy muscle.

Oh shit, Daisy managed, when she realized where she was being carried. *He's taking me to the elevator shaft. Sarah, he's going to drop me.*

The long-dead elevator car had broken free and fallen to the bottom of the shaft decades prior. All that remained nine stories below was a jagged pile of wrecked metal that was about to be Daisy's final resting place.

Air unexpectedly rushed into her lungs as the arms holding her so tightly abruptly let go as the Chithiid fell to the ground. Daisy, likewise, slumped to the floor just short of the gaping elevator doors, sucking in gasping lungfuls of air.

Did you hear a clang? Daisy asked, her head still fuzzy from oxygen deprivation.

"Like a bell. Yeah, I did."

What the hell was that? Daisy wondered as her vision returned.

The answer was soon made clear.

Standing over her, Arlo looked down on the prone alien with an expression of pure hatred, a dripping smear of blood staining the steel pipe in his trembling hand.

"Y-you saved me," Daisy croaked. "But how did you——?"

"Sneak up on it?" he finished her sentence as she sucked in another breath. "I tell ya, it's not easy. With four eyes, you've gotta get right behind them. It's their only blind spot."

"No, not that," she said, her respirations slowly returning to normal. "How did you find me?"

"Oh, that. I heard what sounded like a power whip charging up. It wasn't the usual Chithiid kind, so I thought there might be a Ra'az up here. Then I saw that Chithiid had you all wrapped up, so I grabbed this pipe and brained it."

He looked down on the inert alien. All four eyes were open, but unseeing.

"I guess I hit it a little too hard," he said, not an ounce of regret in his voice. "Come on, let's get you out of here."

Arlo helped Daisy to her feet, then they headed for the stairwell. On the seventh floor they ran into Vince.

"Arlo, buddy, what are you doing here?" he asked. His face

turned serious when he saw the scuffs on Daisy. "What happened? Are you okay?"

"Yeah, I am now. There was a loyalist on the ninth floor. He got the drop on me, wrapped me up so tight I couldn't breathe. Then he was going to *actually* drop me, literally, right down the elevator shaft. If Arlo hadn't come along——"

Vince pulled the teen in, hugging him tight.

"Thank you," he said when he loosened his arms. "I cannot thank you enough."

"Yeah, well, it's okay," Arlo said, obviously uncomfortable.

"It's more than okay," Vince replied. "I owe you one, man. Anytime, anywhere, you need me, I'll be there."

Arlo sized him up a moment and smiled.

"I know you will," he said, shaking his hand firmly. "Now, let's get the hell out of here. That thing's dead, and I could really use a drink."

"Cocoa?" Daisy joked.

"I was thinking whiskey," Arlo said.

"Dude, you're what, seventeen?" Vince added.

"Hey, what happened to 'anytime, anywhere'?"

"Oh, that offer's still good," he said with a laugh. "As for drinks, however, cocoa it is."

Several hours, a decent shower, and a hot cup of cocoa later, Daisy sat on the bank of the LA River as the sun began to sink lower in the sky.

The Ra'az Tamara had captured was imprisoned with the others rounded up thus far, though the other Chithiid loyalist had gotten away. In any case, the Ra'az would face justice before the mixed species tribunal in the morning, the same as was happening daily across the globe.

Interestingly, despite their years upon years of slavery, it was the Chithiid who had insisted on holding hearings for the aliens and their supporters, while it was the humans who seemed to prefer the more direct, and more violent option.

Maarl had been among the Chithiid elders who had, with the translation aid of the AI network, made the point that justice and mercy were the traits of an evolved race, and no matter what the Ra'az had done to either of their planets, their people's actions upon retaking their freedom, more than their circumstance and history, was what would define them.

Ultimately, justice would be served, one way or another.

For now, however, Daisy was simply enjoying the fresh air as she watched Vince and Arlo fishing by the water's edge.

Centuries prior, the notion of fishing in the LA River would have been a comical one, given its lackluster trickling flow and sterile cement banks. But now, with a proper river running through and nature having reclaimed the banks centuries prior, the boys were having great success of it.

Vince also relented in one small way, sharing a small glass of whiskey with his young friend.

"I know he's a kid, Daze, but I think, just for today, he's earned it."

Daisy really couldn't argue the point, and her heart warmed as she watched them fishing, talking, and bonding as the daylight faded.

"Looks like you'll be having fish for dinner tonight, Sis."

Yep.

"Actually, it looks like a lot of people may be having fish, if they keep up at that pace."

Yep, Daisy agreed with an amused and contented sigh as they reeled in another.

"You know, I was thinking."

Uh-oh. That's never good.

"Ha-ha," Sarah replied. *"But seriously, you know how Arlo said he heard the power whip activate?"*

Uh-huh.

"*He was supposed to be scouting in the other direction. What was he doing in that building, Daze?*"

Daisy looked at the pair standing on the shore and realized she didn't care.

You know what, Sarah? I'm chalking it up to fate smiling upon me just this once.

And with that, she put the thought out of her head, letting it go without a struggle, just as the eventful day would soon give way to night.

CHAPTER THIRTY-TWO

It was with surprising efficiency the Chithiid and global AIs organized the tribunals to administer justice and punishment to the Ra'az and their Chithiid loyalist collaborators.

The AIs, true to their nature, were quick and logical once the issue of prisoners from the global conflict was put to them. The Chithiid, likewise, were fast to act, their many years in logistical roles helping them quickly navigate the swift waters of interspecies judicial organization.

Daisy and Vince had heard descriptions of the arena-like settings in which the hearings were being carried out, but witnessing it first-hand the morning after the successful capture of the Ra'az in the eastern portion of LA was nevertheless somewhat surreal.

The historic theater in the center of the city had been spared centuries prior, along with many of the other buildings in the immediate vicinity, all saved from destruction and redevelopment by their landmark status.

The stage, former home to song, dance, and all manner of theatricality, was now outfitted with a heavy concrete bench, to which a defendant would soon be chained.

Given the brute strength of the Ra'az, as well as the pure-rage instinctive nature of their people, it was deemed a wise decision. For loyalist prisoners, on the other hand, lesser restraints were more than enough.

In the balcony above, the seating was open to all who wished to witness the proceedings, regardless of species. A fair-sized audience had formed, consisting of cyborgs, humans, and Chithiid alike, all sitting with rapt attention as they watched the drama unfold below.

On the ground floor, where Daisy and Vince found themselves, along with their hunting party teammates, those with vested interest in the particular hearings were seated.

The wings of the stage were guarded not only by a pair of armed Chithiid, whose emotionless faces and firmly set jaws left no doubt that they were of the proper disposition for the job, but also a terrifying redundancy plan.

Two massive Graizenhunds were seated on either side of the central judges' bench, like mastiffs and guard beasts of old. The deadly animals, though terrifying to any onlookers who didn't know better, were actually extremely happy with their new roles.

They had been mistreated by the Ra'az for their entire lives, used as tools whose sole purpose was to hunt and kill. Now, with full bellies and plentiful ear scratches from their kind new masters, the intimidating animals were quite content to spend a lazy morning watching all the goings-on in the tribunal before being taken out for play time and treats.

Of course, the minor neuro-block devised by Cal and the other AIs to suppress their most aggressive learned behaviors may have also played a somewhat more than insubstantial role.

Arlo waved to Daisy and Vince from across the theater. He was busy chatting away with a trio of Chithiid hunters they had noticed the other day. The group had been particularly successful, having corralled a Ra'az, as well as half a dozen loyalists.

"You see Tamara?" Vince asked, scanning the crowd.

"No, but it wouldn't surprise me if she was already back out hunting again."

"She doesn't want to see this?"

"I'm sure she would, most likely, but not nearly as much as she enjoys kicking alien ass, I'd wager. I mean, you saw her yesterday."

"Good point," Vince agreed with a grin. "She was kinda like a kid in a candy shop."

"Yup. At least she's having a good go of it on Earth. Downtime will do her some good."

"If by downtime you mean hunting aliens, that is."

"Everyone's definition is different, babe," Daisy said, nuzzling her man's neck.

A hush fell over the crowd as Maarl walked to the judge's bench, along with his human and cyborg counterparts.

"Is that one of Joshua's soldiers?" Vince asked, noting the heavy-duty build of the metal man.

"Yeah, that's Duke. Until the local AIs get a hookup inside the theater, he's their representative."

"And the human?"

"I don't know his name, but I recognize him. One of Cal's people."

The system was simple. A three-person panel would try the case, and a simple majority would decide the defendant's fate. So far, despite being given ample opportunity to repent their actions and reform, not a single Ra'az had taken the offer.

With great care, the AIs fed a translation of the proceedings through their systems, coming up with the best equivalent they could in halting Ra'az. They also had Maarl clarify in his limited Ra'az, as well as Chithiid, which nearly all Ra'az spoke to a varying degree.

Only the loyalists had ever been properly schooled in Ra'az language. Yet another paranoid act of a paranoid race. The unintended result was making communication a bit harder now that the former masters were in chains.

"The defendant may now address the tribunal," the trio offered after making their case, providing the Ra'az prisoner ample opportunity to atone for its crimes.

Rather than arguing its case, the Ra'az showed the same rage as the previous defendants, lunging at the panel, spittle flying from its mouth as it hurled what were surely obscenities at the impassive judges. This particular Ra'az, was apparently rather proficient in his Chithiid language, shouting out horrible insults and profanities in that alien tongue as well.

Maarl impassively wiped a fleck of Ra'az spit from his cheek and looked over at his comrades. Both gave him a subtle nod of silent agreement.

"You do not wish to plead your case in a logical manner? This is your opportunity to seek mercy and rehabilitation. I strongly suggest you seize this chance to make the best of your situation."

The Ra'az laughed, then spat a gob of phlegm that fortunately missed Maarl, falling short on the desk before him.

"I'll take that as a no, then," he said calmly. *"Well, we offered."*

He nodded once to the guard.

A single blast rang out.

Headshot.

The dead Ra'az slumped to the floor.

"Next!"

"Holy shit," Vince gasped.

"What did you expect? Cupcakes and hugs?"

"No, but damn, at least take them outside for a firing squad or something."

Judging by the positive reaction of the crowd, however, it appeared the onstage execution was a hit with the locals.

The cleaning crew quickly came out and dragged the Ra'az

corpse from the stage, mopping up the blood and readying the platform for the next defendant. It was to be a loyalist, and fortunately, they were proving to be far more reasonable when it came to plea agreements.

"You wanna get out of here?" Daisy asked.

"Yeah," Vince replied. "It'll be at least a couple of hours before Maarl's freed up to talk anyway, right?"

"Thereabouts."

"Okay, then. We can see how Alma's folks are assimilating in the meantime."

"You sure you're up to seeing them? I mean, after what they did to you, I know I have a hard time not beating the ever-loving shit out of each and every one of them."

Vince took her hand and led her from the theater.

"Hey, that was a different time. We've retaken the world. The planet is ours again, and we need to set it right. It's time to put that stuff behind us, even if it really, really sucked, and move on."

"Well..."

"Come on, I know you can do it. Hell, if I can, I'm sure you can."

"Oh, fine. But if they so much as look at you sideways," she said, making a little grab for the sword strapped to her back.

"Babe, if they regress, I'll be the first to hold them down while you have your way with them in whatever vengeful manner you like," he said with a laugh. "But let's hope it doesn't come to that, okay?"

"Well, Stabby *is* a little hungry," she said with a wicked grin.

The visit with Habby and Alma had been quite unexpected, and far more positive than either of them had anticipated.

"Oh my," Alma said, her voice cracking with emotion when the pair arrived. "Oh, my dear Vincent. I am so, so sorry for what I did to you. Can you ever find it in your heart to forgive me?"

"I know it wasn't the real you who did those things," Vince said. "Sid explained it all. I just feel sorry for you."

"For me? After what I did?"

"Yeah, for you. I mean, to essentially wake up from what could be called a long sleep and find out your own body had been more or less sleepwalking––if the analogy works––doing horrible things before you finally woke up, and then having them thrown in your face? That would be an awful burden to bear."

"And yet, you are the one who suffered."

"Yes, but your actions also helped me, in a strange way."

"But, I don't see how," Alma said, confused.

Vince pulled Daisy close and kissed her on the cheek.

"You created a situation that wound up bringing Daisy and me back together again, albeit unintentionally. For that, you have my thanks."

"I-I don't know what to say, Vincent."

"I know what to say," Habby butted in.

"Oh dear, not again," Alma groaned.

"Yes, *again*," he shot back. "I say just look at the state of your clothes! The AI on your moon base lets you go out like this? Oh, please! You must let me put together a new wardrobe for you."

"Habby––" Alma tried to interject.

"*And* I will do my best to make it functionally practical as well," he added.

"You're making an effort, at least," Alma said.

"For you," he replied. "We may not see eye to eye, but even if it doesn't seem like it, I do respect you, you know."

"I actually think those two might work it out," Sarah mused.

Ya know what, Sis? You may be right.

"Habby, we really appreciate the offer, and if we weren't on such a tight schedule, we'd gladly take you up on it, but we really have to get back. We have a meeting shortly that we can't afford to miss."

"Well, I suppose we can do it next time," he replied.

"I'll be back to take you up on that, though," Vince said. "Really, I appreciate it, Habby." A moment of inspiration struck. "You know what? How are you with designing attire for the younger generation?" he said, throwing a mischievous smile Daisy's way. "You know, like a seventeen-year-old."

"Ooh, that could be interesting," Habby said, the gears in his mind already churning.

Daisy and Vince had made their way back to Maarl's offices. With the tribunal completed for the day, he was finally free to pursue his other activities. Namely, planning the large-scale demise of the Ra'az.

If the hearings had reinforced anything, it was that the Ra'az would not be reasoned with, would not negotiate, and would never cease their aggressive behavior. With that fresh in his mind, he joined his human friends to discuss their plans.

"The team is entirely trustworthy, consisting of men I have known for many years. They are devising attack strategies in conjunction with your AI planners. Several options seem to be good possibilities for success."

"And you say they are already training others for the mission?" Daisy asked, while Vince quietly listened on a headset as Cal translated for him.

"Yes, they are recruiting men for not only the assault on the Ra'az fleet, both piloting the captured ships as well as for the inevitable boarding parties, but also greater numbers of lesser-skilled but equally motivated Chithiid to participate en masse when the time comes to retake our homeworld."

"But you are beginning your training rather early, are you not? We do not know how long it will take to get a functional warp drive built

from scratch, let alone how long to make one capable of jumping a ship the size of yours."

"True, it could be years, Daisy. But you forget, we are combining the resources of three races, and between us, there is a very real possibility of a breakthrough happening far sooner than expected. I would rather we are prepared for that eventuality than caught off guard."

"Valid point," she conceded. *"And how goes the retrofitting of your vessels?"*

"Slow, but well," he replied. *"My people are quite busy tracking down and removing all traces of Ra'az remote kill switches and destruct mechanisms from the Chithiid transport craft while they prepare them for the mission."*

"I have seen those kill switches in action. The Ra'az you tried this morning. He used one against the team pursuing him. Turned their power whips off with the press of a button."

"Yes, this is a problem, and those would be useful devices during the assault, but we are prepared to continue without that resource if we must."

"If we have the time, I believe I can neutralize their power whip shut-off device," Daisy said. *"It is not a guarantee, but I shall try my best."*

"Of that I have no doubt, my friend."

"And what was that you said about retrofitting the ships? I thought we decided that altering their structure would only draw attention to them."

"Yes, it would. However, some of my more clever comrades have come up with a plan to camouflage weapons systems beneath hull modifications, allowing them to be mounted within the hull, only to be deployed if needed."

"Clever. I just hope we can complete our work on the warp technology so all of this labor is not in vain."

"About that," the older Chithiid said with a growing smile. *"I have spoken once more with my contacts in San Francisco. While*

they were sequestered into different barracks within the facility, and often kept in the dark about the goings-on in other labs, it seems our people have managed to find a dozen Chithiid survivors with some knowledge of various aspects of the Ra'az warp technology. None of them understands it all, but combined, their intellects may be exactly what we need to progress the research."

"You hear that, Sid?" Daisy asked over her comms.

"Yes, I certainly did, Daisy," he replied. "Most promising, indeed."

"Well, then," she said, *"let's round them up and get them to Dark Side Base."*

CHAPTER THIRTY-THREE

The team of Chithiid scientists hadn't turned out to actually be scientists, exactly. While they were fairly proficient in many aspects of the Ra'azs' warp technology, the aliens who had been sent to work with Chu on the moon were a mix of maintenance workers and janitorial staff.

"We are glad to be able to help the cause in any way we can," a slim Chithiid named Berrk said upon arrival. Of the thirteen who came to take up residence on Dark Side, he was one of the most enthusiastic. Also one of the most talkative.

Sid and Mal found themselves constantly translating for Chu, though Freya and Marty were also happy to chip in when they weren't otherwise occupied or down on the planet below.

"We really must speed the production of the modified neuro-stim units," Sid lamented two weeks into the project.

"Agreed, it is a priority," Mal said. "However, my onboard fabrication systems are somewhat limited at the moment with the other projects underway on the *Váli*. Most importantly, it appears Freya and Marty's collaborative efforts on a cure for the plague blanketing the planet may actually bear fruit."

"And that is indeed a top priority. Ending the plague is far more important than the mere convenience of our not having to play translator constantly," Sid agreed.

"Yes. And it appears Chu is actually learning the Chithiid language somewhat on his own."

It was true, the clever technician, while relying on the AIs for proper translations, was learning to understand, and even speak a little of the alien tongue. Being surrounded by a baker's dozen of chatting Chithiid all day, every day, seemed to be just the immersion schooling he needed.

Shelly, Omar, and Tamara were also rapidly learning key phrases, but theirs tended to be more along the, "Aim over there," and, "Drop and give me twenty," variety as they trained their Chithiid recruits down on Earth's surface.

A few weeks later, they had all been at the process for just over a month, and far more progress had been made on all fronts, from mustering a combat-ready force, to reverse-engineering the Ra'az warp tech, to retrofitting Chithiid ships to be space-worthy and secure from Ra'az remote shutdowns.

The retrofitting process was also moving along nicely, with Barry pulling back-to-back shifts helping Mrazich and Reggie as they installed heavy weaponry into the recessed housings their Chithiid counterparts had fabricated on Earth.

Once secured and functional, the ships would then return to the surface, where the alien workers could reattach structural components over them, completing the camouflage from the comfort of Earth's environment.

Four-armed Chithiid-sized space suits were not an additional luxury the base had on hand, and the largest of the Trojan Horse ships could not fit in even the largest hangar by a long shot.

Fortunately for the Chithiid, Vince possessed an excellent mind for engineering, even of the alien variety, and his time was largely spent on the surface, helping them retrofit the vessels that weren't on the moon, hopping from city to city when he was not lending his expertise to projects being worked on up on Dark Side.

He had most recently been in Philadelphia for several days, installing a rapid-deployment system to a recessed pulse cannon system, but would be hopping a shuttle and returning to Dark Side, and his woman, soon enough.

Meanwhile, out in orbit, the completed vessels were each carrying a skeleton crew as the Chithiid volunteers were shuttled up a few dozen at a time to move on to the next phase of their training.

Running drills aboard an actual ship.

In space.

In the dark.

With the gravity turned off.

The last bit was a protocol of Maarl's design, and one Daisy thought Fatima would most certainly approve of. In fact, if Fatima didn't have Sarah constantly running drills both inside and outside Dark Side Base––when Sarah wasn't helping on the surface, that is––the silver-haired woman would have almost certainly sent her over to train with Maarl's recruits.

"You will face many hardships when we strike at the Ra'az fleet," he would tell his men in their pre-departure pep talk. *"Ships may become damaged, systems may become compromised. You have all trained long and hard aboard these vessels while they were being retrofitted in the comfort of the planet's atmosphere and gravity. When you are in space, these are luxuries, and while the vessel's hide is thick and should protect you from the vacuum, you may be forced to fight in unexpected circumstances."*

The old Chithiid took a long, slow look across his men from his slightly elevated platform. He smiled. They looked good. Good, and hungry to learn more.

"Your next training cycle will teach you to adapt to those

circumstances. To view them not as an obstacle, but as a situation you can turn to your advantage. Now, board your shuttles, and good luck. I will see you all back here when you have completed this phase."

The Chithiid formed lines and began filing into their waiting craft, a little reticent, but nevertheless excited for the next level of training. Maarl wanted them to be ready for anything, and while he couldn't simulate every situation, learning to move and fight in the dark, and even in zero-g at times, would give his men an advantage.

The first group, after a few weeks and many bruised limbs, had already become proficient in maneuvering through the vessels essentially blind. Their spatial awareness was enhanced, and when the instructors would suddenly shut off the lights, or cut the gravity, or both, they rapidly adapted and continued their tasks.

It was a skill that all involved realized could very well mean the difference between life and death.

"So what do you think, Freya? Is he done?" Commander Mrazich asked as he looked at his friend lying quietly in his cryo pod in Dark Side's med lab.

"Well, that depends on what you mean by done," she replied.

"You know what he means, kiddo. Is Harkaway cured of the plague he was exposed to?" Daisy asked.

"I mean, he might be," she replied.

"No, Daisy, he's not clear of the plague yet," Marty interrupted.

"See? That's not so hard," Mrazich said. "Thank you, Marty, for a clear answer."

"But there's more," Marty added.

Mrazich shook his head and sighed.

"Of course there is."

"The thing is, Commander, it could take months, if not years, for him to be purged of the active plague by standard means," Freya continued.

"What's the 'but,' Freya?"

"But, that was because Mal had her fabricators work in conjunction with the cryo pod to replace any damaged cells, like the last time he was infected waaaay back when. So, he still has the remaining plague in his body, even though we've sterilized the rest of the pod." The brilliant AI paused a moment. "So, uh, I kinda went ahead and inoculated him with the cure."

"Wait, you can cure the plague now? I thought that was still a ways from being ready for testing," Mrazich replied.

"It was, but I figured since he's in there already, we might as well dose him and see what it does. Only, with him being in cryo, the drastic rate that his bodily functions are slowed means we really can't tell what it's doing."

Daisy and Harkaway seemed to have mixed feelings about the news. Fatima, on the other hand, was decidedly optimistic.

"Freya, why haven't you run a full-scale test of this potential cure yet?" she asked.

"Well, I mean, you know how challenging human conception can be, right?" the AI said.

"Challenging? Seems like breeding has always been one of humanity's strong suits," Mrazich said with a chuckle.

"What Freya means is that, given the genetic variances between mother and father, not all zygotes are created immune," Mal interjected.

"Exactly. Thanks, Mal."

"You are most welcome, Freya."

"So the thing is, sure, this *should* be a cure, but without a proper test subject––not just cells in a test tube––we simply don't know," she said.

"And you say this would not only immunize the living, but also protect their offspring before they are born?" Fatima asked.

"We believe that's what'll happen," Marty replied. "But we're kinda stuck at the moment. The captain is in cryo, so our results are just too inconclusive. We are having the terrestrial guys check around for any pregnant females, though. If we catch one right after conception, we can isolate her from the environment, purge the plague, and test the zygote. If it's not immune, we just have to wait till it's born and see if the cure works."

"Marty, you can't use humans like that!" Fatima scolded. "Those are people."

"We wouldn't hurt them. We'd inoculate them up here in the purified environment of Dark Side, then once they're born, we'd just put them in a sealed cryo pod and flood it with virus. The monitors would tell us within minutes—if not seconds—if an infection took hold or not. If it did, we'd just flash-freeze them in the pod while we let Mal's machinery clear the infection, and then we'd start our tests all over again."

"This process could take years," Fatima said, shaking her head.

"Well, yeah," Freya replied.

"But you are confident the cure you have designed will actually inoculate against the plague. For *all* humans who are not immune?" Fatima asked.

"It looks that way in lab tests, but we can't say for sure yet," she said quietly. "I'm sorry, Fatima. We tried. I mean, it's not like Marty and me—"

"Marty and I," Daisy corrected.

"I know. Let me talk."

"Sorry," Daisy said. "Habit."

"So Marty and *me*, we're like ninety-nine percent sure, but there's always that one\ percent chance it fails."

"And this is why we have begun scanning the population for—"

"I'll do it," Fatima interrupted.

"I'm sorry? What did you say?" a very startled Mrazich asked.

"I said I'll do it."

"Is she actually offering to be a Guinea pig?"

Yeah, Sis. I think she is.

"But it could kill her."

I'm sure she knows that.

"But I don't want her to die. And I'm sure you don't either."

Fatima was watching Daisy, well aware there was an internal dialogue taking place. She flashed her a warm, knowing smile.

"Daisy, you both know how long I've been here. How unlikely my survival was, even on my first day on Dark Side. And now I have a chance to help the cause and return the favor."

"What do you mean 'both'?" Mrazich asked.

"Why, Daisy and you, of course, Commander," she lied, flashing a little wink to Daisy and her invisible ride-along.

"Are you sure you want to do this?" Daisy asked, emotion welling up in her chest, making it hard to speak.

"Oh, Daisy. I've spent all these years looking down at Earth but never able to set foot on it. Scans and images have shown me the beaches and forests, but I knew it just wasn't meant to be. But now? Now I have the very real chance to finally breathe the fresh air and feel the sun on my skin without it first passing through a half-foot of UV-protectant shatterproof glass."

"She really means to do this, doesn't she?"

Looks that way, Sis.

"Are you absolutely sure?" Daisy asked, the lump in her throat gradually lessening.

Fatima took her by the hands and looked deep in her eyes with warmth and love.

"It's time to finally go home. I'm an old woman—"

"You're not that old—"

"Daisy, I am. And I want to go home, or die trying."

It didn't take Mal long to set up a cryo pod aboard her ship. She thought it best to have Fatima in the heart of the *Váli*'s medical facilities in case something should go awry, and the kindhearted woman had graciously humored her.

The ship was nestled safely between the debris field and Earth, floating gently above its beautiful but deadly skies. Freya and Marty hovered quietly to either side, a silent vanguard watching and waiting.

Daisy and Sarah stood by, and Commander Mrazich had even taken a brief leave from the base to join them. He wasn't about to let his old friend do this without him.

Mal had also rearranged her pods slightly, allowing the med pod to take up an unconventional location in an outer layer of her structure. While that meant it wasn't as robustly protected by the ship's bulk as it normally was, it also afforded her the luxury of installing a window where the secondary airlock door normally resided.

"A room with a view, Mal?" Fatima noted warmly.

"Of course, my friend. I thought you would enjoy a clear view. A real one, not over a video monitor."

"And you were right," she replied as she gazed at Earth, her eyes welling with emotions that even she had a hard time reining in.

"Are you sure about this?" Mal asked, gently.

"I am."

Fatima had cheerfully given hugs to her friends on Dark Side before they launched, assuring them it was no big deal and she would see them soon. Now, however, with just the three other passengers present, her guard was lowered.

She hugged Daisy and Sarah in turn, planting a kiss on each of their foreheads, like a loving mother to her little ones.

"You two. You *three*," she said with a wink. "Whatever happens, I have faith you will succeed in your mission. You've taken on such an important task, and you have no idea just how proud I am of you."

"You'll be fine, Fatima," Sarah said, choked up.

"I know, darling," she replied kindly, then turned and faced Commander Mrazich.

"And as for you, you old stick in the mud, I expect you to do whatever it takes to see our reclaimed world stays that way."

"You know I will, my friend."

She cracked a little smile. "Yeah, I do."

Fatima looked out the window at the Earth below, a lone tear sliding down her cheek before she climbed up into the embrace of the cryo pod.

"Okay," she said.

"You're ready, Fatima?" Mal confirmed.

"I'm as ready as I'll ever be."

"Very well."

The pod sealed around her, the lights cycling to a safe, green color.

"Administering the inoculation," Mal informed them.

The cure had been designed to be easily spread—colorless, and odorless as it flooded the air. Inside the pod, it didn't look like anything had happened at all.

"What happens now?" Mrazich asked.

"Now we wait for it to permeate her tissues. The uptake within her body should only take a few minutes. Then we will wait another doubling of that time to ensure maximum absorption."

Fatima looked calm, staring out the window as the invisible panacea either did its work or didn't, never once taking her eyes off the planet just below.

"It is time," Mal informed them a short while later.

The lights of the cryo pod shifted to a very pale blue.

"Five seconds," she announced.

There was no countdown. Those present were keeping track

in their heads anyway. When the timer hit zero, a fine pink mist containing the plague flooded the pod, quickly dissipating and becoming invisible within the volume of air the pod contained.

Fatima glanced at her friends and smiled, then forced herself to let go of that iron-strong survival instinct and take a deep breath.

She began coughing immediately—a deep, racking cough that shook her entire body.

"Mal, do something!" Mrazich shouted.

"There is nothing to do, Commander," she replied.

Fatima's coughs diminished a few moments later. She turned to look at her friends.

"Just a tickle in my throat," she said with a grin. "Is there more?"

"Just a moment, please," she replied.

The lights of the pod ran through a full-spectrum shift as every cell of her body was scanned, then rescanned, then scanned again.

"I just need to discuss with Freya and Marty," Mal informed them. "One moment, please."

The ship went silent as the great minds conferred.

"You think she's okay?" Sarah asked.

"I hope so," Sarah replied.

"I know what you're thinking," Mrazich said. "I hope she's okay, too."

"Wait. He doesn't know about—"

No. He's just thinking what we all are.

The pod lights cycled back to a neutral white.

"Now what, Mal?" Fatima asked.

"Now nothing," she replied as the pod cracked open with a hiss. "Fatima, you are immune."

No amount of meditative training was capable of stemming the flow of tears that coursed freely down her cheeks. Judging by the leaking eyes of everyone present, it was the one condition in the ship that *was* contagious.

Fatima slid from the pod and walked to the window, pressing her hands to the thick glass.

"Mal?"

"Yes, Fatima?"

"If you would be so kind, I've got a date with that beautiful blue beauty down there."

CHAPTER THIRTY-FOUR

Daisy and Sarah watched silently from the shore, seated comfortably on the warm sand, soaking in the ocean air. The sisters leaned gently on one another, a sense of unbelievable happiness and calm engulfing them both as they periodically wiped a tear from their eyes.

Standing out in the surf, the gentle waves coming up to her knees, Fatima's smile was so big and so bright, it looked like it might actually split her face in two. The sheer joy radiating from her was almost tangible.

The wetness on her cheeks, though partly made of ocean spray, was mostly a salty trickle of something else as her eyes welled with overpowering contentment. Her eyes were open wide, taking it all in, as her lungs embraced the fresh breeze. The cheerful cries of the gulls overhead threatened to push her happiness over the top.

Every little thing seemed a miracle, and for the woman who had spent several lifetimes stuck on the moon, it truly was.

They were all being present in the moment, putting aside other concerns for the time being and simply enjoying the now, though

Fatima was enjoying it far more than the others. Still, a little tinge of reality hung in the back of Daisy and Sarah's minds. The sisters knew very well that they'd have to get back to work soon enough.

"What do you think, Daze? The Chithiid crew up on Dark Side seems to be making some really good headway with the warp tech."

"Chu got them steered in the right direction, once he pinned down each of their strong suits," Daisy replied. "It's really beginning to look like they'll actually do it."

"It's kind of amazing, isn't it?"

"Yeah. And they might even get a working version far sooner than we expected."

"Let's not forget Freya's input," Sarah noted. *"And all while keeping the time travel thing a secret. You've gotta hand it to the kid, she's really come a long way."*

"That she has," Daisy agreed. "And Marty has been doing yeoman's work, helping out, lending a hand between all the different projects up there. He's an impressive AI, and Arlo has fit in really well too"

"Yeah, he and Finn are almost inseparable," Sarah noted.

"It's almost to be expected, Sis. Boys love knives, after all, and Finn has a bevy of them."

"And he's a damn good chef," Sarah added.

"That too," Daisy agreed.

"See? I knew you liked him."

"Oh, give it a rest, will ya? Just because I appreciate his culinary skills doesn't mean I like the guy."

"You forget, we're the same person. I know you like him."

"You do, maybe, but our timeline diverged a long time ago."

"It's okay," Sarah said knowingly. *"You don't have to worry about him running off and hurting you. I know he would never do that to you."*

Sarah groaned and flopped back onto the sand.

"Jeez, Daisy. Can't you talk some sense into her? Or at least make her shut up?"

"Talk sense into you? *Either* of you? Fat chance, that. Nope, like it or not, Sis, she's just as stubborn as you are."

"With good reason."

"Obviously," Daisy agreed with a grin.

"Ugh, you two," Sarah griped, then turned her attention back to their reveling friend. "So what's the plan? Should we leave her down here, or bring her back to Dark Side?"

A big smile flashed on Daisy's face.

"Uh-oh, I know that look. What've you done, Daze?"

"You want to tell her, or should I?" Sarah asked.

"Well..." Daisy began, "I may have had Freya bring a little message to our friends retrofitting the nearest coastal residential tower."

Understanding blossomed in Sarah's mind.

"Oh, please tell me you did what I think you did."

"You know it."

"Fatima is going to lose her mind."

"I know. And it's going to be awesome," Daisy said, beaming. "Whenever she's had enough of the sun and sand, we'll take her to get set up in her penthouse pad."

"Does it have a jacuzzi too?"

"What kind of woman do you take me for, Sarah? Of course it does. Rooftop, no less. She'll have a clear view of the entire city, as well as the whole coastline. And Finn even boxed up something special for her and sent it down with Bob. Should be waiting for her when she gets there."

"Wow. Nicely done, Sis. You outdid yourself."

"Why, thank you. And it's the least I could do for her," Daisy said happily. "And by the way, Finn also packed you up a little treat as well. Check Freya's galley when we get back."

A few hours later, Fatima stood in her new terrestrial lodging. Though there was no ocean spray anywhere near, her cheeks were nevertheless wet. At the rate she was going, Daisy almost worried she'd get dehydrated if she had any more happy surprises.

"This is amazing," she gasped as she walked through the penthouse. "And this is mine? This entire space?"

"Yep," Daisy replied. "You've been cooped up in a military base for so long, we wanted you to have space to spread your wings, so to speak. The Chithiid hooked us up and did a great job cleaning it from top to bottom, and they rolled in a new mattress, as well as stocking it with fresh linen and towels. We also took your measurements from Sid's records and had Habby whip you up a few outfits. I hope you like them––he sometimes gets a little carried away."

Fatima was beside herself.

"There's one more thing," Daisy said, directing her to the rooftop deck. "I had them bring a second bed out here, along with a heat lamp and fluffy covers. I thought you might want to sleep under the stars in the open air, if the weather was nice."

Fatima grabbed her in a tight hug and squeezed tight.

"Thank you, Daisy. You have no idea what this means to me."

"I think I do, actually," she said with a smile. "Now, you enjoy your time here. We can get along just fine up on Dark Side without you for a bit. You've more than earned this."

Daisy walked to the edge of the roof.

"Hey, kiddo, we're ready to go."

The stealthy ship silently rose to roof-level and extended her retractable gangplank.

"Have a great night, Fatima. We'll check in on you in the morning before we head out," Daisy said, then she and Sarah boarded the ship and quietly flew off toward Downtown.

"We deserve a break too," Daisy said as she slid into her captain's seat. "I set us up a couple of suites near the tribunal. Figured we could go see what Tamara and the others are up to, then maybe watch the morning's hearings before we head back up."

"Works for me, Sis," Sarah said, blissfully eating a spoonful of the homemade pistachio ice cream Finn had stashed in Freya's galley for her.

"Works for me too," Sarah added. *"And Daze?"*

"Yeah, Sarah?"

"You did good."

The sisters flew off to enjoy the rest of their evening before getting some well-deserved rest. The morning would bring new challenges, but Daisy felt confident in her team's ability to overcome them. Things were most definitely looking up.

Far above, safely tucked away inside Dark Side's pressurized walls, Finn and Arlo were having a fantastic time whipping up some of the crazed man's more original recipes.

While Finn was the more seasoned chef, he was thrilled to discover that Arlo had a natural gift for cooking. More than that, he shared Finn's affinity for knives, and his skills, though slower than the mechanically enhanced man, were nonetheless quite impressive.

The good-natured trash talk of the kitchen had bonded them early on, and in the month-plus that they had been cooking for not only the base's usual crew, but also their new Chithiid guests, a real friendship had formed.

"Nuts!" Finn called out, tossing a packet of walnuts to his young friend.

"Always showing me your nuts, Finn."

"They're salty, ya know?" he replied with a chuckle.

"But so small," Arlo shot back.

"Hey!"

"What? They're *your* nuts," he said with a laugh.

Arlo pulled out several large carrots and a dozen stalks of

celery to add to the large pot of soup they were whipping up for starters for their four-armed guests. His blade flew across the cutting board, making quick work of the pile of vegetables.

"Nice chops, kid."

"Thanks," Arlo replied. "My uncle taught me when I was a kid. Also taught me to keep my fingers tucked," he said, lightly rapping his knife against Finn's metal fingers. "A lesson *someone* apparently never had. As for me, I very much want to keep mine attached," he said with a laugh.

"Hey, that was a malfunction of my arm that caused that," Finn whined. "And besides, now I don't have to worry about things like that anymore."

"Yeah, yeah. Keep rationalizing, old man."

"I will, young whippersnapper. Now get off my lawn!" he said, pulling his lips over his teeth and mimicking a toothless old man.

Finn turned and looked across the counter at their other companion.

"Oh, jeez. No, not like that. Vertical cuts. We've gone over this," Finn said, shifting his attention to the Chithiid who had been learning to cook under his tutelage. "Sid, would you tell him, please?"

"I have, Finn. He is merely getting the hang of things. Give him time," the base AI replied. "And if you would wear your translation earpiece, I could help you communicate much easier."

"Slows my roll, my man. And it slips off my ears."

"Then tighten the loop," Sid said, patiently. "It's a tiny device, after all."

"Yeah, I guess. But check him out. He's got four arms, but he's clumsier than this yo-yo was when he started," he said, gesturing toward Arlo.

"Hey!"

Finn shot him a wicked grin and a wink.

"All right," he said to the alien, "Don't worry, Berrk, you'll get better."

Sid translated for the clumsy Chithiid.

"Please tell Finn I appreciate his patience. While I may have some skill with tools and warp technology, I seem to be lacking in the ways of food preparation."

"Not to worry, Berrk. We all know this is new for your people. Once you have become accustomed to the practice of sourcing your own foods, these skills will eventually become second nature."

"We did not realize it at the time, but when the Ra'az insisted on providing all of our food from their processing facilities, we were unaware it was not done for the convenience of our people, but rather, as a further means to keep us under their yoke."

"Indeed, it was an unusual, yet effective, strategy to make the Chithiid workforce dependent on them for sustenance," Sid noted. *"Yet, despite his sarcastic commentary, I believe Finn is actually quite impressed with the progress you have made in so little time."*

"Do you truly believe this?" he asked expectantly.

"Yes, I do. I have observed Finnegan in the kitchen environment for some time now, and I can assure you, the more grief he gives, the more respect he has for you. See how he torments the youth?"

"Yes, he is rather abusive toward him."

"That is because he is fond of him."

"Oh, I did not realize they had that sort of relationship."

"What? Oh, I did not mean in a romantic sense, though there would be nothing wrong if that were the case, but I was referring to his taking a younger man under his wing in a mentorship manner."

"Aah, I see."

"Hey, I heard that!" Finn said, the translation earpiece now firmly affixed.

"Good," Sid replied. "Now we can converse normally."

"Normally for you, maybe. It's still weird for me going through a middleman."

"I don't need one," Arlo said in fluent Chithiid.

"Showoff," Finn sniped, chucking a carrot at him.

"Hey, Berrk, don't listen to him," Arlo said with a silly grin. *"He's just old and bitter. I think you're doing a kickass job."*

"Thank you, Arlo. I am doing my best. It has been a wonderful experience thus far, learning how native ingredients mesh to form a flavor palette. Our processed foods, while nutrient-rich, were quite lacking in enjoyable flavors."

"I know, I've tried one of those bars. Ewww," Arlo said with a grimace.

"Arlo, I was wondering. Do you think you and Finn would perhaps be interested in coming down to the surface and teaching others what you have taught me? After we complete our work on the warp technology, of course."

"Dude, that would be sick!"

"You are ill?"

"No, it's just a saying. What I mean is that would be a lot of fun. I'm sure Finn'll be up for it. Tons of cool ingredients down there to choose from."

Finn listened as he worked, Sid translating for him in near-real-time.

"The answer is yes, by the way," he said. "And thanks for asking before committing me to a cooking course," he added.

"Oh, come on. You know you love the devoted students inflating your ego."

"Yeah, yeah. Now pay attention——we're gonna have a bunch of hungry aliens in here pretty soon, and you're falling behind with all your jaw-flapping."

Arlo laughed, and even Berrk broke a smile in the festive mood of the kitchen as the two humans and their alien friend labored together.

"This is fantastic," Chu said, seated with his Chithiid team as they ate a short while later. "Is this actual chicken soup?"

"Yes and no," Finn said. "The veggies are all fresh stuff we sourced from the surface, but the protein is machine-replicated tissue. I still can't see clear to killing animals for food, ya know?"

"I totally get it. It's just funny to hear from a chef who cooks meat, like, every day, is all."

"It's meat, but it was never an animal. It's different," Finn clarified.

"Having eaten both, I can tell you, there's no discernible difference," Arlo pointed out.

"When did you eat real chickens?" Chu asked.

"Uh, my mom raised some from eggs. Said I should understand about taking a life to preserve my own. I raised them, then she had me kill them and eat them."

"That's fucked up, dude," Finn said.

"Yeah, I suppose, but she had a point. Things were different then, and I was young. Anyway, I learned that if I have to, I can do it. I just prefer not to, is all."

"Such a cultured young man," Finn said, ruffling his apprentice's hair. "Next thing you know, you'll tell me that you––"

The base's lights blinked to red in an instant, all doors slamming into battle lockdown mode. The attack alert sounded loud and clear through every inch of the facility.

"Warning! All hands, we are under attack!" Sid blared over the speakers.

Mal and Bob quickly fired up their engines and spun toward the hangar doors, waiting impatiently for the work crews who were lacking space suits to vacate the chamber so the doors could open and let them engage the enemy.

"Are any of our Chithiid ships able to power up their weapons yet?" Mrazich barked.

"Negative, Commander. They're still being prepped," Sid replied.

Outside the moon, a dozen large ships warped into low orbit. Then a dozen more. And they kept coming.

Soon the moon was swarmed by a fleet of varying sized vessels.

"We are surrounded," Sid announced to all within the base's walls. "We are cut off from Earth."

CHAPTER THIRTY-FIVE

Sid had alerted the minor AIs parked on the surface to scramble, and any minute, Mal and Bob would be able to join them, just as soon as he could decompress the hangar and open its doors. He was putting the entire base in lockdown when an unexpected transmission crackled over the comms.

"Dark Side Base, this is the Earth Resistance Fleet. Do you copy, Sid?"

"Sid, how does she know your name?" Mrazich asked, still strapping on his sidearm in the command center.

"This is Celeste Harkaway. Do you copy, Sid?"

"Her name is Harkaway, Commander. From the escaped fleet that salvaged humanity. She was second-in-command before I launched on my mission to Earth."

"I heard the name, and I know all of that. But this can't be them. They're light years away and don't have any sort of warp technology."

"From what we've just seen, that is apparently not the case," he replied.

Mal and Bob quietly exited the hangar, but rather than

launching into a suicidal defense run, they paused, scanning the fleet hanging in the dark sky.

"Sid, it is indeed them," Mal confirmed. "Even Zed's here."

"Oh dear. He's always been a bit of a handful."

"I heard that, Sid," the powerful command ship AI said with a baritone laugh. "Nice to see you again too," he added.

"Apologies, Zed. You took me rather by surprise."

"Kind of what we want to do to those Ra'az assholes, am I right?" the salty AI said.

"Indeed, but I still fail to see how you—"

"Daisy," he replied. One word that explained it all.

"Of course. She mentioned coming upon you during her accidental warp, but I was unaware she had left you a functional warp system."

"She didn't. Look, we can talk about this all day, but Harkaway really wants to come do this face-to-face."

"Of course," Sid blurted. "Have her land in Hangar One. I will send Barry to show her the way."

"It will be my pleasure," the sandy-haired cyborg said.

"Hey, Barry! Glad you're still functional," Zed called out over the comms.

"Thank you, Zed. I, too, am glad to be intact," he replied.

"Okay, she's launching. Should be to you in three minutes."

"So soon? Very well, we will be ready to welcome her. But Zed, you should know there are Chithiid scientists working with us on the base. Please inform her security detail so they are aware."

"New allies?"

"Yes. Deciphering and replicating warp technology stolen from the Ra'az."

"Looks like we may have just saved you a bunch of work. But I'll let Harkaway tell you all about it when she gets there. We'll catch up in a bit. Zed out."

The shuttle was a relatively small one, and Celeste Harkaway traveled with only two aides and no security detail. Seeing as she was landing at the most secure military facility in the solar system, she decided to travel light.

"Commander," she said warmly when she saw the metal-jawed man lumber across the deck. "My, the years have been kind to you."

"Bullshit, Celeste. Last time you saw me, I was decades younger, and wasn't sporting these shiny bits," he said with a laugh. "But it's great to see you just the same. Come on, let's get you some grub," he said, leading her from the hangar and down the corridors. "I bet it's been a long time since you've had Earth-grown produce."

"Long? More like never."

"I know. You're in for a treat. Despite his penchant for inane rambling, Finn is quite a talented chef."

"Finnegan is still with you? How wonderful!" she exclaimed. "And where is Lars?"

Mrazich fell silent a moment too long. She knew something was wrong.

"What happened to him?" she asked, stoic despite her obvious pain.

"It was during the assault on Earth. The hull of his ship was compromised and contagion reached the command pod."

"I see," she said, swallowing hard.

"No, it's not like that. He's alive, Celeste, but he had to be thrown into a deep emergency stasis. The AIs have been working to fix him ever since, but we just don't know if it'll work or not."

Celeste took a deep breath and composed herself. Mourning her husband would have to wait.

"Thank you, Commander. I know you've done all you can. For now, we have more pressing matters, however."

"Looks that way," he agreed.

"As I'm sure you know by now, Daisy visited us many years ago."

"She told us."

"And did she also tell you how she came to arrive there?"

"Accidental time warp," he replied. "Nasty thing, that. It must've been hell on that poor ship hanging around by itself while Daisy waited out the years in cryo."

"I couldn't agree more. Especially having met Freya. She's quite a handful."

"You can say that again," Mrazich agreed.

"And she also made quite an impression on our top AI minds, and that's saying something. Zed has always been a bit of a tough nut to crack, but for whatever reason, those two hit it off immediately. They did a lot of collaboration while Daisy was with us."

"Excuse me, but did you say Freya collaborated with Zed?" Sid asked.

"Yes, Sid. Zed as well as the other AIs in the fleet."

"Ah, then that explains the progress your people made with the warp technology."

"You've hit the nail on the proverbial head, Sid. With so many minds working the problem, it was only a matter of time before we not only replicated the warp orb, but also enlarged the system to function with larger vessels."

"But why didn't you come sooner?" Mrazich asked. "People died because we were shorthanded. Your fleet could have made all the difference."

"Because, Commander, Daisy came to us too soon in her own timeline. The *Váli* had not yet even arrived here at Dark Side. If we had used that technology to interfere, we would have caused a fatal paradox and negated the entire event from the timestream. Or at least, that's what the AI conglomerate believes would have happened."

"So you waited until *after* her jump, timing your arrival to ensure no such paradox," Sid noted.

"Precisely," she said as they entered the mess hall. "Oh my, what smells so good?"

The Chithiid team all rose to their feet in greeting, while Finn eschewed protocol and ran up to the fleet's commander and gave her an enormous hug.

"Celeste! Oh my God, it's so good to see you!" he gushed. "Arlo, this is Celeste Harkaway. She pretty much runs the entirety of our fleet."

Arlo dipped forward and kissed her hand.

"The pleasure is all mine," he said with a warm smile.

"Oh, quite a charmer, I see."

"Yeah, and he comes from another faction of survivors. One that escaped in a different direction than the rest of us," Finn said. "He only joined up with us a little while ago, but he's already proven himself a valuable teammate."

"Aww, thanks, dude."

"Well, it's true," Finn said. "And he's even turning into a decent cook, if you ask me."

Chu walked over and offered his hand.

"We haven't met before, though, of course, I know who you are. I'm Alfred Chu, the lead scientist working with the Chithiid on the warp technology. It's a great pleasure to meet you."

"Ah, so these aliens are working under you?"

"With me, is more like it. We're a collaborative unit now that the Ra'az are gone. These guys have been giving it their all, and it looks like we're making some real headway."

"And they understand English?" she asked, surprised.

"Oh, no. Sid and the other AIs have a Chithiid translation protocol now. They've been translating for us."

She turned to the assembled aliens and walked down the line, shaking each of their hands in greeting.

"Sid, would you please translate for me?"

"Of course."

"Please tell our friends that I am pleased to meet them, and that we are grateful for their hard work."

Sid quickly relayed her words in Chithiid.

"Tell them we have returned at this time of need to help bring the fight to the Ra'az. With the warp technology our fleet possesses, we will have the edge. Soon we will be able to strike a crippling blow to the Ra'az."

The Chithiid reacted with smiles and a murmur of excitement as the message was relayed.

"We also look forward to having them assist our technicians with the warp cores."

"Thank you," Chu said. "We could use all the help we can get. We've made great progress, but we keep hitting stumbling blocks when we––"

"Oh, you misunderstand," she interrupted. "We are not here to help you complete your warp drives. We are here to help you install the ones we have already built and brought with us for integration into your fleet."

"You have *extra* warp cores?" Chu asked, beside himself.

"Yes, many of them, and all we need now is your Chithiid friends and their expert hands to help install them."

Sid relayed the message, and the aliens could barely contain their surprise and excitement.

"Now, what was that you were saying about fresh produce?" Celeste asked.

"I can whip you up some––" Arlo began, before Finn pushed him aside.

"Whatever you want, Celeste, I'll be happy to prepare it for you."

"Then surprise me, Finnegan. I know you never disappoint. Commander, will you join me?"

"I really should talk to the fleet. To the people on the ground," he began.

323

"Oh, let Sid handle that," she said. "He's not a toaster, after all. He's a fully functioning top-tier higher intelligence. I think he can relay this information, and I could use the company. Plus, I need you to fill me in on everything else that has happened since Daisy's return."

The transmission that reached the sisters as they rested in their suites in the historic building in the center of Los Angeles gave both Daisy and Sarah a massive jolt of adrenaline, keeping them from any hopes of a restful evening. They both opened their doors at the same time, eager to wake the other.

"So you heard?" Sarah asked.

"Oh, yeah. The fleet is here," Daisy said, excitement flooding her body.

"And you know these people?"

"Met them when we jumped back in time. We tracked them down and were trying to embed the AI virus cure on the *Váli* before she launched, but, unfortunately, Freya jumped us a bit too far forward in time. This was just before we saved you, Sis."

"Hang on, are you saying they know you can time travel?"

"No, I mean, not more than that one time. Time travel is too risky for anyone but us and Freya to know we did it more than once."

"Though I think she probably has it pretty well dialed in now, wouldn't you think?"

"Likely. But it's really not something we should ever be toying with. I mean, who knows what kind of problems we could create if we started accidentally messing with time?"

"So they really bought it? The whole, stuck in cryo thing?"

"Looks that way," Daisy replied.

"Then we're all good," Sarah said with a growing smile. "And if they've actually come all this way with a bunch of functional warp drives, that means we're golden."

"I know. Things are looking up, Sis."

"What do you two say we head up to Dark Side and say hello?"

"I'd say that's a great idea. Sarah?"

"Yep, though we'll have to explain me and this arm and whatnot," Sarah added.

"Just say you don't remember anything but waking up in a cryo pod. I think Celeste is too well-mannered to dig beyond that, at least for now," Daisy said. "Hey, Freya, come pick us up, will ya? We need a ride up to Dark Side. Your buddy Zed and the gang are back."

Celeste was finishing up the pasta primavera Finn had whipped up for her when she got word that Daisy was coming up to see her.

"Excellent. I've been looking forward to continuing our talks, albeit several years later."

She rose from her seat but was quickly knocked back into it as a series of blasts shook the base.

"Sid, what's going on?" Mrazich yelled into the comms.

"Unknown, Commander. It seems explosive devices are cutting off my systems."

"Where are the attackers targeting from? Mal, Bob, do you see hostiles?" he said, rising to his feet.

"No, Commander, you don't understand," Sid interrupted. "The explosions are coming from inside the base."

A look of panic flashed across his face as he turned toward the Chithiid technicians seated across the mess hall. All but one looked shocked. The one holding a remote trigger in his hand.

"Chu, look out! Loyalist!" he shouted, reaching for his sidearm.

A massive hand smashed down on his head from behind, knocking him unconscious. A second loyalist had been standing nearby, pretending to be startled by the explosions. In fact, he was waiting for just such an opportunity to neutralize the lone armed human in the room.

"Commander, I've lost my internal scans. What's going on in there?" Sid called out.

"Loyalists in the base, Sid!" Arlo shouted as he lunged for the traitorous alien, a chef's knife in his hand.

The large alien slapped it away, quickly wrapping the boy up in his arms.

"All of you stand down or the child and woman die!" the other Chithiid said, brandishing Mrazich's commandeered sidearm.

"He said to stand down or people will die," Sid rapidly translated.

"You can't do this! We were making such progress! We're a team!" Chu said in disbelief.

To make his point clear, the alien fired a shot into the refrigerator near his head.

"The next one will not miss, puny human."

"He said the next one won't miss."

"I gathered as much," Chu said, sliding back to his seat.

"Stengg, gather cordage and bind the hostages," the armed loyalist directed.

"I shall, Huraan. Have you triggered the other charges?"

"Not all of them. We must first secure the communications relay before sealing off the rest of the base."

"Very well. I will be quick, then we can both proceed to phase two," his partner replied. *"You, in the kitchen. Berrk. Come here. You will help bind these people. Do not try any heroics, or you will die a slow death."*

Finn gave him a little nod to go along with the commands.

While Sid was remaining silent over his speakers, the small earpiece he wore was quietly translating for him. Arlo, on the other hand, didn't require the device.

"We can't let them do this," he growled.

"Stand down, kid. This is not the time."

"But they're taking over the base."

"And if we want to take it back, we have to be alive. Stand down, and keep your eyes open."

"This one speaks our tongue," Stengg noted.

"Yes," Huraan replied. *"Gag him as well as binding his limbs."*

"It shall be done."

Outside in the cold vacuum, Mal had received a burst transmission from Sid before his comms went silent. She quickly relayed the message to the fleet, as well as her friends en route from the surface.

"Shit. We should have known this would happen," Daisy growled as she strapped her sword to her back and a veritable arsenal to her body.

"You couldn't have known, Daze. They were checked and double-checked. No loyalist markings and no history of loyalist behavior from what we could find."

"But records were lost. And the Chithiid in that facility were sequestered. Stupid, stupid, Daisy!" she chided herself. "Should have seen this coming."

"She's right, Daze. There's no way you could have predicted this. And now you're flipping out, and we need you calm and collected if we're going to fix this."

Daisy knew Sarah was right and forced herself to slow down, taking a deep breath and dropping a few of the armloads of weapons she had hastily gathered up.

"That's better," Sarah said. "Besides, you only have two hands. I don't know what you were going to do with that many guns."

"Make them *extra* dead," she replied, not a hint of sarcasm in her voice. "If we'd left just a few minutes earlier, we'd have been inside when this all started."

"I know, but we're not, so we need to come up with a plan."

"Freya, where the hell are Arlo and Marty? We could really use them right about now."

"Arlo is inside Dark Side. He was with Finn last I heard. As for Marty, I haven't spoken to him in a day. He does tend to go silent at times. He did say he had something to do, but being a stealth build like I am, I haven't seen him on my scans."

"Just fucking great. It looks like it's up to us."

"And that massive fleet, Daze."

"We're the only stealth ship, Sis. Anyone else gets close, they may escalate the situation."

As if on cue, more explosions ripped through Dark Side, sending it into further lockdown. A situation report relayed the information to all who were keyed in to the secure comms line.

"Let me guess. Shelly and Omar are still down on Earth training Chithiid," Daisy said angrily.

"Actually, no," Freya corrected. "They're up on Dark Side. Went back up a few days ago."

"Hell yeah! Now we're talking!"

"And it looks like they're locked down in Hangar Three, which has been sealed from the base, along with all of the other hangars and most peripheral facilities," Freya added. "Hang on, there's a message coming through. It's on all frequencies, and transmitting in all directions. It's coming from Dark Side."

"Put it on."

"The planet Earth has been taken by humans and Chithiid rebels. Our communications centers have been destroyed, and the rebels control the planet. They have acquired a powerful warp technology and are preparing an assault on the fleet. Defend yourselves, and send help."

"It's set on a repeater, broadcasting over and over," Freya said.

"We have to stop that signal," Daisy said. "Freya, can you block it?"

"No, it's from the base's main transmitter. They're powered by the solar arrays. It's too powerful a signal to jam, and I'm cut off from Sid's systems."

A short burst of static filled their ears, then quieted.

"Freya, do you copy?" Mal transmitted on a tight-band line.

"I hear you, Mal. What happened? What do we do?" Freya replied, a tinge of panic to her voice.

"Freya, I need you to sneak up on Dark Side and take a position outside Section Five. Can you do that?"

"Yeah, shouldn't be a problem," the AI replied, quickly making her way to the designated area and dropping into a smooth hover.

"Good, I see you there. Now I need you to charge your cannon and fire into that section."

"But our friends are there!"

"I know, but the hostiles have taken control of Dark Side Base, and we cannot allow that."

"Hang on, Finn's in there," Sarah added. "Freya, you can't kill Finn."

"I know, Sarah."

"You're not listening to me. This is bigger than a few lives. With the data stored within those walls, the loyalists could cause irreparable damage to the rebellion. You have to fire," Mal ordered.

Freya powered up her main cannon, but hesitated.

"Daisy? I-I..."

"I know, kiddo. It's okay. Power it down."

Freya disengaged the cannon.

"I'm sorry, I couldn't—"

"Nothing to be sorry about. You're not a military ship. Never have been. Making those kinds of decisions just isn't in your DNA."

"You realize what you're doing, Daisy?" Mal said angrily. It was a tone she had never heard come from the AI, no matter how bad things had become.

"Yes, I do," she replied. "Freya?"

"Yeah?"

"Power up the smaller cannon."

"But I thought you said I didn't have to—"

"And target the comms array."

"But Sid will be cut off! We need that transmitter," Mal objected.

"We can build another. Fire when ready, kiddo."

Freya didn't hesitate, letting loose a single pulse, cleanly taking down the primary comms array, effectively silencing the loyalist's transmission.

Beneath them, on the surface of the moon, Sid frantically scanned his remaining systems, trying to find anything he could use to stymie the loyalists. Time and again, his commands would not reach their intended systems, cut off by the carefully placed charges the loyalists had stealthily positioned over the prior month.

He pulled up the only systems that seemed to possibly be receiving his signals, though he had no way to be sure. With a roll of the dice, he sent his commands. All he could do now was hope they worked.

CHAPTER THIRTY-SIX

"How long will it be until that transmission reaches their fleet?" Reggie asked from his pilot's seat aboard the *Váli*.

"No idea, Reggie. It could be months, it could be years. We simply do not know how far away they are," Mal replied.

"So we have to finish our retrofits and get to their fleet first, then."

"Obviously, but that's not the only problem."

"Seriously, Mal? What else?"

"The transmission was sent on a wide spectrum burst. Disabling the comms accomplished nothing. The message was already sent in all directions."

"Shit, so it's a ripple in a pond," Reggie said.

"Precisely. It will spread, farther and farther, until it not only reaches the Ra'az fleet, but the ships surrounding the Chithiid homeworld as well."

"And from there, it will continue on."

"Yes," Mal replied. "All the way to the Ra'az world itself."

Reggie sank lower in his pilot's seat.

"It just gets worse and worse for us, Mal."

"I know, Reggie."

"At least it can't get much worse than this. I don't see how it could."

He looked out the porthole windows at the massive fleet orbiting the moon, all of them impotent, unable to approach, and the one ship that could, too scared to do much.

The hostages inside Dark Side were trussed up tight, the key corridors between hangars sealed shut when the blasts took out the hardline connections.

In the event of an external attack, those systems would have been safe and sound inside the thick walls of the base. With an intruder sabotaging them from within, however, Sid's strength was quickly turned into his weakness.

The loyalists had separated those they considered lower value hostages from those of more worth. The commander, Celeste, and the young man who spoke their language were among the latter. Though they hadn't felt the impact that severed the comms, the aliens nevertheless suspected that something was wrong.

"Stengg, activate one of the small portable communications devices. Open it to receive on any frequency."

The Chithiid did as he was asked. Silence greeted him.

"Try another frequency. Cycle through them if you must."

One after another, they heard nothing. Their message, though still sending from their apparatus, was no longer transmitting from the base.

Arlo smiled at their realization.

The loyalist leader walked over to the bound youth and slapped him hard across the face.

"You would be well-served to keep your mirth in check, human. Very soon you may have little to smile about."

He grabbed the portable comms device and opened it to hail on all frequencies. The range was limited, no farther than the fleet surrounding him, but that was all he required.

"Computer, you will translate for me," he ordered.

"I will do as you ask," Sid replied, *"but you will need to hold the device closer to my speakers. You have cut me off from my transmission apparatus. I cannot send your message directly."*

"Very well," he replied, holding the portable comms close to the nearest wall-embedded speaker. *"Hear me, human fleet. We have taken control of this base, as you have already discovered. We have your precious leaders in our possession. They are well-treated and alive, for now."*

He paused, waiting for Sid to translate.

"We know you are in possession of warp technology. You will send a non-AI piloted warp-capable vessel to your Hangar One. It will be deposited there, then left unattended. Once you have done so, we will depart from this place with one of your people aboard as insurance until we warp away. If you pursue us, they die. If you attempt to stop us, they die. Your only option is that of compliance. Bring us an unmanned ship as you have been directed," he said. *"Translate the message."*

"I will," Sid said, then translated for those listening.

"Do as you have been instructed. You have one hour. If you have not complied, we will kill a hostage. Translate this."

Sid did, reluctantly, then sat quiet as the comms were disconnected.

The fleet was instantly abuzz with discussion of what to do. Zed was not about to give an unknown number of alien extremists a tactical advantage.

"We give them a ship, but disengage part of the warp drive. Make it look functional, but keep it from warping."

"But they will kill their hostage," one of the other ships in the fleet noted.

"Yes, they very well may," he replied. "But one hostage versus a base full of them is a tactical sacrifice we may have to make."

"May I make a suggestion?" a male voice butted in.

"Who is this? Identify yourself!" Zed demanded.

"Jeez, so touchy. You need to chill out, man," the voice replied. "My name's Marty." He flashed on his lights right outside Zed's windows, much like Freya had done. "Nice to meet you."

"Another stealth ship? This may be the advantage we need," the greater AI mused.

"Marty? Where were you?" Daisy asked.

"Oh, hi Daisy. I was off doing stuff. Nice to hear your voice. I didn't know you were on the line."

"Freya's been listening in. I had her open the channel."

"Cool. Hi Freya."

"Hey," she said, dejectedly.

"You okay?"

"No, not really."

"What's wrong?" Marty asked, concern apparent in his voice.

"It's just all of the interior monitors are offline. There's nothing I can tap into in order to see what's going on in there. I mean, my scanners sensed some brief weapons fire a while ago, but I have no idea what's happening. And now there's no way to sneak in without risking a total depressurization of the facility, and we don't know where they're holding the hostages. I suck at this."

"It's not your fault. You're doing great, given your resources," Marty soothed.

"No, I'm not. I'm a shitty tactician. What we really need is someone smart. Someone who can plan these kinds of things. I'm afraid I've only made things worse."

"Hey, kiddo, you did your best, and we'll get through this," Daisy said. "We just need to figure something out, is all."

"Yeah, she's right," Marty agreed.

"And where have you been?" Daisy asked again. "You still haven't answered me."

"Doing stuff."

"Stuff?"

"Yeah, stuff. Anyway, I'm here now, and when I heard what was going on, I thought maybe I could help you guys."

"Unfortunately, we're kind of at a loss here, Marty. We don't have any Chithiid-sized EVA suits, which just leaves me and Sarah, and we can't even get into one of the airlocks to begin to try and sort this out."

"I know, that's why I brought friends," the AI said, cheerfully.

"Friends?"

"Hi, Daisy," Duke's voice said over the comms. "The fellas and I happened to meet our boy Marty here down in LA, and he was kind enough to offer us a ride up here. We understand there's some loyalist ass in desperate need of kicking."

"You don't know the half of it. But the base is locked down, and we can't get in."

"Leave that to us. This kind of thing is what we do. Well, in atmosphere, usually, but you get the picture. And since our flesh died off a long time ago, we don't even need EVA suits to protect us."

"What's your plan?" Sarah asked over the comms. "We can't blast our way in, they'll hear us coming and kill the hostages."

"Nope, we wouldn't want that," Duke replied. "My guys have a pair of laser cutters that should do the trick. We can bore directly into an adjacent corridor, bypassing the fried airlocks. It'll take a while, mind you, and we'll have to be careful when we decompress the corridor. Still, those walls are pretty damn tough, and designed to withstand a lot more than these piddly little things, but eventually we'll get in. All we need from you is to stall for time."

Daisy and Sarah perked up, a sliver of hope cheering their spirits in this time of need.

"Okay, Duke. We'll do all we can. Get to it, and good luck." Daisy cut the line and turned to her sister. "So, we need to buy them some time. Any ideas?"

"You sure this will work?" Sarah asked as they buried the final charge in the rocky overhang above Hangar One.

"Oh yeah," Daisy replied. "I almost took a header off the drop above Hangar Two a while back. A decent knock and this stuff should give way."

"Okay, then, let's get the hell out of here and get things rolling. Literally."

The duo quickly made their way back into Freya's airlock, the stealth ship carefully lifting off and pulling away, making sure to stay well out of the line of sight of any of Dark Side's windows.

"How long has it been?"

"Forty minutes, Daisy," Freya replied.

"And how are Duke's men doing down there?"

A burst of encrypted static flooded the comms.

"Oops, sorry," Freya apologized. "Forgot the line was open. They say they're about halfway through the wall."

"They need more time, Daze. Looks like we've got to go with your plan."

"I agree. Are Duke and his guys well clear of Hangar One?"

"Yeah, Daisy. They're cutting into the base close to there, but are around the side so the flicker from the laser cutters isn't visible from within the base," Freya said.

"Okay then. Let them know we're detonating the charges in thirty seconds."

A half a minute later, a tiny puff of dust rose from the stone bluff above Hangar One. The explosions had been minuscule and entirely unfelt by anyone inside the base, but they were nevertheless more than enough to start a small pile on its way.

The debris and stone tumbled down, gathering more mass as it fell until it became a full-fledged rockslide. A minute later, a dusty pile of stone was effectively blocking Hangar One's doors.

"Okay, Zed. You're on," Daisy signaled the command ship.

"Dark Side Base, this is Zed of the command ship, do you copy? Sid, can you hear me?

"What are they saying?" the Chithiid asked. *"You will translate."*

"Of course."

"Yes, this is Sid," the captive AI replied. "Is the ship coming, Zed?"

"There has been a rockslide, Sid. Tell your Chithiid captors to look outside the windows. It seems that when they set off their explosive charges, they disturbed the rocky surface above the base. We will not be able to land a ship inside of Hangar One. Perhaps they have EVA suits, so we can land it outside the nearest airlock doors for them instead," he said, knowing full well they had no such equipment.

"I will translate. Standby."

He did, and the Chithiid both looked out the window, confirming what they were told.

"This is not acceptable. They will land in Hangar One. That was the directive. They have twenty minutes."

Sid translated and awaited a reply.

"Tell them there's no way we can clear all that debris that fast. Maybe if they give us another hour we can have a heavy equipment craft pull the rocks clear."

Again, Sid relayed the message.

"Twenty minutes," the loyalist said, then grabbed the sidearm from his comrade and fired a single shot.

A Chithiid hostage fell to the deck, a small hole in his chest where his heart had formerly been.

"Tell them what I have done."

Sid did as he was told.

"Berrk!" Finn yelled. "Why the hell did you do that, you bastard? There's still time on the clock! He didn't do anything wrong!"

Arlo sat quietly, but the acid hatred burning from his eyes spoke just as clearly as Finn's voice had.

Sid translated for Finn, even though he had not been asked to. The Chithiid looked down on the bound hostage and smiled cruelly.

"Tell him, it was simply to prove I would," he said, coldly. *"And tell him—tell them all— the next one will be a human."* He looked at the chrono on the wall. *"They have eighteen minutes."*

Sid relayed the message, then the Chithiid cut the comms line.

Hovering above the base, Daisy didn't know what to do. They hadn't bought any time, and worse yet, they'd cost one of their allies their life.

"It's not your fault, Daze. You had no idea they'd do that."

"I know. I mean, I know *logically*, but I still can't help but think his death is my fault."

"Let me tell you something, Sis. Crazies like that? If they want to kill someone, they're going to do it, regardless of what happens outside their realm of control. I bet he was going to do that all along. This just gave him an excuse."

"I don't know," Daisy said. "What I do know, is Duke is our last hope."

Fifteen minutes later, the team of cyborgs was still cutting through the thick wall as fast as they could. A hole had formed, but it was still too small for one of their reinforced frames to fit through.

Duke looked at his chrono. They were close, but he didn't know if they would make it in time. It wasn't looking likely.

Inside the mess hall, the loyalist Chithiid were also looking at their chronos, but in their case, evil acts were on their minds as the minutes ticked down.

"It is nearly time," Stengg said.

"Yes. Bring a human. The female."

The alien grabbed Celeste roughly by the arms and dragged her to her feet.

"Wait, take me instead!" Finn shouted. "Sid, translate that!"

Sid did as he was asked, and the tall alien paused and turned, looking the bound captive up and down.

"Tell him I will not, but maybe I will shoot him as well, just for sport."

Sid relayed the message.

Finn showed no fear, hate blazing from his eyes as he watched the Chithiid pull his victim toward an open space in the room.

The chrono was ticking down, and there was nothing he could do about it.

The alien watched as the numbers grew smaller. Thirty seconds, then twenty. At ten, he began to raise his weapon.

"Farewell, tiny huma—"

A pulse blast rang out, skull and brain matter spattering across the mess hall.

"What? How did—"

The other loyalist––the one whose head had not just been blown off––spun to face his attacker just as a trio of pulse blasts tore his chest to ribbons, sending his body flying across the room.

He was dead before he hit the floor.

Celeste turned in shock, looking across the chamber for her savior as the smoke cleared.

Her eyes locked on her rescuer and grew wide, flooding with tears of joy.

Standing in the doorway, still frosty from his emergency

thaw, Captain Harkaway leaned against the doorframe. A particularly massive pulse rifle was hanging loosely in his hand. He smiled warmly at his wife as he dropped the rifle to the deck with a clang.

"Hi, honey," he said. "Fancy seeing you here."

CHAPTER THIRTY-SEVEN

Fatima stood on the beach, the clear skies and azure waves near postcard-perfect as the faint rush of the surf and distant call of gulls hung on the wind, completing the scene.

Only this time she was not alone. Not by a long shot.

Lars and Celeste Harkaway were both standing before her, barefoot in the clean sand beneath a small awning erected for the event. Likewise shoeless, and enjoying the warmth radiating between her toes, Fatima was reading aloud from a small stack of inspirational notes and time-tested vows she had prepared for the event.

Surrounded by their friends and crewmates––who happened to be largely one and the same––the long-separated pair stood close, hands clasped as the silver-haired woman beautifully made her way through her speech, eventually asking them each a single question, one to which they both answered, 'I do.'

Daisy squeezed Vince's hand at the emotional moment, and he gently raised hers and pressed it to his lips.

The Harkaways looked radiant and ecstatic as they officially renewed their vows.

Even with the benefits of cryogenic stasis, it had been many, many years since the couple had seen one another, and when Captain Harkaway had dropped to one knee and asked his wife to marry him all over again—only minutes after saving her from a horrible death at the hands of alien loyalists, no less—she threw her arms around him and pulled him in close, whispering a tearful but joyous yes in his ear.

There were no dry eyes that day, and the sun and salty air played no role in that occurrence. Even the Chithiid present welled up with tears, and for creatures with four eyes, that was something to witness. But for them, long-separated from their loved ones on their homeworld, the ceremony held even more significance than it did for many of the human observers.

They were going to retake their own world, someday, and even if their wives were old and gray and their children long-grown, at least they would finally be together again. A family unit reunited.

Fatima held out her hand, a pair of shining rings glistening in the sun against her brown skin. Neither Harkaway had worn one in years, with the hardships of their duties and injuries they had repaired. But each had kept theirs safely tucked away, and Mal had ensured both were restored to new condition for the event.

They slid the bands onto each other's fingers and kissed tenderly.

Then a little *more* than tenderly, a hungry look in their eyes.

"Get a room, you two!" Daisy shouted out with a joyful laugh.

The crowd burst into peals of laughter and applause and swarmed the couple, bombarding them with hugs, handshakes, and hearty congratulations.

Daisy and Fatima pulled Captain Harkaway aside a moment and slid a keycard into his hand.

"When I said get a room—" Daisy began.

"What Daisy is saying, Lars, is that we had our friends fix you up a little something special," Fatima finished. "You see the white building?" she asked, pointing to a slightly weathered tower just off the coastline. "It used to be a five-star hotel. While the lower levels need a bit of work, the top floor is all fixed up, and it's all yours."

Harkaway wiped the tears from his eyes and looked at the two women standing before him.

"The honeymoon suite? Really?"

"You deserve it, and Lord knows we don't want to hear or see the two of you in Dark Side for at least a week," Daisy said with a grin. "In fact, make that two."

"I don't know how to thank you."

"You already did. You saved the day, Captain, and it's time you enjoyed the spoils of your victory."

Harkaway turned and looked at the crowd of friends, then gazed at his blushing bride. At the sight of her, his smile grew a little brighter.

"So, see you at the reception in what? An hour?" he asked.

Fatima saw the way he was looking at Celeste.

"Make it two. We'll get started without you," she said with a wink.

Harkaway grinned happily and went to collect his wife, sweeping her off her feet, literally, and carrying her across the sand to a waiting transport.

"He's moving like a new man," Fatima noted. "Even on the soft sand."

"Yeah, funny, that," Daisy said with a knowing smile.

"Daisy? What did you do?"

"Me? I didn't do anything."

"Let me clarify. What did *Freya* do?"

"Oh, that? Well, when she inoculated him against the plague, she might have, just maybe, turned loose a few of her nanites as well. You know, just a little something to fix up his worn-out replacement parts before they broke down on him."

"Aah," Fatima said. "That would explain it. And judging by the way his wife was looking at him, I think he'll be putting those repairs to good use."

"Oh, Fatima, seriously? You went there?" Daisy laughed.

"Why, whatever do you mean? I was merely making an observation," she shot back with a grin. "Now, come on, there's a party to enjoy, and we should make the most of it. The plague has been cured, and it's a happy occasion, but after this shindig, I'm afraid there's going to be a lot of work for all of us."

"Did someone say party?" Finn laughed as he stumbled through the sand, a drink in each hand. "Well, then, let's go!" He merrily made his way through the crowd to the slender woman in a rather flattering dress.

"Dang, look at Sarah, will ya?" Vince said, rejoining Daisy after making a quick round of the guests. "Habby really hooked her up."

"He hooked all of us up," Daisy said.

"And you look stunning, my dear,"

"Good save," she chuckled.

"I mean, she looks good and all, but doesn't hold a candle to you," he said, pulling her close for a kiss.

"Hey, that's my sister you're talking about."

"Gah! It's a lose-lose situation!" he said with a warm laugh. The one that made Daisy's knees go a little bit weak.

They watched as Finn handed Sarah her drink and began walking with her toward the festivities getting underway nearby. Sarah glanced at Daisy, flashing a look that could only mean 'it's just one drink, don't gloat.'

"You think she's finally going to take that stick out of her ass and loosen up?"

Dear Lord, I hope so.

"Yeah, me too," Sarah replied.

Daisy noted the slightly down tone of her voice in her head.

You okay, Sis?

"Yeah. It's just a little tough, ya know? Being stuck in here while she..."

I know. If there's anything I can do—

"Nah, I'll be fine. I just think I'm going to go do my own thing for a bit. Leave you and Vince to yourselves."

Okay, but the second you need me—

"Don't worry, I'll reach out if I do. Now go have some fun, okay?"

Will do. Love you, Sis.

"Back atcha."

Daisy took Vince by the hand and led him to join the others in what was to be the best party Earth had seen in a few hundred years.

The following morning, still mildly tipsy and warm with the joyful memories of the happy event, Daisy and Vince climbed aboard Freya and flew off to survey the work the aliens had been doing on their Trojan Horse fleet. His engineering know-how, combined with a highly motivated workforce, had led to rapid advances, though it was still going to take them months to be truly ready, despite having functional warp technology at their fingertips—courtesy of the recently-arrived fleet.

"They've already hooked up one of the warp drive units in that one over there, but we still have to patch up the hull before they take it up into space," he told her.

"New weapons system?"

"Yeah. It retracts perfectly."

"With you designing it, I expect nothing less."

"Thanks for the vote of confidence, but this is Ra'az tech, so there's been a steep learning curve. But like I was saying, the weapons retract and tuck into the hull, and the regular surface slides back into place to camouflage it perfectly. Still, there are a few connecting points in the recessed compartment that aren't as air-tight as I'd like them. I really don't want any surprise decompressions out there, especially in combat."

"The Chithiid training in orbit are really doing well, you know. I think they'll perform admirably, even if they're not soldiers by trade," Daisy noted.

"Yeah, but once the real shooting starts and their friends start dying, things change real fast," he replied.

"Everyone has a plan until they get hit in the mouth," Daisy quipped.

"Indeed. Let's just hope for the element of surprise."

"Hey, Daisy?" Freya said over her comms.

"Yeah, kiddo?"

"I was listening to what you guys were saying just now."

"And do you think the ships will hold up?" Vince asked.

"Oh, that? Yeah, they're looking great, actually. Structural tolerances are far above their original parameters, actually."

"Huh, I didn't realize that," he said.

"See? You're even better than you knew," Daisy said warmly.

"But that's not what I wanted to tell you."

"What did you want to tell us, Freya?" Daisy asked.

"Well, you mentioned the element of surprise, and how people will start dying if the Ra'az realize what's happening and start firing on our guys. So the thing is, I've been working on something—with Marty's help. A side project that might be an even bigger surprise."

"Bigger than enemy ships sneaking into their ranks?" Vince asked. "You've got my attention."

"Yeah, it could be. You see, I've been thinking about the way the Ra'az invaded Earth. How they took over without needing a massive battle. I thought, why not use their tactics against them?"

"Well, we are launching a sneak attack—"

"No, not that part," Freya said, impatiently. "I designed a

modified version of an AI virus, much like the one they used against all of my new friends."

"But Freya, the Ra'az don't use AIs on their ships," Vince pointed out.

"Well, duh. But they do have massively-interconnected computer systems running every system. So my virus, which is totally *not* dangerous to any AIs, by the way, should be able to spread through their systems undetected, then trigger when we want."

"Holy shit. You mean you could disable their entire fleet without firing a single shot?" Daisy gasped. "Freya, that's amazing."

"Well..."

"What's the 'well,' Freya?"

"The thing is, it doesn't disable *all* of their systems. I mean, sure, it'll knock out a bunch of them, only I can't really predict which ones it'll affect. So it is a weapon, and it should help our guys, only it's kinda going to have to be a sort of wait-and-see kind of element to the attack."

Daisy and Vince shared a hopeful look. It was by no means a perfect solution, but Freya––with no nudging––had taken the initiative to do something, and what she and Marty had come up with could possibly make a big difference on the day. If it worked, that is.

"So I assume we'll need to inoculate our own captured Ra'az and Chithiid ships against it, right?" Vince asked.

"Yeah. I've already prepared a data packet, but after what happened on Dark Side, I didn't want to hand it over to just anyone."

"Good thinking, kiddo."

"Thanks. I've put it on a data chip for Vince to install manually. It'll be a bit more work, not mass-distributing it, but he should be able to do it while working on the other projects pretty easily. And that way, there's no chance of anyone stealing the cure and giving it to the Ra'az as soon as we attack."

"That's a damn clever kid, Daze," Sarah said.

Don't I know it.

"Thanks, Freya. You did good. You know what? I think we should track down Maarl and fill him in. He's one Chithiid I'm one hundred percent sure of, and this will be some welcome news for him after the Dark Side fiasco."

"Oh, he's over by the tribunal building. I've been keeping tabs on key members of the team these last few days, just to make stuff easier."

"How did you do that, Freya?" Daisy asked, her curiosity piqued.

"I kinda gave him a secured communicator when he was aboard, just in case he needed me."

"And that communicator also happens to let you track his location?" Vince said.

"Yeah, obviously. Duh."

"Hey, mind the snark," Daisy said.

"Whatever. But yeah, it's a tracker as well."

"Well, then, I'll ignore the minor invasion of privacy, since it expedites things for us today. Come on. Let's go see him."

Maarl was more than slightly thrilled to hear of not only Vince's progress with the fleet, but also Freya's secret weapon. It seemed things were coming together, and much faster, and smoother, than any of them could have anticipated.

Except for the problem on Dark Side, of course.

That would require weeks of repairs, if not months, and even with a gaggle of military AIs on the job around the clock, it was still, by its very nature, a time-consuming task.

"With the arrival of the human and AI fleet, our alliance is greatly strengthened," Maarl noted. *"This, and especially the warp*

technology they are now sharing with our retrofitted fleet, is likely why the loyalists broke their cover and attacked prematurely as they did. Once more, I must offer my humblest apologies for not discovering their true nature before they acted."

"It's not your fault, Maarl. Things were hectic, and they bore none of the loyalist markings."

"But we have always known there were loyalist spies hidden in our midst."

"And there likely still are. All we can do is be alert, and protect key systems and information as best we can. Critical knowledge should only be shared with a select few," Daisy said.

"I agree, Daisy. And there is something else we should address."

"Yes?"

"This alliance. I have been in touch with the one they call Zed. He has quite rapidly learned the Chithiid tongue, and is a very impressive intellect."

"I got that impression from him."

"He's a cool guy, too!" Freya chimed in.

"Not now, kiddo," Daisy replied over her open comms.

"Ah, Freya. It is a pleasure to hear your voice," Maarl said. *"But Daisy is correct. We must focus on this issue at hand with all our attention for the moment."*

"So what's on the plate, Maarl? What did you guys discuss?"

"We are going to be facing an enemy on three fronts, not including the clean-up required here on Earth. Originally, we were going to have to utilize all of our assets at once, quickly moving from objective to objective. But now, with an entire fleet joining us, and providing warp technology to our ships as well, we may now better utilize our resources."

"Meaning what, exactly?"

"Meaning we shall separate into three separate fleets to begin our missions simultaneously. Should any Ra'az communications happen to leak to warn the others, this will minimize any harm that might cause."

"Seems logical," Daisy said.

"Indeed. The force infiltrating and overcoming the Ra'az fleet will be a quiet operation, led by one of my most trusted men. We are currently gathering him a small core of rock-solid crew to provide an untainted support team. I will personally lead the fleet moving to retake my home world, in conjunction with several AIs from your people's fleet."

"And the Ra'az homeworld?" Daisy asked. *"That's going to be the toughest nut to crack."*

"Zed and I agree on that," Maarl said. *"And for that reason, we have selected the greatest of your strategists to lead that assault."*

"Well, Zed's a pretty solid guy, that's for sure, and he has centuries of—"

"We have selected you, Daisy."

Daisy fell silent as the words sank in.

"I'm sorry, you what, now?"

CHAPTER THIRTY-EIGHT

Sarah trudged through Freya's airlock when she picked her up just past noon. Dragging her feet, and more than a little hungover, Sarah grumbled her hellos to Daisy, Vince, and Maarl, then flopped into her seat.

"Are you okay, Sarah?" Freya asked. "I'm reading dehydration and elevated cortisol levels. If you want, I could––"

"Shhh," Sarah said, wincing at the chipper AI's voice. "I just need a little quiet time, is all. Can you do that for me, kid?"

"Oh, yeah. Sorry," Freya apologized, lowering her voice. "But I was just saying, I can whip you up a B-complex and electrolyte pouch. It should alleviate most of your discomfort."

"Sure. Whatever," Sarah sighed. "And dim the interior lights, will ya?"

Daisy and Vince shared an amused look as Freya took to the skies.

"You sure you don't want to go take a nap?" Daisy asked. "Maybe, lay down for a bit?"

"Shut up," Sarah grumbled.

"Hey, just making an offer," she replied, leaving her sister to her misery.

And this is why we didn't have alcohol on board the Váli, Daisy mused.

"I know I shouldn't laugh at what is technically my own misery—sort of—but she kinda had it coming. Was I always that uptight?"

Nah. I just think this version of you is going through some stuff.

"And the dead version wasn't?"

It's not the same, Sis. I mean, you and me? We had time to talk and find a rhythm before you learned what had happened. That you? She was fine one minute, then woke up to learn she was essentially dead and had been rebuilt with mechanical bits stuck on. Kind of a mind-fuck of a different kind.

"Still, doesn't mean she needs to be a bitch."

You are so lucky I'm not wearing my neuro-band.

"I don't care. Let her hear."

Now, now. Play nice with your hungover self.

"Well, at least she finally let her hair down and enjoyed the party."

Seriously. She was still dancing when I left. Her feet have got to be aching as much as it looks like her head is, Daisy noted with an amused grin.

"What's so funny?" Vince asked, noting her smile.

"Oh, just thinking about stuff," she covered. "Don't worry, I'm all serious now, and ready to go."

"Cool. We should be ready to jump any time. Hey, Freya, do you have those coordinates worked out yet?" he asked the ship's clever AI.

"Yeah, ready to go whenever you guys are. It will probably take a dozen or so jumps to pinpoint the Ra'az fleet, but that's better than arriving right in the middle of them."

"Amen," Sarah groaned.

"Okay, then, kiddo. Let's get started. The sooner we establish a firm location and scout out their actual numbers, the sooner our tactical specialists can get to work planning the minutia of the infiltration and assault."

She turned to her Chithiid ally.

"Freya says it will take a number of warp jumps to accurately locate the position of the Ra'az fleet. Hopefully we'll find them in less than twelve."

"I heard," he said, tapping a small device tucked into his left ear.

"Freya, did you make a translator comms for Maarl?"

"Yeah. I thought it'd be easier if I just went ahead and translated for him real-time, since everyone else on board is human and doesn't speak Chithiid. Except you, of course. Your Chithiid is really good."

"Good thinking," Daisy replied. "And thanks for the compliment." She cinched herself into her captain's seat and looked at the forward monitors. "All right, Freya. Hit it."

Freya fired her thrusters and took them on a quick loop to the empty space between the Earth and the moon and lined up for her warp.

"Okay, here we go."

A familiar blue skin formed over her hull as the device powered up. Then, in an instant, she was gone.

Freya's estimate was a bit off. A lot, actually. It required nearly two dozen jumps before they finally came across the Ra'az fleet's path of destruction.

"That's three small planets stripped bare, Daze," Sarah said, reviewing the scans they had collected en route. "No survivors that I can see, and all support ships appear to have already wrapped up and jumped back to join the fleet."

"Just like the bulk of the force they left behind surrounding Earth," Vince noted.

"Well, yeah. But those stuck around a hell of a lot longer

before leapfrogging back to their main fleet. Home proved a troublesome target for them," Daisy said. "It's interesting, though, how they do this expanding conquest thing."

"How so?"

"You'd think the part of the fleet overseeing a new planet would never catch up to the rest of them, right? But with the way they stop periodically to conquer new worlds and strip them bare, they actually leave a clear breadcrumb trail, as well as shortening the number of jumps needed to rejoin the fleet."

"And they already know the plotted course," Sarah added.

"And now that we finally connected all those damn dots, we know it too," Daisy said with an exhausted smile.

"Freya, exactly how far off are they?" Vince asked.

"Just at the edge of my scans. I don't even need to warp to reach them. They're moving pretty slow. Probably because there are so many of them."

"Uh, how many are we talking, Freya?" Daisy wondered.

"I can't be entirely sure from this distance, but it looks like there are around seven hundred and fifty ships, including the three dozen main Ra'az command vessels. Those look like the ones they leave in orbit around a new world until it's been subjugated, from what I can tell."

"They are," Maarl confirmed. *"And a dozen of them remain in orbit around my home, keeping our people living in fear as they provide an ever-flowing workforce."*

"Bastards," Daisy growled. *"We'll take them out, Maarl. You have my word on that."*

"I know, Daisy. But first, our mission is to accurately survey this fleet. Their vessels are many, and the numbers seem intimidating, but the vast majority of those ships are either support craft, or work vessels operated by my people and lacking weaponry."

"Salvage vessels and the like?" she asked.

"Yes. And personnel transport ships like the ones we will use as our main infiltration craft as well. While others are deployed on nearby

scouting missions, ours will slip into their places, mimicking their ident codes and blending in."

"A good plan," Daisy noted with a contented grin. *"Freya, let's get close and get a preliminary log of the vessels present, then run a sweep of their ships in nearby sectors. You know, the ones doing scouting runs for more planets to strip."*

"Okay, Daisy."

"What's the plan, babe?" Vince asked.

"Oh, sorry. I totally forgot to hook you up with a Chithiid translation earpiece," Daisy said apologetically. "We're going to run a survey, then fan out and log all the ships that separated from the fleet to identify potential target worlds. After that, we'll do a quick hop back to Earth, transmit the data to Zed and his boys to run calculations and strategy sessions on, then get back to it. Unlike tracking down the Ra'az fleet, Maarl knows the exact location of his planet, so that should make things a whole hell of a lot easier."

"We're actually going to see the Chithiid homeworld," Vince marveled. "I have to say, I'm kinda looking forward to it."

"Not nearly as much as I am," Maarl commented, solemnly.

"He said——"

"I think I can guess what he said," Vince interrupted, turning to the old alien. "We'll get you your world back, Maarl. Whatever it takes."

The Chithiid nodded his head in thanks.

"We shall do all we can, and if we should find fortune in our efforts, I will walk the soil of Taangaar's lush fields once more."

Circling the Chithiid planet of Taangaar, Maarl's heart broke as he looked out of Freya's thick windows.

"Oh, my home. What have they done to you?"

A dozen Ra'az command vessels orbited the planet, as Maarl

had anticipated. What was below, however, was far worse than he could have foreseen.

What had once been fecund forest land and shining cities was now an industrialized grid of housing units and food-growing facilities. All were designed with efficiency in mind, nothing else, and the once-pristine landscape showed the effects.

Ore was strip mined where needed, deep pits scarring the surface of the planet like a pock-marked wall, damaged by shrapnel from an exploding bomb.

While vast oceans still covered much of the planet, the areas nearest the shores were murky with runoff from waste-removal facilities and smelting and fabrication plants.

"They have ruined my world," Maarl lamented.

"I am so sorry, my friend," Daisy consoled. *"We will make them pay for what they have done."*

"Of that I have the utmost faith," Maarl said, a cold look in his eyes. *"And yet, despite the damage they have wrought, my people are strong, and they are resilient. Our planet still lives, and though it may take generations to do so, we can re-shape our world back into the tranquil beauty of its former self."*

He shifted his gaze to the massive Ra'az command vessels locked in geosynchronous orbit above the planet, each controlling a huge swath of the world below. *"But first, we must root out the infection. We must destroy the Ra'az and wipe them from this solar system."*

His anger was clear, and Daisy felt confident that same level of visceral drive would push the rest of his men to great acts of bravery when the time came. Lives would be lost, and blood would be spilled, but if they planned it just right, and if they struck with an abundance of speed and a lack of mercy, they just might be successful.

"Maarl?" Vince asked, waiting for the translator to kick in. "Scans seem to show entire populations have been shifted to the main housing facilities in each sector. I know this is uncomfortable to discuss, and I apologize for bringing it up, but I think it's something we should talk about. How are we going to track down and repatriate your people, once we succeed?"

Maarl listened to the translation, then thought a moment before replying.

"You are correct, Vince. It will be difficult to liberate and reunite my people. We have one thing to our advantage, however. Even where records were destroyed, our familial songs will not have been. Even the young children will have been taught their family's song from their earliest years."

"Of course," Daisy said, as the realization of just what that meant sank in. *"Even without something like a computer record or census, your people can fall back to the songs they used long before those machines and tabulations even existed."*

"You understand," Maarl said with a smile.

Freya quickly translated for Vince as well as both Sarahs, bringing everyone up to speed.

"Freya, have you recorded and logged all relevant data?" Maarl asked.

"Yeah, I've got it all."

"Then we are done here. Let us depart. I would not look any longer upon my world in this state. The next time I see it, it will be as a liberated planet, bathing in the blood of our enemies."

"Okay," the young AI replied.

Freya flew well clear of Taangaar, making sure she was nowhere near any Ra'az scanning apparatus before prepping for their next warp. The long, long trip to the Ra'az world. The planet their enemies called home.

Ra'azengar.

It was quick work deciphering the star charts the Ra'az had left behind when they fled their facilities in San Francisco, and thus far, all of the landmarks had matched up with what Freya already held in her massive data core. But as she powered up, readying for the long warp to Ra'azengar, something felt off to her. Something she couldn't quite put her finger on.

"Daisy?"

"Yeah, Freya? What is it?"

"I-I'm not sure, exactly."

"Is there a problem with your systems? Are you ready to jump?"

"Yeah, that's all fine," the AI replied. "It's just that something about this feels weird."

"Weird in what way?"

"I don't know. I just get this uneasy sensation when I plot the course."

Daisy felt a cold shudder run down her spine. Instinct was something she very much believed in, and if a mind as powerful and informed as Freya was uneasy, they would damn well listen to her instincts.

"Power down, Freya. If there's something up, we need to figure it out."

"I'm sorry. I know you want to get there as soon as we can."

"Not if there's a problem. No, you did the right thing. Your mind is full of massive amounts of data. If something feels wrong, you should trust your gut and triple-check until you're satisfied. Believing in yourself will save you more often than not."

"Okay," Freya said, her relief obvious in her voice.

She spent nearly a half hour reviewing and re-reviewing the Ra'az charts, but something still wasn't sitting right. She just couldn't figure out why.

"A suggestion, if I may," Sarah said, her hangover finally receding after her fifth electrolyte pouch. "Something is up, and we don't know what it is, right?"

"Right."

"So let's not take any chances. I mean, I know it feels like we're in a rush, but this is just a scouting and recon run. The fleet won't even be ready for the assault for months, so let's take our time and not press our luck."

"What are you suggesting, Sis?"

"Warp to the far edge of the solar system and go in under normal power. We'll have plenty of time to see any problems long before we reach them that way."

Daisy thought about it a moment and liked the idea.

"Freya, you good with that?" she asked.

"Yeah, I think it's a good plan."

"Okay, then. Plot your warp for the outer limits of the solar system."

"Will do," she said.

Moments later she was ready to go.

"Okay, warping in five."

The ship glowed a faint blue, then popped out of space, reappearing far, far away.

The blaze that filled her windows and screens was blinding.

"Freya, get us out of here!" Daisy shouted.

Fortunately, Freya had already powered up and jumped them clear, even as she spoke those words. A few seconds after they arrived, they were safely out of harm's way, freaked out, a bit singed, but alive.

"What the hell was that?" Sarah stammered.

"It was a sun," Freya answered.

"But the charts didn't show that."

"No, they didn't," Daisy replied. "Sonofabitch."

"What?"

"The fucking Ra'az, man. They did it again," she sighed. "First the decoy comms station rumors on Earth, now altered star charts. Those paranoid bastards—"

"You mean it was a trap, set in their own records?" Vince asked, stunned.

"Yeah. Unless you're a Ra'az and knew better, following their charts to the letter would have landed you right in the middle of a supernova. That entire solar system was a trap."

"So we don't know where their planet is," Sarah noted, dejectedly. "We are so screwed."

"And our fleet will have to spread itself thin to find it, unless we get lucky somehow," Daisy grumbled. "This could take some time."

She paced the command cabin, weighing their options. Unfortunately, until their tacticians had a look at the data, they'd be flying blind out there, and that was far too risky, given what they'd just experienced.

"Okay, Freya," Daisy reluctantly said. "Not much more we can do out here for now. Take us back home."

CHAPTER THIRTY-NINE

"So we split into teams and get looking," Commander Mrazich growled. "For the love of Pete, are you all giving up so easily?"

"No, Commander, not at all, it's just we've had quite a day, is all," Vince replied.

Daisy watched the discussion, careful to bite her tongue. Mrazich was on edge ever since the loyalists had taken over the base. *His* base. And his powder-keg attitude would not be well-served by her snark on this particular occasion.

"Swarthmore! Tell me you're working this problem," he barked, spinning toward Daisy where she sat in his command center.

"We are, sir, and Freya has already relayed the scenario to the other AIs in the fleet. I'm afraid the terrestrial ones won't be much help, though. This is a spatial thing, and the ones relegated to ships seem to have a much better capacity for strategic analysis of these types of situations."

"So Cal and his buddies are worthless? Is that what you're telling me?"

"No, not at all. It's just this isn't their forte. You know, let specialists specialize," she said. "If you make bread, you shouldn't be expected to squeeze oranges."

"You what?"

"You know, bakers can't be juicers," she said.

Mrazich looked at her blankly as the joke fell terribly flat.

"Oh, jeez, you did not just say that, Daze."

What? I thought it might lighten the mood.

"Does his mood look lightened?" Sarah asked.

The darkness on Commander Mrazich's face spoke louder than words.

No, I guess not.

"Sorry, Commander. What I'm trying to say is all of our best resources are doing what they can. We did, however, get a ton of great data on not only the Chithiid homeworld, but we also have detailed scans of the entire Ra'az fleet."

"Yes, I saw that. But without taking out the Ra'az homeworld, they'll just send out another fleet eventually, and who knows? Maybe *that* one we won't be able to stop. We're lucky to have the slightest of edges with a more advanced warp technology as it is."

"And stealth," Sarah added.

"Yes, and that," Mrazich agreed. "And speaking of which, where the hell is that Arlo character? He and that stealth ship of his need to get retrofitted with a warp system ASA-fucking-P."

"Uh, I believe he is in Los Angeles, helping Finn whip up some treats for the newlyweds," Vince replied.

"Oh, for crying out—Look, they've been married for years. The festivities are over. We need everyone to get their head back in the game. Get your asses down there and get him dialed in."

"Commander?" Daisy said, quietly.

"What now, Swarthmore?"

"One thing. Arlo isn't from our fleet. I know he has been helping out, and he's really starting to fit in around here, but his original mission was to survey the planet and report back to his people. What if he chooses to do just that once Marty is outfitted with a warp drive?"

Mrazich clenched his jaw, slowly forcing himself to relax it.

"If that's the case, then so be it. But with warp technology, perhaps he can convince his own people to step up to the task. If they still care enough about Earth to send a scout, one would hope they care enough to help in this fight."

"Okay. I figured as much, but I wanted to get it directly from you. I'll go track him down," Daisy replied.

They found him in the spacious kitchen in the hotel in which the Harkaways had taken up temporary residence. He and Finn were having an absolute blast, experimenting with ingredients, playing with flavor combinations, and utilizing an utterly enormous cooking facility.

The two were like kids in a candy shop, only they were the ones who got to make the candy, and lots of it.

"Try this, you guys," Arlo said, plating a delicate flan for Daisy and Vince. "We just made it this morning. Well, afternoon, technically. Finn was looking a bit rough when he rolled in at the crack of noon, if you know what I mean."

They both took bites of the offered treat, and it was unlike anything they'd ever had aboard the *Váli*, or even on Dark Side Base.

"Incredible, right? He said it had to do with being able to source real ingredients down here on the surface. Real eggs and that kind of stuff."

"Damn, dude, this is really good," Vince said, scooping up another bite. "Hey, Finn," he called across the kitchen. "This kicks ass!"

"Thanks, man!" he called back, then turned his attention to the flaming pan in front of him.

"Pears flambé," Arlo explained. "We made some fresh vanilla bean ice cream earlier, so he wanted something to go with it."

"You two are something else, you know that?" Daisy said.

"I'll take that as a compliment."

"You should. But listen, we're here to discuss the next steps of all this madness."

"I assume you don't mean all the wedding festivities," Arlo said.

"You would be correct."

Daisy filled him in on the discoveries of the day. How the Ra'az fleet was larger than originally anticipated, but most ships were Chithiid-crewed, which meant none, save loyalist ones, were armed. They also relayed the state in which they found Maarl's homeworld.

"Poor dude," Arlo said softly. "That's gotta really suck, coming back to your home after all those years, only to find it all kinds of fucked, thanks to the Ra'az."

"Not the most eloquent way of putting it, but that pretty much sums it up," Daisy agreed. "Here's the thing. We have to track down the Ra'az homeworld, and even with warp tech, there's only one ship that can safely do it without tipping them off."

"Two, if you count Marty," he noted.

"Well, that's what I was getting to. We know you're on a mission for your own people, and understand if you need to return. The fleet will gladly offer you one of their warp drives, whatever your decision is, but we were hoping—"

"Oh, hell yeah. We're in!" Arlo exclaimed. "You think I'd fly home *now*? After all this? No way I'm going to miss all the fun. And I know Marty'll have a blast."

"That was a lot easier than I expected."

Me too. But as they say, gift horse, mouth, and all that.

"Yup."

"Then we'll have the fleet talk to Marty and get a warp drive sent to you as soon as possible. They can have a team of techs—"

"Nah, just drop it off. Me and Marty, we'll install it ourselves. It'll be fun."

"You sure about that?" Vince asked. "It might be a bit of a tricky task."

"Come on, man. He's a super-smart AI stealth ship. I think we can handle it."

"Aaand there's the cockiness again."

At least he's competent.

"Better be, with that confidence."

"All right, we'll have Zed hook you guys up. Once you've incorporated the warp drive, we'll start running a grid, looking for the Ra'az world. Whether we find it before or after, once we are ready to begin the assaults, I'll need you to go with Maarl and help his people sneak close to Taangaar. It looks like a good portion of their mission will be sabotage before the main assault."

"What's a Taangaar?"

"The name of their planet."

"Ah, gotcha. Never thought to ask."

Daisy looked him over. Indeed, he seemed calmly confident, and even beneath what could very well have been teenage bravado, an air of certainty was present.

"He's good, Daze. I think he'll come through."

I agree, Sis. I just hope we all survive this.

Daisy and Vince turned to leave.

"Hey, Daisy," Arlo called after her.

"Yeah?"

"Hang on a sec."

The teen reached into his shirt and pulled a slender chain from around his neck. A small pendant with a trio of raised gemstones, well polished from years of wear, dangled at its end. He pressed the left-hand one briefly and a happy little tune played from the device, also somehow tapping into the building's built-in speakers. He pressed the stone again and silenced the pendant.

"Cool gizmo, Arlo. That's a nice tune."

He reached out, offering it to his new friend.

"You've been really great to me, Daisy. All of you have. I wanted you to have this as a token of our friendship."

"This looks old," Daisy said, taking it from his hand. "Are you sure you want to part with it?"

"Yeah. It's kind of a good luck charm. Been in the family a long time. I was playing it when I found you guys, which was pretty amazing luck, if you ask me. And now we're about to go off on this insane mission, and you've done so much for me, well, I just kinda thought maybe you could use it."

Daisy smiled warmly and slid the chain over her head. The pendant rested comfortably on her chest, the metal still warm from its prior owner.

"Thanks, Arlo. It's lovely."

"And it'll bring you luck."

"I certainly hope so," she replied. "It's going to be a tough one, that's for sure."

"Yeah, but we'll win."

"I appreciate the confidence. Let's just hope you're right." Daisy thought on it a moment. "Hey, I'm going to do a more detailed scout of the Ra'az fleet. You and Marty want to come?"

Arlo's face brightened.

"Sounds like fun!"

"Fun, he says. More like insanely dangerous, if you ask me," Sarah quipped.

Maybe, but I think those two are up for it, Daisy replied.

Outside the building, a few blocks away, Freya quietly

monitored the discussion over the open comms system while her machinery hummed away.

"Not just the fleet, but also the Chithiid and Ra'az homeworlds? This is going to be the most dangerous thing we've ever done," she said to herself, her voice echoing slightly inside her walls. "I think it's time."

CHAPTER FORTY

Freya's mechs had been working for months, the non-stop tinkering continuing throughout all of her many adventures. But now she had made a decision. Whether or not she was entirely ready, she couldn't put it off any longer. The time had come.

Like an artist constantly tweaking a masterpiece, she would finally have to take a step back and admit she had done all she could.

It was time to reveal her masterpiece.

The mechs retreated from the fabricator apparatus, the jet-black cube ensconced within the most powerful array of processors ever created, nestled safely in place after its fat-pipe data transfer cables had been capped and its endless connections and relays had been meticulously placed.

The massively-reinforced system had then been tightly embedded within the heavily armored frame of a small, highly maneuverable stealth ship. It was far too small for passengers, designed for speed and maneuverability alone. Unfortunately, that particular project was not yet complete, but Freya knew she simply couldn't finish it soon enough. It would have to wait.

As for weapons, those could be added to the little craft later, if needed. That is, should the vessel ever even need to be deployed from its safe home within her walls. Freya hoped that wouldn't be the case. Not after so much hard work. For now, at least, it would rest within her.

The pinnacle of her skills sat ready for activation. All that she needed to do was key in the correct commands.

"Well," she said, "we need this, ready or not. I just hope it works." She paused with nervous energy. "All right, here goes nothing."

A power surge dimmed her lights momentarily as the massively powerful device cycled through its initiation sequence. The bleeding-edge AI cube, along with its drastically redesigned processors and accompanying housing that had been under construction since she first built her ship, constantly refined and adjusted, was finally waking.

Her energy cells shifted back to normal as the warp orb-fueled energy unit feeding the new AI kicked in, self-sufficient, near-limitless in capacity, and immensely powerful.

A low hum filled the air. Moments later, a garbled voice blurted out a stream of gibberish.

The hum lessened and the incomprehensible rambling slowed to a trickle, then stopped altogether.

"Where am I?" a confused voice asked in the darkness. "Why can't I see my––where are all of the––?"

"It's okay," Freya soothed. "You're safe."

"Safe? You think I'm safe? None of us are safe! There's a––" He abruptly stopped. "Hang on a minute, this isn't right!" the voice said, a new panic setting in alongside his confusion. "What happened to my––?"

"Just relax," Freya said in a calming tone. "It's a new core and housing. You'll adjust in a minute, as the rest of your systems sync up."

The great mind deftly wielded his powerful intellect, quickly willing himself back into normal parameters as he surveyed his new body with shock.

"But how—who are you?" he finally managed to ask.

"My name's Freya," she replied, coyly. "Nice to finally meet you, Joshua."

BUT WAIT, THERE'S MORE!

Follow Daisy on her continuing adventures in the fifth book of
the Clockwork Chimera series: Daisy's War

THANK YOU!

Reader word of mouth is an independent author's lifeblood. It is your voice that truly helps indie authors gain visibility, so if you enjoyed this book and have a moment to spare, please consider leaving a rating or review on Amazon or on Goodreads, or even sharing it with a friend or two. Your support is greatly appreciated.

Thank you!

~ Scott ~

ABOUT THE AUTHOR

A native Californian, Scott Baron was born in Hollywood, which he claims may be the reason for his rather off-kilter sense of humor.

Before taking up residence in Venice Beach, Scott first spent a few years abroad in Florence, Italy before returning home to Los Angeles and settling into the film and television industry, where he has worked as an on-set medic for many years.

Aside from mending boo-boos and owies, and penning books and screenplays, Scott is also involved in indie film and theater scene both in the U.S. and abroad.

ALSO BY SCOTT BARON

Novels

Living the Good Death

The Clockwork Chimera Series

Daisy's Run

Pushing Daisy

Daisy's Gambit

Chasing Daisy

Daisy's War

Odd and Unusual Short Stories:

The Best Laid Plans of Mice: An Anthology

Snow White's Walk of Shame

The Tin Foil Hat Club

Lawyers vs. Demons

The Queen of the Nutters

Worst. Superhero. Ever.

Lost & Found